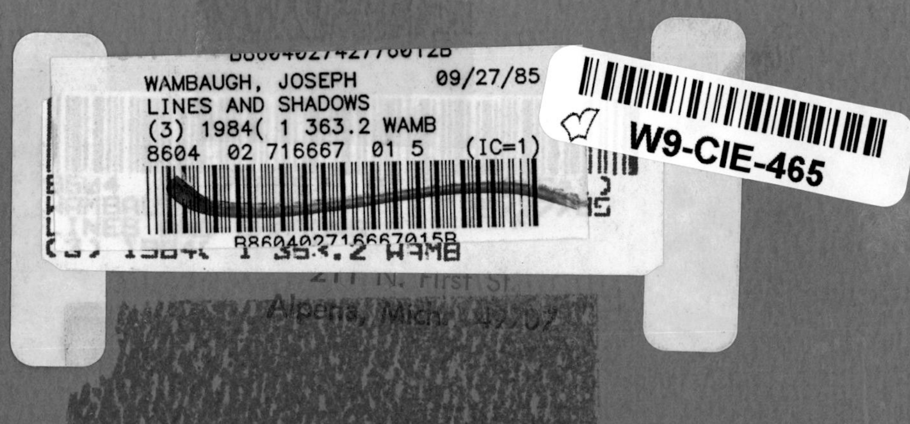

LINES AND SHADOWS

Books by Joseph Wambaugh

FICTION

THE NEW CENTURIONS
THE BLUE KNIGHT
THE CHOIRBOYS
THE BLACK MARBLE
THE GLITTER DOME
THE DELTA STAR

NONFICTION

THE ONION FIELD
LINES AND SHADOWS

LINES AND SHADOWS

Joseph Wambaugh

A PERIGORD PRESS BOOK

William Morrow and Company, Inc.
New York 1984

Grateful acknowledgment is made for permission to reprint on page 379 lines from the song "Sunny," Words and Music by Bobby Hebb, copyright © 1965, 1966, Portable Music Company, Inc., All rights reserved.

Library of Congress Cataloging in Publication Data

Wambaugh, Joseph.
Lines and shadows.

"A Perigord Press book."

1. Police patrol—California—San Diego. 2. Undercover operations—California—San Diego. 3. Border patrols—California—San Diego. 4. Alien labor, Mexican—California—San Diego. 5. Mexicans—California—San Diego. I. Title.
HV8148.S32W35 1984 363.2'32 83-13313
ISBN 0-688-02619-2

Printed in the United States of America

First Edition

1 2 3 4 5 6 7 8 9 10

BOOK DESIGN BY LINEY LI

For those who lived it, on both sides of the line

This is a true story.

PROLOGUE

THE BRIDAL SUITE

IN 1982, THREE SAN DIEGO AREA POLICE OFFICERS UNDERwent psychological counseling in an effort to assess some traits that might cause either embarrassment to the police department or danger to the officers themselves.

The three officers in question were all convinced that disturbances in their lives were related to police service. At least two had experienced some episodes of weeping, which is predictable in police stress cases. At least two had some thoughts of self-destruction, which is extremely predictable in police stress cases. The only other thing the three officers had in common was that they were all part of a little experiment conducted by the San Diego Police Department. The experiment lasted eighteen months, ending in April 1978. It was a strange experiment, the results of which are still being debated on both sides of the Mexico-United States border.

Ten officers of the San Diego Police Department were asked to walk a foot beat. It may well have been the most bizarre and remarkable foot beat walked by American policemen in modern times.

In addition to being the story of that walking beat, this is also a tale of two cities. Each of the city's metropolitan areas houses about one million people. One city is geographically small and the people live in close proximity. One city is large and sprawling.

In one city, inhabitants still suffer diseases considered exotic in the other: cholera, polio, typhus, tuberculosis, rickets. In the other city, separated from the former mostly by an imaginary line, lies some of the richest real estate in the richest half of the richest state in the richest country on the face of the earth.

Within a two-hour drive north from that invisible line there float unbelievable armadas: yachts and pleasure craft, half a million of them. And no less than 150 *builders* of yachts and pleasure craft striving to fill the insatiable need.

Although it's difficult to say where unusual ideas originate, this one may have been born many years ago in a hag of a hotel near the Mexican border. The top floor of the hotel in San Ysidro housed "the bridal suite." The sole occupant was an officer of the United States Border Patrol. He could cross the floor in two strides. He was a very big man living in a very small room, wryly named.

Dick Snider recalls his days in that hotel vividly. The floor outside his room ran downhill so that he had to *skate* to the slime-green bathroom down the hall. Slipping and sliding back *up* the floor to his coffin of a room was another matter, especially when he'd been putting down tequila and mescal and Mexican beer at The Playland Club, a theater-cum-saloon run by an ex-tightrope walker.

Maybe that's how it all seemed to the twenty-five-year-old border patrolman on his first assignment, trying to live and support an estranged family on $75 a week, reduced to eating cheese sandwiches three times a day, listening to the ex-tightrope walker recall her good old days walking wire.

San Ysidro is not an incorporated town; it's mostly a

Spanish-speaking community within the city limits of San Diego. One can, they say, hit the United States port of entry with an empty tequila bottle thrown from any house in San Ysidro. An exaggeration, but one gets the idea. Back when former border patrolman Dick Snider was pinwheeling down the halls of the little hotel it was mostly cesspools, train trestles, stucco or cinder-block beer bars, and streets as greasy and blistered as fried tortillas.

Burl Richard Snider was born in southern Arkansas, in the tiny town of Silva, a crossroads that time and cartographers have obliterated. His family were farmers and mostly raised him in southeastern Missouri, the "lapland" where Missouri laps into Arkansas. It was a Mississippi River backwater which flooded yearly and caused his family to make several trips to California, their "*Grapes of Wrath* trips," to find work in the San Joaquin Valley. One of those trips lasted two years, and during that time the youngster had occasion to play with Mexican children whose families had also made journeys from far places—cruel, hard journeys. The lapland farmboy found they were very much like himself, those Mexican children. He began picking up bits of their language and he studied Spanish in school, discovering that, because of Spanish, other studies clicked.

"For the first time in my life even English seemed to jell for me," he recalled. "Spanish classes were a snap when I later entered the Border Patrol academy. While other guys were washing out because of it."

But there was some living in store for young Dick Snider before joining the U.S. Border Patrol. He got married at seventeen and began working in the California oil fields, making quite a bit of money for a boy—a very large boy to be sure. He and his bride had two babies and everything was coasting along about as smooth as buttermilk. Then his oldest child, Ricky, got a strep infection of the larynx.

A generation later he looked, well, *baffled* when he tried to describe it. Ricky was just three years old. Ricky had trouble breathing one night. The next morning it was worse. Dick Snider rushed his son to the hospital. Ricky began choking. Ricky began *strangling.* Dick Snider watched his son's face go blue-black before his eyes. His boy wanted his father to save him. The doctors cut open the boy's throat and did a tracheotomy. The life support machine broke down. The boy died six hours later at two o'clock in the afternoon.

"It's confusing," he remembered. "I'd go out a my head for several minutes at a time. Then I'd come back. Out and back. I can't remember the details. I can only remember that he recognized me at the end. The doctors tried to tell me that he couldn't have. I believe he knew me at the end. His hair was wheat-blond and his eyes were brown. He always tried to do what I did. Once he scared me to death by running into a corral full a horses. He was going to wrangle them, he said. He said if his daddy could do it . . . well . . . he was *some* kid."

Dick Snider and his wife also had a baby daughter, but nothing was the same after the boy's death. There were some years of misery, then divorce.

He eventually found himself absolutely alone, in a mean little room in a hotel in San Ysidro, draping his large frame out the window on cool San Diego nights, watching the glow in the sky from Tijuana.

There had been no Hispanics in Dick Snider's border patrol class. In fact he was the best Spanish-speaking recruit in the El Paso barracks during training. The United States government had not thought it necessary to recruit officers who fluently spoke the language of the border. Dick Snider, who always hankered to be in law enforcement, made investigator very quickly.

"I used to watch the San Diego cops chasing aliens down the streets a San Ysidro," he recalled. "I'd sit in that sorry little room and look out at them. It made me think a lot about the alien plight."

And it wasn't easy supporting his estranged wife and

daughter. Hence, cheese sandwiches and some milk when he was lucky. And booze because it was sometimes more necessary than food—that is, when you tended to think of a family destroyed and a dying son crying out for help. It's not hard to imagine the fantasies in a cockroach hotel in the night, always an arm's length from a service revolver, closer than that to the memories of a dead child. *I couldn't save him.*

So, lonely and frightened men must think of other things. They get strange ideas. They drink, and they gaze out the window at wormy mongrel dogs dragging infected bleeding anuses across stippled pavement, dogs who cross the imaginary line at will to scavenge. And they gaze at cops chasing aliens in a crazy game more akin to present-day Pac-Man than anything else. At least when seen from the vantage point of a coffin of a room called the bridal suite.

The idea he got a generation ago was this: *There is not a significant line between two countries. It's between two economies.*

"I kept thinking, what if I'd been born a hundred yards south a that invisible line? As long as it's the haves and have-nots side by side, they're gonna come."

There was a lot of anguish and misery out there in the night on the frontier. And it may be that this is where the idea for the later San Diego police experiment was born. While watching an early version of Pac-Man, where American lawmen ate up Mexican aliens only to spit them back south. And ate them up the next night only to spit them back south. And the next night.

It's easy to see how a young border patrolman might start to identify with these *pollos* driven north by circumstance. And to wonder how many of *them* had seen a dying son cry out. *Save me.*

The border patrolman in the bridal suite began to concentrate on the anguish of illegal aliens. So as not to contemplate his own.

CHAPTER · 1

OBSESSION

BURL RICHARD SNIDER HAD JOURNEYED HALF A LIFETIME from the hotel in San Ysidro. He had gone from the U.S. Border Patrol to service as a park policeman on the other side of America, in Washington, D.C. He had remarried, returned west and had two more children. And he had joined the San Diego Police Department.

In the fall of 1976 Lieutenant Dick Snider, now a sixteen-year police department veteran, old enough to know better, was lying flat on his belly in a canyon watching a nightly ritual. The aliens gathered by an imaginary line between two cities, two countries, two economies, and when the sun was about to set they moved. In the old Border Patrol days a few dozen might try it on a given night. Now, in a zone of only a few square miles, in effect a no-man's-land between the cities of Tijuana, Mexico, and San Diego, U.S.A., they came. Sometimes ten thousand per *week*. And in those canyons lurked Tijuana bandits and cutthroats who fed off the *pollos* as they crossed the frontier in the night. One of the slashes of earth in this no-man's-land is called

Deadman's Canyon, for good reason. It is a mean, blood-drenched gash of mesquite and cactus and rocks within the city limits of San Diego, one of the richest cities in the richest state in the richest country. . . .

The illegal aliens saved and borrowed and sold and carried the net worth of their lives in their socks and underwear, and sometimes in bags and bundles. Bandit gangs formed near that imaginary line and enjoyed a nightly bonanza in the canyons. Aliens were ambushed, robbed, raped, murdered, occasionally within screaming distance of United States officers at the land port of entry.

The bandits were no fools. They lived in Tijuana but operated on the American side where it was safe. Tijuana lawmen can be very unpleasant, as the bandits well knew.

And the bandits were without mercy. During one robbery, a young *pollo* father was shot with his baby in his arms. He lay dying ten feet inside the promised land while the bandits stripped everything of value from the living members of his party. An orphaned blood-spattered baby with fat knees was carried screaming in agony back to Tijuana with shotgun pellets in his eye and brain.

All of this troubled Lieutenant Dick Snider, just as it had troubled him twenty years earlier. He lay in the scrub at night, alone in those canyons, the binoculars cupped in his big leathery paws, watching through slate-colored eyes forever squinting from the smoke of a dangling cigarette. His life had changed very much for the better in these intervening years. But the aliens? The Mexican economy was fearful. The rest of Latin America was desperate.

In 1976 there was already lots of rhetoric about the alien phenomenon. The American State Department had been forced to admit that the overall dilemma was insoluble, and was publicly promising to try to "manage" it a bit better. The five hundred Border Patrol officers in the Chula Vista sector were catching more than twenty thousand aliens a month, almost all of them having crossed in those few square miles of canyon inside the city limits of San Diego, near the busiest land port of entry in the world. The agents used helicopters, horses, four-wheel-drive vehicles, infrared scopes, magnetic sensors, seismic sensors.

Sometimes a border patrolman had been known to stroll into an asparagus field on the west side of Interstate 5 and illuminate a *pollo* with his light, commanding him to stand and submit. After which he would suddenly find himself surrounded by fifty other aliens who thought he was talking to *them.*

The nearby city of Oceanside, for example, had a population of some seventy thousand and grew by fifty thousand during fruit-picking season, from undocumented stoop laborers. The law said that a farmer was not violating the law by hiring the illegals, but was by *housing* them. Therefore they slept in the brush, under trees, in cardboard boxes. The nights in San Diego County can get cold.

And it came to pass that labor organizers and farmers did much shouting into the wind. The farmers said that if they must pay and house American workers (assuming they would *do* stoop labor) a strawberry would cost what you now pay for an avocado. An avocado would cost what you now pay for a Mercedes. And so forth.

And Chicano activists entered the picture and argued that the American government could not separate a Chicano from a Mexican (with which most native Mexicans would disagree) and called the frontier "The Vietnam of the Southwest."

The director of the Immigration and Naturalization Service had, by 1976, publicly commented that the alien situation appeared almost hopeless, far beyond the control of his uniformed force, the U.S. Border Patrol.

In the summer of 1976 Dick Snider was forty-five years old, too old to be lurking around the boonies, they said. Pretty dopey, they said, to be taking the department's four-wheel-drive Ford Bronco to clatter up into those godforsaken canyons, one mile and one century away from the Southern Division substation of the San Diego Police Department. But he did it with ever more frequency, usually alone, and pondered the fate of those pollos being brutalized out there in the darkness as he lay concealed in foxtail grass and cactus and tumbleweeds.

Sometimes in the late afternoons, while he watched the multitude of aliens gathering on the mesas and plateaus waiting for sunset, he would see groups of Mexican schoolchildren being led across the invisible line by teachers conducting excursions into the canyons for flora and fauna. Oil-rich jojoba beans grew wild. Wild anise flourished, and scrub oak, stunted and tough, relentlessly surviving. And everywhere the threat of cholla cactus. Dick Snider watched through binoculars the throngs who played soccer and baseball and bought tamales and soda pop from the Tijuana "roach wagons" which also came to take a buck or two from the pollos before the canyon crossing.

He watched children with empty jars, and milk cartons full of water, flooding the burrows of tarantulas and scorpions, capturing the wretched creatures alive to peddle to Americans in the bars or to Mexican entrepreneurs who ensconced them in plastic molds to sell to tourists as paperweights. *Everything* was for sale to Americans in the border city.

It was not more than a short walk from a low-rent hotel where a young border patrolman once occupied the bridal suite. And in essence, he was still contemplating the same dilemma: the aliens.

It occurred to him that almost nothing had changed in all those years. It was as though, well, something as uncoplike as *destiny* had marked him, linking him to this place, near that imaginary line. But there had been *one* change in recent years: the bandit gangs. And it was insupportable to him that some pollos were actually attacked within screaming distance of *his* substation. Even Deadman's Canyon was only one mile (and one century) away.

It didn't seem to trouble very many other people. After all, they were *illegal* aliens, criminals by definition. But some of the criminals were only three years old, and some were younger. And the bandits were not sentimental about mothers and babes. Finally he became obsessed with the incongruity of it. This was the prosperous, beautiful, tourist-filled city of San Diego, U.S.A. *His* city. His outrage agitated the cerebral cortex where ideas live. And one came to him.

The best way to convince bureaucrats of anything is to quote statistics. Police administrators can toss around more numbers than baseball managers. And like baseball managers, pollsters, politicians, or Pentagon generals, they can make statistics do just about whatever they wish. But there are certain statistics which even the most resourceful police pencil pusher would have trouble explaining away. One is homicide. There *is* a dead body on your beat or there *isn't*. And too many of them were turning up around an imaginary line which Dick Snider had long believed was used to divide two economies. No one knew for sure how many murders actually occurred on American soil, because there were verified episodes of bereaved pollos carrying their slain husbands, wives, brothers, sisters, children, back over to the Mexican side for burial.

And every cop who has ever worked among illegal aliens knows that pollos assaulted in the night would not routinely report the crime to the U.S. authorities, since these people generally feared the authorities of both countries, not to mention deportation. Therefore, the San Diego police statisticians only got wind of the crimes where the Border Patrol or police stumbled upon some victim who had been gutted like a fish, or hamstrung by the bandit wolf packs, sometimes making bloody circles in the dust before bleeding to death. Sometimes raped so brutally that hospitalization was required prior to deportation. The *real* body count was anybody's guess.

Dick Snider finally tired of crawling around those canyons at midnight, listening to gunshots and cries in the darkness. He remembered the old Border Patrol days when they used to track one alien ten miles because illegal entry was then considered a big deal. He wondered if nowadays any overworked, frustrated, dung-shoveling border patrolmen unconsciously approved of the Tijuana bandits for culling the migrants in no-man's-land. In fact, he wondered how many ordinary compassionate citizens would tolerate the bandit gangs, who probably scared away a fair number that might otherwise have joined the ragtag migratory battalions of the night.

That year the U.S. Border Patrol was estimating that they would arrest more than 250,000 aliens. The wishful statistic they always gave to the press was that they probably caught one third. Which the cops called "a hallelujah batting average." Prosecuting aliens for illegal entry was a nightmare. After three or four arrests it was possible to get a conviction for a misdemeanor, which *might* mean five days in jail. Reentry after formal deportation was technically a felony, but very hard to prove. The Border Patrol investigator would have to get certification of the existence or nonexistence of records in Washington. Aliens are rarely fingerprinted, don't carry identification, and often change their names on later tries, so it was nearly impossible to prove identities. If the Border Patrol caught 10 percent of all pollos, they were doing remarkably well, the cops figured.

Border patrolmen talked wistfully of *La Ley de Fuga*, The Law of Flight. If you flee you are shot. The law of Mexico. The law of *many* "developed" countries. But alien smugglers have been known to make a million dollars a year. It's lucrative, and everyone knew that if the aliens were somehow miraculously all rounded up, half the restaurants from San Diego to the Oregon border would have to serve buffet style on paper plates. And wealthy Californians would suddenly be washing their own cars and cutting their own grass and cleaning their own houses and tending their own children. And who in the hell would pick the crops? And what of the small factories? And what would happen to the garment industry? And so forth.

So with this incredibly complicated headache, only too familiar to the people of San Diego living just north of that imaginary line, it wouldn't do for Dick Snider to approach the police administration with do-gooder talk about the tragedies inflicted by bandit gangs. The way to approach it was to present cold, incontrovertible *numbers,* and to tell the police administration how he could make those big numbers get smaller.

It wasn't easy, in that things move very slowly in a bureaucracy. At first the brass was not particularly troubled by the numbers. But the reported alien crimes, which Dick Snider had always estimated to be a tenth of the actual occurrences, were causing some damage to the overall portrait of "America's Finest City," whose tourist bureau touted the most temperate climate on earth. A city where tourism was huge. A great retirement community and an enormous military base. Very unlike the bigger city "up the road"—meaning Los Angeles—San Diego was advertised as being lovely and smog-free. And *safe.*

But the San Diego Police Department daily occurrence sheets were telling another story:

> Saturday, 2300 hours. Spring Canyon, alien robbery. Two males armed with a gun. Three victims.
>
> Saturday, 2100 hours, Deadman's Canyon, three suspects, two victims. Knives and machetes used.
>
> Wednesday, 2000 hours. Alien robbery, E-2 Canyon. Clubs and rocks used. Ten victims. Five suspects.

And the aliens were not only being robbed by bandit gangs, but *others* were finding the pollos too tempting to resist:

> Wednesday, 1930 hours, alien robbery, Monument Road. Three victims. *Armed Tijuana police officer* ambushed them.
>
> Wednesday, 2245 hours, alien robbery. Three victims. Monument Road. Border Patrol interrupted robbery. Tijuana auxiliary policeman (unarmed) in custody. Other uniformed officer (armed) escaped into Mexico.
>
> Friday, 0700 hours. Alien robbery. Suspects were two Tijuana police officers. Victim struck in face, threatened with gun, maced in eyes.
>
> Thursday, 2230 hours, alien robbery. Three victims robbed in gully by two male suspects dressed in tan Tijuana police uniforms.

Then the robberies began getting steadily more ferocious, the log entries more grim:

> Wednesday, 0950 hours. Body found ⅓ mile east of Hollister, 200 feet north of border fence. Male, Mexican, 30's, throat cut.
>
> Friday, 1430 hours. Border Patrol found body on mesa near mouth of Spring Canyon. Badly decomposed male.
>
> Tuesday, second watch. Border Patrol says Tijuana Police Department notified them of murder by soccer field in Spring Canyon, 0100 hours.

If the pollos were lucky enough to run the gauntlet in the canyons, there awaited the Mexican-American youth gangs of San Ysidro. Who could resist? The pollos were so timid. So *easy:*

> Wednesday, 2300 hours, alien robbery, San Ysidro View Park. Victim struck from behind. Face beaten in. Hospitalized.
>
> Friday, alien robbery, 0100 hours, 8 male susps, 17–20 years. Armed with knives and clubs. Two victims and their children robbed.

And if the pollos were lucky enough (and fit enough) to outrun the bandit gangs in the canyons, or the moonlighting Tijuana cops, or the Mexican-American youth gangs, or the helicopters and four-wheeled vehicles of *la migra,* they found other perils awaiting them in their crossing:

> Saturday, third watch, Interstate 5 under pedestrian bridge. Alien struck while running across freeway.
>
> Monday, third watch, Otay Mesa Road, vehicle ran over fleeing alien. Broken pelvis.
>
> Saturday, third watch. Another alien hit by car on Highway 805, running across freeway. Taken to Bay General. Not expected to live.

And if the male aliens managed to survive the bandits in the canyons and the moonlighting Mexican cops, and the Mexican-American youth gangs, and the speeding cars, there were additional perils for females between the ages of ten and seventy:

> Sunday, 2300 hours, Border Patrol chopper interrupted gang rape. Five suspects. Spring Canyon.

And so forth. There were some San Diego police administrators starting to get a very large headache from all these statistical entries, and the last thing in the world they needed while they pondered the border phenomenon was civilian pressure. But that's exactly what they got. Articles started appearing with regularity in the San Diego newspapers:

ALIEN BOY PARALYZED BY ROBBERS
Sixteen-year-old has spinal cord cut
Seventh alien robbery this week

During the summer, investigative reporters interviewed a Mexican-American youth gang member in San Ysidro for his lurid account of alien robberies. In a short career he had beaten and robbed countless victims, and raped fifteen alien women, one for every year of his life.

By midsummer 1976 the Tijuana mayor was sweating out all the reports of his police officers ambushing aliens on American soil. A spokesman for Mayor Fernando Marquez Arce told U.S. reporters: "We are sure these are bandits impersonating Tijuana police and not members of our department. There are stores in Tijuana where uniforms resembling police uniforms can be bought and we are sure there are people buying these and posing as police."

Finally, by summer's end Mexican President Luis Echeverria Alvarez addressed the U.S. government on the fate of pollos being robbed, beaten, raped and murdered at the American border.

He said: "They deserve the respect accorded to human beings by every civilized society," and he added that the attitude of the Mexican government "has been and will continue to be uncompromising" on the safety of these aliens.

And while some U.S. citizens said who gives a shit what some boss beaner in Mexico City found "uncompromising," there were those in Washington who listened to everything said in Mexico City these days. The beaners at last had something the gringos *needed* at this point in history: oil. No one knew how much as yet, but it was there. *Oil!*

So, with ever more frequency the San Diego press and indeed the national press began to pay attention to the reports of border bandits, and in virtually every local article and every television interview (sometimes three a week) there was some statement by one Southern Division lieutenant named Burl Richard Snider.

"Only ten percent of the crimes are reported," he liked to say. "Here's a picture of a fourteen-year-old girl when they finished with her. Here's what they did to a man who didn't have enough money to satisfy them. Here's . . ."

Oh, they just *loved* him for that uptown. Cops generally trust the press about as much as they trust politicians, judges, lawyers, psychiatrists and the Red Army. Dick Snider was conducting a one-man publicity campaign. He was even quoted in a *business* journal as to the impact of millions of aliens in America.

"You'd have to build a Chinese wall two thousand miles long to stop them," he said. "To tell the truth, pard, I don't know if *that* would do it." And not that he'd stoop to overkill, but he once perversely noted that when Joseph and Mary fled King Herod they were illegal aliens.

And when asked for the solution to the grave dilemma, Dick Snider would just squint a slaty eye at his interviewer and roll the ubiquitous cigarette from one side of his mouth to the other and rock back on his cowboy boots and say, "Pardner, I don't think I *have* a solution. I just don't want people brutalizing them on my beat. In my city. In my country."

In *his* country! That did it. Uptown, in the corner pocket, the department brass started ricocheting like snooker balls. Who *is* this son of a bitch? *His* freaking city! *His* freaking country! You ought to be able to trust a goddamn Okie with a goddamn dust-bowl kisser not to make speeches on behalf of the goddamn *country*!

Nevertheless, his publicity campaign was working with a vengeance. He was appearing on television more than Mayor Pete Wilson. And some of the high-ranking officers—who didn't trust *any* middle-level management person who would crawl around the hills like a rattlesnake—these same brass hats had to become instant border-crime experts because slavering reporters were demanding answers to the questions Dick Snider was raising.

Even Chief of Police William Kolender, known as a progressive police administrator, telephoned Dick Snider with his jaws a bit torqued, complaining that he was made to look bad during one of the lieutenant's impromptu press interviews.

It wasn't that Dick Snider disliked the chief; in fact quite the opposite was true. He thought he might have a chance with his secret scheme precisely because Kolender *was* the new chief. So he chose his words a bit more carefully, but continued his publicity blitz, supplying any journalist who called with all the lurid details of alien ambush by bandit wolf packs.

And the top brass of the San Diego Police Department found themselves paying visits to Southern Division to tramp around the goddamn hills and canyons, slipping in coyote crap, trying to become instant border-crime experts, thanks to one bigmouth lieutenant named Snider.

One of the more critical reporters of the police beat overheard a deputy chief bitching about Dick Snider, and the reporter remarked that it goes to show you can't trust any white man that talks good Spanish. And the deputy chief stopped nodding like a dashboard doll and said *that* was about as humorous as a prostate probe.

But Dick Snider hadn't been in law enforcement most of his adult life for nothing. He understood the workings of the bureaucracy well enough to mitigate any radical notions of fighting border bandits simply for the sake of saving illegal aliens. Especially at a time when Californians were talking about taxpayer revolts. He did what every wise civil servant would do: he found a buzzword.

"We need a *federal grant,*" he told reporters. "To create a . . . sort of task force."

Dick Snider envisioned a force of men, comprised of San Diego cops and federal officers from the U.S. Border Patrol and U.S. Customs. But during any discussion of his idea he'd toss around his buzzword: federal grant.

The fact is it was virtually impossible to receive a law-enforcement federal grant. But he bandied numbers about, and was quoted in several interviews as to the modest amount of money he would need to field a force of men to deal with the bandits. And journalists ran to U.S. Customs and U.S. Border Patrol to discuss the merits of proposals being put forth by a San Diego police lieutenant who seemed to have "his finger on the pulse of the border," as they put it.

In police circles what Dick Snider was doing is called washing dirty laundry. And cops just don't do their duds in public, not if they care about their police careers. Not if their pension is not secure. And his wasn't. But there had always been a certain naïveté about the big lieutenant. Other policemen talked about it. He tended to believe that if your cause is just, you can't get hurt too badly. Which caused more cynical colleagues to show white eyeballs.

The federal grant went nowhere. However, after the media barrage Chief Kolender fulfilled Dick Snider's hopes and dreams. He began discussing with federal authorities a task force to cope with the crime problems of the border. And to Dick Snider that meant at long last he would deal with the bandits. He had an idea whose time had come—a generation later.

CHAPTER · 2

THE INSIDERS

ANY COMMENT ABOUT WHAT HAPPENED IN THE NO-MAN'S-land by the international border usually begins and ends with a judgment, critique, debate about one Jesus Manuel Lopez, the police sergeant chosen by Dick Snider to ramrod his fledgling Border Crime Task Force.

It would be a mistake to try to understand Manny Lopez too quickly.

"The better we came to know him, the bigger the question mark," is how one of his men would later put it.

And the metaphor could not be more appropriate. Manny Lopez was *marked* by the interrogation point. He was only twenty-nine years old, with a hairline already retreating on a small head. He had nearly Asian eyes, a nose more Middle Eastern than Mexican, slightly pocked cheeks, a gap-toothed impish grin. He would have looked at home selling carpets at a bazaar in Izmir, and there was probably never a rug peddler who could have outtalked him. But what one would not forget about Manny Lopez was the question mark. When he was in any way aroused, his right eyebrow did the most remarkable reptilian sidewinding crawl up up *up* his forehead until it formed a perfect question mark across his skull.

Many a man in the months to come would be amused, bewildered, *terrified,* watching that right eyebrow begin to slither, creep and crawl until the interrogation point was formed. And then you had an indelible portrait of Manny Lopez. A question mark. He, staring intently, the right eyebrow curling, squiggling, *locking* in.

"Manny Lopez kept turning me down at first," Dick Snider said. "He was a hard-charger and superambitious. He wanted to be a plainclothes investigator. He didn't seem too impressed with what I was selling. But he was my only choice from beginning to end. It wasn't just that he was the only Mexican sergeant crafty and crazy and gutsy enough to pull it off. He was the only sergeant *period.*"

All of the task force members would call Burl Richard Snider "Lieutenant" when they addressed him directly. But when talking about him to others it was "Burl the Pearl."

"Dick Snider *is* a pearl," Manny Lopez always said. "I worked for him back when he was a sergeant and I was a rookie. The guy could never be anything except outfront. But that can be a *fatal* flaw in police work."

During his police career Manny Lopez was elected president of San Diego's Latino police organization, *not* an important career step given the makeup of the department. In a force of 1,365 men and women, on the very fringe of a sea of Latinos stretching from Baja California to Tierra del Fuego, less than 5 percent of the department were Mexican-Americans. There were four sergeants. There were no lieutenants, no captains, one inspector, no deputy chiefs. Incredibly enough, there was only one in homicide, and none working burglary or robbery.

The large city of San Diego has been accused of nourishing a village mentality in areas of social progress, tucked away as it is in a far corner of America. And a police department always reflects its community. The Mexican-American cops did not refer to themselves as "Latinos" or "Hispanics" or "Mexican-Americans." They called the majority "whites" and they called themselves "Mexicans." And yet even this might be refuted by those people living south of the imaginary line who feel they are nothing like the northern "coconuts," who are brown on the outside but white within.

Linguists say that there are not many people who are truly bilingual—that is, foreigners who can fool a native speaker by conversing in the mother tongue unaccented. Manny Lopez was one who could. And he was a *talker* in both languages. He had also been director of the San Diego Police Officers Association, the first Mexican-American to hold this post. And the Police Officers Association represented *all* cops: white, black and Mexican. He was also on an advisory panel to the chief. So Manny Lopez knew something about politics. He had career ambitions and wasn't impressed with Dick Snider's obsession with aliens being victimized on American soil. But when Dick Snider showed Manny Lopez some photos of an alien who'd been robbed and had his face ripped away by a two-by-four studded with nails, Manny looked at the pictures and said, "Okay, you got it. Count me in."

And Dick Snider was ecstatic. He had the man to ramrod the task force. And he figured that the man of his choice had been persuaded by the very thing which so obsessed him: the agony of aliens.

Except that Manny Lopez *wasn't* persuaded by that. He privately said, "Dick Snider coulda shown me a picture of an alien with his head cut off. I woulda said that's tough. Life's tough."

The truth is, he was sick of waiting for an investigative job and he was sick of Northern Division with its bloated whiny millionaires. He was even sick of ogling all the bikinis stuffed with surf bunnies that littered the streets of La Jolla. He was almost thirty years old and wanted some *action* before he settled down and made a real run at promotions.

"I was bored. *Real* bored," he admitted. "*That's* why I joined Burl the Pearl's task force."

And that decision would completely change the direction of his life.

It was jointly decided by Dick Snider and Manny Lopez that the Border Crime Task Force should probably be composed of Mexican-American cops. As it turned out, this was a fortunate decision, given the radical change in direction the experiment would take. But at the start the search for Mexican-American officers began only because Dick Snider was one of the few in middle-level management who spoke Spanish and realized its importance here where the ocean of Latinos was flowing inexorably north.

He assumed that all Mexican-American cops would at least understand Spanish well enough to do the job as he had conceived it. He and Manny Lopez were going to lie in wait in the canyons, much as Dick Snider had done alone these many months. They were to listen and observe and catch the bandits smack in the middle of their robberies. They would ambush the ambushers. That was the *plan*.

The publicity blitz by Dick Snider had not been lost on U.S. government law-enforcement officials. Two customs officers and two border patrolmen were being loaned by the government to Dick Snider to augment his task force. The city of San Diego was giving him ninety days to produce results in the bandit-plagued hills and canyons. That was a very short time to turn a squad of city policemen into . . . what? Canyon-crawling commandos?

They all wondered early on if they were destined to be bastard children. The amorphous experiment was being seriously questioned even before it began. Their budget was being trimmed before they spent any. Their training time was being cut to five days, giving them a weekend to rest before going out in the canyons at night to do whatever the hell it was they were going to do. And they had only a vague idea of what they were going to do out there. Oh, they were going to curtail the marauding bandits through some sort of commando ambush, but not in any way that remotely resembled tactics they'd used in street police work.

And they took a verbal beating from the rest of the cops who got wind of the training camp at the U.S. Marine Corps facility at Camp Matthews, some ten miles north of downtown San Diego. They were outfitted in black navy watch caps, goggles for brush crawling, camouflage fatigues, combat boots. A few tried blackening their faces like military raiders they'd seen in a hundred war movies, and directed obligatory cracks at those with darker skin, just as they'd seen in a hundred war movies.

Even Dick Snider, who finally had his dream realized, wasn't sure how to train his new task force now that he was being given his chance.

"I remember the first briefing," he said. "I told them it was gonna be very unpredictable out in those canyons. I told them chances are somebody was gonna get hurt. I wanted them to believe it from the beginning. If someone had to get hurt it should be the bad guys."

And they looked at him and nodded respectfully, and he saw them roll their eyeballs and heard the puff of a dozen involuntary sighs and he thought, "They *have* heard this speech before." In a hundred war movies.

Manny Lopez came to doubt it from the start. He looked at them in their camouflage and goggles. These weren't marine raiders. These were city *cops.* And other cops howled when out of curiosity a few heard about Camp Matthews, or got a look at them when they made the mistake of wearing their John Wayne suits to the police station on the way home. But they were an eager band of young policemen and they just grinned and shrugged and ran it off all day in training.

Eddie Cervantes was, in addition to being a dedicated Marine reservist, a very fast runner who cheerfully punished the out-of-shape street cops by setting a fleet-footed pace all over the hills, yelling, "On, ter, thrp, frp!" like every leatherneck since the Boxer Rebellion, while the out-of-shape street cops dragged ass up and down the canyons.

There were two policemen in the group who had seen combat in Vietnam, both ex-Marine drill instructors: Ernie Salgado and Fred Gil. Since Manny Lopez admitted that he didn't know diddly about guns and ammo, Ernie Salgado volunteered to help with the weapons training. It seemed likely that out in bandit country they might need more than their police service revolvers, but threading one's way on treacherous trails in the night would make it pretty tough to lug around standard police shotguns. And SWAT rifles would probably be dangerous for everyone concerned.

The task force decided to use a High Standard, model ten, 12-gauge shotgun, which was equipped with a flashlight, a pistol grip, and a short barrel for concealment. It was essentially a sawed-off 12-gauge shotgun that could be held in one hand and fired at very close range. The ammunition used in police department revolvers was 158 grain, roundnose lead. Most policemen, though they carry handguns as tools of their trade, are not technically versed in firearms. Ernie Salgado was, and wondered from the beginning how effective two-inch gun barrels would be, since ordinary police department ammo already had little punch. He wondered if, what with the shorter revolver barrels and the inevitable waste of gas, the 158-grain ammo might lose *too* much power. That they might be better off with four-inch or even six-inch revolvers out there. And that the sawed-off shotguns might expand the bird too soon; thus anyone hit with projectiles from their short-barreled shotgun-handguns might be able to pick the lead out of his navel like belly-button fuzz and throw it right back at them.

There were two things noteworthy about these opinions on the efficacy of sawed-off shotguns and snub-nosed revolvers: 1. No one even dreamed *how* close their confrontations would get. 2. No one *completely* believed there was going to be heavyweight gunplay out there in the first place.

The fact is, most policemen can go an entire career without firing a weapon outside of the pistol range. On any police department there are a few officers who seem to become involved in multiple shootings, but there were none of these on the task force.

So there was a great deal of running and firing during those five days at Camp Matthews. And everyone treated the whole exercise in the best of humor most of the time. Except during one of their night exercises when they simulated sneaking up on bandits who were sneaking up on aliens. It was good boyish fun until someone almost stepped on a rattlesnake. A *live* rattlesnake. Very few of these city boys had ever seen a rattlesnake, living or dead.

Dick Snider had seen his share, from the *Grapes of Wrath* days up to and including his stint as a border patrolman so many years ago. And even in the past few months while conducting his one-man creepy crawly campaigns in the canyons at night, he had seen and heard the reptiles.

Rattlesnakes? *Real* rattlesnakes. This got their attention all right. Bandits were one thing. They weren't truly expecting much trouble from a bunch of raggedy thugs, all horsed-out on Mexican brown. They were just planning to kick ass and take names, as they say in the business. But *real* rattlesnakes? And how about tarantulas? Can they kill you? And what about those freaking scorpions they'd heard about? Were there really scorpions out there? When somebody started asking if rats carried plague, Dick Snider had to give his young city boys a few reassuring words about the *other* dangerous creatures of the canyons, who had been there far longer than the bandits.

The border patrolmen assigned to the task force taught the cops a few tricks that at the time seemed of doubtful value but, as the task force experiment took its radical turn, proved very valuable indeed. Things such as hunkering down: The illegal aliens ordinarily squat when approached by suspicious or threatening persons. So the cops had to learn to squat. And to try and *feel* the docility of pollos, to learn the gestures of submission and to talk shyly, with proper humility, the timbre and tone of voice modulated accordingly. About the exact opposite of a Japanese sushi chef, they were told.

Even the use of the hands was completely different south of the imaginary line. A real Mexican would call to an adult with the fingers pointed downward. *"Ven aquí"* would be softened by that waggling of down-turned fingers. A dog or a child would be called with the fingers up. They were starting to learn just *how* a Mexican differs from a Mexican-American.

And just in case they were called upon to do a little undercover work, they were taught a few short phrases using the vernacular of real Mexicans. Anglicized slang was nearly as much in evidence among law-enforcement officers and street people in Tijuana as it was on the American side of the border. But *campesinos* fresh from the interior would certainly not be asking for *mechas* to light their cigarettes. And if one was going to use the word *frajo* for cigarette, there would be subtleties involved. Why does this pollo from Durango know the slang of the border? Indeed the slang of the Mexican-American barrio? Has he made multiple crossings and come to talk the language of smugglers and guides, or is he some kind of law-enforcement informer or police agent?

And if any of them was ever asked to impersonate an alien from the interior, what kind of cigarettes should he carry? What brand of matches would likely be sold in a *pueblo* in Chihuahua?

And what of the language of guides and smugglers? *¡Trucha!* (meaning "Be careful!") was not a word many of them had heard, yet it was *caló* or barrio slang in Los Angeles, referring to a sharp dude who kept his eyes open.

The living language of the border, a patois of Spanish and English and bilingual slang, leaped whole areas of the California southland, came in and out of vogue, traveled back south prowling the border, crisscrossing as effortlessly as the scabrous mongrel dogs of the frontier. They listened and thought it was sort of interesting, but what the hell did it have to do with a bunch of street cops who were going into those hills to kick ass and take names?

One old policeman at Southern substation, when he got his first glimpse of the cop commandos, put it this way: "Black Jack Pershing was the last asshole *dumb* enough to go chasing Mexican bandits around the hills. And it ended up with Pancho Villa being played by every movie star from Beery to Brynner. What'd Pershing get out of it? A statue of himself in a wino park up in L.A., with a million pigeons shitting on his hat."

Nobody wanted to think about it, but the fact was General Pershing and the U.S. Cavalry never came *close* to catching Pancho Villa.

"We don't really know what we'll be doing," Renee Camacho told his father as he was getting the last haircut he would have for a while. Renee had a boy-tenor voice, though at twenty-eight he was actually one of the older men on the squad.

Herbert Camacho was a barber whose shop was located near Thirteenth and Market Streets, only eighteen blocks from the central police station. Renee and other cops often stopped to have a beer with the barber.

Herbert Camacho thought that the task force would be

a good thing. "They're your people," he told his son in reference to the alien victims. "Somebody has to protect them."

Renee had been a natural choice for Dick Snider. He was an energetic cop and, like Dick Snider himself, had a softer side which appealed to the task force lieutenant. A side not often apparent in policemen, and often decimated when young men do police work on city streets.

There was more. Dick Snider had known Renee's father some sixteen years, since Snider was a rookie himself, patrolling Thirteenth and Market Streets.

The older man had always liked the tall lieutenant and told Renee that Dick Snider was *simpático* with the Mexican culture. The barber liked it when Snider would unashamedly offer an embrace and even a kiss, Mexican style. But he had reservations.

"Do you think it might be very . . . dangerous out there?" he asked Renee, his only child.

And one night while the barber was working at his second job, clerking in a liquor store, Dick Snider happened by to get some beer on his way home. Herbert Camacho surprised Dick Snider by blurting, "You better take care of my boy out there!"

"I'll take care a him," Dick Snider promised the barber. "I'll take care a them all."

"None a the guys wear bulletproof vests, goddamnit!" Tony Puente repeated it a thousand times during the formative days of the task force.

"I'm buying the bulletproof vest," his wife, Dene, insisted.

"I won't wear it."

"Are you crazy?"

"I won't wear it."

"Do you wanna die?"

"The other guys might laugh."

"The *other* guys might . . . *laugh*?"

She was "white," but understood *machismo* as far as the Mexican male was concerned. They may not be *real* Mexicans in the eyes of those living south of the border, but the concept of *machismo* is alive and well on both sides of the imaginary line.

She insisted. He refused. She bought the vest. He wouldn't wear it. She called his mother—"a typical little Mexican spitfire mother," as he described her—and then the yelling and screaming *really* started.

"You'll wear the bulletproof vest!" his mother said.

"I *won't* wear the goddamn vest!"

"I hope you get shot, then!"

"I'd rather get shot than wear it!"

And so forth. In the end of course his mother told him she didn't mean it. Still, he *would* rather get shot than wear it, he said. This was in the early days of the experiment. He didn't know so much about getting shot.

When all else failed, his wife wept. "You're not gonna die and leave me with three kids. You *have* to wear it!"

And this did get to him. Grievously. He believed he had robbed her of her youth. Dene was fifteen years old when they married. He was an eighteen-year-old Marine.

It seemed to him that he had always been taking care of women and arguing with them. He was an eldest child with five younger sisters. It was never apparent that he was as bright as he was. He was shy and soft-spoken. He graduated from high school before his seventeenth birthday and joined the Marines with his mother's written consent. He couldn't *wait* to get away from home, away from an alcoholic father who embarrassed him. The embarrassment was the worst possible kind because it was laced with guilt and remorse. The old man used to humiliate him by coming to the Little League baseball games to watch him play for a team sponsored by the San Diego Police Department. The team was managed by police detectives, and young Tony Puente imagined that they had probably arrested the drunken man sitting in the stands cheering him on. Lots of policemen had booked him for being drunk. Tony Puente would forever be easily embarrassed and quick to feel guilt.

The Marine Corps was not an escape. He was beside himself when the Cuban crisis broke in 1962. The Marines were going to Guantánamo! He couldn't wait. But he and his teenaged girl friend had already set the date. He went to his commanding officer to see what he should do.

"Should I bug out to Guantánamo or should I do the *right thing*?" the young Marine asked his officer.

The answer was of course implicit in the question. He did the right thing, as usual. He got married and served his three-year enlistment in Santa Ana, California, a short drive from home. They had three children, and would have a fourth before the border experiment was over. He had robbed her of her youth, he believed, so that when she warned that he was not going to be shot dead and leave her alone to raise the children, he *almost* agreed to wear the vest. He would later change his mind about *machismo* and bulletproof vests.

In some ways Tony Puente looked more Mexican than any of them. His face was rather flat with small Indian eyes peering out through rimless glasses. When his hair grew long and he sprouted a Zapata moustache, he looked like the classic renderings of Mexican revolutionaries. But he spoke Spanish very poorly when recruited for the task force by Dick Snider and Manny Lopez.

He had other things to offer, such as experience. At thirty-three, he was next to the oldest man recruited, and he had seven years of police work. He had never gotten to Guantánamo Bay. He had never gotten anywhere. But at least he was getting out of uniform duty, whether Dene liked the idea or not. And he wasn't going to be wimpy and wear that bulletproof vest.

Yet there *was* something he did not, could not, deny her. And it was something that came to be more crucial to every aspect of life than a thousand bulletproof vests. Dene became immersed in a fundamentalist church. Her life, and his more than hers, would never be the same again.

"She was a young woman with kids," he would say gravely, trying to describe the religious crisis that would soon consume him. "Here I was off at night doing police work and she was forced to raise the kids herself. It seemed to me at first that the new religion was a . . . phase. A *growing* experience. She needed *something* on those lonely nights. It seemed okay that she read the Bible two hours a night. Better than TV when I was off doing police work, I figured."

At this time in his life the faith of Tony Puente was moribund. It had never been the same really since his father died a death hastened by alcohol abuse. The Puentes called the nearby rectory for the priest to come. A white priest told them he'd be glad to oblige—for seventy-five dollars.

Tony's mother then called a Mexican priest, who came at once without mentioning money. Nevertheless, Tony Puente's faith was severely shaken, and in fact was never restored. As he tried to explain the profound, irrevocable change in his marriage and life, he put it this way: "I said okay to her new religion but nixed the bulletproof vest. If I had it to do over I'da wore the goddamn vest to *bed* if she woulda shined-on the God Squad. But how could I know what would happen?"

The oldest cop among them was Fred Gil. He was an ex-Marine drill instructor who had served in Vietnam and hence was expected to assist with the quasi-military training. Fred Gil was thirty-six years of age, even quieter and more soft-spoken than Tony Puente. Fred Gil was known for a shy smile with a sense of humor buried deep. And he was perhaps the only ex-drill instructor in the history of the U.S. Marine Corps who used epithets like "heck" and "goldang." He was one of the poorest Spanish-speakers among the Mexican-American cops, and was so diffident with superior officers that he avoided eye contact and frequently put his hand in front of his mouth when talking to anyone above the rank of sergeant.

Fred Gil's passiveness seemed at first rather astonishing, in that during his service days he had been All-Marine Judo Champion in the open class for heavyweights. And at two hundred pounds this was not easy, since he had to compete with monster Marines. Fred Gil was pleasant, likable, physically fit. Many cops were surprised that at his age he'd join this outfit to run around in the cactus and lizard shit, freezing in the night. But it was personal with Fred Gil. He was affected by the brutality of the bandit gangs in the canyons. Dick Snider's pictures of pathetic alien victims made an impression on old Fred Gil. Perhaps he and Dick Snider had lived long enough to know something about unfulfilled dreams and to empathize with those who had none. Perhaps he was approaching mid-life crisis. At thirty-nine years his wife, Jan, was probably into hers. They fought most of the time. Their marriage was miserable.

Joining the task force was *his* idea, he said. He was going to do something with his police career before he was too old to bother.

"After Vietnam, I just didn't *strive* at much of anything," he said. "I was just so glad to be *alive* it was enough for a long time. Ordinary police work seemed peaceful after the war. Just living without the daily fear of someone trying to kill me."

So Fred Gil found himself in the task force, but he didn't want to *lead* anyone anywhere.

The tallest of them, Ernie Salgado, was their weapons expert. Like Fred Gil he was an ex-Marine who had been in

Vietnam at the beginning of the Tet offensive, and in Da Nang with the 7th Marines. He had been an infantry squad leader and had seen his share of combat during his thirteen months over there. He often wondered if the canyons at night would make him flash to Nam.

Ernie Salgado hailed from Marfa, Texas, population 2,600. It was mostly a Mexican town with some whites and no blacks. He had lived with anti-Mexican sentiment most of his life and decided to settle in San Diego after being stationed there in the Marines. But even with five years of police service, city life was still not completely comfortable. He was the only one of them who didn't like to join the beer busts after work. He might sip a brew if the peer pressure got to be too much, when they ragged him endlessly about Marfa, Texas. Where, they said, your ordinary evening was spent watching cement harden. He made the mistake of telling them about his hometown one night after he'd had about one and a half cans of suds, which loosened his tongue. He would endure Marfa jokes from that night on.

Ernie Salgado had a long face, with a jutting chin and protruding overbite. Wisecracks about his teeth and jaw would come to get on his nerves more than the gags about Marfa, Texas.

Joe Castillo had a lithe athletic build and was the kind of young cop the groupies might ogle. And did he *ever* appreciate that. He was twenty-five years old and by his own reckoning was still in the "black glove" phase. That is, the period of street adjustment when young policemen feel the enormous weight of the new shield on their chests. When some cops quite literally find it imperative to buy and wear black leather gloves, and would probably carry a riding crop if the department would approve.

Joe Castillo was a poor report-writer and had some fear of Manny Lopez' reputation for being the kind of sergeant who was strict on reports. Still, the task force seemed like it might be a stepping-stone to some *good* plainclothes job.

Maybe he wasn't a bookworm, but anything physical was his cup of tea, he figured. Like Fred Gil he spoke lousy Spanish, but in the beginning he thought: What the hell, how much Spanish do you need to jump out of trees, or whatever, onto the heads of a bunch of Tijuana junkies and kick their strung-out asses? Joe Castillo was *extraordinarily* macho.

In the months to come, when the camaraderie was to take a few unexpected twists and turns, Joe Castillo frequently gave vent to frustration and rage. He was wont to say to his colleagues: "You don't like it? Let's step outside!"

Unfortunately, it sometimes caused hoots of laughter from all hands when Joe Castillo would momentarily forget that they were *already* outside.

Carlos Chacon finds himself suddenly confronted by horror. His sister is being attacked by three men. They force her to the ground. One of the assailants is trying to stab her. Carlos goes for them. One of them raises a long knife. Carlos Chacon runs forward but he's too late. The knife is plunged into the belly of his sister, who begins screaming. The scream is for pain, for help, and a cry of *outrage* at being murdered.

He's screaming too, so loud he can't hear her anymore. He lunges at the heap of bodies. He pulls the knife from his sister's heaving belly. It sucks from her guts and splatters blood all over their faces. There's a lot of blood.

Now *he* is the assailant and the three men are fighting for *their* lives. He's relentless, without pity. *They* scream. He holds the heavy knife. The knife feels like . . . justice. He slashes the throat of the man who stabbed his sister. The man cannot even cry out. He just looks at Carlos in horror and accepts his fate. Carlos is big, weighing well over two hundred pounds. He is twenty-three years old. The second assailant is no match for him. He plunges the knife into the throat of the man. Up to the hilt. The man does not even *try* to scream. The third assailant gets away. Carlos' rage is unspeakable, worse than anything he has ever experienced.

He wakes up. The dream is one of many that recur. He dreams of violence a lot.

"My mother was a *real* wetback," Carlos Chacon liked to say.

She had four children in the Republic of Mexico when she was still a young girl. She crossed into Texas by way of the Rio Grande—hence, a *real* wetback. But she had only three children with her on that crossing. Her husband gave one of them away, a daughter. Carlos' mother would eventually have four more daughters and two more sons. She would raise nine children and think about the one left in Mexico.

She settled in Brownsville, Texas, close to her native land, and got a job washing and ironing for American G.I.'s. She met and married a man named Chacon. Among her children was Carlos, who always wanted to become a policeman.

"I was delivered into this world by a cop," he said. "When my father was in jail. I never met my father."

Carlos Chacon was one of three task force members who spoke good Spanish, growing up as he did with Spanish as the language of life, and dream, and fantasy. His mother took her children and migrated to the San Diego area.

"I always appreciated the Richard Pryor joke"—he grins, showing wolfish white incisors—"where the kid says, 'That's my *mom* you're beating up,' and the man says, 'That's my *woman,* kid.' "

His mother lived with a man named Geronimo who used to beat her regularly, and Carlos as well. But the boy inherited some size from the father he never met. Carlos was growing quite large and finally Geronimo found himself overmatched. He was beaten by the boy.

When Carlos went to sleep that night, having just successfully conquered a man he so feared, he dreamed of violence. He was awakened in the middle of the night uncertain whether he was still dreaming. The face of Geronimo was grinning at him. Leering, really. Geronimo began wiggling his crooked finger for the boy to come. Geronimo was holding a machete. Carlos leaped screaming from bed and grabbed a metal bar he had lately kept beside his bed for protection. Geronimo was a bully and a coward. He fled cursing, taking his machete with him.

Geronimo blessedly left their lives for some time and the children settled down a bit, but one day he returned. He tried to resume where he left off, by beating Carlos' mother yet again. But now Carlos was a tenth-grader.

"This time I beat him up *bad,*" Carlos Chacon remembered. "I was so big by then I was looking straight down at him. It was in the room where I used to hear my mother screaming."

They lived in Otai, near Chula Vista. It was a gang-ridden Mexican neighborhood. The people distrusted police, but Carlos did not. "The police came and they sided with me. I beat him *bad.*"

The eyes of Carlos Chacon were not something to forget. He had well-shaped expressive brows, a low forehead, wavy black hair parted in the middle. He talked with his hands, a Mexican trait. But the eyes, well, they were so liquid as to be flowing. Perhaps Valentino had eyes like this, Son-of-the-Sheik eyes which can look startled, fiery and more, while he shows the lupine, very white incisors.

"My mom is the greatest ironer in the world," he liked to brag when he joined the Chula Vista reserve police.

She did her son's police uniforms just as she had done the uniforms of American G.I.'s many years earlier in Brownsville, Texas. He had the sharpest military creases of any cop in San Diego County, reserve or regular. He also had a six-inch Colt Python, .357 magnum.

He was twenty years old then, and like all the other

young police reservists he was trying to master pistol shooting. Dry firing an hour a day was nearly as good as firing a hundred rounds on the target range, they told him. And who could afford a hundred rounds of practice ammo? To dry fire, one simply aims at a spot on the wall, small enough to simulate a bull's-eye at twenty-five yards. It is to condition the eye, mind and hand to a slow, gradual trigger squeeze, and not to jerk involuntarily while anticipating the kick of a handgun during actual firing.

Carlos had a best friend at that time. The friend's name was Michael Clarence Jackson. He was a high school classmate and they did everything together. Michael was black, but he had a lot in common with Carlos Chacon. For one thing, neither had known a father. Carlos once thought he was going to get to see his father for the first time, but the old man died just before the planned visit, cheating Carlos to the end.

They fantasized: Michael about going to law school and being a judge, Carlos about becoming a police chief.

Michael also loved the .357 Colt Python and Carlos let him dry fire it whenever he liked. The action on the .357 magnum was satin-smooth. Carlos ordinarily opened the cylinder and threw the rounds into a box just before the dry firing sessions.

There is controversy as to how it happened. Young men playing quick draw? Carlos said he was dry firing. If so, he obviously didn't look at his target, only at the beautiful Python. He squeezed off an imaginary round. A *real* round exploded from the Python's muzzle.

Carlos Chacon remembers the next part vividly. Michael fell to his knees, his chest smashed open. He wasn't making any noise at first.

"I'm sorry!" Carlos Chacon cried to his friend. "I'm sorry!"

Michael never answered. Finally he started moaning. The moaning sound is what made Carlos run to a telephone.

"He's dead," a deputy sheriff said to Carlos Chacon at the hospital. And that was it. An accidental shooting.

Carlos went with the coroner to the home of the dead boy who had dreamed of being a judge. Carlos insisted on telling Michael's mother himself. He kept saying, "I'm sorry! I'm sorry!" until the black woman swept him into her arms and then they both held each other and cried.

Carlos Chacon had another dream. It was a straightforward dream, virtually devoid of symbol. In the dream Carlos sits on the edge of very dark woods. Michael comes out of the woods to greet his friend. He says, "How you doin? Everything's *great* with me!" They talk about trivial things and Michael goes back into the woods. The dream is not unpleasant, but it recurs. It is always exactly the same.

Despite the accidental shooting of Michael Clarence Jackson, Carlos Chacon was accepted by the San Diego Police Department two years later. He was still a rookie when asked by Dick Snider and Manny Lopez to join the border squad. He enthusiastically accepted.

Carlos Chacon would name his first son Michael, for his slain friend. But he still loved guns. And Carlos Chacon still had *lots* of violent dreams.

CHAPTER · 3

THE OUTSIDERS

ROBBIE HURT WAS TWENTY-FIVE YEARS OLD, STILL A PROBATIONARY policeman with less than a year on the department. At first he hadn't known if he'd like it when he was assigned to Southern Division. It was isolated, geographically cut from uptown San Diego by the towns of National City and Chula Vista. On the other hand there were only eight to twelve men on a shift. This meant he wasn't just a badge number, as some of his academy classmates complained of being, those who were assigned uptown at central headquarters. There were certainly no lieutenants like Dick Snider uptown.

"He was very easy to be around if you were a working cop," Robbie Hurt said. "Uptown you didn't talk to supervisors like you could talk to him. And then he asked me to take a little walk with him."

One night before the task force was formed, Robbie Hurt and Dick Snider took off their uniform shirts and Sam Brownes, and with their service revolvers tucked in their belts they took a stroll up to Deadman's Canyon.

Dick Snider was very outspoken, Robbie Hurt remembered. He was opinionated; he was frustrated. The rookie cop stood with his tall lieutenant and watched him gazing off at the Tijuana night lights and listened to him talk about his obsessive dream of ridding the canyons of bandits.

"The aliens have no one in their corner," his lieutenant told him. "Imagine these peaceful people coming through these canyons. They only wanna feed their families. Imagine the fear and the abuse they suffer down there."

It was tremendously flattering for a rookie cop to be spoken to like this, to hear the dream, to be asked his opinion.

Robbie Hurt had lived in Oakland, where he was raised by a grandmother, and he had attended the University of California at Berkeley for one year. He had been in San Diego for four years, working at the North Island Naval Air Station and for the U.S. Post Office. He had gotten married and one day when career plans seemed tenuous and confused, he applied for the San Diego Police Department.

Robbie found police work to his liking and, since he had studied English at Berkeley, was a good report-writer, but he hadn't had time to distinguish himself in his brief police career when his lieutenant seemed to see something in him. He impressed Dick Snider when he found a discarded wallet on one of those nights while they prowled the perimeter of the canyons. It was later determined to be part of the loot in the murder of an alien. Finally his lieutenant told him what was on his mind.

"I'm thinking about getting a group a guys together to patrol these hills and *handle* this thing," Dick Snider confided as they stood on a hilltop overlooking Deadman's Canyon, on a misty summer night when the lanterns glowed murky just across the imaginary line. In the district with a grand revolutionary name: Colonia Libertad—home of smugglers, addicts, bandits and the hopeless poor.

"I was thrilled to have a lieutenant confiding in me," Robbie Hurt said. "I was floored when he asked me to join the task force. A plainclothes job while still on probation!"

"That job was the beginning of the end of us," Yolanda Hurt recalled. "It took a while to see how he was affected by it. Not in any way I'd expected. But in other ways. He was more affected by the experience than any of them, including Manny Lopez."

Yolie Hurt was a year younger than Robbie and they'd been married five and a half years when Dick Snider's experiment began. "We met when I was eighteen," she said, "and we got married the next year. So we grew up together . . . or did we *both* grow up?"

A tall, slim young woman, rather attractive, and more so the more you were around her. It didn't take the other cop wives long to figure out that she was absolutely genuine, very easy to take, and possibly ten years more mature than her husband.

The experiment was exciting for all the wives at first. These were not your cotillion-trained Junior Leaguers with orthodontic smiles. These were young cop wives, and their husbands, with the exception of Robbie Hurt, were of Mexican descent, several from broken homes, most from relatively poor backgrounds. Yolie Hurt had never in her life been farther than Los Angeles.

She met Robbie when he was in the Navy. Almost instantly her Mexican mother took a liking to him. She called him *mi hijo* even before they married. Yolie didn't like Robbie very much in the beginning, but he was mad about her and told her that repeatedly, and told her mother and sisters and brothers. And he bought her flowers and opened the car door for her. He was a happy, charming young fellow in those days, and didn't appear to have a moody side.

Robbie was a product of a broken home and she pitied him for not having had the parental love she had always known. Yolie, who was always a hyperactive worker, was only too glad to work all the harder for him after they married. She brought home a good paycheck. She kept an immaculate house, as did the other task force wives. Sparkling homes, clean babies and a steady civil-service paycheck being a symbolic leg up into the middle class for all these children of the working class. She also managed the money, did the laundry, cooked the meals. She and Robbie remained childless, and he became a kind of surrogate child.

"I spoiled Robbie *bad,*" she says. "When I look back I just don't know how I *did* that to him."

Yolie had gone to the same high school as Robbie's police academy classmate and fellow squad member, Carlos Chacon. When the experiment began, she and Robbie spent many hours talking about it. She learned of terrible things the bandits did to aliens, and how this squad of cops was going to do something that had never been attempted before. There was something else, something that Yolie was uniquely equipped to understand: Robbie Hurt, almost from the beginning, was feeling like an outsider.

"The jokes they tell in Spanish," Robbie complained to her. "I never know if they're about me. Then I have to have them explained."

"That's a little thing," she'd tell him.

"It's not so little," he'd answer.

And as the days passed, the others, some of whom at first spoke very poor Spanish, began boning up. They had to learn how the Tijuana *cholos* talked. It was to become critical that they learn.

"I'm sure that talking Spanish makes them feel . . . closer," Yolie Hurt told her husband. "It's kind of . . . *endearing* for them."

The wives of Tony Puente, Renee Camacho, Fred Gil and Manny Lopez were white. Carlos Chacon's wife was of Filipino descent. The wives of Eddie Cervantes, Ernie Salgado and Joe Castillo were the only ones of Mexican descent. Yolie Hurt was from mixed parentage: her mother was Mexican, her father black, and physically she was a blend of both. She understood culture clash and how it feels not to precisely belong among whites, blacks or Mexicans.

Robbie was proud of the fact that he was a good writer. "At least I can do the best reports," he said to her. "They come to *me* for help with their reports."

"Those Mexican cops haven't had much in their lives," Yolie told him. "You got to be patient. This is *real* exciting for them." Robbie Hurt's young wife had no idea as yet how exciting it was going to get.

Except for Dick Snider, Robbie was the only one of the original officers on the task force whom they called an O.T.M., which was how the U.S. Border Patrol labeled aliens who were "other than Mexican." He was the only one not to understand Spanish, since Dick Snider did speak the language. There were forty black cops on the department. There were eight black sergeants and one lieutenant, so the blacks were only slightly better represented than the Mexican-Americans.

"How can any rookie say no to this job?" he asked his wife. "Especially a black rookie?"

This black rookie didn't say no. He *leaped* at the offer.

They called him King Kelly. "Guys that ride bikes get handles like *King,*" he said. "And a biker always gets a rep, a jacket. Even a cop biker. Me, I had a cock jacket. They thought every broad that rode my bike, with the exception a my mother, got laid. Like I had a cock bike with a trick seat on it! I'm a married man with three children. Just because I'm a biker I get a cock jacket and a handle: *King* Kelly."

There was a gaggle of waitresses at a certain restaurant near Southern substation. The cops had handles for *them:* Fat Mindy. Thin Mindy. Lana Banana. Two or more waitresses were always ready to party after work, to go to The

Wing, a nearby park named in honor of early glider flights wherein daredevils soared fifty feet above the earth. The cops and waitresses would drink beer at The Wing and commiserate about their respective jobs and about how unappreciative the public is, and pretty soon they'd be soaring at five thousand feet without benefit of glider.

One night King Kelly went for a run on his screaming 550 Honda with a blood alcohol reading of about .18, he believes, and his passenger, Lana Banana, was even drunker. Everyone loved that Honda and the bright-orange snowmobile suit that went with it. It was fun to see how fast the Honda would roar by the base of Otai Mountain. King Kelly found out how fast it would go while he was breathing .18 blood alcohol: exactly 105 miles per hour. It only works if you're without goggles and without a helmet and you're blowing about .18.

"If you lose it at one-oh-five," he said, "you go down in a tumble a sparks and you don't have to worry about comas and IV's and paralysis and irreversible brain damage."

It made perfect sense at the time. The night wind was frosty and Lana Banana put her icy hands inside the orange snowmobile suit just as a rabbit ran out and froze in the beam of light.

Ken Kelly's last thought was: We're gonna hit a rabbit at one-oh-five. My wife's gonna be mad because even though I'm innocent they're probably gonna find us with her hand inside my pants, wrapped around my balls. The rear wheel's gonna slip out and we're gonna die now. Good-bye.

Except that he reflexively swerved just enough to go into a deadly high-speed wobble.

"More! Do it more!" Lana Banana screamed, later describing the wobble as something akin to straddling the world's *biggest* vibrator.

And thanks to the volume of alcohol in his body, his reactions were so *slow* that they rode out of the deadly wobble which would have killed a sober man. Lana Banana said it was a hell of a sexy ride, a 550cc Japanese *dildo,* is what it was. And that Ken Kelly was a prince! No, a *King*!

He was a sturdy blond with lank straight hair combed back flat but always falling over his ears. After a few drinks he loved to take both palms and pull his hair back tight on his head and leer, with darting pale-blue eyes. His Jack Nicholson impersonation. But actor Jack Nicholson *never* looked as deranged as Ken Kelly, not in his most eccentric performance, not when Ken Kelly let go with his demented scream: "Sex! Drugs! Rock 'n roll!"

He was known as a talented cop. He was smart and gutsy and spoke in colorful, profane, grammatical English. Ken Kelly wanted to join the new task force badly. He was twenty-eight years old with plenty of police experience, having been a cop for nearly six years, and he knew the canyons better than anyone. From the time he was a boy until he joined the San Diego Police Department, Ken Kelly had hunted doves in Spring Canyon, and north of Airport Mesa, and even in Deadman's Canyon and Smuggler's Gulch. He knew he could find his way around those hills night or day.

The task force was another chance, he felt. He had tried dozens of times without success to get to Vietnam while in the Air Force. He always wanted to do something *significant* and fate was denying him.

"If you *ever* decide to give a white boy a break," Ken Kelly pleaded to Manny Lopez, "I know one loony enough to go out in those canyons." Then he'd do a Gunga Din and say, "I'll carry water, sahib. Take me *with* you!"

Ken Kelly was not one of the original San Diego cops selected for the experiment, but he wasn't about to give up. He could be found leaping out of police corridors at any hour of the night crying out to Manny Lopez, "Take me with you, bwana. I'll be your gun bearer. If you don't, I'll go bad, I swear. Sex! Drugs! Rock 'n roll!"

He never gave up. He figured: Who knows what might

happen out there in those canyons? Somebody might get stung by a scorpion and they'd need to send in a bench warmer.

Manny Lopez couldn't go to the john without a voice from the next stall whispering, "If you don't take me, I'll go wrong. I'll wear a blindfold and a garter belt and star in stag movies. Take me *with* you!"

Manny Lopez would giggle and promise Ken Kelly that if there was ever an opening . . .

CHAPTER · 4

EXODUS

IT WAS THE FIRST WEEK OF OCTOBER WHEN THEY FINALLY got to do it. There were jokes and chatter and excitement during the briefing that afternoon. There were lots of cracks from the other patrol cops as the task force gathered shotguns, revolvers, flares, first aid kits, goggles, flashlights, binoculars, ammo, radios, handcuffs.

As sunset approached, Eddie Cervantes, the Marine reservist, said, "Time to saddle up," and someone pissed him off by noting that in *The Sands of Iwo Jima* that was John Wayne's line.

Then Dick Snider—who was as big as John Wayne, with more lines eroding his dust-bowl kisser—said, "Let's go out and put some crooks in jail."

It didn't sound right coming from someone dressed in camouflage fatigues and a black woolen watch cap and combat boots, and armed to the teeth. It sounded like *cop* talk just when they were starting to think of themselves as some kind of commando raiders, ready to outswat SWAT.

The whole operation sounded military enough on

paper. Renee Camacho, one of the first men chosen by Dick Snider, was going to work a support team with a border patrolman. They'd handle the equipment, and God knows what-all they had that four-wheel-drive vehicle loaded down with.

"Everything but frigging C rations!" one of the patrol cops said when he looked into the Bronco. And he called them "Flea SWAT-ers."

Eddie Cervantes was working the other support team with a U.S. Customs officer. One observation team would be manned by a big young cop named Felix Zavala and a border patrolman. The main observation team would be handled by the supervisors, Dick Snider and Manny Lopez. They had the valuable commodity: a starlight scope for nighttime observation work.

The arrest team would be manned by the two ex-Marine D.I.'s, Ernie Salgado and Fred Gil. They would be assisted by rookie cops Robbie Hurt and Carlos Chacon. The victim team, which would be responsible for corralling the alien robbery victims, was worked by another rookie, Joe Castillo, who was disappointed that he might not get enough action, along with the other U.S. Customs officer, who spoke the good Spanish needed for victim interrogation.

There was a continuation of chatter and jokes as they took the short ride to the canyons, impatient for sundown. There was plenty of reconnoitering to do once they got there and placed the teams where they could observe unobserved after darkness. And though some of the cops of Southern Division had occasionally driven up those bone-jarring rock-clay trails, which were slimy-slick in winter and cement-hard in summer, they hadn't really seen and heard and smelled this patch of land when it came *alive.*

It was not a large area of responsibility, not geographically. Just a few square miles of low hills and shallow canyons, full of dry brush in Indian summer, and cactus. And mesquite losing its vitality and balling up into prickly tumbleweed. The parched vegetation was stunted but surprisingly relentless and enduring, like the scorpions and tarantulas. Wind rattled the dry brush. Every rattle was spooky because of snakes.

First impressions: two hawks wheeling in the sky through smoke plumes drifting north from the Mexican city. Then a pack of coyotes, brown shapes and gray, slinking across the trails at dusk, eyeing these humans with indifference. The overriding image at dusk was of shadow. Looming shadow, fleeting shadow, silvery light and cloud shadow in the canyons. Sometimes brassy light as the sun rested suddenly on the ridge. Then shadows crossed the sunball on the horizon. Silhouette shadows. Human beings.

An unbelievable tableau to digest all at once. The garishly painted shacks blanketing the hillsides across the imaginary line quickly assumed the color of urban smoke. Smoke at dusk in the shadowlight. There was the "upper soccer field," a plateau so called because the aliens did indeed play while they waited. And the lower soccer field, a smaller plateau. And Deadman's Canyon, Spring Canyon, Washerwoman's Flats, where an old Mexican squatter used to live and do her laundry in the dirty trickle flowing through the U.S. canyons.

The unbelievable tableau: the throngs, the multitudes, the masses! They were everywhere: huddled by campfires, squatting, playing, buying tamales, selling soda pop, chatting, laughing, swapping clothing, exchanging money with guides, singing, weeping, getting *ready.* The nightly army of aliens was readying itself to come. All of this only several hundred yards across the canyons. All of this just north of the invisible line, on U.S. soil, in the no-man's-land tacitly relinquished to them by the United States government, which had decided that its border patrolmen would avoid these few square miles of miserable earth and wait farther north, on more accessible land.

Even through binoculars it looked for all the world like

an enormous sprawling picnic. There was a game of baseball in progress. There was an astonishing number of women and children among them, not to bid the men farewell. *They* were coming too. Perhaps they had tried it last week and been caught? Or been turned back? Or robbed? Or raped? Perhaps they had tried it *many* times.

And there were pregnant women coming for the sole purpose of giving birth to their babies in the home of some barrio midwife. To have a child who is a U.S. citizen, entitled to all the rights and privileges accorded same. To register the birth and perhaps return with the child to Mexico, *that* child's future guaranteed should things get worse.

"I couldn't *believe* it the first time I saw it," Renee Camacho said. "And I'd lived in San Diego all my life. It was like . . . did you see the old movie *Exodus*?"

So the task force assembled across the canyons and chose their observation points, from which they would support each other, observe crimes, arrest bandits and corral victims. And they would look at one another in wonder when hundreds of other aliens suddenly materialized in the dusk. Human beings of all ages would rise up as though from the earth itself. People who had been invisible—resting, sleeping, eating, praying. Up from the mesquite and the rocks and the skeletal oaks. They would simply rise *up*!

And then it was dark. Just like that.

The hills began to *move*. The masses began to surge northward on their journeys to the land of plenty. It was dark. Darker than they dreamed it would be. Dick Snider had told them over and over how dark it was in the canyons, but Jesus Christ! This was *dark*. Could an ordinary night *get* this dark? There was even an early moon. But it was *dark*. And they weren't alone, not by a long shot.

The *Star Trek* lights attached to the sawed-off shotguns were of no value whatsoever and were quickly removed. The radios were faulty in the canyons. The starlight scope was seeing only shapes. They saw what looked like a guide meeting a group of fifteen. Some looked like children. They saw what could be three bandits waiting behind a rock pile. Then the shapes disappeared. Then the *rocks* disappeared.

It was not quiet but it seemed quiet. There were the ever-present dogs barking in the canyons, delirious with joy at the scraps left by the aliens beginning their march. The kerosene lamps were glowing all over the hills to the south, which was Colonia Libertad, home of bandits and smugglers and drug dealers and addicts. What looked sordid in the day was beautiful by night. The kerosene lamps flickered. The squalor was transformed.

The music began, radios mostly, but they could hear some live voices singing, all from the hills south of the imaginary line, from the shacks and cantinas of Colonia Libertad. Then they started hearing the *clicks.* At first it scared the hell out of them. The safety being taken off shotguns? The bandits have shotguns? No, castanets! That's all it is, castanets. What the hell's this? Somebody's doing *flamenco* in the canyons?

It was stones. The clicking of stones. Or sometimes they snapped their fingers. They did not talk, these masses coming toward them through the canyons. They signaled to each other by clicking stones together. All of them: the aliens, the guides, the *bandits.*

Cadaverous dogs who accompanied them a short way suddenly did not bark or growl or whimper. Children didn't cry. All creatures of the canyons seemed to revere the ritual, played out each night of the year when there was neither flood nor storm. The silence of the masses was eerie and made the cops very uneasy. Click click click and no other sound from them.

The city cops couldn't see twenty feet in front of them. And it got darker. Then they couldn't see *ten* feet in front of them. And it got darker.

Tony Puente, the only one among them to wear corrective lenses, removed his glasses, wiped them and put them back on because he could see only eight feet in front of him. Within one minute he could not see *five* feet in front of him. And neither could the others.

The San Diego newspapers carried heroic headlines for a few days: POLICE PUSH TO WIPE OUT BORDER BANDITS. And STALK BANDITS AT BORDER. And CRACK DOWN ON BORDER BANDITS.

But the sad fact was painfully clear their third night out: The commando raiders could not find their dicks in that darkness, let alone bandits.

One task force member claimed he heard a rattler. Another ran his hand into some cactus and required first aid. Another was forced to arrest three aliens who literally stumbled over him in the darkness. Reluctantly, disgustedly, he had to turn them over to the Border Patrol to get them out of the way.

Dick Snider tried to prove that middle age was insignificant and went chasing a group of fleeing shadows, ending up on his face, saying, "I'm okay, I'm okay," through a mouthful of mesquite.

In less than a week the commando raiders were no more. There was nothing left but the derisive hoots from their peers which echoed from central headquarters to the Mexican border. Everyone giggled and asked if they could use the raiders' sexy camouflage fatigues for camper tarps.

So much for plan A. The contingency plan, if Dick Snider was not to fall on his sword after the commando debacle, was to have some of the task force members dress as aliens and act as robbery decoys. In fact, this was much closer to proper police work and something the cops were not unfamiliar with. Vice cops, narcotics cops, detectives, all have occasion to decoy bad guys, and what was the difference, really, whether you did it at Eleventh and Market Streets or in a vermin-infested gully called Deadman's Canyon?

But first they were going to test their decoy techniques on San Diego city streets. On October 11 five of the task force cops, dressed more or less like aliens, took a stroll through the streets of San Ysidro looking as diffident as possible.

It was about 11:00 P.M. when the five of them walked along Kostner Drive. They saw three young men standing by a parked car. The young men were Mexican-Americans. Just like them. The three young men, who'd been smoking a joint or two, were totally fooled by the mannerisms and the ragged clothes.

Tony Puente removed his wire-rimmed glasses, realizing that few aliens could afford *any* glasses, let alone gold wire rims. In the slang of the streets a young man asked if they'd like a ride north, but the cops ignored them and kept walking, in the manner of pollos. Then the three young men strolled up beside them and one of them said in Spanish, "Come with us. We'll protect you from *la migra*"—which was what the pollos called the U.S. Border Patrol or anyone dealing with aliens in either country.

But the cops just lowered their gaze and walked a little faster. Then one of the young men said, "They're going to arrest you *cabrones*!"

But these dumb pollos seemed way more scared of them than of *la migra*. Still, he tried once more and said, "*¡Vengan carnales!*"

But calling them brothers didn't help either. These pollos picked up the pace. Finally one of their benefactors, who was wearing about a hundred jailhouse tattoos on both arms and hands, started running toward them. A funny thing happened. The cops began hotfooting it down Darwin Way and they started *feeling* like pollos. The five of them were running from three lowlife *vatos* who were cursing and threatening them—but not yet demanding money, a crucial element in the crime of robbery.

One of the street thugs got sick and tired of this and, cornering them in a cul-de-sac, picked up some rocks from the ground. Then the hoodlums were looking at shiny brass shields and realizing they had really screwed up, and the pollos-cum-cops began chasing the thugs back the way they had come.

Tony Puente was very surprised to have felt, however briefly, like an illegal alien. To feel threatened by everyone. To be abused by petty hoodlums who probably could have been bought off by a few extorted dollars.

It was only a "probable cause" arrest. The thugs had not as yet demanded money. They would not be charged with robbery and were released the next day. It was an unremarkable encounter except that it proved that they *could* look like aliens. But there was the other thing, the strange sensation as they got into the parts they were playing. They told Dick Snider to get them union cards from the actors guild.

They tried it again the next night. Two men with the look of smugglers offered to give the pollos a ride to Los Angeles for $100, and were arrested for a violation of the "wildcatting" law in the California penal code: that is, offering transportation for money, without a license. Not a great pinch, but their alien disguises and mannerisms were working.

Within the next several days on the streets of San Ysidro they had broken up into groups of three or more and had been accosted by many street hoodlums, ranging in age from thirteen to twenty-nine years. They had been threatened with knives, sticks, rocks, screwdrivers, and asked to give up money. A couple of the Mexican-American street crooks had tried to escape and a couple had succeeded. Otherwise there was no problem arresting them. The decoy business was a piece of cake.

There were lots of show biz gags about who was going to be the next Robert De Niro. Then they decided to take their act on the road, into the canyons where the *real* bandits did business, the banditos from the *other* side who sometimes left their victims rotting in the mesquite.

They were already beginning to form a class structure. At this stage of the experiment there were three walking teams. The first was inevitably comprised of Manny Lopez, Tony Puente and Eddie Cervantes. Tony Puente was one of the senior men in terms of police experience. Eddie Cervantes, the smallest, was the most aggressive and outspoken. He was from Texas and talked a slightly accented Tex-Mex English. He had grown up speaking Spanish and was fluent.

The fourth member of "the varsity," as they began calling themselves, would vary. Manny Lopez would give the others a rotating shot at walking with the varsity. On this night it was Carlos Chacon, and very soon his extraordinarily expressive eyes would get about three times as big as the muzzle on the sawed-off 12-gauge under his coat. And the slithering question mark of a right eyebrow would be crawling all *over* the balding forehead of Manny Lopez. This, when a Tijuana bandit walked up and introduced himself.

At dusk the varsity had begun walking their new foot beat on the top flatland along the international border between the Tijuana airport and Deadman's Canyon. They were about one hundred yards inside the line and were walking west. They were tense, excited, alert, but not very afraid. This was their first night posing as pollos in the canyons but they were already finding enough confidence to talk with parties of real pollos heading north. Manny Lopez and Eddie Cervantes could fool anyone. Manny did most of the talking. Tony Puente spoke such poor Spanish he was ordered by Manny to keep his mouth shut. Carlos Chacon carried the sawed-off shotgun under the oldest and funkiest jacket he owned.

The happening of note on that very first evening occurred in the vicinity of the Tijuana airport. The four cops were walking like a covey of quail, alien style, when just before nightfall they saw a blue and white Tijuana Municipal Police car on a dirt road south of the fence. There were no cops inside. The cops were behind them talking through the fence to three girls who had just crossed into the United States. Three Tijuana policemen then stepped over the barbed wire fence onto American soil. One of the cops caught his tan uniform pants on the wire and began to curse.

One Tijuana policeman said, "*¡Vengan!*" but Manny Lopez and his three men continued walking.

Then all three Tijuana cops, without wasting any more breath, simply drew their automatics, jacked rounds into the chambers and said, "*¡Vengan, cabrones!*"

And the neophyte pollos responded. They said:

"Holy shit!"

"Hey! Hey! HEY!"

"What the fuck!"

And while the Tijuana cops were puzzled by these weird pollos babbling in English, Manny Lopez pulled his badge *and* his gun. Then his three subordinates drew *their* guns.

The first evening in the canyons, their first *hours* in the canyons, there were seven cops pointing guns not at bandits but at each other.

"That's what you'd call a *righteous* Mexican standoff," Eddie Cervantes later said.

But not at the moment. Nobody was thinking up gags at the moment. They were all staring down very large gun barrels and getting very tense.

"*¡Policías!*" Manny Lopez warned. "*¡Somos policías!*"

"Ooooooh! *¡Policías!* Well, we thought you were *banditos.* You weren't acting like pollos! We wanted to get you back to our side," the cops told them.

But Manny Lopez wasn't buying any of it. There had

been too many reports of Tijuana policemen robbing aliens.

"Why don't you control the bandits from *your* side. That's where they're from," he told them in Spanish. "Now let's see some identification."

They, being on American soil, reluctantly obeyed, and Eddie Cervantes took the Handie-Talkie out of the plastic drawstring "pollo bag" he was carrying and relayed the names of the Tijuana cops to communications.

Then there were many apologies while the Tijuana cops tried to convince Manny Lopez that they, too, were after bandits.

"Cops and robbers," Manny said disgustedly in English. "These motherfuckers're cops *and* robbers! Take a walk, Jack," he said finally to the senior Tijuana policeman, who understood *that* well enough.

"What the hell kind a job is *this* going to be?" Tony Puente wanted to know as they resumed walking. He thought about Manny drawing down on them while facing their guns. He thought maybe he should start wearing his glasses even if it did blow their cover. Then it got so dark that glasses wouldn't have helped much.

When the sun dropped, the huddled masses unhuddled to begin the nightly crossing ritual. One of them was a twenty-five-year-old *campesino* named Lino Ariza. Lino Ariza was of course very frightened to begin with, and even more so when he and his party were instructed by their *coyote* to remain near the international border until their guide came for them. Lino was from Durango, as was one of his companions, Luis Rodrigues. A third man, who had introduced them to the *coyote* in Tijuana, was from Jalisco. There were also three women in this crossing party whom Lino did not know.

There was so much for Lino to fear waiting there—just

seventy-five yards inside the line, yet so close to the lamps and noises of Colonia Libertad—that he had to relieve himself repeatedly, making many trips down the trail to disappear behind the bushes for a few moments. After his journey, and the money he had already been forced to pay, Lino had only 24 U.S. dollars left, and a $15 wristwatch, his most prized possession, and a leather cowboy belt with a big metal buckle. That and the clothes on his back. Yet Lino Ariza was by far the richest in his party that night. And somehow these border people, the *coyotes* and guides and criminals, seemed to sense it. Or so Lino imagined.

At 10:00 P.M. they were standing on the rim of Deadman's Canyon with their backs to the flickering lamps of Colonia Libertad. They crouched when a blue and white Tijuana police car drove slowly past the fenceless invisible line and flashed a perfunctory beam of light toward some children playing with an old truck tire.

Then the party of trembling aliens saw three shadows approaching slowly in the darkness. It was so dark the shadows were only a few yards away when they materialized. Lino immediately suspected the worst because the three men were dressed slightly better than the pollos. They wore tight jeans and warm Pendleton shirts. All had long hair past their collars and two had bandannas tied around their heads in the manner of movie pirates. And they didn't walk like pollos. They strode boldly toward them so that Lino and his party instinctively crouched down to show their submissiveness.

Lino wasn't sure who saw the knives first, but one of the women stood up screaming and began running back toward the border. It probably prevented a multiple rape, because the other women panicked and followed her, leaving the bandits to deal with the squatting men.

The bandits were of course more than a bit angry at having lost the women, but there were lots more where those came from. The leader, who wore a scraggly goatee, suddenly stepped behind Lino's friend Luis and placed the blade of his knife against the throat of the terrified unprotesting alien. Lino saw a trickle of blood and when Luis began to cry, another bandit smashed him in the face with a huge rock. Luis fell to the ground whimpering and pleading.

The bandits never said anything except *"Danos tu feria"* the whole time they searched them. Only that slang demand for money. And only once. They were efficient. They didn't waste movements or breath. They got the $24 from Lino and his treasured watch and his leather belt. Luis Rodrigues, happy to be alive, gladly surrendered the only thing of value he had left, a cowboy belt with a big metal buckle. It had cost him 5 American dollars in Tijuana when he first arrived.

The cops all wore the oldest grubbies they owned and the rattiest tennis shoes, but still were not quite properly costumed. Manny Lopez was thinking of making a Salvation Army or Goodwill run to outfit his troops like proper aliens. As they got to the rim of Deadman's Canyon, they were startled by three shapes squatting in the manner of pollos.

Manny Lopez, who was getting the docile inflection down pat, simply said *"Buenas noches"* very respectfully as they passed. The squatting men did not reply respectfully, nor at all. The three were wearing jeans and had collar-length hair and two wore bandanas tied around their heads.

One of the squatting men stood up. He had a scraggly goatee that fluttered in the wind. He told them in Spanish to watch out for *la migra.* And when they saw a pair of headlights in the distance which could not have been Border Patrol, he told them to duck.

And then, sick and tired of the charade, and more than satisfied that these pollos were pluckable, one of the bandits walked up to Eddie Cervantes and introduced himself in a manner that the cop had never before experienced.

Eddie Cervantes had sad eyes that turned down at the corners. He was short enough to be the brunt of all the Munchkin jokes, and his gung-ho Marine haircut was boyish. He looked perhaps the easiest for the bandits to intimidate. The bandit merely smiled and brought a blade straight up, glinting in the moonlight. Without warning he grabbed Eddie Cervantes by the throat and whispered in his face, *"Hórale, cabrón."*

That quickly. To be grabbed by the throat. To be staring at a blade. No by-your-leave. No how-about-a-cigarette? No foreplay.

The cops would learn about bandit styles. The style of this trio was to intimidate through violence, not just the threat of violence. The goateed bandit swung the heavily buckled belt he'd just stolen from Lino Ariza at the face of Manny Lopez.

The bandits could not have been more surprised. There was a hell of a lot of yelling and screaming when Manny whipped out his two-inch revolver, and as it later said in the arrest report, his bandit "suffered a slight injury to his forehead as he struggled for the weapon." Which, translated into regular English, meant that Manny Lopez smacked him right between the freaking eyes.

Eddie Cervantes did not use his weapon. It happened instantly. The flash of steel, the hand at his throat. Manny yelled something, the gun cracking the bandit between the horns. Eddie Cervantes had his gun in his hand but instinctively grabbed for the knife. He kicked his bandit's balls clear up around his head rag.

The arrest report would also say, "Only the force necessary to effect the arrests was used by the arresting officers."

But these three bandits got a *whole* lot of lumps. They were the first real bandits the cops had encountered. And they had scared the living shit out of Eddie Cervantes. And people who are scared often play catch-up.

The fact is that after Eddie Cervantes threw a shoulder into his bandit and knocked him flat and pounced on him and beat the living crap out of him, he was still very tense and very mad. He shoved his snub-nosed revolver into the teeth of the bandit and said, "I could *kill* you right now!"

And it dawned on him. He could! Out in these canyons, in the darkness, with the others still handcuffing and wrestling and beating the hell out of the other two, he *could* kill this bandit right now. His hands were shaking. He had never fired his gun outside of target practice.

"I could kill you right *now*!" he repeated, bumping the bandit's teeth with his gun muzzle.

"Don't kill me, *'mano*!" the bandit pleaded. "Don't kill me!"

"I could, you son of a bitch!" Eddie Cervantes said. "I *could*!"

But he didn't.

"We were afraid to use our guns at first," he would later say. "We were still *normal* policemen."

At about the time that Eddie Cervantes was flossing the bandit's teeth with his gun muzzle, the other teams found a brace of dazed and bewildered pollos not a hundred yards away in the darkness. One of them had a knife wound on his throat and a contusion on his forehead where he had been smashed by a rock. Lino Ariza and his party were driven to the substation, where they identified the bandits who had robbed them.

Lino Ariza told the cops that he would give one leg and one arm if he could just make enough money to survive in Durango. He didn't see how a person could ever be happy in such a violent country as America.

When Tony Puente got home that night from the beer party to celebrate the bandit bust, he was hoping that his wife, Dene, would be awake. When he wanted something badly enough, he'd *hope* for it. He never prayed for anything since he had stopped being a Catholic. And anyway his wife—who had plunged into tract-dispensing, Bible-reading, self-denigrating Fundamentalism with a vengeance—was praying enough for both of them.

"Maybe I coulda stopped it in the beginning," he would say over and over to his comrades during the months to come. When he'd been drinking enough.

Sometimes he wondered if he should have married a Mexican girl. Would it still have happened? She was, after fourteen years of marriage, not yet thirty years old. She was slender and still looked to him like the child he had married. The fact is, Tony Puente was mad about her and would remain so even when her plunge into religion would come to dominate not only her life but his. When in fact her faith would become the single most important force in *his* life.

She was not awake. It was just as well. He was drunk. But she looked *so* young. He didn't go to sleep. He went unconscious. The next day he couldn't remember driving home. For a while, he couldn't find his glasses.

During the last week of October 1976 there would be no less than seven newspaper stories dealing with rather routine arrests made by the new Border Crime Task Force. The wives and the cops themselves began searching the department stores for suitable scrapbooks.

They all knew that Manny Lopez was a friend of the San Diego Police Department's press relations man, Bill Robinson. Manny called Robinson, and a good account was released to the newspapers about their first *real* bandit arrest.

Eddie Cervantes, whose down-turned eyes were a little baggy that morning from booze and a nightmare, couldn't wait to get a copy of the newspaper. He wondered if he should maybe buy a *leather*-bound scrapbook. He opened the newspaper. There was a terrific story dealing with the attack on Manny Lopez by a bandit swinging a belt buckle. And of how Manny Lopez and his men disarmed and captured the crooks, who turned out to be heroin addicts. There was no mention of the knife at Eddie Cervantes' throat. There was no mention of Eddie Cervantes' throat, nor of the rest of him.

And his sad eyes turned down a little more and he thought maybe a plastic scrapbook would be good enough.

And he wondered if Manny Lopez had *stolen* his glory.

CHAPTER · 5

¿SABES QUÉ?

THERE WAS ONE SIGNIFICANT INCIDENT IN THE MONTH OF November which influenced the way future cards would be dealt and played in those canyons in the months to come. For the second time in their short history the squad became involved in a dangerous Mexican standoff.

Manny Lopez was not teamed with the varsity on this particular night. He was leading a walking team consisting of one customs officer, a border patrolman and two of the San Diego cops. An illegal alien they had encountered earlier, thinking they were fellow pollos, had warned them that there were two Tijuana policemen robbing aliens near the railroad tracks on the Mexican side.

The reports of rogue cops from Tijuana had been mounting. Technically such police officers were not robbers but extortionists. It was uncommon for a Mexican cop to shove a .45 automatic in somebody's face and empty his pockets, bandit style. They *suggested,* under color of authority, that the pollo get his ass back to his own country unless he could make the cops' miserable job worthwhile. After all, the cops had kids too. The Mexican police might reason that they were charging a tariff to close their eyes to something their government didn't discourage in the first place: the migration of its boldest and most desperate citizens.

The alien had warned them to watch for a station wagon on the Mexican side. They were about two hundred yards from the railroad tracks and walking east at 11:00 P.M. but did not see any cars south of the fence. When they were one hundred yards closer to the tracks they saw a vehicle, maybe a station wagon or van, crawling along the tracks without headlights.

They heard a car door slam just south of the international fence. They continued walking and saw two figures running westbound in the darkness as though to cut them off. They froze and watched two dark figures climb through a fence hole just above the Border Patrol's welded landing mats. The figure in the lead was wearing the black uniform of a Tijuana auxiliary officer.

He charged forward, yelling: *"¡Vengan acá!"*

He brought up a four-inch .38 revolver and pointed it at the face of Manny Lopez. And for the second time, the sergeant was staring down the muzzle of a gun, and for the second time he made a decision others might not have made: he did not explain who they were. Just as he had done with the Tijuana cops near the airport, he looked straight into the gun barrel, and risked being shot to death by reflex or design.

While facing the gun he jerked out his own revolver and badge and said: *"¡Policías!"*

A *second* Mexican standoff. Manny's men followed suit. The black-uniformed Mexican did not jerk the trigger through reflex or design. He looked at the handguns and shotgun facing him. He heard someone say he would die at once unless he dropped his gun. He stepped back two paces in the moonlight. His gun was still aimed directly at Manny Lopez. Then he lowered it.

The second man turned and ran to the fence. There was some confusion then in the darkness as the cops fanned out, dropped down, fearing a sniper attack, but heard the door slam on a vehicle and got to the fence in time to see a jeep wagon with white numbers on the side. The second man powered that jeep up the hill, lights out like a movie stunt man. Backward. Within seconds he was *gone.*

Manny Lopez jerked the gun out of the auxiliary officer's hand and decked him. Manny Lopez was pretty mad all right when he cinched the iron on the wrists of the protesting Mexican, and called him about a hundred kinds of thieving crooked bastard cop.

The man was twenty-three years old and was *not* a cop. In Tijuana, people pay the city treasury for special patrol by auxiliary officers. There are no privately hired rent-a-cops as there are north of the line. Yet auxiliary officers are to the municipal police what privately employed security officers are to the San Diego Police on the American side of the border—private citizens in uniform.

The Mexican auxiliary officer was carrying about $60 in U.S. currency and about 630 Mexican pesos. He may have been extorting aliens in the canyons. He said he thought Manny Lopez and his men, due to their strange behavior in walking *along* the border fence, were not aliens but robbers of aliens. He said he should not have crossed through the fence, but that he was not a bandit.

The auxiliary officer was arrested for robbery-related crimes, but all charges were dropped by the district attorney, since nothing could be proved. The Mexican had only crossed the border while armed. He had only said "Come here!" Nothing more.

"If I'da waited I might a got *shot,*" Manny Lopez protested to the investigating detectives.

"He *may* be a robber, but we'll never know," was the answer.

"*I* know," Manny Lopez said, "that Mexican's a *crook.*"

And when he thought about it, that was redundant. To Manny nearly all Mexican lawmen were crooks, auxiliary or regulars. They were thieves and worse. Manny Lopez was feeling more and more *alone,* and strangely enough there was something exhilarating about it.

One evening a lieutenant wrote a strange acronym on their chalkboard. It said: B.A.R.F.

When asked what it meant the lieutenant said, "Border Alien Robbery Force."

Border Alien . . . BARF? Was he jiving them? How would that look in the papers? BARF? Bullshit! They called themselves something infinitely more romantic, The Task Force. Screw this BARF shit.

And then one night shortly after Eddie Cervantes met his first real Mexican bandit and flossed the robber's teeth with a gun muzzle, the boys were doing a little walking in a San Ysidro gang neighborhood preparatory to going out into Smuggler's Gulch and Deadman's Canyon. If they couldn't get righteous robbers there, they hoped for an easy wildcat bust, since like all public servants, they needed to pad the stats to justify their existence.

There were lots of wildcatters, real and bogus, offering rides to the multitudes of pollos passing through. In fact, many of the wildcatters were actually thieves and robbers and rapists, and the aliens never had a chance for a real ride at all.

On this particular wildcat outing, the varsity, with Joe Castillo as the fourth team member, walked from the train trestle to the streets of San Ysidro, where they were confronted by two men who had the look of Tijuana guides.

One of them stopped the four pollos by asking for a cigarette. Manny Lopez produced a proper pack of Fiesta Mexican cigarettes. Another asked for a match. Manny Lopez produced a proper Mexican matchbook.

"Where do you come from?" one of them asked, putting

the Mexican cigarette in his pocket and lighting an American smoke from his own pack.

By now, Manny Lopez was enjoying his thespian talents and he switched from the familiar places, Tecate and Mexicali, and said, "El Salvador. We came all the way north through Mexico from El Salvador. It's very bad in our country."

Then the guide said to Joe Castillo, who spoke Spanish about like Rosalynn Carter, "Got any *pisto* on you?" We'll give you a ride to Los Angeles for fifty dollars each."

Joe Castillo didn't answer, but put his thumb up toward his mouth in the drinking gesture, laughed nervously and shook his head no, since *pisto* in barrio slang refers to an alcoholic drink or a drinker.

The guide said, "I don't want something to drink. I want some *money*. In El Salvador, *pisto* means money. I don't think you're from El Salvador."

Then the other guide said to Joe Castillo, "Say something, brother. Let's hear you talk."

And Manny Lopez, who had a temper like Idi Amin, said to the guides, "*¿Sabes qué? ¿Sabes qué?*": You know what? You know what?

Then in English he said, "You know what? Fuck this!"

And the wildcatters were in short order flat on their bellies wearing iron on their wrists. After the two were booked and it was time to go out into the canyons, the entire squad was informed about the episode where Joe Castillo "fucked up."

Still a rookie cop, Joe Castillo had not yet started calling his sergeant by his Christian name. He said, "But, Sarge, how was I supposed to know that *pisto* means something else in El Salvador?"

"Goddamn it!" Manny said, with his eyebrow squiggling into half a question mark. "I told ya to shut up and not talk. Let *me* do the talking."

"But, Sarge, I *didn't* talk!"

"This is kind a like in the old war movies," it was observed. "Like where they ask ya who Betty Grable was married to and who's Mickey Mouse's girl friend, and like that."

"Who's Betty Grable?" he was asked, and Manny's twenty-nine-year-old reptilian eyebrow settled down, and he started feeling *old.*

"We need a code word when we're ready to take them down," Manny decided. "How about *¿sabes qué?* When I'm talking to these assholes and I got the elements for a righteous bust, I'll say *¿sabes qué?*"

"What's that mean exactly?" Robbie Hurt wanted to know.

"You know what? That's what it means. You know what? So listen for *¿sabes qué?*" Manny Lopez told his men. "When I say *¿sabes qué?* get ready, cause a bust is going down."

"Then we need *another* signal to know when to pull our guns or grab them or whatever," it was noted.

Robbie Hurt felt left out because the Spanish conversations in their hole-in-the-wall squadroom were getting as prevalent as the English, making him even more of an outsider. He said, "How about *Barf*?"

"*Barf?*"

"Yeah, Manny says *¿sabes qué?* when it's time to get ready, and *Barf!* when it's time to jump on their heads or draw down on them."

"Barf?"

"Barf."

It was *very* unromantic but there it was. Barf! They decided to give it a try. And they could call themselves *The Task Force* for the rest of their natural lives, but it soon became abundantly clear that to the rest of their world they were *Barf.* So the Barfers loaded up and headed for the canyons and very soon one of them thought he might be spending Christmas of 1976 in the county jail. For manslaughter at least.

It was 9:00 P.M. when the varsity was walking just fifteen yards north of the imaginary line. They were approaching E-2 Canyon, so called by the Border Patrol. E-2 Canyon was about one-half mile east of the port of entry. There were lots of bandit gangs working E-2 and the other canyons, most of whom lived in nearby Colonia Libertad. On this particular night Manny Lopez, Tony Puente, Eddie Cervantes and Carlos Chacon were stumbling along a trail in the darkness when two men approached, and they figured to get their second wildcatting pinch of the night.

The two men stood while Manny and his Barfers squatted in submission. They were asked for a cigarette and a match, and Manny The Actor produced the proper cigarette and matches from his prop department. And then they were offered a ride to "Los," as they refer to Los Angeles on the streets. The tariff was to be $100 a person.

And since the wildcatting violation was technically completed, Manny Lopez was about to say *¿sabes qué?* Except that one of the men said there were some other pollos going in the same truck and he had to give them a whistle.

Tony Puente squinted through the darkness and saw that the other shadow figure seemed to have something in his hand. Eddie Cervantes offered him a cigarette. The man came forward, put something in his pocket and accepted the cigarette with the same hand.

The startling flare of a match. A canine smile. The face of a jackal. They started getting nervous.

Tony Puente was wishing he could wear his glasses, especially when the first guide returned with three more pollos to join their crossing group. Except that they didn't walk like pollos. And they began chatting to the Barfers in a very friendly fashion. And there by the trail in the blackness, with a cold wind blowing up, they began, ever so slowly, to move into positions behind the cops, all the time talking about the easy trip they would have to Los.

And despite the chilly wind, the varsity started to sweat. Glasses or not, it looked to Tony Puente like they were *all* holding something in their hands. And though no one had made a demand for money or produced a weapon with a threat of force, thereby satisfying the requirements of the crime of robbery, Manny Lopez thought that this circling pincer movement had gone just about far enough, and he'd settle for a wildcatting bust because he was feeling very uncomfortable.

When the five men who were ringing them on the moon-swept trail began talking to each other in very low voices, Manny Lopez said, "*¿Sabes qué?*"—not a moment too soon as far as his troops were concerned. Two of them saw clearly that one of the "pollos" who had joined them was wearing a *ski mask.* And they were two hours and two months from hard powder and chair lifts.

"Barf!" Manny screamed.

Four snub-nosed revolvers and one shotgun were already showing when Manny yelled "*¡Policías!*"

Each cop went for the nearest robber. The man who had accepted one of Eddie's cigarettes began to run. Eddie Cervantes, the smallest and fastest Barfer, started after him. They were only a few yards from the border. The robber was twenty-two years old and could really move. Eddie Cervantes caught up with him at the line and the young man reached for his rear pocket, which contained a bone-handled knife. Eddie Cervantes yelped, "Barf! Barf! Barf!" and swung his revolver down on the robber's skull and heard the loudest explosion of his life.

The robber screamed in the face of the shocked little Barfer. The bandit's eyes slid back and he said, "Ayeeee! You *killed* me!" And he fell to the ground and was absolutely still.

When the junior varsity walking team came stumbling,

cursing, falling, through the mesquite and rocks and cactus toward the sound of the gunshot, Renee Camacho found Eddie Cervantes gaping at the bandit corpse. Eddie Cervantes was saying, "Oh, shit! Oh, fuck! I didn't *mean* to kill him! What am I gonna do now? What am I gonna *do*?"

Eddie Cervantes' sad down-turned eyes had dropped to his lip. There were a lot of things going through the young cop's head, of course. Technicalities, for one thing. The robbers had never actually demanded money. They had never made an overt attack. Was it only wildcatting, a misdemeanor? Then he didn't even have the *legal* right to shoot him—never mind the moral right!

"What am I gonna do?" the littlest Barfer cried. "Am I gonna go to jail for manslaughter?"

The corpse's name was José Gutierrez. The corpse moaned. The corpse started getting up.

"He's not dead! You're not dead!" Eddie Cervantes screamed to the bandit.

But the crook *thought* he'd been killed. He was more certain than Eddie Cervantes. He sure as hell had a big headache, and a lump on his skull about the size of a tequila glass.

After figuring out that he'd been knocked cold and had not died after all, he said to Eddie Cervantes, "I give. I *give*!"

They arrested the bandits for wildcatting, since they didn't have the needed elements for a robbery charge. They made a police report to cover the accidental discharge of one department-issued Smith & Wesson two-inch revolver. They didn't bother detailing some damage done to the revolver. It seems that when Eddie Cervantes, using the gun as a club, coldcocked the bandit, he bent the trigger guard into the trigger, causing the gun to fire.

No one had been hit by the round and the bandit was glad to be alive and wasn't complaining, especially since they were charged with only the petty crime of wildcatting.

A day or two in the city jail and then back to Mexico and taking more care *next* time he robbed some pollos.

The cops had another fine time after work and this time Eddie Cervantes got blitzed. They did lots of Marine reservist/midget jokes: "What do Eddie Cervantes and King Hussein have in common?" "They're military lions?" "No, hydrocephalic dwarfs."

Then Eddie, with lots of help from Manny Lopez, would turn on the tallest Barfer, of prominent jaw and crooked teeth, and do their Marfa, Texas, jokes: "Hey, Ernie, I hear a big night in Marfa is when the Coke machine's working." "Hey, Ernie, were you the champ bottle opener with those teeth?" "Hey, Ernie, what's armadillo chili taste like?" And so forth.

They also made a lot of jokes about the guy in the red ski mask who had gotten away, and who was called "El Loco" by the ones they'd caught. They had found the mask in the brush by the international border. There were plenty of gags about how "Loco" would have to buy a new one when he went to Aspen for the season.

Except that a smile would freeze momentarily as a Barfer would think about this new job soberly. About the mean, lonely, godforsaken canyons, where a shadow might appear in the darkness and be right in your face before you even saw it. A shadow becoming a man smiling, who talked reassuringly. Behind a ski mask.

The drinking picked up considerably after that.

CHAPTER · 6

MILAGRO

THE CANYONS WERE QUIET TOWARD YEAR'S END. THE REASON was written by Manny Lopez in one of the activity reports: "It was *too cold* for the bandits to be out."

But their experiment didn't have much more time to run. The chief of police had promised Dick Snider only ninety days to clean out the bandit gangs. He complained that it wasn't their fault if activity was slow and they hadn't been able to arrest enough bandits to prove that their presence had caused the real drop in reported robberies.

They started walking in San Ysidro to build up the stats. Ernie Salgado, the tallest Barfer, and Manny Lopez, his car pool companion, got assaulted by a middle-aged Mexican-American who tried to extort some beer money from them and slugged Ernie with a flashlight. Which was at least good for a yuk since he was arrested for *battery* on a police officer. And Joe Castillo was struck on the foot by a rock thrown by someone in the darkness. And one seventeen-year-old San Ysidro street thug tried to muscle a few bucks out of the varsity one night and, after realizing that his pollos were cops, threw a fist at Eddie Cervantes and kicked him in the face before receiving his in return. Eddie Cervantes just seemed to be the natural choice of the real bandits in the canyons as well as the play bandits of San Ysidro. He'd suffered most of the minor injuries to date.

At month's end, Manny Lopez wrote disgustedly in his log: "The most exciting part of the evening was when I ripped my pants jumping over a fence."

Which made Manny decide to outfit his ragged band properly. After nearly two months in the hills they were getting ragged and grubby and *wild* looking. Pollos all wore two or three pair of pants. Women often wore two dresses and long pants underneath, since they couldn't depend on being able to carry clothes on their journeys north. When they arrived at their destinations they could peel off one layer of filthy clothes, leaving a layer of cleaner clothes for seeking employment.

The Barfers didn't shop at Abercrombie & Fitch. They shopped at the Veterans' Thrift Shop. They had fun fighting over coats and pants and shirts, and shoes with platform heels, the kind aliens liked, which would soon be reduced to ragged strips of imitation leather by the cactus and rocks in the hills.

Manny Lopez justified the expenditure of department funds by saying, "They're getting so scroungy I'm afraid the bandits won't *wanna* hit on us. These fuckers look too low-life to have any loot."

The bill for all of their clothes was $26 and some change. The new old clothes helped their morale. But they were going to lose their Border Patrol and Customs officers very soon. Dick Snider was desperately hoping that before the ninety days were up his men could do something spectacular to convince the chief of police and the mayor that the city cops should keep BARF going even after the U.S. officers left. Ninety days just wasn't *enough*.

The thing that might save his experiment, he believed,

was media coverage. They weren't accomplishing a hell of a lot, because it had simply quieted down out there in the hills. Still, whatever they did the newspapers loved. If they so much as took down a couple of wildcatters, or San Ysidro teenyboppers trying to hustle them for 35 cents, it would make the papers. There were fifteen newspaper stories written about them in a month wherein they did not make one significant bandit arrest. The media were trying to create something, it seemed. What, the Barfers didn't know. And Dick Snider didn't *care.* His experiment was born of publicity and politics, and it might not die if he could somehow manipulate publicity and politicians. He encouraged his sergeant to grant a few requests from service clubs that wanted to hear about this band of cops called BARF. But Manny Lopez didn't need encouraging.

Chief of Police William Kolender was a departure from prior chiefs. He was up from the ranks, a large man with wavy brown hair styled just over his ears. He owned a good speaking voice and looked like the Hart Schaffner & Marx executive models. He was known as the first police chief in San Diego history with progressive ideas. He was skillful enough to be liked by his men, by City Hall, *and* by the media, no mean feat for a police administrator. It was not a secret that he might aspire to political office upon the completion of his police career.

Bill Kolender had in his office two flags, one of Ireland and one of Israel, a private joke made public at every first meeting. The chief invariably let a reporter, interviewer, community leader, know that he was at heart an Irish cop, but in reality a Jew, the first ever to attain such an office in this city. And he'd let you make of that what you would.

Until of late he had been the object of just about any speaking request made of the police department. He was good. But now there was somebody better. Chief Kolender and all the department brass had to pay attention because Manny Lopez could wow them. A natural storyteller, Manny was in his element up there, say before a Kiwanis luncheon, pointing his finger like a gun, eyebrow crawling and squiggling like crazy whenever any female caught his evil little eye. His hands flying all over the place as he dramatized how they handled this band of cutthroats in Deadman's Canyon or that band of killers in Smuggler's Gulch. And if they had another Chivas Regal handy, yes, he'd have one.

Manny knew how to live: a Chivas in one hand, a Santa Fe Corona Grande in his mouth, dressed for these occasions like John Travolta in *Saturday Night Fever.* This police sergeant, not yet thirty years old, was a smash on the local lecture circuit. And for at least fifteen minutes after he got to the station in the afternoons he would, while sobering up, regale his scruffy, ragtag, flea-bitten, cactus-stuck squad about the scotch they practically *poured* down his golden throat at the luncheon. And of how the ladies *loved* his performance. And the Barfers would maybe get a little envious, but they admired him. Some of the younger ones like Joe Castillo and Carlos Chacon admitted that they worshiped him.

The chief of police and other department brass *had* to notice that this Mexican-American sergeant wasn't hurting the department image, not a bit. Maybe this experiment might turn into something halfway decent after all.

Right around Christmas 1976, they met the border version of the Artful Dodger. One night the varsity—Manny Lopez, Tony Puente and Eddie Cervantes—were not in the canyons but walking in San Ysidro when an eight-year-old yellow Ford pulled up beside them. The car stopped and the occupants looked at the pollos, drove off, circled, parked on a side street and waited.

The Mexican woman behind the wheel studied Manny Lopez, who wore against the cold his alien field jacket, a woolen cap pulled down over his balding head, two pairs of shiny dress pants, and plastic platforms which were breaking his freaking ankles.

She said, in Spanish, "Do you know where Enero Street is?"

"Oh, no," Manny Lopez told her. "We're not from here."

She smiled and said, "Where do you come from?"

Pointing south, he said, "We've just come north."

"Do you have a ride?" she asked.

"No, no ride," Manny Lopez answered.

"My mother will take you to Los Angeles," the driver's companion offered.

"Get in," the driver said quickly. "*La migra* and city police are all around."

The three cops jumped shivering into the Ford and she drove the residential streets of San Ysidro for several minutes, explaining to them that she was looking for two women and one man from El Salvador whom she had transported from Tijuana to the vicinity of the borderline at the Tijuana airport, where a guide was to bring them through the canyons. The woman had a forged passport which allowed her to cross legally.

They were not able to connect with the Salvadorans. They drove instead to a home in San Ysidro where she had to make certain arrangements preparatory to taking them on to Los Angeles. She went into a modest house, leaving her daughter Olivia in the car with the three passengers. Olivia was articulate and spunky. When Manny Lopez asked her if she wasn't afraid to be left alone with three strangers, she smiled prettily. Obviously she was not.

She told them her life story. They had been smuggling aliens for about five years. She often rode with her mother around Tijuana during alien pickups. Olivia was a third-generation smuggler whose father and grandmother were still at it. Her father was living in Texas on parole for smuggling. Her grandmother was on probation, having been caught with a load of two dozen aliens. And alas, even her mother, now in the house exchanging money with other smugglers, had been the driver in that particular operation and was also caught.

"Mamá must be very careful," she informed them. "The hardest part of the journey to Los Angeles is the San Clemente checkpoint."

Manny Lopez, Tony Puente and Eddie Cervantes nodded soberly at this revelation and even more so at the next when she revealed more smuggler lore: "*La migra* and the San Diego police are on constant watch and they beat up prisoners!"

She also informed the cops that the resident of the safe house had gotten rich by smuggling and had bought a restaurant, but had squandered his fortune in that business. Lousy restaurateur, good smuggler.

When the girl's mother returned, the deal was struck. She normally charged $250 a head for O.T.M.'s and $200 for Mexicans. In the spirit of the holidays she offered the boys a ride to Los Angeles for $150 apiece, and she was suddenly very surprised to see the shield of a San Diego police sergeant in the hand of Manny Lopez. Olivia followed in the footsteps of two generations by getting busted.

Normally, wildcatting arrests were okay for the stats but not worth an officer's report. This one was, because of Olivia and her life story. It was two days until Christmas and the cops were feeling sentimental. And perhaps they were a bit smitten by her looks. She did, after all, have a beautiful smile and eyes like a jackrabbit. And she was just slightly larger than one, this *very* artful dodger. The littlest smuggler was ten years old.

This particular arrest was at least mildly depressing to one of the Barf squad who put it this way: "I was bummed. I watched *Oliver* that year on TV and all of a sudden it *sucked.* I couldn't figure out what was wrong with me till I started thinking about that little smuggler Manny and the guys brought in. I switched off *Oliver* to Donnie and Marie or something, *that's* how bummed I was. I kept asking myself what kind a job *is* this? What's it mean out there on that border? What is this alien business all about? Does it *mean* something? Is it some kind a weird comedy? Why wasn't I laughing?"

There were only six unsensational newspaper stories about BARF during the month of December. They were only two weeks from their ninety-day moratorium. They faced imminent disbanding and at least one of them had said he was more than ready to move back to *real* police work. The border patrolmen and U.S. Customs officers were gone in any case. Dick Snider needed a *sensational* bandit arrest. Or a public relations miracle. Something to bolster flagging media interest. He still believed totally in his experiment. He knew that given time he could curtail the bandits and save many people much anguish and death.

And he got what he was looking for: a goddamn exploitable Christmas *miracle,* they called it. At least one person would for the rest of her natural life believe that it was a real one.

It was twenty minutes till midnight on the night of December 27th. Manny Lopez and fellow varsity members Tony Puente and Eddie Cervantes were freezing and flapping their arms and blowing steam as they walked on the American side of the Tijuana highway, which was separated from the United States of America at this point by the sorriest, hole-riddled, Erskine Caldwell wire fence they had ever seen. In fact, the fence was an *insult.* They figured that for a country that could put men on the moon, *no* fence would be infinitely more dignified than *this* one, for chrissake.

It was cold; it was damp; it was *boring.* Only one thing made any sense at all. Pick up some brews and scotch and pack it in early. In fact, maybe pack it *all* in. Dick Snider was about the only police lieutenant any of them had ever really felt affection for, but let's face it, what were they doing that they could point to and say, "Look what we accomplished"? They might as well be writing parking tickets.

It may have been a downbeat Christmas season for the Barfers but nothing like what it was for Rosa Lugo, who stood trembling on Monument Road holding the hand of her thirteen-year-old daughter, Esther, looking wistfully toward the land of silk and money. It was no doubt very difficult for Rosa Lugo to keep her teeth from chattering, because not only was it cold but also she was wrenched and frozen by fear. She had chosen this night to offer her daughter Esther a chance in life. They were going to *cross,* and maybe Christmas of next year would be a different story.

One thing sure, it took more than a little nerve just to be there in the darkness on the highway, owning nothing but the skirt on her body and a nondescript faded poncho, shivering in the sudden gusts which perhaps blew hard enough to make her hip-length braid shoot out like an arrow, an arrow pointing north like an omen.

The logical place to cross was through a big drainage pipe five hundred yards east of the intersection of Monument Road and Dairy Mart Road on the U.S. side. The tunnel was a popular place for pollos to duck across the line, which was slightly more than imaginary at this place because of that dilapidated wire fence. The tunnel was a place where human beings squatted, hunkered, crawled, waited, urinated and defecated from fear and tension and sickness.

And where bandits lurked.

There were twenty men waiting in that drainage tunnel for a guide who never came. It was not just a cold night; it was a clear night, not velvet-black but hard-black. Sea wind blew away the Tijuana smoke and San Diego overcast, and the night sky shone down on crossing aliens, making life a bit easier for the Border Patrol. It was one of those nights when the moonlight in the canyons and hills, and on the west side of I-5 here by the asparagus field, made shadows hard-black like anthracite. And the drainage tunnel was so black inside that it was easier to *smell* the presence of another human being than to see him. And that was possibly the most fearful thing. To be there inside the pipe, in the darkness that was far blacker than the night, and to *smell* another human being you could not see, could not hear.

Rosa Lugo of course wanted to turn and run from the tunnel the moment she smelled the first human beings. But she was undeniably brave, and though her hands were no doubt drenched, she held her daughter's ever tighter and crept forward into the black void toward the smell and hot breath of human beings.

It turned out that there were twenty pollos in there who had not connected with their guide. Some of them were later very hard-pressed to explain what they did and did not do in that tunnel after the arrival of Rosa Lugo and her daughter Esther. This was the beginning of an attempt by some of the Barf squad to understand a terrible and tragic phenomenon that recurs throughout time. The Innocents/Hostages/Victims say to the conscienceless sociopath: "You won't dream of hurting me when you see how submissive/meek/obedient I can be!" But of course the victim has no more understanding of the sociopath than does the average citizen. That is, the victim cannot really believe in the *existence* of a true sociopath, let alone fathom the fact that they are everywhere, some antisocial, some not. Sociopaths, who often are attractive, intelligent, sane, and utterly without a sense of guilt, or superego—call it what you will.

And if the average citizen knew anything about the omnipresence of sociopaths, and the mentality of Innocents/Hostages/Victims, they would never play brain-numbing games like What I Would Have Done Differently at Auschwitz.

And so forth.

The fact is that the most meek and docile and submissive people of Mexico were not among the aliens in the tunnel. Those remained in despair. The boldest came, and one cannot doubt their courage. Man for man, the children and grandchildren of Mexican aliens have accounted for more Medals of Honor fighting for the United States than any other ethnic group. It's just that the aliens in the tunnel responded to sudden naked violence and force with an instinct to submit, and to win over the aggressor through docility. Like millions of Innocents/Hostages/Victims before them.

Rosa Lugo and Esther were already too deep within the bowels of darkness to retreat when the five intruders burst into the other end, smashing into the covey of waiting pollos with curses and kicks. There was glass smashing. There were dull thuds and cries of pain. And threats to shoot and cut and maim if the pollos did not submit at once.

And twenty pollos, except for one who fled in terror, *did* submit, and still the beatings and screams continued. Just for good measure, or for fun. And Rosa Lugo pressed her daughter back against the urine-splashed tunnel walls and dared not breathe and prayed that the violence would stop, and that the assailants would not press forward in the darkness. Whoever they were.

Five of these pollos would later make a police report. These five men ranged in age from eighteen to thirty years. They were just average run-of-the-mill aliens who had been fighting the night cold by enjoying fantasies of jobs paying, say, $15 a day, and trying to keep their bowels in check when the intruders exploded into the tunnel. The intruders absolutely cowed and *terrified* these *campesinos,* though these wiry men could lift and pull and push like worker ants and were far stronger than the average American of comparable size. They thought at once that the intruders were bandits but hoped they were not like the bandits from the canyons who, they'd heard, would shoot you in the knees or slash or hamstring you just to intimidate the rest of your party. Bandits who had killed Juan or Ernesto or Julia, or whoever, in the stories passed around campfires at night. But these intruders were not even *men.*

They were boys. Teenage hoodlums from the Tijuana streets. They could have been eaten alive by the many strong men in the tunnel that night but they had an enormous advantage over these pollos and they knew it. They were mean and aggressive and violent, without a trace of compassion or pity. They were exactly unlike these older stronger men; hence they were perceived as overwhelmingly powerful. To be obeyed without question.

Their leader said, "We have guns and knives. Who would like to *feel* our knives?"

The aliens moaned and murmured and a man began to plead for his life, saying that he had eight children. One of the little thugs thought this was funny as hell and had a drink from a bottle of Russian vodka (*anything* can be had in Tijuana) and toasted the eight soon-to-be orphans. They were having a good old terrorizing time, these five hoodlums, who probably did *not* have guns and possibly did not even have knives, since the boy bandits learn very soon that a herd of thirty pollos will easily submit to three attackers armed only with *rocks,* if the attackers have big enough *huevos.* And these assailants were about to prove just how big their *huevos* were, because they could sense something new. A presence in the tunnel as palpable as blood: women!

The oldest of the aliens was named Reynaldo and he had lived thirty years without ever feeling someone breathing liquor in his face in the black of a tunnel, talking about how a knife would feel slicing open his belly and throat. He later was terribly ashamed and remorseful and *bewildered* when he admitted that he was relieved when the band of boy bandits found the women and released him.

Rosa Lugo made a decision to run, but it was too late. Rosa Lugo felt hands on her breast. Two pairs of hands. She screamed and someone put his hand over her mouth and began whispering obscenities. Her legs went weak. Then her legs went out from under her. She could hardly breathe.

Rosa Lugo suddenly couldn't see Esther! Her daughter began *screaming.* The child was being dragged through the tunnel away from her. They were dragging Esther away. The leader of the boy bandits was overjoyed. While rubbing and fondling the breasts of Rosa Lugo, whom he held by the mouth, he found twenty American dollars and two religious medals, maybe silver, that he could sell to the whores in the Colonia Coahuila brothels, since whores were mad about religious medals.

He released her mouth when he found the money. There was lots of time. Rosa Lugo started pleading. She was calling to the bandits in the tunnel. She could see shapes. Terrible shadows. Her daughter was sobbing hopelessly, crying out for her mother. Rosa Lugo never asked for mercy for herself. She offered to submit to rape and even murder, *anything* if they would release her daughter. They thought this was *really* funny. What? Rape an old woman when there was this sweet little *pollita*? Maybe later, *vieja.* Maybe *after.*

The rapist dragged the whimpering girl to the mouth of the tunnel. He pinned her against the wall with the weight of his body. Keeping her upright he worked with her long pants and his. The words of the rapist were transcribed later that night on a police report. He was heard by witnesses to say: "How pretty you are. You'll like a cock once it goes in. How *pretty* you are!"

Then Rosa Lugo really began to scream. They might have heard her screams in the brothels just south. She shrieked at the beaten, cowed group of men around her.

She screamed: "Somebody help her! Don't let them do this to my daughter! Please!"

But the rapist had Esther's pants to her knees and was preparing to mount her from the rear, and now the girl was totally hysterical and was only able to whisper, "Mamá! Mamá! Mamá!" As the rapist was heard to say: "You're going to like this fuck, you pretty . . ."

Then Rosa Lugo did something extraordinary, something she later thought was unbelievable. She stopped pleading to the bandits for mercy and to the other alien victims for help. She spoke straight to God, ordering nothing less than *un milagro.* Perhaps, in that it was just two days since the birthday of Jesus Christ, she'd done *enough* pleading for the courage to make this journey. Well, she wasn't pleading now. She was *demanding.* She was heard to say: "God, you *must* save my daughter! You *will* save my daughter!"

And lo! At this precise instant, not a handful of yards away in the darkness, and not ten feet north of the *Tobacco Road* wire fence, there squatted three sorry, ragged, wild-looking little spectators with woolen caps pulled down over freezing little ears. With nothing hanging out anywhere but maybe a Zapata moustache or two, and Manny Lopez' pseudo-Armenian nose, frozen red and dripping. The varsity was trying to see what the hell was going *on* in the freaking tunnel on the wrong side of the line.

When they heard the words of the rapist, Tony Puente couldn't *believe* it. He and Eddie Cervantes looked at Manny Lopez but the black woolen cap had been pulled so far down over his balding little skull that the only things showing were that droopy moustache and that dripping nose. He looked like Yosemite Sam in the old Bugs Bunny films.

They couldn't see it, but they knew that eyebrow was probably clear back to the crown of his skull about now and that his little eyeballs were laying on his cheekbones. He was eye-popping mad. That was Mexican soil over there and they were ordered never to cross, *but . . .*

"*¿Sabes qué?*" Manny Lopez mumbled. "*¿Sabes qué?*" He was possibly talking to the young bandits, especially the one who was just about to penetrate Esther Lugo. He didn't say "Barf!" He said, "FUCK THIS SHIT!"

And then there was *lots* of screaming and yelling, as a *hurricane* hit that tunnel. There were pollos and boy bandits flying in all directions. There were people getting slugged and kicked and sapped and punched and pistol-whipped—the right people, the wrong people. There was chaos in the tunnel, and Rosa Lugo ran to her daughter Esther and helped the hysterical little girl dress herself. Rosa Lugo could not even cry. Not at the moment.

Tony Puente was true to his costume designer, Manny Lopez. He was wearing something like Tijuana disco shoes that night. Just like some dumb shit pollo in from the country with his brand-new big-town platforms. And he was so mightily pissed he started chasing one of the boy bandits. He could hear Eddie thumping the head of another with the shotgun as he skidded past them in the darkness and out. He had his two-inch .38 in his hand and he was moving those plastic skates and the highballing boy bandit was screaming, "Leave me alone! Leave me alone!"

And Tony Puente was running blindly and screaming back: "I'm gonna *kill* you, you bastard!"

The three cops were all family men, Tony Puente having been married so young that he even had a child the same age as Esther Lugo. "I'm gonna *kill* you!" he bellowed at the bandit as he smoked down a street in his disco shoes.

A *street*?

Suddenly he took a look around. He was running on a *street.* He was hotfooting by four lanes of traffic. He was taking a jog through the streets of Tijuana, in the country of Mexico, right beside a shantytown *full* of pals of the guy he was trying to catch.

Tony Puente passed a power station. Funnels and stacks rose up, blowing pollution on a lonely city park nearby. Why didn't he wear his goddamn glasses? His feet were killing him and he couldn't run anymore, but he limped very fast back to that big drainage pipe. The thug who disappeared near the brothels of Colonia Coahuila might shoot him down with ease when he crossed the highway. He peered short-sightedly toward the dark shanties. *Why* didn't he wear his goddamn glasses?

When Tony Puente got safely back, the melee was over. There were five aliens giving statements to the junior varsity, which had been summoned by Handie-Talkie and was on the scene. Only one of the boy bandits had been caught, but he was the one who had been trying to rape Esther Lugo. He was looking like a train wreck by now and this made Tony Puente very happy. He hoped that the ones who had escaped back to Mexico would also need some suturing and maybe plasma.

Manny's fists looked like dog meat and there was a *most* interesting conversation going on, a conversation that Tony Puente and all the cops might remember for the rest of their days.

Manny Lopez was giving his usual twenty orders per second, telling this one to call for transportation, that one to check for the motherfucker he'd busted his knuckles on, another one to get the pollos' names for statements. And where the hell's Tony? There he is. Where you been? Where's Robbie Hurt with the transportation? Why doesn't nobody listen to me? Are they all dead at communications? And the inevitable "Listen, fucker!"

Manny Lopez was least of all aware of the *other* half of a conversation that the Barfers were seeing and hearing amidst his litany of profanity and commands. The entire squad, varsity and junior varsity, all of them bloodied, bruised, freezing, were spellbound, because how often do you see a *miracle*? At least, how often do you see someone who is seeing a miracle?

The child Esther Lugo was still crying, though not so much now. But it was Rosa Lugo they were all looking at. She had attached herself to Manny Lopez. She was on her knees, there in the glass-littered, rock-jutting gully. She was on her knees and Manny was tethered to her and didn't know it.

Manny Lopez was just doing what he does: motherfucking somebody for incompetence, threatening to open up the would-be rapist's skull for spiders to crawl into. Manny wasn't paying much attention to the fact that he was attached to Rosa Lugo.

The woman had him by the hand. His raw, swollen hand was being cradled in both of hers. She probably didn't hear him cursing and screaming and fussing and fuming. She was on her knees looking up at Manny Lopez and she was apologizing to Him who had sent Manny.

She said to the sergeant: "God sent you to us. I dared to demand and in His great mercy He sent you to us!"

And Manny Lopez only became aware of the miracle that had occurred for Rosa Lugo when she continued to enrapture the squad of Barfers by taking the raw and puffy mitt and raising it to her face like a relic.

With tears streaming she kissed the hand of Manny Lopez.

"Hey, cut it out, lady!" Manny said. What *is* this shit?

She never heard him. She probably heard an angel song. Rosa Lugo had her miracle.

The Barfers thought they were *really* getting weird out there in those hills. A couple of them actually started talking about it like it *was* some kind of miracle. And about what's a miracle anyway? Try telling Rosa Lugo she didn't get a miracle. Just *try*.

When they got off duty they knocked back a couple bottles of *hard* booze. After all, it wasn't every night you got sent Special Delivery by the Man Himself. And they talked about how twenty men could let themselves be terrorized by a few punks, and be willing to let a little girl be raped. Were they all cowards, these docile aliens? And what was courage? And what was survival? And what was a frigging miracle anyway?

The job was making their heads crazy. They were talking about things cops don't usually talk about. This wasn't like police work. A few of them were really *glad* that the ninety-day moratorium was approaching.

The rescue at the tunnel came to have some significance for Manny Lopez later that night when he had time to discuss it with Dick Snider. A dramatic rescue of a little girl just two days after Christmas? A goddamn, almost bona fide, freaking Christmas miracle? Even the Mexican state judicial police who came to collect the victims and witnesses and suspects were *very* appreciative, and did not criticize the San Diego cops one iota for entering Mexican territory. They don't *like* rapists in religious countries like Mexico. Not one little bit.

And it was clearly possible that Dick Snider had his public relations miracle to show that his squad was doing valuable work. And that the moratorium should be lifted to give them more time to disperse the bandit gangs.

When the story was told and retold, the Barfers would invariably mention the unforgettable sight of the "old woman" kneeling at the feet of Manny Lopez and kissing his hand. It was always "the old woman."

When asked how old they thought this woman was, they usually answered, "Well, with such a young daughter, she was probably only fifty. But she looked at least sixty. It's a hard life down there."

The official police report lists the correct age of Rosa Lugo. She was thirty-one, just slightly older than the "angel" whose hand she kissed. It was indeed a *very* hard life down there.

CHAPTER · 7

PARADISE LOST

EVEN THE MIRACLE COULDN'T SAVE THE TASK FORCE. THE rescue at the tunnel was given some publicity, but only on the south side of the border. It seemed that the department brass wanted this one kept as quiet as possible. It was a good piece of work all right, but they had crossed into Mexican territory to do it. It would be better to leave this one alone.

The border patrolmen and U.S. Customs officers were pulled out by their respective agencies and reassigned. On the last afternoon of the ninety-day experiment, long before sunset, the Barfers observed a group of men standing two hundred yards west of Deadman's Canyon. They were standing by a pickup truck on the Mexican side of the border. The cops heard a gunshot, and after hitting the ground they watched the group through binoculars. One of them was calmly shooting in their direction. Target practice on the pollos in the canyon? Just then a Border Patrol observation plane flew over. They heard more gunfire. They didn't know if the men were shooting at the aircraft or just having a little more fun shooting at aliens. They were probably bandits who *owned* that section of canyon. They could shoot at anyone they damn well pleased in this no-man's-land.

The Barfers were pretty disgusted when they hung it up that night. They hadn't actually accomplished much in ninety days. The freaking bandits still owned a hunk of San Diego.

But they had a whale of a party to celebrate the closing of their show. They had tried in vain to convince one another and the brass that they had been boffo in the canyons. At the party everyone got good and blitzed and all the wives got very well acquainted just as they were about to part company. The U.S. Border Patrol and U.S. Customs said that they'd all done a good job and the government agencies took their men back for good. Manny Lopez was a hell of an emcee, and ad-libbed like crazy with a Santa Fe Corona Grande between his teeth and a water tumbler full of Chivas Regal in *each* hand, because someone told him this might keep him from unconsciously pointing his finger like a gun and saying: "Listen, fucker!"

He called little Eddie Cervantes to the head table and gave him a pair of baby shoes with platform heels. He gave Renee Camacho and his pal Joe Castillo a pair of his-and-her champagne glasses. He gave Robbie Hurt an old Chevy hubcap, a ratty pair of huaraches and a switchblade knife, making him an honorary Mexican. Manny had something in his bag of tricks for everybody.

Dick Snider proved to be an excellent sport and dressed up as an Arab sheik, letting a hired belly dancer wiggle her gluteus all around him. Actually, Dick Snider was a most unhappy man. His grand experiment had not been given a chance, not as he saw it. They *could* have damaged the bandit gangs, given more time. He expected that now, with milder weather, the bandits would renew their attacks with a vengeance. And in fact they did.

Very shortly after the Barfers returned to ordinary sane police duty a couple of crazy things happened. It was as though the madness in the canyons was following them.

Junior varsity member Ernie Salgado was thrust into a moment of violence never experienced before nor after in his police career. He remembered watching a television interview wherein the most decorated police officer in San Diego was being given an award for lifesaving. The policeman had fatally shot a bank robber. The irony of the moment was not lost on that policeman, who commented to the interviewer: "Here I am getting an award for lifesaving. I only had to kill to get it."

Ernie Salgado, like almost all policemen, had never fired a weapon at a human being, not since Vietnam. If it were to happen, he figured it should have happened in the canyons. Outside of the accidental shot fired by Eddie Cervantes when he used his revolver as a club, nobody had popped a single cap in the canyons.

He was sent to Northern Division and was assigned to SWAT. It was a typical San Diego Sunday morning, which meant fair weather and a quiet city. He was ordered to accompany a detective and another uniformed cop to a house where an escapee from the juvenile detention center was supposed to be hiding. He was along for this ride because the teenager was supposed to have a shotgun in his possession. Cops are, from the first day in the academy, admonished that juveniles must not be shot unless in dire emergency, but there was no sense taking any chances. And though everyone knew that escaping from a juvenile detention center was a "crime" punishable by loss of bubble gum for the week, you never knew about squirrelly kids.

Ernie Salgado's gun was loaded first with a .54-caliber rifle slug. The next rounds were buckshot, the SWAT theory being that in a confrontation with a barricaded suspect the slug would be of some value, since officers would be at a distance. If it was a situation where a suspect was in normal shooting range, ten feet or less, the buckshot would be much more useful.

Ernie Salgado was supposed to be covering the house from the outside when they announced their presence—hence the rifle slug. Two of the people in the house came out and met the cops, who were told that the kid inside *did* have a shotgun. The detective wanted Ernie and his shotgun right next to him that Sunday morning.

They entered through the back door into the kitchen. The last resident to leave the house told them that the boy was in the bedroom. "The one on the right," he said.

They crept toward that bedroom. It was getting extraordinarily warm in the house. It was oppressive, in fact. Then they saw that another bedroom door was ajar. It was the wrong bedroom. Ernie didn't like the wrong bedroom door being ajar. Neither did the detective, and he was going to push it wide open just to feel a little better about it when . . . WHAM! the door slammed in his face.

Several things happened superfast for Ernie Salgado. The detective jumped to the side of the door and yelled at the kid to come out. Ernie stood in front of the door with his shotgun at the ready. The detective pushed the door open and Ernie was face to face with the kid.

It was every cop's nightmare. The kid was standing on the bed. He was looking down at Ernie in the doorway. The boy had an over-and-under .410 shotgun of his own, and he was bringing it up to the face of the cop.

Ernie Salgado only heard one explosion. One *long* explosion. The longest explosion he'd ever heard outside of Nam.

But it *wasn't* one long explosion. There were three rapid explosions. The boy fired both barrels. One blasted out the doorjamb just above the tall cop's head. The other took out part of the wall and ceiling. Ernie fired once. The .54-caliber rifle slug, seven-eighths of an ounce of lead, hit the boy full in the chest and blew a hole clear through him.

There was also a visual explosion. The huge slug, which might knock down an elephant at that range, hit an aorta. The boy exploded in blood.

He died within seconds. When asked later how he felt about it, Ernie said he felt indifferent about it. He said that shortly thereafter he made a promise to himself and kept it. He said he wanted never to think about it and never did.

The violent episode experienced by Ernie Salgado during their return to ordinary sane police duty was perhaps not nearly so bizarre as an encounter by varsity member Tony Puente, whose wife was overjoyed now that the ninety-day experiment in the hills had come to an end. Maybe their life could return to normal. Maybe he'd stop coming home in the middle of the night smelling like an alien—smelling like a *drunk* more often than not.

It was the thing to do after they got off duty. After all, they were part of a unique police experiment and a guy *needed* a taste or two when he'd been stumbling around for hours out there in the black of night with strange people all around him in the darkness. How could she understand the canyons? Even *he* couldn't understand the goddamn canyons.

Part of him was glad it was over. They had never, any of them, admitted how scary it was out there in no-man's-land. Some of them hinted at unpleasant dreams. But they were baaaaad-ass cops. Way too macho to talk about it. He wondered if some of the others were relieved that it was over, no matter how much they complained about not having a fair chance to take those bandits down.

He was not glad to be back doing dreary, boring uniformed patrol, but he could always hope that some plainclothes job would open up for a Mexican. When Tony Puente had joined the San Diego Police Department eight years earlier, only 4 percent of the department had Spanish surnames. In one of America's ten largest cities, on the very border of Mexico, the gateway to *all* of Latin America.

Even under the new chief there was only one Mexican out of twenty men in Homicide, one in Burglary, one in Narcotics. The Mexican cops hoped that Chief Kolender could institute some changes in the department. He had come up through the ranks. He was smart and he was no redneck. But America's Finest City, and the police force that protected it, were very slow to change. This was a prosperous, isolated, provincial corner of America.

So if he wanted a plainclothes job, he'd better find one that was presently held by a Mexican. And he'd better wait until that Mexican got promoted, moved out, or died. Traditionally, the only chance for a Mexican was to replace another Mexican. He'd hoped that the experiment might prove something to the rest of them: that a bunch of Mexicans could go out there in those hills and do a *job.*

And that was another odd thing about those hills: dressing, talking, *smelling* like an alien was very very strange. Really, trying to *think* like someone else for the first time in his life. It made you understand that you are *not* a real Mexican, not even close. And yet the white majority thought of you as one. It was very hard out in those hills for some of them. It produced a culture clash in their heads.

And then on top of it he was having to cope with a *religious* crisis at home that was driving him goofy.

When as a boy Marine he married his child bride, his new father-in-law wouldn't even speak to him. Bad enough the premature wedding, but to be marrying one of *them*? The man was eventually won over by young Tony Puente, who understood that it might not be easy for a West Virginia hillbilly to accept the prospect of "half-breed" grandchildren. Tony won him over not by being more "white" but by being more Mexican. Though his Spanish was lousy he spoke it as often as possible for his new father-in-law in those days, and the old boy was delighted by the sound of it in Tony's soft, crackling, quiet way of talking.

And after he'd become a cop it was apparent that he was going to be a good husband to Dene and a good father to his children. Everything was going along fine for Tony Puente until she took the plunge into the all-consuming, tract-disseminating, Bible-thumping, Fundamental religion. It was mildly annoying at first, but what the hell, she'd been such a young wife and mother. He had police work and was gone much of the night, but what did *she* have?

But then he started reading the tenets of this religion. Only the missionary position? Wives shouldn't undress in front of husbands? Unnecessary provocation? BULLSHIT!

Except that it was too late. She was immersed ten fathoms deeper than John the Baptist. And in the holidays just past, she said she didn't want a Christmas tree in the house because it violated the dogma of her new faith.

So he immediately went out and bought a Christmas tree about the size of a California redwood. He had to saw half the limbs off the goddamn thing just to get it in the door. He was going to show her a Christmas, all right. He was going to hang mistletoe and holly and colored lights in the *john*, for chrissake!

But despite a Christmas tree sticking out half the windows in the house, despite more lights than the San Diego airport, Christmas was a bust. They argued; she cried; he felt guilty. Christmas sucked.

She had to suppress and humble herself to be pleasing to God, he was told.

"But I spent half my life trying to *better* myself!" he told her. "I wanted you to have *more* than my mother, married to that drunken Mexican!"

"Lately I think *I've* been married to a drunken Mexican," she informed him.

"BARF's finished. I'll stop drinking so much," he promised.

She read the Bible for two hours each night and there was nothing he could do about it. And really, when he dared admit it, there was something creeping into his hatred of her church. He despised her new religion, all right. But if someone needed to *believe* in something, what could he offer? He still remembered the white priest: "Your husband's dead, Mrs. Puente? I'll come at once . . . for a seventy-dollar donation."

He didn't know if he believed in *anything* supernatural, so what could he give this girl who needed something more than he had?

Well, maybe things could improve now that BARF was over. Now that he was once again in uniform doing regular police work. Maybe he could work a day shift? Then with the drinking cut out of his life, things *would* get better. Maybe she wouldn't need her new Bible-banging pals so much. Maybe he could wean her away from them.

So it was back to ordinary, dull, boring, *sane* police work. And then, on his very first day back to ordinary dull boring sane police work, he received a radio call. Later, it didn't seem possible. He wasn't sure it was happening while it *was.* It was like when he woke up drunk after the nights of boozing. What happened? What was real? What wasn't?

The radio call was given to him in broad daylight. There was a family disturbance. There was a fifty-nine-year-old man fighting with his sixteen-year-old son. No big deal. It was a middle-class white neighborhood. *It was his very first radio call* after leaving the insanity in the canyons.

"I can't reason with my dad," the boy said to Tony Puente when he opened the door. "He's getting more senile every day!"

He was just your run-of-the-mill sixteen-year-old, all fuzz and zits, patched blue jeans, a T-shirt. Just bitching about his "senile" old man with whom he shared the house.

Just like a teenybopper to call the old man senile, Tony Puente thought, wondering when his kids would call *him* senile.

Tony Puente looked at the man standing in the living room in his bathrobe, enjoying *All My Children* or something on TV. He was fifty-nine years old, too young to be senile.

He *was* senile.

He said, "Hello, you!" and brought out a little gun and pointed it right smack at Tony Puente's shiny badge, which he'd taken the trouble to polish this first day back in uniform.

"I don't know shit about guns," Tony Puente later said. "At first I didn't think it was real!"

It was real. It was a very cute derringer, a *magnum* derringer. Tony Puente squinted through his glasses. He homed right in on that funny little gun in the man's hand. It was looking more and more real all the time.

Tony Puente had a strange thought the whole time he was in that room. In fact, he couldn't think of anything else for what seemed like an hour but was really only a few minutes. He had never worn the bulletproof vest during the ninety days in the hills. The thought was this: My wife's gonna get mad at me. She'll say I died because I wouldn't wear that goddamn bulletproof vest!

"I think *All My Children*'s a groovy TV show," Tony Puente said. "Don't you?"

"I'm not watching *All My Children,* you dumb son of a bitch," the man said, making little circles with the derringer.

"I sure like *As The World Turns,*" Tony Puente said, sweating buckets. And just that fast, his glasses were fogging.

"I don't have to take your shit!" the man told him.

"No, sir!" Tony Puente said. "So maybe I better just boogie on out and let you enjoy your . . ."

"Don't move!" the man said. "I think I should kill you right *now.*"

And the cop flinched when he heard the word. He was desperately trying to avoid any statement, sentence, phrase, word, anything that included terms like *shoot, kill,* or . . .

"Dad, don't *kill* him!" the kid screamed suddenly, and Tony Puente flinched again and wanted to scream back at the kid: "DON'T SAY KILL, YOU ASSHOLE!"

Instead he said, "Well, now, your dad and me, we're just gonna talk. Hell, we probably have a *lot* in common and . . ."

"I hate niggers!" the man said.

"That lets *me* out!" Tony Puente informed him ecstatically. "I'm a Mex . . ."

"Dad, he's *not* a nigger! Can't you see?" The kid was screaming it. "He's a *cop,* Dad! And he's a Mexican! You're a Mexican, ain't you, Officer?"

"Uh, could you just let *me* handle this, my boy?" Tony Puente said to the kid, who was jumping up and down and tucking his hands between his knees and under his arms. But then the kid shrieked, "You can't kill a cop! He's wearing a uniform! He's a cop, Dad! Don't *kill* him!"

And Tony Puente's shirt was soaked, and he realized the horrible truth of the situation. The *kid* was a banana! Bonzo. Loonier than his old man. He was alone in a house with *two* psychos, not one!

The kid started spinning like a top. The old man started babbling something else about niggers. Tony Puente was thinking how he'd survived three months in the hills and canyons with nothing worse than a fading scar on his ass from falling on a rock with his badge in his hip pocket.

He had to think! He thought of inching his hand closer to his Handie-Talkie, of keying it open. He thought of going for his gun and leaping to his left, since right-handed people usually jerk rounds to *their* left. He couldn't swallow the spit in his throat.

"Don't *shoot*! Don't *kill*!" The kid kept screaming it, and Tony Puente was starting to hyperventilate and could think of only one thing: to take that fucking kid with him when he died!

Then the man got tired of all this screaming and yelling and jumping around, and he strolled over to a chair and made himself comfortable.

And Tony Puente leaped on his head. And, true to form, the kid leaped on Tony Puente, yelling, "Don't you hurt my dad, you son of a bitch!"

"I didn't know *anything* about guns," Tony Puente later said. "I especially didn't know anything about derringers. I had hold a the gun with one hand and managed to get my radio out with the other. And there I was with maniacs hanging all over me, and scared I'd shoot myself with this nutty little gun, and I somehow get a screaming call out to communications. And the communications operator said: 'Is this urgent?' "

That evening an inspector came to the station to ask about Tony Puente's encounter with the father and son, who were both in custody and would no doubt be treated like what they were—nuts. The inspector didn't ask him many questions. He said he was glad no one got hurt. The sergeant thought it was kind of a funny deal. Ditto for the lieutenant. Nobody seemed to care very much or notice that Tony Puente was having trouble keeping his mouth moist.

He realized he couldn't even tell his wife about it. She'd get mad about the goddamn bulletproof vest. Tony Puente thought he might as well be back in the canyons. Things were no more real and explicable out here in the city. He came home very late that first night back in patrol. He did the sensible thing. He went to a cop's bar and got smashed.

CHAPTER · 8

PARADISE REGAINED

IN MID-JANUARY THE NEWSPAPERS ANNOUNCED THAT BARF had been disbanded. Dick Snider was disconsolate. Manny Lopez was frustrated. Some of the men had mixed emotions. Felix Zavala said he had no desire to return even if the department should change its mind. He was gone for good.

They were flea/chigger/mosquito-bitten, cactus-stuck, kicked, punched, threatened by scorpions, rattlesnakes, tarantulas, men. Some of the newspaper stories were getting dubious as to whether BARF was ever a sensible police experiment to begin with. Letters to the editor complained about the waste of taxpayers' money to protect illegal aliens. There were newspaper stories such as DOUBTFUL TACTICS. And, BORDER FORCE TERMED EXPERIMENTAL.

But then suddenly, very suddenly, other newspaper stories started appearing: GANG STABS, ROBS YOUTH AT BORDER. And, MAN ROBBED NEAR BORDER. And, ILLEGAL ALIEN STABBED AND ROBBED.

Dick Snider was desperately trying to convince his superiors that perhaps banditry had slowed *because* they were effective. Manny Lopez said the word spreads fast in Colonia Libertad and the bad guys had boogied because of BARF's presence. Dick Snider could point clearly to the drop in reported robberies, so wasn't *that* an indication of their effectiveness? They hadn't made any big dramatic bandit arrests, but was that their primary function? Or was it to curtail alien robberies? If the bandit arrests they'd made persuaded the robbers to cool it, they'd done a job. Would it have been better if they'd shot down a dozen bandits in canyon firefights? They'd saved some people. Ask the mother and child at the tunnel.

"Saving people?" Manny Lopez said privately, shaking his head. "*Helping* illegal aliens? The police administration laughed at Dick Snider behind his back." Manny Lopez puffed on a Santa Fe Corona Grande as he said it, and his eyebrow went sidewinding into the question mark. "When I was director of the San Diego Police Officers Association, I had to work with the brass and the politicians every day to get what cops wanted. I knew how to deal with these fuckers in the real world. You don't talk about *helping* people. You talk about influencing the taxpayers. The voters. You don't get things done *helping* illegal aliens. I talked about the *media.* About making the media love us. I talked about City Hall and how if we could reinstate BARF I'd guarantee we'd get the kind a press relations to make them give anything the department wanted in our next budget request. That's how you accomplish your goals in the *real* world. I played *hardball* with these fuckers."

Then the eyebrow of Manny Lopez settled down where it belonged and he said, "Dick Snider? He looks like he'd *never* fit in a business suit. They thought he was just some big old country boy who liked to run around those hills. They didn't understand his fixation with helpless aliens. They never could understand that Dick Snider actually believed that everybody uptown was basically a nice man like himself.

" 'What's he trying to *do,* Manny?' they'd ask me. 'Does this Okie mean what he says?' They didn't respect him and they didn't like him. We all had our reasons for wanting BARF to start back up again. I had mine, and most of it had to do with ambition . . . and maybe *something* else. The fact is, I was starting to like it out there in those canyons. There were . . . strange kinds a payoffs. In your head. We all had our reasons, but only Dick Snider's reasons were . . . *pure.* You had to love a guy like that. He stayed *pure* till the end."

The efforts of Dick Snider and Manny Lopez to reactivate BARF were given some help by the bandits themselves. Very suddenly the newspaper stories told it: BANDITS STAB AND ROB AT BORDER.

Whether or not the disbanding of BARF was known by the bandits—and it's doubtful that it was—the robberies began in earnest. And they were *violent.*

City Hall was besieged by the media, who wanted to know if America's Finest City was just going to concede the border canyons to the cutthroats in perpetuity. It could get uncomfortable for Mayor Pete Wilson, who was, in a few years, going to make a successful run at Washington, D.C., as a United States senator.

In less than three weeks everyone caved in. BARF was reactivated. Manny Lopez was back, but Dick Snider was ordered to keep himself occupied as a uniformed watch commander, *indoors.* Total control of BARF should be left to Manny Lopez, he was told.

Dick Snider never complained much. He was content to help and advise in any way he could. He would like to have been out in the canyons, but the fact that BARF was there was a great victory for the alien victims.

Yet he knew it would never be the same. Manny and

the others kept him informed, and yet he was also starting to feel like an outsider.

Ken Kelly was having lots of domestic problems. As he put it: "I was running with this fast bunch a cops who went through a couple shifts a waitresses at our fast-food emporium."

He was getting off at 11:00 P.M. and getting home at daybreak. Some of that "fast bunch" were Barfers. And they were *very* fast and the waitresses loved to hear the exaggerated stories of bandit arrests in Deadman's Canyon. Ken Kelly could see that an aura was starting to form around these canyon hardballers with their funky alien rags and wild hair and moustaches and whiskers. God, he wanted to be one of them.

"Be nice to Lopez," they all told him. "When there's an opening we'll talk for you."

"But will he *take* a blond white boy?"

"We'll talk for you," they promised him. "He might."

Ken Kelly was a hard-charging cop, and he was glib and articulate, much like Manny Lopez himself. He continued bombarding the sergeant with one-liners but he also wrote a persuasive officer's report stating a host of reasons why he should be a Barfer. Manny was impressed by anyone who, like himself, could wield a pen as well as a sword.

"And then fate sprung the trapdoor and I fell in a vat a drizzly shit and almost drowned!" Ken Kelly wailed at the memory.

He was working night patrol and took a drive down by the U.S. Customs secondary inspection area. It's the place where tourists pay duty on goods brought back from Mexico, or have their cars torn apart if it's suspected that they're carrying contraband. It's the place where trained dogs sniff for drugs, away from the mainstream of traffic.

Ken Kelly was only an hour from getting off duty. He had a reserve officer riding with him, and as all regular officers do, he had a tendency to be a tour guide for the citizen cop. He was driving the patrol car south on I-5 by the old border check station when they saw a commotion near the bus circle where Tijuana tour buses and regular city buses drop their passengers. They could see some U.S. Customs inspectors milling around a gathering crowd in the darkness.

It turned out that a man had driven back across the border the wrong way on I-5. He tried to avoid the customs line and drove northbound on the Mexican side which was open only to southbound traffic. He was not stopped by the Mexican authorities, but the Americans halted him before he could get his car onto the proper side of Interstate 5.

He was not drunk. He was not carrying contraband. He just didn't feel like waiting in the customs line. And he was screaming his head off at everybody within earshot. He was, in the words of Ken Kelly, "a real number one prick asshole."

So Ken Kelly did what cops generally do to number one prick assholes who have committed a traffic violation they didn't observe. He started looking for a violation he *could* observe. He found that the car's left taillight was out and he began writing him a ticket, for failing the attitude test, as they say.

But this driver's attitude didn't improve. He kept chipping away. He had a *big* mouth. Ken Kelly started getting a tension headache like the one on television. He wondered if he'd *ever* get on the Barf squad. He wondered if he'd ever get away from number one prick assholes like this one. He'd rather be facing bandits in the canyons. He'd *much* rather be facing bandits in the canyons.

The man said he would not sign the traffic citation. Ken Kelly informed him that it was only a promise to appear and not an admission of guilt. The man said he still wouldn't sign.

The man was told that he'd have to be arrested, rather than released on the promise. He signed. Then he wanted to void the signature. Then he relented. Then he didn't want to take his citation copy. Then he changed his mind.

And suddenly his attitude altered miraculously. It was so sudden Ken Kelly couldn't believe it. And shouldn't have. The man took the ticket and began to apologize. He apologized more than profusely. He smiled and told Ken Kelly that he had been out of line and that Ken Kelly was one of the most professional lawmen he'd ever met. Moreover, he put out his hand and told Ken Kelly that he was one of the *nicest* cops he'd ever met.

And there are moments like this in every policeman's life, when the adrenaline surge is simply squeezed off. When the tension instantly subsides and you're not sure if you're relieved or disappointed. When all that was wrong in your angry cop's world becomes inexplicably right. In short, when some citizen cons the shit out of you.

He gripped Ken Kelly's hand and said, "I mean it. You're the *nicest* police officer I've ever met."

And Ken Kelly just stopped being a cynical cop and reeled back on his heels and generally behaved like a dumb ass *civilian,* saying, "Well, that's okay. Sometimes I do things I regret, so I understand. It's okay and I'd like . . ."

But the man, continuing to hold the grip, cut him off by leaning closer. And he breathed into Ken Kelly's face and told him something that all policemen have been told. It wasn't the worst thing that was ever said to him by a citizen. It was just that, at this time in his life, he was vulnerable. The man leaned very close into his face and said something like: "You're so nice that I wonder when you're gonna stop fucking little animals, you slimy lowdown . . ."

Suddenly Ken Kelly was doing his deranged Jack Nicholson impression without even knowing it. And he saw the man tumble over backward and land flat on his back. The right side of the man's head was gashed open and bleeding.

Why was everyone looking at him like he ate chicken heads? What *was* this guy yelling about?

Ken Kelly said to his astonished partner, "What's he yelling about? I didn't hit him!" Then to the fallen citizen he said, "I didn't hit you!"

He hit him all right. Ken Kelly's flashlight looked like an eight iron. Later, he sat in the watch commander's office, smoothing his limp blond hair back over his ears, and told his sergeant: "*Obviously* I hit him with my flashlight. I *must* have. But I *swear* I don't remember! Would I do something like that on purpose in front of a million witnesses that all looked like lawyers with hemorrhoids? *Would* I?"

The sergeant answered dryly, "Why didn't you just take a hammer down to the nearest A.C.L.U. office and lay your cock on the desk?"

Ken Kelly was destined to become a police department celebrity. He was the first San Diego cop to be criminally indicted as a result of a citizen's complaint. It was a bifurcated complaint in that he was also charged by the police department with using excessive force.

The mother of Ken Kelly was diagnosed that year as having terminal cancer. He had to hire a lawyer and the case dragged out for months during that terrible period of waiting. He pled no-contest to simple assault and went to a probation interview like any common criminal. He was the first in San Diego to do so dressed in a police uniform.

He also had to go to the police credit union and say that he needed desperately to borrow a lot of money: "No, not for a new car, asshole! To keep from wearing stripes!"

Manny Lopez could understand that there are moments in a man's life. He had a moment or two he wanted back. He had long since decided that Robbie Hurt could not be on the walking teams because he was black, and that Robbie needed a regular partner on the cover team. It wouldn't hurt if the partner was a white guy who also couldn't be a decoy in the canyons. He could be another *outsider.*

Ken Kelly was told that when there was an opening he would be nominated by Manny Lopez and maybe voted into BARF by the others who knew him. If that happened, the next guy he smacked with a flashlight wouldn't be dragging him into court. Canyon bandits don't make citizen complaints. Of course the next guy might just *shoot* him to death, but Ken Kelly figured that the way his life was going these days the guy would be doing him a favor.

On their second night back in the canyons, an otherwise uneventful Sunday evening, they began to suspect they had taught the bandits a trick or two. Manny Lopez was walking with the junior varsity that night. Renee Camacho and Carlos Chacon were his partners. Despite uptown orders Dick Snider would not stay in the station and decided to join Robbie Hurt on the cover team.

Just before dark, Dick Snider spotted a man near E-2 Canyon about half a mile east of the port of entry. He was lurking near a large hole in the fence and he looked like a very wrong number. Pretty soon he was joined by four other men, and as darkness fell, Dick Snider contacted Manny Lopez by radio and told them to take a little walk in the direction of the fence.

Manny and the junior varsity paralleled the fence, and when they neared the entry hole where Dick Snider had spotted his man, they were confronted by a figure in the darkness. He wore a blue tank jacket and jeans. He was a teenager, as it turned out, but looked older. He was also a strung-out, tattooed, drippy-nosed Colonia Libertad heroin addict who needed something to eat, and who needed a fix even more. When he got within twenty feet of the Barfers and they could not detect a weapon in his hand, they squatted and got into character.

"Where're you going?" he asked.

"San Diego," Manny Lopez said.

"I can take you," he said. "How much money do you have?"

"Two hundred dollars," Manny told him, "but I need it to get to Los Angeles."

"How much do you have?" he asked Carlos Chacon.

"Seventy-five dollars," Carlos answered in good Spanish.

When Renee Camacho was asked how much he had, his boy-tenor voice climbed into an alien singsong and he said, "Fifty dollars," with an accent that sounded unauthentic to Manny. Still, the kid was forcing him to talk.

The young man seemed satisfied. "I'll be right back," he said.

The Barfers remained squatting, just ten feet from the international border, there by the man-sized hole in the fence. When the kid returned he was not alone. There were three men with him and another teenager. The group stopped a few paces away in the shadows and the other young man said something to his pals that puzzled the Barfers. He said, "What did El Loco say?"

It was the second time they'd heard this name "Loco" —the bandit who'd tried to rob them and escaped, leaving his red ski mask behind. Then the first young addict did something no one else had done thus far in the canyons. He said to Manny Lopez, "Stand up. I have to search you for weapons."

And of course Manny tried everything but method acting. Weapons? Poor pollos like ourselves? What would we be doing with weapons? Poor *campesinos* like us? And so forth.

Manny's performance was convincing. The five walked a few steps back to the ominous hole in the fence and talked to a shadow figure just beyond, a man who remained at all times in the country of Mexico. A man who had already experienced the shock of meeting "pollos" who turned out to be San Diego policemen.

When they returned, the young junkie lost his patience. He was now wearing a black glove, and they saw a naked blade in the gloved hand. He wanted some money *now* and said so.

And that was it. Manny Lopez said, "*¿Sabes que?*" to get ready. And a moment later he said something none of the bandits understood: "Barf!"

And all three cops leaped to their feet, baring blue steel gun barrels, and the three older bandits flowed through that fence hole as sleek as seals. The two young junkies didn't move fast enough.

They were strung-out hypes, but desperate and very game. Renee Camacho yelped when he got kicked. Carlos Chacon grabbed one kid while the other made for the fence hole yelling, "*¡Socios! ¡Socios!*"

It was a word they were to hear many times in the months to come. The bandit cry for partners: "*¡Socios!*"

There was a lot of stomping and punching and biting and gouging going on out there, and lots of other Barfers running across the canyon to assist them. The young junkies got pretty well thumped. But the thing that made the incident memorable was that when the kid yelled "*¡Socios!*" the shadow figure approached the fence. And with his feet planted firmly on Mexican soil he momentarily disrupted the bruising struggle by firing a gun point-blank right at them. He missed and vanished into the Mexican night.

Then there was *real* screaming going on.

"*Barf! Barf! Barf!*"

"Goddamn! Son of a bitch! *Barf!*"

They managed to hold on to the two young addicts, and there were bumps, bruises, contusions and lacerations on both sides. The addicts were almost unrecognizable when later seen in court. Renee Camacho woke up the next morning feeling like he'd played the Chargers that Sunday.

And there was one topic of conversation that night at the booze party. "Loco"? Who *is* this bastard with the ski mask? Even when he knows who we are, he's not afraid to shoot.

Renee Camacho made a cogent observation that night. He said, "It used to be sticks and stones and maybe knives out here. Now is it gonna be guns? What're we doing, teaching the bandits to use *guns* to match us?"

Was that to be their legacy? The Barf squad helped *arm* the bandits? Everyone thought that was very ironic and funny. Sort of.

CHAPTER · 9

MORDIDA

THERE IS AN INCREDIBLE ENERGY FLUX SIZZLING through the United States of America. That, and an unreasonable belief in limitless possibility mark the Americans abroad like a branding iron, making them seem even less like the cousins they find in ancestral homelands than other foreign tourists. One has only to visit, say, Ireland, and watch an Irish-American in a Dublin pub, tears gushing as he listens to some rebel ditty about shooting Englishmen to death. Or in Tel Aviv to observe a tour of American Jews, eyes agleam, dancing the hora with some real live Sabras who are getting free drinks to do it. Or Mexican-Americans in those cantinas in Tijuana that advertise "authentic" Mexican food, which generally means gristly *carnitas* and so-so *salsa,* too hot for most gringos.

The Barfers themselves on occasion were part of the latter *turista* group. And tourists they were, getting loud and buzzed, amateur boozers warbling off-key to the worn-out crowd pleasers like "La Paloma." Pretending for a rude and bleary evening that they were real Mexicans like the *mariachi* who was raking it in with both hands and feeling that he had about as much in common with these Anglicized coconuts as he did with the Chinese restaurateur who was paying his salary, and who was at least born and raised in Mexico.

The natives of Ireland, Israel, Mexico and other countries frequented by roots-hunting Americans have a term for them. It has exactly the same meaning in Hebrew, Gaelic, Italian, Greek, Swahili and Spanish. The term is *Yankee dipshits.*

And even though a bunch of Americans of Mexican blood can dress up and fool desperate people for a few minutes in the canyons, real Mexicans know instinctively that all Yankee dipshits, regardless of where their parents or grandparents were born, are indelibly marked by the unbelievable energy flux and unreasonable belief in limitless possibility surging through that strange country to the north. They know instinctively that Mexican-Americans have *less* in common with them than the dipshits will ever know.

In a matter of a few days after the Barf squad was reorganized and returned to the canyons, none of them would be crossing that line for evening fun. The Barfers were beginning to learn that Mexico belongs to Mexicans, *real* Mexicans. Though some Barfers would forever judge Mexico by American standards, some would not, and would become troubled and confused by what was about to happen. But one thing for sure, almost none of them would be going back across that border for cheap tequila and beer and nights of singing "La Paloma." They'd be too goddamn scared to be caught dead over there.

One way in which Mexicans differ markedly from Americans is in their concept of law and order. That is not to say that their law enforcement is inefficient. Armed robbery, for instance, is considered a huge crime in Mexico, where guns in the hands of the masses terrify the government. In December, traditionally the worst month for bandits in American cities, Tijuana had a single armed robbery one year. In San Diego or Los Angeles or San Francisco, robbery is as common as fornication, and a tourist, if he's going to get drunk and flash money and raise hell, would be far wiser to do it on the streets of Tijuana than on certain streets in San Diego or Los Angeles or San Francisco, where he'd have about as much chance of survival as Gloria Steinem in Tehran.

The Mexican police share some attributes with their Yankee counterparts. Defensive humor for instance. There is a statue of a patriot priest in Tijuana, and it was a cop who first decided that the statue's hand was not pointing to a better day for Mexico. The padre was simply saying, "Look out, pollos! Here comes *la migra*!"

Ditto for the bold sculpture of the Aztec chief Cuauhtemoc holding his war club aloft. Cuauhtemoc, the cops say, is yelling, "Get your raggedy ass *out* of this country! *That* way through the fence!"

Then there's the policemen's story of the drug dog. Perhaps an apocryphal tale, it illustrates many things, not the least of which is the underlying sadness of living cheek by jowl with not just a rich nation, but the richest half of the richest state of the richest nation. . . .

It seems that the mayor of Rosarito was having one hell of a time getting across the international border to do business in San Diego. He would present his identification at the border and, with reserve and good manners and patience, inform the U.S. Customs officers that he was the mayor of Rosarito and that he made numerous crossings. And His Honor would invariably find his ass in the secondary inspection area with a German shepherd crawling all over his car sniffing for contraband.

Of course Mexican-Americans are much like other Americans—not very reserved and mannerly and patient. However, the mayor of Rosarito was a real Mexican, and silently endured the humiliation each time he crossed. Then one day when he was doing city business back in Rosarito, one of his cops came to his office with a livid American who was hollering, swearing, threatening. The American's car had been illegally parked and was impounded. He was outraged because the car bore U.S. Government license plates. It seems that the livid American was a U.S. Customs officer.

The mayor nodded politely and let the customs officer scream himself hoarse, until the American made a huge mistake by saying, "I demand to be treated the way *you would be treated* on our side of the border."

And all at once he was looking at a grin as wide as Baja California. There hadn't been a Mexican politician grinning like this since the country struck oil. His Honor had a private conversation with his cop, who had had it up to his chin strap with this gringo, U.S. *migra* or not.

Upon the orders of the mayor, the Mexican cop went out and rounded up the mangiest, scabbiest, wormiest stray dog he could find. When the customs officer and the mayor showed up at the impound yard, the cop was waiting with this twitching, cowering cur, who was introduced to the *migra* by His Honor.

"Thees ees our marijuana dog," the mayor informed the customs officer. "I am sorry but he must sneef een the car for drugs."

And then while the American official went up like rocket's red glare, the Mexican cop dragged the howling dog into the front seat of the U.S. Government car. And the terrified animal pissed all over the place.

The customs officer of course was strangling on his own bile when the cop hauled the poor creature into the back seat. And the dog continued pissing a river.

The customs officer could not even manage a croak

when the mayor turned to him and said brightly, "But, señor, joo should be bery happy! Eef he had smelled contraband our marijuana dog would have *cheet*!"

The other thing about Mexican cops and people in general down below that imaginary line is that they don't try to *understand* lawbreakers. And though the Mexicans' ideas of what constitutes crime might differ from those of their colleagues north of the border, they have no trouble at all with a dichotomy.

There is a saying among Mexican cops: *El pájaro mas pendejo sabe volar.* The most dumbbell bird knows how to fly.

And Mexican cops do not intend to be earthbound from the moment they pin on the badge. To accept a "gratuity" from a smuggler, guide or pollo, for example, does not seem to be a terrible offense, not when they are paid barely enough to keep a family fed. Not when *la mordida*—payoffs, bribery, *the bite*—has been a way of life since the *conquistadores* began the systematic extortion of the Aztecs. It is *expected.*

If the Mexican cops seize a car stolen in the U.S., for example, they know full well that the American owner has received an insurance payment for that car, so they figure what's the harm in keeping it for official business? The police service did not supply nearly enough cars and even required them to pay for their own gasoline for official business if they exceeded their modest gas quota.

Mexican cops usually try to understand the gringo cops, knowing that it's hopeless for gringos to understand *them.*

The felony crimes in Tijuana are investigated by the *judiciales,* the state judicial police. The uniformed cops in the tan uniforms seen by the *turistas* are municipal police responsible for traffic control and keeping the peace.

An American tourist would not know a *judicial* upon seeing one. For instance he may be one of a group of young men at a table in one of Tijuana's several good restaurants.

He may be wearing a *guayabera* shirt made popular by President Echeverria. The shirts are usually white or tan, with side vents and pockets on the outside, sometimes with epaulets. Or he may be one of the handsome young dudes sitting at the bar at one of the surprisingly tame skin-show saloons on Avenida Revolución, where tourists invariably start bitching because they could see hotter acts in Davenport, Iowa.

And many a secretary from Kansas City has had her heart set aflutter by this young fellow at the bar or that one who clearly isn't watching the show and isn't paying for his drinks. One looks like a young Tyrone Power with a designer haircut. One's wearing a purple art-deco shirt and they're both wearing Sergio Valente jeans. One has a gold chain and a religious medal of soft Mexican gold hanging from his throat, and the other's wearing mirror shades on top of his head. And they're both sporting white imitation-lizard cowboy boots and belts with silver buckles about the size of a football.

And then a secretary from Kansas City may notice something bulging under the shirt of the one who looks like Omar Sharif and, my God! It looks like a gun!

It's a .380, or a .45, or a 9mm pistol. An automatic for sure, in that they're more macho than revolvers, and Mexican cops are macho. Which you *better* believe.

Also, they're proud of the low crime rate in Tijuana. They generally distrust the municipal police and blame them for everything from traffic chaos to robbing corpses on homicide cases. These *judiciales* investigate all major crimes except narcotics, which are handled by the federal judicial police.

Life isn't easy for these cops either, not when they know it's absolutely impossible to have anything approaching a decent life without *mordida.* The bite is their "bonus" for doing good police work.

All residents living below the imaginary line understand exactly what will happen if they indulge in behavior that generally constitutes serious crime in civilized countries, but sometimes Americans get the idea that because the Mexican tourist business is so vital, they can grossly exceed the drunken, noisy, insulting behavior that Mexicans have come to accept from them. Sometimes a software salesman from Silicon Valley with a skinful of scotch may make an *awful* mistake. He may grab the tit/ass/snatch of a housewife coming to pick up her shopkeeper husband after a fourteen-hour day. And when her husband runs to her rescue, the little greaseball may get four knucklebones in the chops, after which the software salesman may dig out for the border in his Hertz rent-a-car and nearly cream a motor cop.

Then the software salesman will be totally *amazed* by his windshield exploding before his eyes and he'll jump on the brakes with both feet because they're shooting at him! And he may find himself in the headquarters of the *judiciales* and be staring at two handsome young dudes, one who looks just like Omar Sharif and the other who's a ringer for Tyrone Power. And they tell him that it's a serious crime to assault women in Tijuana, and he tells them he didn't and he's not talking. He's demanding to call the American consulate.

The dude who looks like Tyrone Power then shrugs and begins to unbutton his purple art-deco shirt. When the software salesman asks him why, he says it's so he doesn't get it spotted by Coke.

"Coke?" the American says. "You aren't setting me up on a phony drug bust! I *demand* to make a call."

But the one who looks like Omar Sharif just smiles and fetches the Coke—Coca-Cola, a whole six-pack.

They're gonna ply me with soft drinks to break down my resistance, the American thinks. And he couldn't be more right.

Sometimes with ordinary recalcitrant prisoners, *le dan*

agua. A drink of water. From a hose. Lots and *lots* of water. After some water interrogations, the cop in charge comes out looking like Mark Spitz. And the prisoner looks like a water bed, all shuddery and quivering, as he lies on the floor bloated by about five gallons of T.J.'s H_2O, guaranteed to give him the drizzles.

As to the Coke, well, when there was the riot at La Mesa Prison in Tijuana, there were lots of gringo reporters on hand and they all wondered at the strange habits of the Mexican soldiers who were marched into that prison carrying ginger ale.

Ginger ale? These goddamn Mexicans must be crazy for ginger ale, they said. There were thirty cases of the stuff. The prisoners knew better and surrendered right *now.*

So the software salesman is getting ready to make some smartass remark, like "How about some Jamaican rum in my Coke?" when the Tyrone Power look-alike throws a wristlock on him and handcuffs his hands behind his back. Then, while he yells and screams for his rights as an American citizen, his arms are looped over the back of a swivel chair and he's tilted back. Way back. And then he gets his Coke. Right up his *nose.*

His head is held by Omar Sharif, and Tyrone Power starts shaking up that Coke until it's ready to explode, and then the cop shoots a jet right into his snoot. And he has to breathe through there because Omar Sharif has just shoved a little hand towel down his throat.

You don't like our soda pop? Would you prefer some Bubble-Up? How about a Bubble-Up margarita, hold the tequila, hold the salt?

He is treated to various flavors of soda pop but he feels the same way about all of them.

The sensation has been described by prisoners. Some have said it's like a volcano erupting in your brain. In any case he starts confessing, but of course they can't hear him. And they don't stop right away, because some guys have told them lies during confessions, so they give him a few more bottles.

And pretty soon he's confessing like crazy but nobody can hear with his mouth full of towel. They're just going about their business talking about jai alai or something and he's kicking and screaming and thrashing and confessing and nobody's *listening*! And Kilauea has erupted thirty-four times right behind his eyes, which are filling up with molten lava. And he's crying and trying to scream and silently confessing. To *anything*.

When they let him up and dry him off and he finally stops sobbing long enough to be intelligible, another one of the *judiciales* walks in. He's not as young and handsome as the guy who gave him the soda pop. In fact, this one looks like someone who would sidle up to you and try to sell you a lame horse, or a TV crate filled with bricks, or a Porsche with a VW engine. In short, he looks like Wayne Newton.

He has a pencil and note pad. He asks the software salesman if he would like to confess. And he starts. Still crying, he begins with the time he stole a yo-yo from a Sioux Falls five and dime. Then he confesses that when he was little he flogged his dummy maybe a thousand times and didn't tell the priest in confession. Then he tells about all the cheating on his wife.

Wayne Newton's used to it. He lights a cigarette and sits back staring at the ceiling and after listening to every single crime, every sin, every peccadillo the salesman can remember in his whole life, he asks a few perfunctory questions about the attempted rape of a Mexican citizen. And the salesman stops and stares beseechingly at Tyrone Power because he's *not* a rapist!

All Tyrone Power does is smile encouragingly and cup his hand as though he's holding a bottle with his thumb over the mouth of it. And he shakes the imaginary bottle a few times. That's all. It's something they do often when interrogating hardball Mexican criminals who are not cooperating.

The little smile. The gentle shaking of the cupped hand with the thumb crooked over the mouth of an imaginary bottle.

And the software salesman's on his knees saying, "Yes, yes, yes, I did it!" And he confesses to the Lindbergh kidnapping. And to the Boston stranglings. And then he remembers the time he let his hand slide across the ass of a redhead at that computer convention in Atlanta and he *tries* to tell them about that, but they don't *care* about a bustle rubber in Dixie.

In fact, Wayne Newton's looking bored and he glances at his watch and hands over the note pad all written in Spanish and the salesman signs it without being asked. And he begs to sign a check. And can he sign over his mortgage? And his car? Will they accept his Hertz car? As a fucking gift!

Finally, he ends up paying a modest fine, but while they're "processing the paperwork" (which takes about a week because it's true these folks are not intimidated by time) he learns a few new tricks. In that he shares a ten-by-ten-foot cell with fourteen other guys, the most aromatic of whom smells like the bubonic plague, he learns to sleep on his feet like a cockatoo.

And for the rest of his life, or maybe for ten or twenty years at least, a funny thing happens. Whenever he hears the Coca-Cola song he starts to confess. He might be back home in a Silicon Valley drugstore minding his own business and the girl at the cosmetic counter is playing a radio, and he hears: "It's the reeeeel thing, Coke is . . ."

And he's weeping and screaming and throwing himself on the floor. On his knees! Confessing to the pharmacist! To the cashier! To a goddamn notary public, who runs screaming out the door when he tries to confess to his Pekinese!

By the time the cops arrive he's kneeling in front of the health-aids counter spilling his guts to a hot water bottle on sale for $5.98.

And should a *real* American rapist—like the ones who routinely prowl the Southern California streets and freeways committing multiple murders—decide to cross the imaginary line looking for dark-eyed beauties and sexually harm a *child,* well, there is absolutely only one sensible course of action. He must quickly run and find the most dilapidated, sputtering, smoky Tijuana bus on the road and start giving the exhaust pipe a fast blowjob while it's stopped at a red light. The way those things spew carbon monoxide he should be safely dead before the light changes, and that would be the only sensible place to be if he gets arrested for molesting a child: dead.

That's one way that law enforcement differs south of the imaginary line, but Mexican cops had always extended great hospitality to their San Diego colleagues. Pretty soon the cops down there would come to *hate* some of their brethren north of the line, those who dressed up as pollos and walked at night in the canyons.

In the twilight hours of February 1st, the Barfers hit the canyons as usual. Dick Snider, technically not the BARF supervisor anymore, but still a Southern Division shift lieutenant, decided to come along to work the cover team with Robbie Hurt. The only varsity team member on duty that night was the BARF supervisor, Manny Lopez, and he decided to let Joe Castillo walk with him. Carlos Chacon was walking with Renee Camacho.

Fred Gil walked with a new member of the junior varsity, brought in to replace the cop who had quit during the BARF hiatus. His name was Joe Vasquez. He was twenty-six years old, a burly fellow with a large shaggy head and small hands. Not a big man, but he *seemed* like a big man, with a face like a wanted poster. In fact, when they were asked to help with a stakeout on a robbery series in uptown San Diego, they were shown a composite drawing of a suspect who was robbing fast-food restaurants. The suspect was described as "big and ugly." The composite drawing looked just like Joe Vasquez, who immediately became known as "Big Ugly." Or, when his fellow Barfers were feeling more charitable, "Quasimodo."

Joe Vasquez took it with good humor. He was by nature a loner, not one to sit and rap with the boys. Not one to booze it up after they got off duty, in a ritual getting manic. He once said that he had only one close friend, his wife. The others thought that was pretty weird kind of talk. Definitely not macho. A wife for a best friend? But he was reliable and brave. You had to like Big Ugly.

Wind tore the clouds to shreds. The canyons were a patchwork at dusk, silver light and shadow. Sound on the wind: loud radios playing sad Mexican music. Glasses breaking. Beer cans popping. The smell of beans cooking. The smell of city smoke. There were people playing and watching soccer games on the upper field, a hundred people. Colonia Libertad was jammed with cars. It was going to be a bad night for the Border Patrol, they said.

Joe Vasquez and Fred Gil climbed to the top of Airport Mesa to work their way toward Deadman's Canyon. Dick Snider and Robbie Hurt established themselves and the Ford Bronco where they could watch most of Spring Canyon, the upper soccer field, and the mouth of Deadman's Canyon, along with the hill leading north from Colonia Libertad. Manny Lopez and Joe Castillo walked past Washerwoman Flats and headed east toward Deadman's Canyon.

There were children all over the hillside just above Spring Canyon and on the dirt road that parallels the international border. Canyon children as wild as hawks. Suddenly, Dick Snider and Robbie Hurt, concealed in the brush and mesquite, met a group of seven kids and four dogs sitting quietly behind them, watching them watch the aliens. After a time the kids and dogs got bored and ran off yelling or barking toward Spring Canyon, stopping only to warn a pair of pollos that they were being observed through binoculars by *la migra* on top of the hill.

The pollos who got the friendly warning were Manny Lopez and Joe Castillo, who was carrying his little pollo bag over his shoulder on this rather warm winter afternoon. The bag contained a Handie-Talkie, flares, first aid kit, and flashlights, all of which would be used on this memorable evening.

While Dick Snider and Robbie Hurt were watching the alien movement in the canyons they saw three men walking down the road from the top of Airport Mesa. Two of the men peeled off onto a trail overlooking Spring Canyon in the direction of Manny and Joe. One of the men was too well-dressed to be either a pollo or a bandit. He was wearing a creamy leather jacket, slightly belled mocha slacks, and cowboy boots with stitching to match the jacket.

Clouds like banks of foam blew in over the canyon mouth when Manny and Joe Castillo started in. Stunted trees with withered fingers pointed up and away from the canyon floor. Joe remembered the trees.

Manny and Joe walked about 250 yards along the creek bottom and soon they came to a curve in the creek where the trickle of polluted water snaked sideways and the brush grew thick. There seemed to be cloud shadow everywhere. Then from the twilight shadows a very ragged alien stepped from behind a hill of mesquite and stood silently staring at them. Then another man, this one twenty-three years old, the same as Joe Castillo, and wearing a creamy leather jacket, mocha slacks and boots. Joe admired the young man's clothes. There was never a pollo *or* bandit dressed like this. His left hand was down at his side. When he brought it up and extended it, they saw that his taste extended to firearms. He was holding a beautiful .45-caliber automatic pistol with silver grips. He was pointing it right at Manny Lopez' right eyebrow, which had leaped into a shocked and spiky interrogation point.

The two Barfers went instinctively to their haunches and tried to get into character, which wasn't easy. Joe Castillo customarily talked with his hands, long graceful fingers fluttering like bird wings. Ordinarily he was the world champ of body language. He hunched his shoulders, dipped his head, swayed his torso, squirmed his hips, always with the hands fluttering and gesturing. But not now. This was the first time in his young life that he had ever been face to face with a gun muzzle. Joe Castillo had turned to stone.

The gunman said, "*¡Migra!*" letting them know he was an immigration officer—from which country he didn't say.

The shafts of light from half a sunball dropping below the hills glinted on the blue steel barrel of that gun and Joe Castillo remembered thinking: That's such a *pretty* gun.

It was something that was to happen a great deal from this moment on, a game they would play in their heads. The game was called, "What was I thinking *when*?"

"I like guns," Joe Castillo said later. "That's why I thought: That's a *pretty* gun, with the light bouncing off the barrel. And those silver grips."

The man held the gun in his left hand. He kept it just a few feet from the face of Manny Lopez. This was the third time a man representing himself to be a Mexican lawman had shoved a gun into the face of Manny Lopez. But this time Manny didn't pull a gun and badge and have a Mexican standoff. Not by a long shot. This time Manny had a very bad thought about himself slithering through his brain. The thought was this: You're gonna *die*.

Manny Lopez had not been in Vietnam. Manny had never shot at a human being before, only at targets on the police pistol range. Manny didn't even know much about guns except for his own service revolver, and he wasn't that great a shot. He could only think that very evil thought:

You're gonna *die.* It's too bad. It's too bad you're gonna die.

The .45 was cocked. Then for some reason the dapper stranger moved the gun to his left and pointed it at the face of Joe Castillo, who squatted four or five inches to the right of his sergeant.

It was all happening so slowly that Manny Lopez couldn't believe it. It *is* like in the movies, he thought. Time *does* slow down. And then Manny stopped thinking that he was going to die and stopped thinking about time slowing down and stopped thinking about anything but the two-inch Smith & Wesson .38 in his shoulder holster. While the .45 was aimed at the face of motionless Joe Castillo, who thought of inching his long fingers toward his own gun, Manny snatched the .38 from his holster and began jerking the trigger as it came up.

PLOOM PLOOM PLOOM PLOOM PLOOM! is the way it sounded in the ears of Joe Castillo. Then things speeded up for him as the dapper stranger began whirling, spinning, jerking. He was jerking back and forth like a wolf in a shooting gallery. Then Joe heard a BOP! as he saw the dressy dude going down.

The shot was from Joe's own gun and he found himself firing at the raggedy partner, who was flying across the creek bed, screaming his head off. Joe popped another cap and the raggedy partner went down.

The only transmission received by the frantic cover team of Dick Snider and Robbie Hurt was Joe Castillo yelling into the Handie-Talkie: "He's shot! We need cover!" which sent the Barfers running in all directions, mostly wrong.

Joe Castillo was, in his words, totally *bughouse.* He didn't know if he was alive or dead for an instant. He went running after the raggedy alien he'd just shot down and remembered jumping on the screaming ragbag and beating the living shit out of him. The slightly injured alien started fighting back but Joe Castillo was past rage. He wanted to beat the guy to *death.* He stopped when the adrenaline seemed to gush out his fingernails. He'd never felt like this. He hardly had the strength to drag the guy back to Manny.

Manny Lopez was on the ground holding the dressy dude by the shirt front. Manny was also bughouse and found himself yelling into the guy's face. "You asshole! You asshole!" Then Manny Lopez remembered that *the only word* the guy said was *migra.* "Are you *really* an immigration officer?" Manny asked him.

"Yes," the man answered. But he was turning gray.

"You stupid bastard!" Manny said. "Why did you *do* this?"

"I thought you were smugglers," the man gasped, and somehow he managed to pull himself up on one elbow.

"Bullshit!" Manny Lopez said. "You're a thief. You carry a badge and you're a thief!"

"How bad am I?" the man asked, and he was panting heavily.

Manny looked at the blood-soaked, bullet-riddled body. The guy was body shot three times, one through the right nipple, two in the groin. He was also arm shot. He was even ass shot, caught by a slug while spinning like a wolf in a shooting gallery. He looked *bad.*

And Manny Lopez, never having been accused of sentimentality, shrugged and said, "You're gonna die."

"Oh, nooooooo!" the guy cried out. But he pulled up his own blood-soaked shirt and examined the wounds. In fact, he sat up. In fact, he was trying to get to his *feet*!

Except that Joe Castillo, breathing like a marathoner, with eyes all beady and scowling like the boss ayatollah, came raging back to the creek bed, dragging the handcuffed, bloody partner of the dressy dude. He saw the guy from behind just sitting there talking to Manny Lopez. And Joe Castillo, with his ears still ringing from the gunshots and his face full of lead shavings and the smell of gunpowder running clear through his nasal cavity to his brain, thought that Manny had missed. This son of a bitch had a cocked and loaded .45 in our faces and we almost *died* and Manny missed!

Then Manny was stunned to see the handcuffed alien go hurtling through the air and land belly first at his feet, while Joe Castillo, looking wild and bughouse, took three steps and kicked the dressy dude right in the chest, doing more harm, it turned out, than the tit shot which ricocheted off the breastbone and came out the chest cavity, causing very little damage.

"What're you doing, fucker?" Manny yelled. "The asshole's *dying.*"

"Oh," Joe said, looking at the Mexican immigration cop, who was writhing on the ground in more pain from the kick than from the gunshots.

When the other Barfers came panting across the canyon toward the direction of the gunfire, they found Joe Castillo putting surgical dressings on the man, trying to apologize for kicking the shit out of him while he was dying.

Except that he *wasn't* dying. He pushed Joe away and got to his feet on his own. Then he waved away *all* help and said, "I can do it myself."

And he walked with them out of the canyons to the nearest dirt road just as the ambulance came bouncing over the horizon.

And he continued a running dialogue with Manny Lopez all the time he was leaking blood, saying things like: "Yes, I know it's a bad way to work smugglers." And, "Yes, it was stupid to be on U.S. soil." And, "It was wrong of me to draw my gun on you even though I thought you were smugglers." And, "I really screwed up and understand perfectly why you shot me."

He understood *perfectly.* He was full of holes and dripping all over the canyons and he could cook up a story as he walked out unassisted.

The Barfers were amazed. By now Carlos Chacon was

on the scene trying to direct the Border Patrol chopper via Handie-Talkie. Joe Vasquez was stumbling around with a radio earpiece in his ear and the cord dragging the ground, thinking that his new job might be interesting. Darkness had fallen and they were staggering all over the place trying to fight their way up the embankment with two prisoners, one on a gurney. Everyone was yelling and bitching and slipping and falling and finally the wounded Mexican said, "Leave me alone! I can do it better *myself!*"

Shot full of holes, he apparently had only one worry: that these coconut assholes might accidentally drop him over a cliff and kill him. And in fact he climbed the escarpment better than any of them and walked all the way out.

There was of course pandemonium on all police frequencies. The Border Patrol chopper was WOP-WOP-WOPPING over their heads. The Mexican *judiciales* and municipal police had heard the action on their frequencies and were pouring into the canyons from the direction of Colonia Libertad. There were rubberneckers flowing out of the lantern-lit shacks south of the line and Manny Lopez was screaming, "Let's get the hell *out* a here!"

Just then some kids from Colonia Libertad decided to have a little fun and set some tires afire, rolling them down into the canyons at them, which made it a bit tough for the San Diego P.D.'s homicide team to come in and investigate, as they must, officer-involved shootings. When they arrived it was all they could do to keep from getting set on fire by rowdy Mexican kids who were bombarding them with rocks and burning tires.

The tire rolling stopped after about thirty minutes, and Carlos Chacon, who was guarding the shooting scene, found another well-dressed stranger making his way down the hill into the canyon. He was a Mexican immigration official and he was carrying a walkie-talkie and speaking into it. He wasn't very happy and advised Carlos Chacon that others were following him into the canyons to find out what had happened.

The wounded immigration officer, Luis Tamez, was booked into the San Diego jail, as was his companion, who told the cops that he was an informant for the wounded *migra.* They both stuck to the story that they were looking for alien smugglers and mistook the Barfers for their men.

There was a bit of difficulty in making a case, since Tamez had never said anything but "*migra.*" It was true that two weeks earlier they had received a report from an arrested alien that he had been robbed in the canyons by an armed man in the uniform of the Mexican Immigration Service. Nevertheless, Luis Tamez had not uttered anything except "Immigration" prior to being ventilated by Manny Lopez.

The assistant district attorney wrote a letter to the San Diego chief of police which made Manny Lopez crazy. It said:

> We have been advised that you and members of your Department have met with officials of the Mexican Immigration Service who have acknowledged the error of allowing their officers (and specifically, Mr. Tamez on this occasion) to operate in United States territory. You have advised us that you believe the interest of important law enforcement cooperation between the Republic of Mexico and your Department would be adversely affected by a prosecution of Mr. Tamez. We must consider that interest as well as maintenance of harmonious relationships between the United States and Mexico.
>
> In view of these considerations and the technical nature of possible criminal acts for which Mr. Tamez probably has a legitimate defense, we be-

lieve the interests of justice dictate that no criminal complaint or prosecution should be instituted.

The story even received a big play in out-of-town newspapers. *Stern* magazine sent German reporters to do a story on these lawmen who were shooting down other lawmen on the border. Pete Wilson, the mayor of San Diego, asked President Jimmy Carter for federal assistance with border crime which had directly led to a tense international situation.

There was no getting around it; these Barfers were getting ink. They were hot. They were turning into something like media darlings. Maybe they were . . . *useful*?

When Manny Lopez heard about the district attorney's refusal to issue charges, he immediately resigned from the Barf squad. He put it in writing to Dick Snider. Manny received an urgent telephone call from the chief of police.

Chief Kolender said, "What do you think about us not issuing charges against the guy?"

"Chief, I think it's *fucked,*" Manny answered. "It makes it look like *I* screwed up! I hear his father's a big government official in Mexico City. So what? He's a *thief* with a badge. The *worst* kind a thief anyone can be."

"You can't quit this squad," Chief Kolender told him.

"Yes I can, Chief. I quit," Manny said.

"What do you want me to do?" the chief of police asked.

"I don't know," Manny Lopez answered. "You're the chief."

"I *know* I'm the goddamn chief. What do you want me to do?"

"My guys feel like nobody's backing them up," Manny Lopez said. "I want you to come . . . to my *house* and explain to my guys, and maybe . . . *apologize* if you feel we deserve it?"

"How about Sunday?" the chief of police quickly asked.

And he did it. Chief Bill Kolender *also* knew a thing or

two about machismo and stroking. He almost apologized twice. Despite the district attorney's letter to the contrary, he said that the police department took a strong stand but that there wasn't any way of convincing the district attorney to issue criminal charges. He said that he was sorry if they felt let down, because he thought they were the ballsiest bunch of cops he had ever encountered in his entire police career. He said that he appreciated the job they were doing out in those hills. He said that he would never have the nerve to go out there in those godforsaken canyons at night and belly up to armed desperados.

They had never had a high-ranking officer talk to them like this, let alone the chief of police himself. Manny beamed and passed around the beer and everyone looked at him in wonder. He could quick-draw looking down the throat of a cocked .45 automatic. He could even persuade the super-chief himself to come to his house. And *almost* apologize. He was some kind of hardball motherfucker, this Manny Lopez! He had prunes, they whispered to one another. Manny's prunes were big as honeydews. Manny Lopez had balls to the *walls*!

There was one thing that really pissed off the chief though. He said that the head of the Mexican Immigration Service told a lowdown lie about one of the Barfers. It seems that there was a rumor going around down south that a Barfer ran up and kicked the wounded officer who was lying on the ground shot to pieces. Chief Kolender assured the squad that he told the Mexicans what he thought of a preposterous story like that.

It was the first shootout for the Barf squad. Manny Lopez said, "We'd been in fights. We'd been threatened by Mexican cops with guns and by robbers with knives. We'd even been shot at by Loco through the fence. But I'd never faced anything like this immediate deadly threat. I *knew* that fucker was gonna shoot. Don't ask me how, but I knew it. And I didn't try to run. I didn't cry. Who knows, maybe I was a split second from crying or running or pleading, but I *didn't.* I *knew* I could do it now. Whatever happened—rain, blood, shit or flood—I could deal with it. I never felt like this before. I never felt so confident. Or *something.*"

Manny told Dick Snider to tear up his resignation letter. He was going to stick with BARF to the end. Then he had to run off because a local network affiliate wanted a television interview.

CHAPTER · 10

LAST OF THE GUNSLINGERS

SOME WAGS HAVE SAID THAT THERE ARE TWO THINGS TO talk about in America's Finest City: the predictably even temperature and the San Diego Chargers. And that when football season is over there is only the temperature.

San Diego is truly a scenic place, virtually perfect for the armies of joggers who live there. But sometimes the resort mentality seems to run amok and permeate everything, including the police force. It's almost as though the city is a thousand miles from the Baja Peninsula, gateway to all of Latin America with its millions of have-nots. For example, when Tony Puente first joined the police department and was sent to the border substation, Manny Lopez was the only other Mexican-American there. Including Dick Snider, that made three Spanish speakers, and Tony's Spanish was minimal.

Yet that was nothing compared to how it was in the bad old days. Manuel Smith, one of the cops working "Mexican Liaison" for the police department, remembered how it was. He'd been a cop for exactly twenty-one years on the night that Mexican immigration officer Luis Tamez was shot by Manny Lopez and survived. The surnames of Manuel Smith and his partner Ron Collins were a big joke around the department in that they were both of Mexican descent. Manuel Smith's ancestor James Wilcox Smith came to the Baja Peninsula from England in 1810, converted to Catholicism, married a Mexican girl, and stayed. The Baja Peninsula is full of Mexicans with Anglo surnames: Collins, Johnson, Blackwell, Simpson, Smith.

Manuel Smith was a second-generation San Diego policeman and had relatives throughout the Baja Peninsula as well as around the border on both sides. He was a shrewd, jovial cop with wavy hair and great white teeth. And he was *big,* nearly big enough to be protected by the Greenpeace ship, they used to say. His partner, an ex-football player, was also so big that this pair could wear out the shocks of a Plymouth in about two weeks. Their combined weight was somewhere between five hundred and six hundred pounds. Everyone said that if the San Diego naval base would just lash them together and float them, they could afford to decommission the U.S.S. *Enterprise.*

Both cops were of patrolman rank, Ron Collins having been a liaison officer longer but Manuel Smith generally thought of as the spokesman by virtue of his incredible connections south of the imaginary line. He had a cousin in the *judiciales* and another in the municipal police. Just watching him operate was a thing to behold. Manuel Smith couldn't even cross the border without having to pause and chat with the Mexican border guards, who normally only stopped cars heading south when they wanted to peddle some tickets to the police rodeo at the downtown bullring.

And when he got to the headquarters of the *judiciales* it was as though Santa Claus had arrived. Tijuana cops had a thousand problems that needed solving up north. There were personal problems, relatives who needed assistance with documents, immigration problems, insurance problems, employment problems. There were professional needs, the endless information search by cops who had no access to computers. There was impounded property linked to persons who traveled south to do business, legal and otherwise. The Mexican authorities had to labor under a maddening information gap that Manuel Smith and Ron Collins could help them narrow through American sources.

By the time he could even step foot inside state judicial police headquarters, Manuel Smith had a laundry list hanging out every pocket, and more to come when he got inside. An F.B.I. agent coming to the same headquarters might cool his heels in the lobby for a whole afternoon, while Manuel Smith had ten *judiciales* falling all over themselves just to help him locate the son of some American cop who was last seen smoking pot laced with PCP and running naked through the Tijuana cemetery on a big frat weekender.

He'd often worked San Diego homicide cases that took him south, and he admired the cunning ways of cops who have no crime lab and have to make do. When the Tijuana cops came to San Diego for tours, Manuel Smith would show them the police department's crime lab and computers and communications center and other law-enforcement gadgetry, and they would say, "Yes, it's just like ours."

It would make Manuel Smith sad because he knew that he was showing them *wonders,* and they were embarrassed. And they *always* called him *'mano* and *pareja,* "brother" or "partner," affectionately.

He understood the need for liaison between two countries living cheek by jowl, and he understood how delicate was his position. Former San Diego police administrators did not even *want* a Mexican-American cop being the liaison with Tijuana authorities. "They" might think of the possibility of profit and corruption if "they" got together with "their own kind."

Manuel Smith was old enough to be very careful. He well remembered a promotion board when a former deputy chief had said to him: "Smith, what're *you* doing trying to make sergeant? *You* people ought to be happy you have a *job.*"

And how it still was when a Mexican-American cop would say to another: "When're you gonna retire so I can go to homicide?"

Manuel Smith and his father before him had experienced a lot of that during their careers as San Diego policemen, so he had learned to tread softly. He would not join San Diego's Latino law-enforcement society.

"It was hard enough trying to get accepted all those years," he told them. "I can't see segregating ourselves again."

He knew about Mexican protocol and understood how Mexicans differ from Mexican-Americans so profoundly. He appreciated their hospitality down south and was embarrassed that Mexican lawmen could not come to a San Diego police station and be treated with the respect they showed him.

He remembered a homicide case prosecuted in San Diego where at his request a pathologist from Mexico volunteered to come and testify for the San Diego police about a man, injured in San Diego, who died in a Tijuana hotel. It seemed that a border patrolman ruptured the spleen of an alien who managed to get back across the border to the hotel before dying. There was no way that a U.S. officer was going to be convicted of killing an illegal alien, but when the judge said in open court, "I'm sure glad I don't live in Mexico and have to go to a doctor like *that,*" Manuel Smith wanted to *crawl* out of the courtroom rather than face the pathologist.

Once, when he was on holiday working at his ranch in Baja, he had occasion to see a dilapidated pickup truck break down on the rutted dirt road by his property. It was obvious that the truck's starter was inoperative, and while Manuel Smith considered giving a push with his own four-wheel-drive vehicle, he was surprised to see two little Mexicans start working like ants without looking for help. First they stacked flat rocks under the rear axle; then they dug holes under both rear wheels; then they took a length of rope and wrapped it around the wheels much as you'd string a yo-yo. While one man sat in the truck, the other grabbed the rope and took off running down the road.

The wheels started spinning. The man in the truck popped the clutch. The engine fired up at once. The two little Mexicans refilled the holes and moved the truck off their rockpile, chugging away never to be seen by him again. It reminded him of the way the *judiciales* had to work homicides and other crimes. They made do, and did it surprisingly well.

Manuel Smith clearly understood Mexican lawmen and their bewilderment when they were criticized in the north for, say, shooting a kidnapper dead as he tried to retrieve the ransom, *after* he'd confessed where the victim was.

"A man like *that*?" would be the inevitable response to northern critics. "Why would *anyone* care about a man like that?"

Well, it was their way and their country. He wouldn't want to be *suspected* of being "a man like that," but given their resources they kept a teeming city relatively crime-free. By American standards, Tijuana was pristine.

But he was a San Diego cop, second generation, and he never forgot it. "I had to back the play of our men," he said, referring to the Tamez shooting. "When the police down there would ask, 'Why, Manuel, *why*?' I'd always back our play."

Manny Lopez and his men became convinced that Manuel Smith was *not* backing their play. Smith and Collins were ordered to meet with Mexican authorities to deal with the Tamez shooting in such a way that international police relations would be served. Manuel Smith and Ron Collins sat in the headquarters of a deputy chief of Mexican Immigration while he dictated a report to his stenographer. When it got to the part about the guns and shooting, the chief stopped the steno and did some careful editing.

When the report was finished, Manuel Smith and Ron Collins were asked to read it and sign it as representatives of the San Diego Police Department and, by implication, the United States authorities. Ron Collins, who could hardly read Spanish, signed the report. Manuel Smith, who could read much better, signed it anyway.

"They're satisfied," he said later. "They've saved face and we've preserved our relationship, and that's what's important."

But it wasn't important to Manny Lopez, who lost his right eyebrow completely when he heard that the Mexican government had a statement signed by the San Diego Police Department admitting that Tamez was confused and had wandered a short distance onto U.S. soil by accident.

Manny Lopez and his Barfers were in their little squadroom the night Ron Collins came to explain the letter. Manny Lopez was livid.

"What the fuck do you think you're *doing*?" he yelled. "What gives *you* the right? You and Smith ain't even sergeants, for chrissake, and you're signing documents without talking to the Man? That Mexican was a crook! They're *all* crooks!"

Ron Collins said, "If you'd calm down, maybe I could explain."

"I don't *want* your explanation!" Manny Lopez said. "There *is* no explanation. You fucked us!"

"I don't wanna talk to you until you're rational," Ron Collins told him.

"You fucked us!" Manny Lopez accused. "It was a lie! I'll never forget it!"

And that was it. Ron Collins and Manuel Smith were not friends of Manny Lopez after that. In fact, he began to doubt not only their loyalty but their honesty. Manny Lopez himself had done a little liaison work from time to time and appreciated the information and assistance that American police could obtain from Mexico. But he now believed that Manuel Smith and Ron Collins were more loyal to the Mexicans than to their own department. He told his Barfers that they should avoid Smith and Collins completely, and to reveal *nothing* in their presence.

"A crook is a crook," he told his men that night. "And if he's carrying a badge like the dude I shot, he's the worst crook of all. If they point guns at us we're gonna point right back. Maybe we're sick and tired a thieving Mexican cops sticking guns in our faces. Right, fuckers?"

After the Tamez shooting, the newspaper stories and television reports just kept coming. The Barfers were even staging reenactments for the benefit of TV crews. The reporters were hungry for *anything* these hardball border rats were up to. The rescue at the tunnels was rehashed, and other stories of Sergeant Manny Lopez the Gunslinger. A goddamn *saint* whose hand was kissed by a woman kneeling in the dust. The other Barfers wondered if Manny was going to get anointed. Or maybe he'd start making weekly appearances in a fucking *grotto*.

Some of the veterans like Eddie Cervantes would say, "Weren't *we* there? What's it say about *us*? Manny and his *men*. Shit."

But Joe Castillo worshipped Manny Lopez and it showed. Pretty soon the young cop was wearing silk body shirts with collars like the wings on a 747, unbuttoned to his shoelaces to display the dangling gold chains and religious medal. Not only did he dress like Manny but he'd begun to smoke Santa Fe Corona Grandes. He drank Chivas Regal when he didn't even like the stuff.

At one of their impromptu Barf parties Manny guzzled five shots of mescal in one minute to show them how big his *huevos* were. Joe Castillo tried it and kissed the porcelain at once. Manny Lopez had to be driven home at 8:30 A.M. but dragged himself to the Barf softball game that day wherein the canyon crawlers, wearing pukey-yellow caps with BARF on the front, managed to lose to another police team by only one run, mescal or not. Oh, these bandit busters were becoming something *more* than macho.

Then of course they celebrated their near win with more booze, and Joe Castillo, who was trim and fit and who knew something about boxing and martial arts, stood up and shrugged and squirmed and gestured with his long, fluttering fingers and went through his entire repertoire of body language before making an announcement: "My whole body is a weapon!" after which he passed out cold. It wasn't easy becoming police department legends and media darlings.

It was a very active month. With spring approaching and the weather getting milder, they were out there—the aliens, the Barfers, the bandits—all the symbiotic creatures of the canyons.

On one Saturday night in March near the northern slope of the upper soccer field, just one hour after the sun set, two men approached the varsity team of Manny Lopez, Eddie Cervantes and Tony Puente, who were joined by Fred Gil that night. As the Barfers descended a trail to Deadman's Canyon, the two shapes drifted ever closer and loomed, shaggy and smelling like *garbage*. The Barfers squatted in submission and one of the shapes came forward and said, "Give me a cigarette."

Manny complied, handing him a Mexican cigarette, and the other said, "Me too."

They smoked silently for a moment and the first one said, "Give me some money for a drink."

"I only have a little for my journey north," Manny said in his diffident alien voice, and that was all it took.

The second man grabbed Manny by the collar of his jacket, placed a blade to his spinal cord and said they would be requiring either his money or his balls.

The robbery attempt was not unusual except that it presaged an unusual turn of events. Whether the Barfers' growing legend had something to do with it or not, the robbers were definitely eschewing foreplay. They were leaping immediately into armed attacks.

This particular robbery presaged something else—an attitude on the part of Manny Lopez toward imminent deadly threat. With the blade literally at the nape of his neck, there in the darkness—smelling what? garbage?—his right eyebrow squiggled into the most perfect question mark his partners had so far seen. Manny Lopez rolled his eyes in mock terror and said, "Please, sir! *He* has the money!" pointing to Tony Puente, who was squatting three feet away.

At the moment when Tony Puente and Eddie Cervantes and Fred Gil were pumping adrenaline by the gallon it didn't mean much. Not until later. Because they could almost see the freaking mischief in Manny's little eye under that eyebrow. A guy was about to separate a piece of body rope that could turn him into a dangling puppet, and Manny was not just figuring a way out, he was trying to get a *laugh.*

Of course, after the bandit bought Manny's act and rushed at Tony Puente, Manny Lopez said, "*¿Sabes que,* motherfucker?"

The last thing the bandit heard clearly was "Barf!" Because then he was being pistol-whipped, stomped, slugged, handcuffed, arrested.

The boys had a giggle after hours that night telling what Manny had said. It was good for a chuckle until one thought of it soberly. In Deadman's Canyon in the dark of the night?

With a blade at his spinal cord? Manny can go for a yuk? He *had* to be as scared as the others. *Didn't* he?

Toward the end of the month when the weather was very tolerable, Patricia Ramirez decided it was time to go north and find work. She was twenty-four years old, without skills or education, and reasoned that she was too old to be barely feeding herself in Tijuana. If she was to have a chance in life she had to go. Patricia Ramirez, like most of the others who crossed the canyons at night, wanted *more* and was brave enough to try for it.

It wasn't difficult to find traveling companions on the streets of Tijuana, and it would be foolhardy for a woman to attempt the crossing alone. She barely knew the two pollos she found herself with that night. One was a Tijuana transient and the other, from Jalisco, looked like a *campesino.* They were about her age and seemed strong, and she hoped they might provide her with protection if a guide or, God forbid, a bandit should try to take advantage.

At twilight they were near the borderline about a mile east of the point of entry. There was the unusual carnival atmosphere in the canyons on this clear night as the army of aliens prepared to cross. The three young people stood tensely by a bustling grocery store near the border debating whether they could afford to waste their money on a strawberry soda pop, since mouths got very dry waiting for darkness.

Patricia Ramirez saw four men watching them. One of the men smiled at her. She didn't like his smile, not one bit. They didn't have the docile look of pollos. The smiling man approached and asked if they had any marijuana.

Of course they did not, but the man, still smiling, said, "Then give me some *money,* little sister."

Just like that. And they weren't even in the canyons yet.

They hadn't set foot on United States soil. They were on an unpaved street in their own country. These bandits weren't playing the game fair and square. They were supposed to wait until the pollos were in the United States before they ambushed them.

Patricia Ramirez had exactly 4 U.S. dollars to get her to Los Angeles for some kind of work. She hesitated but gave the man one of her dollars, avoiding his eyes when he touched her. Then he asked her two male companions for money and they silently gave him a few of their wadded U.S. bank notes.

The sun dropped behind the hills. It was time to go. Pollos kissed friends and family and yelled nervous farewells. Patricia Ramirez had not gotten five hundred yards into the darkness when she saw the smiling man again. He was blocking a trail. He had appeared in the night like a ghost. He was still smiling when he said, "Now give us *everything.*"

Then the smiling man's three companions jumped down onto the narrow trail and she got shoved away from her companions. Hands searched her expertly in the darkness while she tried not to cry. She felt her wristwatch going. It had cost her 30 American dollars, months of saving. She felt the necklace slide from her neck. It had cost her $6 in Tijuana, money she felt was squandered frivously. And of course they took her last 3 U.S. dollars. So now she thought she had nothing of value. Nothing they might want. She was not quite correct.

The older man grabbed her by the front of her sweater and dug his hand down inside her bra. He was brutal and it hurt but she didn't whimper. The younger one then laughed and made a remark about how many pairs of pants pollos wear and he put his hand on her body and unbuttoned her long pants.

Then she started to cry. The bandits really got a kick out of it because, sure enough, she wore two pairs of long pants, one to strip away to make herself presentable after arriving from her journey. She wept when they peeled down both pairs of pants and put their hands inside her underwear.

The other bandits were quick and practiced. They used their knives to cut the shoelaces off the terrified companions of Patricia Ramirez. They searched the shoes for money. They made them remove all their clothing, every layer of it. One of the pollos told the bandits that he didn't have any money. Then he, too, began to cry when the oldest bandit smiled and walked up to him and placed a pistol at his temple and said he was going to do something bad to him for lying. Then he stripped the pollo of the few pesos and dollars for which he was risking his life.

The bandits told them to take their clothing and shoes with the cut shoelaces and go barefoot through the canyons. And told them to watch out for bandits—except for Patricia Ramirez, who was standing in the arms of one with her pants down around her knees, crying like a child. He began rubbing her vagina while her companions walked north, avoiding her eyes. They had to live, didn't they? What could they do? They only wanted to survive.

Before the bandits could enjoy the use of Patricia Ramirez, they heard some voices off in the darkness. Someone stumbled and said, "Oops!"

And then someone, who was Manny Lopez, said, "You dumb fucker! Don't say 'oops'!"

Then a voice said, "What should I say, goddamnit?"

And Manny Lopez said, "Say 'oops' in Spanish!"

"I don't know *how* to say 'oops' in Spanish!"

Of course the bandits didn't understand all this chatter off in the night but they understood someone yelling "Oops!" And "Oops!" didn't come from a pollo's mouth, so they knew they were in trouble.

Patricia Ramirez was spared, and while she tried to dress herself and catch up with her fleeing companions, who had run into a couple of Barfers on the trail, the bandits were hotfooting it back to the hole in the fence, where they ran smack into some more Barfers: Manny Lopez and Ernie Salgado.

Two of the bandits, one of whom had the gun, didn't like the looks of two pollos squatting by the fence hole, so they hightailed it east toward the next hole. The would-be rapist with a bar of iron chose to tough it out and take the shortest distance to Mexican soil, right *through* the squatting pollos, one of whom happened to be wearing a red bandanna over his head to keep off the mosquitoes which were turning his balding noggin into an insect fiesta. That night Manny Lopez was also wearing a Pendleton shirt, and so he looked more like a bandit than a docile pollo.

The would-be rapist held a knife beside his thigh and said, "Hey, *socio,* what's happening?" in the familiar bandit greeting. Then he bolted straight for the fence hole swinging his iron bar.

And someone started yelling *"Barf! Barf!"* and the fight was on.

The would-be rapist got pistol-whipped and stomped and was led battered and handcuffed toward a waiting police car later that evening, at which time he had only one thing to say to the uniformed cop who was to transport him to a doctor and jail. He looked *gratefully* at the San Diego police uniform and said, *"Help!"*

"We'll take them down *hard,*" Manny Lopez always said to his men. "Fists, saps, gun butts, whatever it takes. Until such time as the guy's dead or *pretends* he's dead. Or flat-ass surrenders unconditionally."

Patricia Ramirez had to return to Tijuana but was very grateful to be undefiled and alive. And the Barfers had foiled yet another rape, which was good for a few newspaper stories. In fact Manny had to have someone call the press for him, since his arms were too banged up to dial a phone that night from The Anchor Inn in San Ysidro.

That was the night when three passably foxy schoolteachers, one of whom wore a size 40 E-cup, came in and asked if this was where the border "Gunslingers" hang out. That was a *very* late night for several of the boys.

It started getting serious about then—the arrival of groupies, that is. And why not? Weren't they doing television reenactments of their exploits? Didn't all warrior bands deserve camp followers?

At one of their drinking parties someone ate the worm out of a bottle of mescal, and someone was always eating a jalapeño chili like a macho Mexican. Shit, that was *nothing.* Eddie Cervantes topped everybody by picking up a big fat woolly black caterpillar. That sucker was the size of a breakfast sausage, and even the hardest of the hardballers had to cringe when Eddie stuck that wiggly squirming animal between his lips and started crunching it into his grinding molars.

He did it because Manny *dared* him to. Just as young Joe Castillo responded to a Manny Lopez dare to leap over parking meters while they were staggering down the street from one gin mill to another at one o'clock in the morning. The young Manny Lopez clone would vault those parking meters no hands, nuts first, because Manny challenged him. Literally willing to bust his balls for Manny. Oh, he could be a ballbreaker, this Barf sergeant, but hardly anyone noticed yet. They were too busy coping with what the media *said* they were.

So kick open the swinging saloon doors! Stop the tinkling piano. Keep your lizard-shit civilian small talk to front-pew level because you lizard-shit civilians are in the presence of the last of the hardball, cactus-stuck, worm-chewing, chili-sucking, skull-crunching, bandit-busting, ball-clanging Gunslingers in the West.

And maybe that was it. Does America cherish her philosophers, statesmen, artists, scientists? To a *point.* But America *mythologizes* her men of action. Her Gunslingers. America names airports after John Wayne. Could a journalist resist? Think of it: ten little hardball lawmen, shooting down Mexican bandits where they stand, out there in the cactus and rocks and tarantulas and scorpions and rattlesnakes, in a no-man's-land implicitly ceded to the bandits by the U.S. government. If that wasn't a John Ford scenario, what the hell was it? These ten were embodiments of an American myth. And after them, there would be no more.

They had come back nearly a century after the world thought them extinct. These were, by God, The Last of the Gunslingers.

How Ken Kelly wanted to join them. The blond cop would try to show up at nearly every after-hours soiree at The Wing or The Anchor Inn or any other cop's saloon where the Barfers might congregate after duty. There were the regulars: Manny Lopez, dressed like John Travolta with maybe some Merthiolate on his face where he'd been kicked by a robber (groupies absolutely died over visible wounds). And maybe his fists damaged from punching out bad guys. "Could you hold that glass of Chivas Regal up to my lips, my little kumquat?"

And of course right next to his sergeant, young Joe Castillo, ditto for the disco duds but with more gold chains, getting his share of attention because he was the best-looking and had an athletic build and this cute way of talking with his whole body: shoulders hunching, hips swaying, long, graceful hands clenching, unclenching, waving, fluttering. He could have been a mime or a dancer, this young cop.

What a pair: the head Gunslinger and his protégé. Eddie Cervantes was also drinking pretty heavily by now, as were Tony Puente and Renee Camacho. But perhaps the heaviest drinker of them all was the outsider, Robbie Hurt. And whenever Robbie was putting a move on some groupie, it always seemed to be Eddie who would say, "Whadda *you* know about it? You're back where it's *safe.*"

And Robbie would sulk. With good reason. He'd love to

be out there with them. He'd give his Porsche dream to be out there with the varsity or even the junior varsity. As it was he was close enough sometimes to hear them screaming "Barf! Barf! Barf!" And had to run in circles with a shotgun and radio, only to find the voices echoing around the canyons and confusing him. And to end with his heart beating holes in his eardrums, and the adrenaline building without release because he didn't even know what was happening out there in the dark. It was making him goofy. And then to come to the booze parties at the local saloon only to have Eddie Cervantes say, "He's our water boy." Well, it was getting unbearable.

At first Manny let Robbie walk a few times with the junior varsity, but twice, potential robbers who were feeling them out backed off because they had never before seen a black pollo out in the canyons.

Once, when a potential bandit group questioned them, and were seemingly satisfied by a story from Carlos Chacon that Robbie had come from Central America where there were lots of blacks, they backed off nervously before committing themselves.

When Manny Lopez heard that the bandits had almost come close enough to make the necessary threat and demand for money, he said something to the young cops that surprised them. He said, "Listen, fuckers, don't you *ever* do that again!"

When they looked puzzled he said, "Don't you *ever* let someone you *know* is a bandit get away with that shit!"

When they asked what they should do he said, "Beat the shit out a them! Whip their asses and leave them. Maybe then they'll decide to do their stealing back in Tijuana. Maybe they'll start to learn that *we're* badder than the *judiciales.*"

There were some who didn't agree with the way things were going. Ernie Salgado for one. He lived near Manny and drove him to work in a department car. He didn't like the idea of turning into vigilantes. He barely took a drink and Manny and the other hard drinkers got on him pretty good for his temperance. They attributed it to his wife, since once at a Barf party when all the wives were present, Susan Salgado yelled, "Eeeeeeer-nie, get over here!"

And that was all it took with these hardball, bandit-busting, worm-eating Gunslingers. *Pussy*-whipped? Oh, my God!

In any case, Manny Lopez decided that Robbie Hurt, being black, could not be part of the walking teams and would always provide cover when they needed it. Manny told him how invaluable such a service was and how somebody had to do it and how they needed him to run in and save their asses when it got tough. Then Manny would invariably end the stroking of Robbie by dragging some groupies over and saying, "This guy saves my tail out there every night. He is one *bad* dude."

And Robbie would feel better and tell the groupie a few war stories too. And *drink.* Hard liquor. He'd seldom get home before the bars closed. And though he always drove himself home he sometimes couldn't recall doing it. That also seemed macho to the young cop—alcoholic blackouts.

"I don't even *remember* driving home!" Why not? Gunslingers were entitled.

His wasn't the only marriage deteriorating at the time. There was Ken Kelly popping up at nearly every "unwinding" session at The Wing. Asking when oh *when* would there be an opening in BARF so he could join?

He still offered pimping services. "Didn't I tell that new waitress she could meet you guys at The Anchor Inn?"

"But she was a witch! You said she had big tits."

"Zits. I said big zits. Okay, I'll do better."

He tried to please them, but they'd become discriminating: "Goddamn, King! She had a neck like an elephant's trunk!"

"Okay! I'll do *better*!"

Manny Lopez warned Ken Kelly that being a blond white boy, he could no more walk convincingly in the canyons than could Robbie Hurt, but Ken Kelly said he didn't care. He'd be Robbie's partner. He'd be the *other* half of the cover team, freeing up one who *could* walk. He'd carry the goddamn toilet paper.

And one night Ken Kelly got to prove his resourcefulness in the face of danger. A gaggle of waitresses showed up at the park on schedule. They were all there: Fat Mindy, Thin Mindy, Lana Banana, and *another* one.

"She's a ten!" Ken Kelly cried when she stepped out of Fat Mindy's car. She was blonder than Ken Kelly, and she didn't walk, she *rippled*, like a jungle cat. In fact she was like one, in an imitation leopard coat, with dagger fingernails and decadent cranberry lipstick.

The drinking went on until two-thirty and then Fat Mindy made an announcement to Ken Kelly about the leopard girl. "She likes you. She wants to know if you'd like to get better acquainted?"

"Is a frog's ass watertight?" Ken Kelly screamed.

Oh, how the Barfers envied Ken Kelly. She *liked* him! Even after the others had told her 101 exciting shoot-em-up stories, 100 of which were invented. Even though she knew that Ken Kelly wasn't even a Gunslinger, but just aspired to become one.

Since he was really smashed he pulled his long limp hair flat back on his head, and twitched his walrus moustache, and made his eyes buggy in his Jack Nicholson impression. Then he unscrewed the cap on a half gallon of wine saying, "What do you prefer, my dear? Red, white, or beige?"

She said he was so fucking cute!

"I'm all jiggles and wires!" Ken Kelly whispered to Joe Castillo. "I got the war department faked out. I told her I'm working overtime."

Except that another cop's wife who happened to work at the same fast-food joint as Fat Mindy and Thin Mindy and

Lana Banana had made a surreptitious phone call to Ken Kelly's wife telling her where the boys and girls were going to be sometime after midnight.

At 2:30 A.M. Ken Kelly said, "There's a car coming."

And indeed there was. It was driving slowly through the park and up the hill to where they drank. "That sounds just like my Pinto," he said. "The same clinky transmission . . . Naw, that *couldn't* be my Pinto."

It was his Pinto. Driven by his wife, accompanied by their three young children asleep in the back seat. Ken Kelly yelped and made a dive for the bushes. His motorcycle was hidden behind a Barfer's car. The Pinto stopped some twenty-five yards away in the darkness and the lights went out.

The party was *over* and the Barfers started thinking about lipstick stains, and Ken Kelly was crawling on his belly like a tarantula, saying, "Wait! Don't move the car! She'll see my goddamn motorcycle!"

Ken Kelly's wife would turn on the headlights every few seconds and catch them with the beam as they squirmed. Finally, Fat Mindy spoke into the thorn bush that contained the body of Ken Kelly, who by chance was wearing a camouflage army jacket. She said, "Can we smuggle you out somewheres?"

"No! Just leave me alone!" he whispered, and everyone said a fast good-night to Ken after he cried, "Jesus! My off-duty gun! I *know* she has my off-duty gun!"

The last thing they heard him say was: "If I try to haul ass she'll run me down for sure. You don't *know* her!"

So he didn't try to haul ass. He bellied out of the brush in concealment and managed to coast the motorcycle down the hill—a rocky, eroded, unpaved hill. He was so bagged he was seeing two Pintos, four headlights, two wrathful shadows in the front seat. When he made it to the bottom he was sweaty, freezing, thorn-raked. But he'd gotten to the street undetected. He was considerably more sober when he fired up that bike and hauled ass.

When he got home close to dawn she was awake. He was full of coffee and cleaned up and had his stringy hair combed.

"Hi!" he said. "Waiting up for me? I made a hell of an arrest. Been doing reports for hours. Wanna hear about it?"

The Barfers had to admire a resourceful guy like Ken Kelly. And he wanted to be part of their squad *so* badly that they all wanted him.

"I'd like to have you, King," Manny Lopez told him. "But I can't get them to up my personnel quota." Then he grinned and said, "You'll just have to wait till one of us gets shot."

And as a matter of fact Ken Kelly would make the Barf squad before the month ended. Because *two* of them would get shot.

CHAPTER · 11

DRAGONS

ON ANCIENT MAPS, CARTOGRAPHERS OFTEN BORDERED renditions of known territory with a warning: "Beyond There Be Dragons."

There was something odd happening inside the heads of some of the Barfers toward the end of March. It was as though the few square miles of canyons, heretofore ceded to cutthroats by the United States government and the city of San Diego, was *their* territory, their turf, their bloody little patch of land on which they would prove . . . what? They weren't even sure by now. And indeed each man seemed to be out to attain something of value for himself. They didn't necessarily spend a great deal of time during the month of March pondering what it was; they were too busy trying to discover what their leader was up to.

Manny Lopez was driven, restless, searching, probing, praising, scolding, chiding them. He wasn't above humiliating a man publicly for a screw-up in the canyons. One way in which a Mexican-American differs from a real Mexican hardly at all is in the code of *machismo.* It used to be that the vilest, most insulting epithet in the language had to do with being a *puto,* or *maricón,* "queer" being an unforgiveable slash at one's manhood. Simply saying "*¡Eres un puto!*" had in bygone days resulted in many a fight to the death.

In modern times one man could call another *puto* or *maricón,* but even now it's not *that* easy to accept being called, in English, "a pussy"—not if beneath it somewhere is a *real* challenge to one's courage or manhood. "Faggot" was okay, since there was no truth in it. They were always calling each other "faggot." But "pussy"? If Manny Lopez called Joe Castillo "pussy," with the right tone, Joe Castillo might easily risk crushed nuts by vaulting over parking meters. Ditto for Eddie Cervantes eating woolly worms. When things got dicey in the canyons he could make his bandit busters do just about anything by a direct challenge to their *machismo.* And since only he had actually shot someone, and was getting so much media attention for it, deep inside their little hardball hearts they were getting more than a bit jealous of their sergeant.

But he could still keep them quiet by telling them that they were a baaad-ass bunch of hardball motherfuckers. Look out, banditos! Here comes the Cleveland Wrecking Company!

Once when both the varsity and junior varsity were walking on the upper soccer field at dusk they decided to join the throngs of pollos preparing for the night's crossing. They were utterly in character that evening, mingling with the madding crowd, listening to tales by twilight campfires, stories of prior crossings laced with hopes and dreams. Stories of fabulous jobs and great wealth, which in answer to specific questions meant half the pay of a San Diego policeman. In fact, one robbery victim, when he learned that

Manny Lopez was really a San Diego cop, had said sincerely, "I pray to one day become *rich.* Just like you."

During firelight conversations with other pollos, the Barfers mostly had to listen, since only Manny Lopez, Eddie Cervantes, Carlos Chacon, and possibly Ernie Salgado spoke Spanish well enough to fool anybody. But the others understood, and it was sad to listen to the pollos. It also caused things to happen inside their heads and more than once a Barfer would catch himself wanting to tell an alien of certain realities in the land of silk and money.

Sometimes the guides would warn them of San Diego cops who prowl the canyons at night dressed as pollos, about how bloodthirsty these cops were and how they beat and killed pollos just for trespassing on their land.

"They're madmen," the guide said. "They must take them from an insane asylum and bring them out here."

That evening there were at least three hundred people on the soccer field. There were a dozen guides happily jumping from group to group offering their services. There were vendors selling tacos as all waited for the orange fireball to drop behind the hills.

There were peddlers selling soda pop and coffee. There was a man with a guitar singing mournfully of the land he was about to leave. There were five motherless daughters saying good-bye to their father and they were *all* crying.

Easily the most sensitive and sentimental of the Barfers was Renee Camacho. And because of this and his boy-tenor voice which became a soprano singsong when he attempted to talk like an alien, the others called him *maricón* and said he was in love with his pal Joe Castillo. Renee was usually jolly and fun loving and could give it back as well as any. On this particular night as they waited for the curtain of darkness to fall on Deadman's Canyon, he sat by a fire with some pollos and had never felt sadder about all of it. Their role. His role. The entire drama or melodrama being ritualistically played in those canyons at night.

He wondered if it was the season. Spring had brought the desert flowers—purple and white, red as sunset—surprisingly delicate in the harsh canyons, the colors flickering in dusky silver light. Cadaverous, skin-twitching dogs circled the campfires warily. The ground was scabbed up with dropped food and brought the animals, baring their gums in ecstasy.

"I'll never forget it," Renee Camacho said. "This young man, my age, telling us how it was."

"I love my little *pueblo,*" the alien told Renee Camacho. "I love our country, but I must make a home for my children."

Eddie Cervantes was a chatterbox who liked to ask questions. Not entirely familiar with the peso exchange, Eddie asked the alien how much his weekly earnings would buy in his *pueblo.*

The answer was: enough tortillas and beans to keep four children from getting sick. He could buy one scrawny chicken, but only on a good week.

Renee Camacho was deeply affected and even confused. It seemed so hopeless. It made him start to think: what if his grandfather had not got caught up with the nonsense of Pancho Villa and migrated north? He looked around at the soccer field, at the women with babies. At the elderly men and women who were unable to resist the lure of America. He looked at the man beside him and was ashamed. The man was frail, with uncut scraggly hair. He smelled putrid like all the others. Nobody had suitcases. They rarely had bundles. Renee realized something startling from talking to them: first, that they were the bravest of Mexico's poor, to come in the first place. Second, very few *wanted* to come north. They dreamed of making enough money to return to their homeland.

Some had two or three dollars and that was all. Some had several hundred. Renee Camacho always said he never met a mean one, and he kept asking himself, how can *anyone* be cruel to these people?

And after that, when he encountered aliens who had been robbed or stabbed or raped and terrorized, he began to feel what *they* felt. And he wasn't the only one. They all started to *feel* the poverty and fear. It made funny pains in the stomach, they discovered. It made them sigh a lot. Finally it made them mad, but the anger was without direction. And this produced *more* funny pains in the stomach. Renee Camacho, for one, was beginning to change in his treatment of bandits.

Even as a group, odd things began to happen to them. For instance, when the Border Patrol helicopter would make a low-flying pass over a group of aliens, sometimes the Barfers too would begin to run in panic.

"What're we doing?" Manny Lopez yelled one evening when they were doing just that, hightailing it just like aliens. "Why're we running?" he asked them in utter bewilderment. "We're armed to the fucking teeth. We're on duty. We're the *good* guys. Why're we running?"

But of course they figured it out without consulting Lee Strasberg or the Screen Actors Guild. It's just not that easy for a performer to jump in and out of character. And then they talked of how aliens felt like that *all* the time.

Manny would tell them: "It's okay to feel sorry for them, but remember that everyone else is scum. Their government's corrupt. Their cops're corrupt. Don't mix things up or you'll end up dead."

Once, when they were in fact near their substation, starting for the canyons by climbing through a two-strand barbed wire fence, they were surprised by a voice behind them saying, "Okay, motherfuckers! Freeze!" The voice belonged to a border patrolman sneaking up.

The strange part is they threw their hands up and answered in *Spanish*. "*¡Somos policías! ¡Somos policías!*" They were *into* character.

They also had a few laughs on the upper soccer field. Someone made up a name for a little tamale vendor with the chin whiskers of a goat. They called him Chano B. Gomez,

Jr. And on a few occasions some of them actually bought tamales and *ate* them, which Manny Lopez said was the most daredevil act he'd yet witnessed out there, and that it made his gunfight look pussyish.

Chano B. Gomez, Jr., had a transistor radio strapped to his belt and carried some maracas and shook them to the Latin beat from a Tijuana radio station: *cha cha, cha cha cha!*

Sometimes he sold *churritos,* fried sticks of bread dough and chili. And of course a couple of those hardball chili-sucking bandit busters also risked parasitic paralysis by buying and eating the *churritos.* Just like pollos.

Chano B. Gomez, Jr., had an eye for the ladies and he'd skip from group to group hustling his tamales and playing his ghetto blaster and shaking his maracas at any little cutie who caught his eye: *cha cha, cha cha cha!*

And many a time his evil eye would be observed by some father/husband/brother who didn't like his action at all. But Chano B. Gomez, Jr., would just wiggle his goat whiskers at them and play his hissing maracas and skip off as surefooted as a goat on those hilltops.

Someone said, what if he was in cahoots with the bandits and was marking them with his little maracas act? You for rape, my pet. You for robbery. You, pollo, for *death.* Shaking those maracas which sounded like rattlesnakes.

Anyway, they came to make jokes about old Chano B. Gomez, Jr., the goatish tamale vendor, and imagined that he was marking them as they stepped off into no-man's-land: "Beware, beware! Of fiery breath, the monster's lair!"

This was the night that Manny Lopez finally met El Loco face to face. They were walking E-2 Canyon by the hole in the fence. There was a clutch of shadow figures standing on the Mexican side. When five of the Barfers straggled by, they saw clearly that one of the silent shadow figures was dressed all in black and wore a red ski mask!

The man in the ski mask spoke to them. He said, "Do you have a cigarette?"

Manny walked to the chain link fence and got into character and passed a Fiesta cigarette through to the man in the mask. "Do you have a match?" the man asked.

Manny produced an appropriate book of Mexican matches, and when the sulfur flared he looked at the eyes and mouth which were all that showed and he wondered why in the hell a mask.

"Where is your group going?" Loco asked.

"To Los Angeles," Manny told him.

"I might be able to help you," he said. "I have contacts. I work with the *judiciales* as a friend. Why don't you come through the fence and we'll talk?"

"No, señor," Manny said. "We're afraid to go back over there. Why don't you come over here and we can tell you our travel plans?"

And Loco smoked, and seemed to smile but it was hard to tell. Finally, he blew a cloud of smoke and shook his head and said, "On your way, pollos. I don't think I can help you tonight."

Within seconds he had vanished back into the darkness on the Mexican side. And when the others saw Manny up close, they couldn't *find* his right eyebrow. "I *want* that bandit!" Manny said. "That sucker's *mine.*"

Then someone suggested knocking off early and getting some beer and they even offered to chip in for a bottle of Chivas Regal for Manny, but he said they needed a good bandit bust and he put them in the tubes. And that was good for a few yuks.

The "tube," or tunnel, was one of the drainage pipes that ran under the earth from the American side of the fence to the Mexican side. Though the Barfers weren't given to metaphor, it was easy to see that the tube was an absolutely perfect symbol for the international dilemma. The countries of Mexico and the United States were asshole to asshole, and these little alien turds were just rolling out of that tube into the United States, and sometimes the little alien turds just rolled back the other way when the U.S. of

A. was feeling diarrheic. And the bandits knew whereof the countries shat, so they'd wait by the assholes of America and Mexico and search for pearls among the turds.

This was how they described it more or less that night when poor old Fred Gil, the eldest Barfer, reamed out the tube. He was leading the walking team and playing the role of alien guide, staying several paces ahead, stopping frequently to tap stones together or snap his fingers. All at once when he looked back he saw that instead of three shadows there were five! He had picked up two *real* pollos who decided to tag along for the safety in numbers.

Just then a Border Patrol helicopter spotted them and swooped down, and sure enough, the Barfers were so into character they began running with the two real pollos straight toward the tube. Fred Gil was the first one into it. The tube was *full* of human excrement. Fred Gil had a weak stomach anyway. He started gagging. The other pollos, real and bogus, were pushing in behind him. Fred Gil was slipping and sliding in all the feces and yelling out in Spanish and English. Fred Gil's eyes were burning!

Then, after they were all tucked inside, they heard the hovering chopper communicating with a Border Patrol jeep via loudspeaker, and some headlights moved in and the pollos emerged from the tube one by one and were encircled by jeeps.

Before they could warn him, a border patrolman ran up and grabbed Fred Gil and said, "Aw, shit!" It was all over him.

Then, while the real pollos and border patrolman stared in confusion, the other Barfers got hysterical. These little hardball, worm-eating bozos started slapping each other and shrieking and hooting. They staggered around for almost five minutes because poor old Fred Gil had reamed out the fistula.

Later that night, Fred Gil was told to take a crime report from an old Mexican woman at Southern substation.

When she caught a whiff of him, she said she'd come back tomorrow and ran out the door. Fred Gil got the Best Dressed Award at the next Barf party.

One wondered later what the hell Chano B. Gomez, Jr., the tamale vendor, would have thought of this action from his vantage point on the hill, and if maybe *he* could figure out what was going on out there in those loony canyons where the assholes of America and Mexico passed their turds.

Fred Gil was also starting to wonder whether a man approaching middle age was too old to be doing such things. It wasn't just that the job could be hazardous to his physical health; that was only part of it. His home life was a mess. Fred Gil had spent a lifetime proving something or other. Like several of the others, Fred Gil was a product of a broken home and had to be raised by grandparents.

His father had been a U.S. Marine who served at Iwo Jima during that bloody campaign when the Marines did their damnedest to take no prisoners. He gambled and drank and taunted his son. Even after Fred Gil grew bigger and stronger than his father and (much like Carlos Chacon, who had those violent dreams) ended up defending himself by punching the man to his knees, guilt-stricken because this was his *father*—even after that his father would say to him: "You're *still* a mama's boy. Nothing but a mama's boy. You could *never* make it as a Marine."

Fred Gil hated the father who abandoned him. Fred Gil of course joined the United States Marine Corps.

He'd spent half a lifetime proving that he wasn't a mama's boy. He was an all-Marine judo champion in the open class for monster Marines, though he weighed barely two hundred pounds. And the young man who spent most of his life proving something to a man he hated found himself on a very rigorous proving ground in South Vietnam.

Fred Gil's fire team was once temporarily cut off by swift-moving Viet Cong during a Da Nang monsoon. There were five of them on an ammo truck and they thought they were sure to be killed or captured, with most betting on the former.

Until they finally hooked up with their outfit, Fred Gil kept thinking: If I survive this, I'm going to find my father and tell him. Tell him *what*?

He had always been terrified of the man. Too scared even to *show* his fear. Before Vietnam he wondered: Would he run away like his father said he would? Would he fight? Would he, God forbid, *show* fear?

In Vietnam he was lucky. Once while he was headed to Hong Kong for R&R, the plane in front of his crashed and sank in the sea. And while he was gone his unit was hard hit and lost several men. Well, it seemed to run in their family, this kind of luck. His father had survived the bombing of Pearl Harbor and the slaughter at Iwo Jima. In Vietnam his younger brother took three .50-caliber rounds in the back and not only survived but remained a career Marine.

But there was something about the canyon crawling that was very different from war. For Fred Gil, war had been mostly incoming and outgoing rockets and mortars. Formless enemies, shapes sometimes, flashes in the distance. No more. It was terrifying, but it was not . . . *personal.* He had discussed it with Ernie Salgado. Both agreed that this was *not* like war.

Fred Gil said that in Nam when they were hit by the Viet Cong, they wouldn't walk into it point-blank saying, "Here we are!"

As senseless as it was, war made more sense than seeking out armed men in the darkness, never acting, only *reacting.* Ernie Salgado hinted that it was the *intimate* side of this that made it so different. In Nam they didn't really see their enemy except when they counted the bodies. Only once in thirteen months did Ernie see his enemy face to face. His squad was sitting in the jungle at night waiting to move out, and two V.C. stumbled into them. The V.C. got within a few yards before ten Marines shot them to bits. They were living men, face to face. Not movements, forms, muzzle flashes, but *men* armed with AK-47's, young men like themselves. And still it was not the same as the canyons.

During the months to come something similar to this would be articulated by other Barfers who had not been to Vietnam and had no basis for comparison. And if one listened long enough as they tried to describe it, what finally became clear was that along with ordinary terror there was an added element here: *horror.* Because when human beings face violent death, ordinary terror is without another fearsome element: the primordial despair and outrage you feel at looking into the face of another human being who intends to destroy you with malice aforethought. The terror and archetypal horror of being *murdered.*

On the afternoon of March 23rd, Fred Gil got ready for work as usual. Which meant cleaning house and cooking dinner for his wife and family prior to his leaving for the police station. And after his wife, Jan, got home they had their daily ration of bitter arguments. They had decided to stick it out only until the kids were old enough to cope with divorce, a mistake many a cop family seemed to make.

Jan Gil was three years older than Fred and was his exact opposite. She was a woman who looked larger than she was, with sorrel hair, hazel eyes, and a long face. Some of the Barfers noted that at times she resembled actress Lily Tomlin and that Fred rather resembled a diffident version of golfer Lee Trevino. Therefore they were called the celebrity couple.

There was a ton of guilt and recrimination weighing both of them down. There were serious emotional problems involving her son, whom Fred had legally adopted. They argued about that. And she didn't keep the house clean enough to suit him so he took over housecleaning and cooking before he went off to his police duty at night. There were minor things which had become unbearable given their dilemma. She liked to drink and smoke and party and could swear a streak. It embarrassed him. She was as outgoing as he was private.

She could lock eyeballs with anyone. He still avoided eye contact whenever possible. If there was ever a mismatched couple it was this one, but the children begged them to hang in there.

"He changed," Jan Gil remembered. "Before he joined BARF he was always a *very* gentle guy. He was insecure and felt inferior to most people and was gentle. I don't mean candy-ass. I mean gentle. He used to cry and feel bad about himself, that he wasn't going anywhere in life. I started noticing a change after a few months in those hills. He still didn't drink with the others, but he started to get a little bit macho for the first time. He thought BARF was gonna give him a chance to *be* someone. He changed and we fought even *more*."

It might be debated whether or not Fred Gil was getting more macho on the night of March 23rd, but if he was, he was definitely not more macho *after* that night.

That night, the varsity, with Renee Camacho as the fourth walker, was about one hundred yards above Deadman's Canyon at dusk. The junior varsity, consisting of Carlos Chacon, Joe Vasquez, Ernie Salgado, Joe Castillo and Fred Gil, were walking in Deadman's Canyon. Robbie Hurt and Dick Snider provided the cover, with Robbie still wondering how long he could stand being one-who-waits, enduring all the tension and stress without any of the release the others got when something happened. Dick Snider was telling him quite accurately how valuable his job was, and how he must be ready when the others needed him to charge to their rescue. But it was frustrating.

The five junior varsity Barfers were sitting beside a dry creek bed which was six feet wide and no more than three feet deep. Ernie Salgado was on one end of the creek bed and Joe Castillo was carrying the sawed-off shotgun under his coat. The others were in a row except for Carlos Chacon, who was sitting across the gully facing them, with his legs hanging down. It was not only a quiet night but a very still one. There was scarcely a breeze and not much clicking of alien guides and bandits signaling with stones in the darkness.

Across the little gully a huge pile of mesquite soared. The mesquite was nature shaped in the form of a reclining buffalo. It was on such nights that they liked to lollygag right there in bandit country and make cracks about fellow Barfers, or maybe about Manny Lopez, especially if he wasn't around. Big Ugly—Joe Vasquez—was best at the wisecracks. If they were ragging Joe Castillo, who wasn't known for his quick wit, he'd say things like: "Joe's got a candle missing from his cake," or, "His elevator doesn't go all the way to the top," or, "There's a dot missing from his dice." And then somebody would chime in with: "Yeah, there's a brick missing from his retaining wall."

And though it wasn't that funny, pretty soon they'd be lying there snuffling and giggling under a towering moonswept sky, hoping the bandits wouldn't hear them out there in the night.

And then a newlywed like Carlos Chacon might say, "I gotta call my wife with a good story if we're going to The Wing tonight."

And someone would invariably say, "She ain't gonna be home, dummy. The U.S.S. *Kittyhawk*'s in port."

And then everybody would fall back down on the greasy clay trails, or onto dry mud cracked into shards, or right down on the rocks and cactus. When people were unbearably tense, some very lightweight jokes got very funny.

Sometimes they'd just settle back on the eroded hillsides and watch flying insects the color of fire. And look at stellar light over Mexico. At dots hanging in the moonlit sky: nighthawks searching forever.

Sometimes when they were too comfortable they'd discover they had snuggled down among some scorpions, or near an occasional rattlesnake so lethargic it wouldn't even bother slithering away unless you landed in its nest—which happened once to Robbie Hurt, nearly giving him a heart attack on the spot.

Sometimes they'd lie back and listen to voices singing mournfully from somewhere south of that imaginary line. It could make you want to cry if you were in the mood, the achingly lonely music coming from the squalor of the Mexican city. Unless you were Manny Lopez, who would just be off somewhere, pacing, pacing. Looking for *action*.

On the night of March 23rd there by the dry creek bed with their legs hanging down in the gully, the darkness was not velvety black as yet. And it was so quiet after the giggling that someone asked old Fred Gil if he was going to ream out the tube for them again. He was *always* falling in shit, but for all the times he inadvertently sat or stepped in excrement, Fred Gil never once came out smelling like a rose.

Ernie Salgado heard footsteps. He saw two shapes coming toward the huge hairy bush that looked like a reclining buffalo.

All of the canyon brush was hollowed out because people nested there while traveling north. The two figures stopped by the buffalo brush and squatted down in the hollow nest to peer across the little gully at the covey of silent pollos sitting with their feet dangling. One of the figures was later identified as a heroin addict by the name of Morales. He was twenty-two years old, the same age as Carlos Chacon. And in silhouette Carlos Chacon was the first to see that the young stranger was carrying a pistol.

The second figure was later identified as a man named Madrid, and he was carrying a knife with an eight-inch blade. Carlos Chacon made a motion to his partners across the gully. He pointed his finger like a gun and of course all sphincters slammed shut.

Almost all the Barfers were carrying two guns by this time. Carlos Chacon had a two-inch Smith & Wesson in a shoulder holster and a two-inch Colt concealed in the small of his back. He began reaching very slowly toward the Colt, but the young man with the pistol stepped out from behind the buffalo brush and pointed his pistol and said, "Everybody, hands up! Give us your money or I'll shoot!"

The second bandit kept his knife low and jumped across the gully, circling behind the squatting Barfers. Ernie Salgado said to him, "Let me get my money for you." Both bandits smelled like *garbage*.

At this time the varsity wasn't having much luck. They were on an arroyo overlooking Deadman's Canyon and Manny Lopez was griping about what a quiet night it was and that with so little alien activity they probably wouldn't be finding bandits. Renee Camacho remembered that Manny's bitching was interrupted by one sound: KA-PLOOM! The shotgun! And then PLOOM PLOOM PLOOM PLOOM. Then BOP BOP BOP BOP BOP BOP! And then all the muffled and unmuffled explosions ran together and it sounded like a battlefield.

Everyone was running in circles, confused by the sounds of echoing gunfire, and Robbie Hurt and Dick Snider were having the usual fits and convulsions and adrenaline rush because they didn't know what was *happening*. During all this a voice came screaming over the Handie-Talkie, a crackling voice interrupted by static.

Then Robbie Hurt and Dick Snider were both screaming into their own radio, and finally heard the garbled message: "Two down! Two down!"

And Dick Snider yelled, "Officers? Two *officers* down?"

"Suspects! Two suspects down!" the voice cried.

Thank God! But then: "Two suspects down! And officers! Two suspects down and two *officers* down!"

Carlos Chacon would later say, "I could see the pistol in his hand. He was looking right at me when I went for the gun I kept in the small of my back. I thought I was dead."

Carlos had just started wearing a bulletproof vest. Several of them were wearing vests now. Nobody thought it was unmacho to wear a bulletproof vest anymore. And then Carlos Chacon had a fantasy. It was almost as real as the violent recurring dream, where the assailants are stabbing his sister in the stomach and the blood is jetting everywhere, and he takes the knife away and stabs the assailant in the throat and enjoys the spurt of blood.

In his fantasy, time slowed down just as it had for Manny Lopez in the shooting of the Mexican immigration officer. Carlos Chacon had a slow-motion fantasy of a projectile leaving the bandit's little pistol. The pistol was aimed at the face of Carlos Chacon, who, like the others, had been caught unaware with his feet dangling helplessly in the dry creek bed. Carlos could see the lead projectile cracking into his own face. He could see the slug breaking his jawbone. He watched the splinters leaping from his face. Splinters of lead. Splinters of bone. He actually heard the hissing gristle in his face tearing. He listened to the bone shatter. His blood splattered all over his friends. He thought: I hope it doesn't hurt too much.

Carlos Chacon believed that the others on the bandit's side of the gully came out shooting an instant before he did, perhaps while he was fascinated with the gristle and tendons in his own face being ripped and torn bloody. Carlos also in that instant saw that the other bandit was carrying a two-foot machete. It proved to be a knife with an eight-inch blade, but as Carlos later said, "You see *strange* things out there in Deadman's Canyon."

Joe Castillo had his long, fluttering, graceful hands clenched around the sawed-off shotgun under his alien rags. Joe Castillo, ever since he had squatted beside his mentor Manny Lopez and seen a gun aimed at his face, had taken to arming himself rather well. In addition to the shotgun, Joe Castillo wore a gun in a shoulder holster. He carried another in a hip holster, and for good measure he wore a third revolver in an ankle holster. He wore bullet holders stuffed with extra ammo all around his belt. Even so, after this night he would exchange one of the revolvers for a 9mm pistol so that he could have eight in the magazine and one in the chamber. Joe Castillo offered an embarrassed smile when questioned about the arsenal. He would only say, in a masterpiece of understatement, "I'm sort a heavily armed."

It was probably Joe Castillo who fired first, with the shotgun under his coat. He had one thought: Carlos was in his line of fire sitting across the gully. Then he saw Carlos moving to his right. Then he noticed for the first time how vile it smelled in the gully, a dry creek that sometimes carried raw sewage from the Mexican side.

He just stood up, and realizing that the action of the shotgun would probably get jammed by his clothing as it did on the pistol range, realizing that he probably had only one shot, he removed the safety.

"It sounded real *loud,*" he said of that little click.

He pointed the shotgun at the belly of the bandit holding the pistol and unleashed a fireball.

Then it sounded to him like one long burst. First like an automatic weapon, then like one echoing explosion. And instantly there was the unforgettable smell of gunpowder which jetted in his nose and seemed to burn his brain. He *felt* the gunpowder clear to the base of his skull. And he was being hit in the face by lead fragments and muzzle blasts. One long explosion.

Carlos Chacon emptied a gun. Joe Vasquez emptied a gun. Joe Castillo loosed a shotgun round, and Fred Gil, who was standing closest to the bandit with the pistol—just a microsecond before the first explosion or a microsecond after—went for the bandit. Perhaps it was all the years of martial arts, perhaps not, but Fred Gil could clearly remember wanting to drive the bandit down to the ground. He did it just as the bandit was hit by the tremendous blast. And then Fred Gil was blown clear off the bandit's body during that rattle of explosions and he was lying on the ground and the bandit was lying there on top of him, crumpled between his legs, and Fred Gil kept saying over and over to himself: Be cool be cool be cool be cool. DON'T GO INTO SHOCK!

Because he knew he was shot, but didn't know where.

And during all this they were *still* shooting and Carlos Chacon thought he saw a gun in the hand of the second bandit (you see strange things out there) but they never found one and the second bandit began to run and then he began screaming "Aye! Aye! Ayeeeee!"

And through all this someone kept yelling, *"Barf! Barf! Barf!"* and the noise was deafening and then Joe Castillo clearly heard Fred Gil yelling, "I'm hit! I'm hit!"

Joe Castillo had tried to grab the bandit after he fired the shotgun blast and he felt a tremendous shock in his wrist when he reached for the bandit. And the first thing he did was kick the bandit who was lying on the ground. And after he kicked him he wanted to cry, not because he felt sorry for the bandit but because he was feeling excruciating pain, and he had to sit down and say, "It hurts! It hurts!"

And they were *still* firing, and yelling, *"Barf! Barf! Barf!"* And the second bandit was running in total panic by the creek, with Joe Vasquez and Carlos Chacon chasing and firing at him. And Carlos Chacon, clearly the Barfer with the most vivid fantasies, remembers another one at that moment: ducks! Plink the little duck, he told himself. Plink the little duck. And the second bandit, who was younger than the first, cried out, "Aye! Aye! Ayeeeee!" and fell in the cactus screaming.

Then Carlos was on him, kicking him, and Joe Vasquez

was kicking him and he was still screaming. And Joe Castillo was yelling, "It hurts!" and Fred Gil was yelling, "I'm hit! I'm hit!" and Ernie Salgado ran up to Carlos and Joe Vasquez and screamed, "That's enough!" because everyone had lost control, every shred of it.

Joe Castillo was flat on the ground, his wrist shot through and through. The bullet had nicked a nerve that supplies feeling to certain fingers. Those long, graceful, fluttering fingers would never again feel certain sensations. At first Joe Castillo thought he had shot himself. But he wondered how he could have done it with the shotgun. And why wasn't his whole hand blown off if he'd somehow fired with one hand and reached in front of the muzzle? And God, it *hurt*!

By now the varsity had found them. Tony Puente came running up, squinting myopically without his glasses, dropping compresses all over the putrid, sewer-fouled gully, and Joe Castillo was moaning, "You don't know shit about first aid! Gimme it! Put that surgical pad . . ."

But suddenly his fingers shot straight out at an angle, all by themselves! And then they curved into a claw, all by themselves! And he thought for sure he was going to cry, and started yelling, "It hurts! Oooooh, it hurts!"

Still, the oldest Barfer had not budged. Because he *couldn't.* The bandit was lying across Fred Gil's legs and he felt something like paralysis in his lower body. Fred Gil didn't want to look at himself to see how badly he was hit but he couldn't help looking at the body lying across him. The bandit was in pieces. His fingers were blown away and Fred Gil could see the glistening splinters of bone. Shards glinting in the moonlight. In addition to this, the bandit had suffered bullet wounds to the right shoulder, left lower chest, left side of the back, upper spine, left elbow, and two over the right clavicle. He was motionless and his clouded eyes stared at Fred Gil.

Unlike Joe Castillo, Fred Gil was not in much pain. He

was numb. He thought maybe he was hit in the thigh, but still he would not look. Actually, the wound was much higher—in the hip, as it turned out. He was only feeling extraordinarily weak and he kept talking talking talking. He hadn't the faintest idea what he was talking about.

Then something happened that astounded Fred Gil. At first he thought he was slipping into shock and hallucinating. He saw Carlos Chacon come close. After assuring himself that Fred was not vitally wounded, Carlos leaned over the bandit. Fred Gil looked at the face of Carlos Chacon in the moonlight, at this young man only twenty-two years old. At those astonishingly expressive eyes. Eyes of a young man with a violent childhood and violent dreams.

Carlos leaned over the torn and bloody and ragged body of the bandit and began to grin. Fred Gil couldn't take his eyes off Carlos. The very white lupine incisors glistened in the moonlight. Carlos Chacon reached slowly down and poked his finger in the open eye of the bandit. Still grinning wolfishly, he poked the eyeball a second time with the tip of his index finger. Then he looked up at Fred Gil like a character from Bram Stoker and said, "He's deeeeeeeead!"

When Carlos got up and walked away, the bandit gurgled and a little foam spewed out his mouth. Carlos, assuming it was a death rattle, turned disgustedly to say, "What a pussy! Can't even die like a bandit!"

Then it was definitely time to get the hell *out,* because people were pouring from the shacks in Colonia Libertad and someone was setting fire to the old tires on the hillside and rolling them down on their heads.

Manny Lopez arrived, yelling, "Barf Barf Barf!" to keep from getting shot as he ran headlong into the pandemonium. The sheriff's helicopter was also zooming in with its props going WOP WOP WOP and blowing dust and debris all over them.

By now the second bandit was handcuffed and lying face down on the ground. He'd been shot through and through the left side of his neck, causing minor damage. He had what the Barfers thought was an interesting leg wound. A bullet had entered through the *bottom* of his shoe while he was running and traveled up the leg and out the shinbone.

He was also shot in the other leg. The neck wound was from a shotgun pellet, and Manny Lopez, who looked about as rabid as one of the dogs that prowled the canyons, shone a light and saw the pellet protruding from the flesh of his neck. So he *stood* on the neck and said, "You shot my guys, you motherfucker!"

And while Manny was trying to see how loud the wounded bandit could scream, another miracle occurred in Deadman's Canyon. The bandit who was lying across Fred Gil, a bandit literally blown to bits, spoke. He said, "Heeeeelp me!"

They couldn't believe it. Carlos Chacon said, "He's alive! You can't kill them!"

When the sheriff's helicopter, which looked like the old military bubble-tops, finally got landed on suitable ground, Manny Lopez was ministering to this bandit, trying to talk him *into* dying before they loaded him up. Manny was saying things like, "Fucker, you shot my guys! You cocksucker, you're dying! You got a million holes in you! You're bleeding to death!" Then Manny would look over his shoulder at the approaching sheriff's deputies and slap the bandit, who couldn't have felt a hammer blow, saying, "Listen to me, asshole! You're dying! Goddamnit, hurry up!"

He was so shot up that a slug *fell* from his blasted body onto the hospital bed. But he didn't die. He walked into court looking like utter catastrophe. He was in a body cast from the waist up and his shattered arm was raised and casted, with fingers gone, left there in Deadman's Canyon for the dogs. He eventually got sentenced to a couple of years in jail and Carlos Chacon tried to get him to pose for a scrapbook picture.

The detectives weren't thrilled about getting called out to these godforsaken canyons where they rarely had to venture before Dick Snider dreamed up this stupid BARF idea. They were heard that night to mumble things like: "You guys're more trouble than you're worth."

And who could blame them? What with trying to protect the scene and recover evidence while a bunch of kids from Colonia Libertad were having a great old time trying to set the gringos on fire with burning tires. And yelling things in English like: "Motherfuck you!"

The detectives' investigation proved two things of interest that night: first, the bandit Morales did not have a real gun. His weapon was a starter's pistol, and other bandits would notice that it was getting mighty risky to pull robberies with play guns these days. And secondly, it was probably Carlos Chacon shooting across the gully who wounded both Joe Castillo and Fred Gil. The wound of Joe Castillo was through and through with no slug found. The slug in Fred Gil was better left alone according to the surgeons, so they never recovered it. But everything indicated that the shooter was Carlos Chacon.

Fred Gil would shrug and jokingly began to call Carlos "Cop Killer."

And Carlos would call him "Ironsides" or "Lead Bottom."

But Joe Castillo wasn't making jokes. He said that Carlos Chacon was trigger-happy and dangerous. His right hand would never be the same and Joe Castillo began to *hate* Carlos Chacon for shooting him.

Something that *all* the Barfers would begin to hate was about to happen that night. The San Diego newscasters would interrupt regular programming to make a breathless announcement: "Border shooting! Film at eleven!"

And of course ten wives went totally ape-shit and the phones at Southern substation were ringing off the hook and nobody could even tell them anything until everyone got in from the canyons. How the BARF wives would come to hate it, and come to hear it in their nightmares: "Border shooting! Film at eleven!"

The patrol cop driving the ambulance that night was Ken Kelly. They could hear the hoot of the siren and see the flash of lights far off in the darkness from where Ken had to park. When he finally ran down to the arroyo and into Deadman's Canyon he found them lying everywhere. Manny Lopez was screaming up at the kids who were rolling the flaming tires, threatening to kill them all and cursing all the crooked lowlife scum-sucking Mexican cops who weren't there to stop the kids.

Ken Kelly could plainly see that his BARF transfer was imminent.

Manny Lopez had a couple of things on his mind about then, like calling the wives of Fred Gil and Joe Castillo. Jan Gil was easy. She had a tongue as sharp as Manny's and they had been a good match for each other at the off-duty Barf soirees.

When she answered the phone he said, "Hey, Jan, it's Manny!"

And she said what *everyone* says at such moments. She said, "Is he dead?"

Then Manny Lopez said, "No no, he's not dead! He got hurt is all. He's okay!"

And then Manny Lopez tried to think of jokes, and pretty soon Jan Gil was laughing in relief as Manny was saying things like, "Goddamn, he's heavy! How do you handle it? Does he get on top?"

And Jan Gil said, "I just do my best, Manny."

Calling Joe Castillo's wife, Dorothy, was another story. She was a shy little Mexican girl, the prettiest of the BARF wives. He had to be very straight with her.

Then Manny had someone else to talk to. Aside from Fred Gil, the only Barfer not to shoot was Ernie Salgado. Manny Lopez didn't waste time. He confronted the tallest

Barfer in front of the squad, and said, "Goddamnit, why didn't you shoot?"

"There were people in my line of fire!" Ernie Salgado said.

"I think that's bullshit," Manny Lopez said. "I think anybody that works this squad better have the balls to shoot or he better work someplace *else.*"

So, in addition to *very* bad feelings between Carlos Chacon and Joe Castillo, there was something bad developing here between Ernie Salgado and Manny Lopez, the car-pool partners.

Fred Gil had many vivid memories about that night in March. He remembered how they did everything wrong when they tried to get four wounded men out of those canyons. First, they put Joe Castillo on a gurney. Then they put Fred Gil on top of him. And that hurt.

Then they couldn't carry the gurney up those rocky slippery trails, so they tried to carry Fred Gil by the belt. And *that* hurt.

Pretty soon everyone stopped being solicitous and sympathizing with Fred because everyone was sliding and falling on sharp stones and cactus and complaining about Fred's weight and those little Mexicans were still rolling those tires down on them, and Manny Lopez was threatening to kill every Mexican in Colonia Libertad and wishing he had a fucking bazooka! But all that was nothing compared to what was to come.

When they got to the helicopter, the sheriff's deputies made the mistake of trying to load what they thought was a dying bandit first, but Manny's right eyebrow blew clear off his head and he was literally foaming at the mouth when he screamed, "Get that fucker out a there. Get him OUT!"

Manny wasn't doing Fred Gil any favors. What he didn't know was that Fred Gil had acrophobia and didn't like high places. Not one little bit. An airplane was okay, but flying in a litter on the outside of a helicopter?

"Get that bag a puke out a the litter!" Manny Lopez kept yelling, and Fred Gil, who was getting weaker by the minute, croaked, "It's okay, Manny. I'll go in the ambulance."

"You're going by helicopter. Get that fucker OUT!"

"But he's dying, Manny," Fred Gil argued.

"Fuck him!" Manny Lopez yelled.

"Oh heck," Fred Gil said, using his customary epithets. "Goldang it."

The worst was yet to come. Poor old Fred Gil was placed in the outside litter all right, and since it was cold and since he'd be flying for some minutes, they feared he might freeze. So they put him in a warm bag—a *body* bag. He hardly knew what was happening to him until he heard it, the most terrifying sound he'd ever heard in his life.

Worse than an armed bandit who smelled like garbage breathing in your face and saying, "Give me your money." Worse than incoming and outgoing rockets in Da Nang. Worse than a drunken father saying, "You'll never be anything but a mama's boy!" Worse than all those sounds.

Fred Gil felt like one of those poor soggy tarantulas or scorpions that the Mexican kids jarred and sold to tourists. Once strong and venomous, the pathetic insects groped and pawed blindly, not for air but for freedom. They had all the air they needed in those jars but still they looked like they couldn't breathe. Why did their dumb tarantula and scorpion brains convince them that they couldn't breathe, just because their movements were . . .

Fred Gil couldn't breathe! The *worst* sound of his life. He heard a zip. The ZZZIP! of a body bag. And he flashed to Nam. He went totally utterly completely bughouse.

He screamed: "WAIT WAIT WAIT WAIT WAIT WAIT!"

"Wait for what?" Manny asked.

But poor old Fred didn't know for what. He was so terrified and panicked that everything was all wrong—but he didn't know why. And he couldn't think fast enough to say anything at all except: "WAIT WAIT WAIT WAIT!"

Manny Lopez, who had been talking with him all the way up the hills to keep him calm, figured that was it: he'd gone bonzo, some kind of shock or something.

Then Fred Gil—who couldn't sit there and explain to all these dummies that he was absolutely in stark terror of being zipped up in a body bag because of someplace thousands of miles and several years away—said, "My vest my vest my vest! I can't breathe!" And that was true enough because he was hyperventilating like crazy. So somebody opened up that freaking corpse bag to remove his bulletproof vest, and it hurt like hell but poor old Fred didn't care.

And then Manny Lopez said, "There, is that better?"

But before Fred Gil could tell them how much better it was *not* to be zipped up inside that dead man's bag, they did it again! ZZZZZZZZZIIIIIIIP!

Only this time Fred shot past terror. *Way* past. The chopper took off.

"And my mind went on a little trip" is the way he told it.

Fred Gil had a Carlos Chacon-type fantasy, a Technicolor wide-screen hallucination complete with Dolby sound. He fantasized that he was outside his body and could see this poor cactus-stuck, hardball, worm-chewing, bandit-busting, ball-clanging, *hip-shot* little bozo in a wire litter, hanging outside an old worn-out Italian helicopter, skimming over Deadman's Canyon at about five hundred feet, and the wire basket detached itself. In slow motion it just slipped loose because those fools didn't attach it right and why should they since they hadn't done *anything* else right and he watched himself tumbling out of the sky, basket and all. Poor old Fred Gil, a raggedy hip-shot turd-in-a-basket, tumbling end over end down into the godforsaken canyon, maybe by some terrible quirk still alive when those miserable little kids rolled the hot burning tires down on top of his shot-up carcass.

But just then old Fred Gil came around from his little

mind-prodding act. Because for real he could *not* breathe. He was five hundred feet above the canyons, and the rotors were causing such terrible turbulence that the body bag was snapping and popping in his face and his arms were pinned inside and the fluttering flap on the bag was sucking into his mouth! All because he hadn't let them zip it all the way. Fred Gil was going to be the first cop in the history of San Diego, and maybe all of America, to be killed by a corpse bag!

He was starting to faint when they descended and slowed. They made it. To the *wrong* hospital. But Fred Gil didn't care. They were on the ground. His face was fuchsia but he was alive. And the helicopter broke down just minutes after landing and they couldn't even get it started.

Fred Gil looked at the stalled helicopter and said, "I've *always* been lucky," to a nurse who thought he was nuts.

Another nurse thought he was an illegal alien. It was a natural mistake what with all his bloody alien rags and almost smelling like garbage himself and his wild-looking hair and not having shaved for a few days. She thought he was shot in the legs, so drenched was he by bandit blood.

When she started to undress him she discovered one of his *guns,* and screamed, "This wetback's *armed*!"

But old Fred Gil had heard so many terrifying sounds that night he hardly noticed. He was more worried about the catheter that a doctor was sticking in his penis to check for internal bleeding.

"Oh, I don't want that. I really don't!" old Fred Gil tried to tell the doctor, but he was so weak and dizzy he hardly felt it.

Then they were taking X rays and sticking tubes in his arms and nose and mouth as well as his dick, and the pain got worse in his hip and some homicide detective showed up and was trying to question him when he was getting weaker and disoriented.

The bullet merely chipped the hipbone without shattering either bone or bullet. The bullet missed the bladder and everything else. It was just nestled in his body, right in there over his pelvis as snug as you please. As far as the croakers were concerned, it could stay there as long as he didn't get infected from all the debris and trash they scraped off him.

But before Fred Gil could say again how lucky he was, an unlucky thing happened. After they'd cleaned up all the blood and had Fred wheeled back into the emergency ward, they let Jan and the kids come in.

Fred Gil was lying there looking at his littlest daughter, perhaps a bit dazed from the medication, when she said, "Dad, you don't have scrambled eggs, do you?"

And he smiled and said, "No, my head's okay, honey."

And then he considered that. *Was* it? Wasn't Vietnam *enough*? He remembered how it felt for years after Nam. Just being happy to be *alive.* Not feeling overly ambitious. Not striving. Just to be alive with no one shooting at him anymore. Then the police department? Was it that he would forever hear that miserable hateful voice? A voice saying, "You'll *always* be a mama's boy."

Wasn't *ordinary* police work enough? He'd been one of the few who were truly touched by the alien plight, like Dick Snider. He'd hated seeing the terrorized barefoot alien children with hair full of burrs and thorns, watching their mothers weep from just having been raped and robbed in their presence. It was like Nam in that respect: suffering children.

But was it worth dying for? What were they doing out there? It was one thing to get shot. Another not to know *why.* He wanted desperately from that moment on to see his little girl become a woman. It was the only thing that made any sense whatsoever.

And all this was going through his head more or less incoherently when the television news crews arrived and interviewed both Fred and his wife.

He could see that Jan thought it was great. She'd loved the BARF publicity and admitted it, and now they were the *stars.* Their own show! The Lily Tomlin–Lee Trevino hour!

He could see it in her face: their marriage was lousy but this was terrific! The news team came without calling, without permission. They startled Fred Gil by asking pointed, embarrassing questions.

"It looks as though you were shot by one of your partners. How does that make you feel? Is there something wrong with San Diego police training? Do you think more care should go into the selection of men to be out there in those canyons?"

Jan Gil said things like, "He doesn't have to talk to you at all. Fred, don't talk to them if they're going to ask those kinds a questions! Fred isn't going to criticize *anybody* even if they *did* get trigger-happy!"

"I didn't say anyone was trigger-happy!" Fred Gil later tried to explain to Manny Lopez. "I never said hardly anything! It was Jan. AND YOU KNOW HOW BIG HER GOLDANGED MOUTH IS!"

He did say something in answer to their insatiable interrogation. He said what he was *expected* to say when they asked The Big Question, which was: "Are you willing to go back out there in the canyons now?"

He said, "Sure! Soon as I'm back on my feet. Sure I am!"

And then he thought of his little girl. And Fred Gil felt old. As old as war.

Along with Mexican immigration officer Luis Tamez, Fred Gil and Joe Castillo were the second and third lawmen to be shot down in the canyons. So far that made two righteous bandits and three cops. All shot by cops. One might begin to wonder what Chano B. Gomez, Jr., the tamale vendor, would think of *this* from his vantage point on the upper soccer field. All those little hardballs rolling around in Deadman's Canyon, in and out of the canyons and tunnels like so many flinty little turds. Screaming "Barf Barf Barf!" and shooting down people in the night. So far, shooting more cops than bandits.

There is something about violence. Once unleashed, it usually tends to escalate.

CHAPTER · 12

THE BITCH

THERE WAS LOTS OF ATTENTION FOR THE WOUNDED GUNslingers. While Joe Castillo lay in the hospital the next day, with his exploits spread all over the newspapers and television, he was having trouble keeping strangers out of the hospital ward. Hell, out of his bed!

In fact, just before his wife arrived, and even before regular visiting hours, one of the schoolteacher groupies from The Anchor Inn showed up and started looking at him like he was Warren Beatty or somebody, and asked if she could give him a head job. On the spot!

While young Joe Castillo was trying to deal with this little popularity perk, a television news crew caused a ruckus in the hall corridor and a nurse came in to see if the border Gunslinger would consent to an on-camera interview.

"Hell, no," he said. "Get them *out a* here!"

The schoolteacher couldn't believe it. "Turning down a television appearance? Are you *that* famous?" Now she *really* wanted to give him a head job!

And that wasn't the half of it. His phone wouldn't stop ringing. A college instructor called to tell him not to worry about missing classes because he was giving Joe a goddamn *A* for the semester. And every waitress from every fast-food joint and every gin mill in South Bay was asking him if he was the tall one, the heavy one, the nutty one or . . . Christ, they didn't even give a shit *which* Barfer he was, just so they could come and see him.

It was quite a bit to handle for a lad twenty-four years old, all this attention. Of course he didn't understand that he was an embodiment of an American myth, an honest-to-God bandit-busting, badge-toting, shoot-from-the-hip Gunslinger.

All he knew was everyone wanted to give him blowjobs.

And his marriage wasn't worth a shit anymore. He was drunk half the time and the other half he was out in the canyons, or running wild all over San Diego with other Barfers who also didn't understand about American mythology. And he had perhaps the sweetest, shyest, and unquestionably the prettiest wife of any of them. She was being hurt terribly, and she would cry, which would break his heart.

Joe Castillo thought maybe it would have been more tolerable if his wife had been white instead of Mexican, and raised hell and kicked his ass like a Jan Gil would surely do, because he deserved it. The young cop was filled with remorse and confusion and ambivalence about being a real live Gunslinger.

And there was something else—his hand. It sure wasn't right. He was scared that it wouldn't work right ever again. When he was without visitors he'd get very depressed because his hand was no longer graceful and fluttering, and he discovered how hard it was even to *talk* without his fluttering hands. And he'd look over at his roommate in the next bed and say, "I'm only twenty-four years old. What the hell am I gonna do? Retire or what?"

Then he'd pull himself together and realize how *that*

sounded. His roommate was only sixteen years old and had his leg *amputated* because of cancer.

So Joe Castillo blurted his favorite self-deprecatory cry, saying, "My shit is so *ragged*! I'm sorry, I'm sorry!"

But his roommate didn't mind. This kid was jazzed out of his skull from reading all about Joe Castillo in the newspapers and seeing him on television. This kid was in the presence of the first Gunslinger he'd ever met in his life. The kid would pull himself out of bed, still trying to stand on a limb that wasn't there, and answer phone calls for Joe or do other little chores in the room. The kid asked the doctor if he really had to go home as scheduled the next afternoon. He wanted to stay with his new hero, Joe Castillo.

And of course that made the young cop feel just great when he was already wondering what kind of an asshole he'd become out there in those hills. He got a chance to think about it for the next month. He was put on light duty and assigned to be a gofer in the detective bureau. He hated the job.

He started working out with a vengeance. He began punching the big bag and tattooing the speed bag. He found out that he was pretty good. Boxing was terrific. Boxers couldn't be troubled by booze and broads. Rest. Lots of rest. A Spartan life. Just try going into a ring after a binge and watch your little ass get kicked. He loved it. Somebody broke his nose. Who gives a shit? Joe Castillo went to Chino State Prison to box and fought a black inmate. All the Mexican inmates cheered for him, a cop. Later, a snitch he met on the street said, "Hey, man, I *know* you! I saw you throw some leather in the joint!"

He boxed at 156 pounds and eventually won a silver and a bronze medal in the police Olympics. His hobbies became running and boxing. His marriage might just survive the craziness in the canyons, he figured.

When he came back to BARF he had most of the use in that hand. He could sure as hell make a fist out of it and the fingers soon began to soar and glide and flutter like wings, just as before. Pretty soon he was back to his body language; shrugging, twisting, bowing, swaying when he talked to the groupies in the gin mills. He *couldn't* leave the booze behind, not when he was back with the Barf squad. But he said he didn't think he was the prettiest thing to walk down the street anymore. He didn't think he'd ever be a cocky, black-glove kind of cop ever again.

But one thing didn't change: his feeling for Carlos Chacon. When he'd get drunk his eyes would smolder almost as much as Carlos' eyes *always* smoldered. Carlos Chacon had shot him, no matter how much Carlos claimed it was inconclusive. Joe Castillo *knew* it was Carlos who did it and there was no remorse in Carlos for shooting him. He was going to watch Carlos Chacon *very* carefully in those canyons.

A few things happened to the squad while Joe Castillo and Fred Gil were off recuperating. One thing was that Ken Kelly was brought in as a replacement. Like Robbie Hurt, Ken Kelly had to be convinced that he was the wrong color to walk as a decoy with the others. Ken Kelly figured that Robbie, being black, couldn't do a proper makeup job to pass as a Mexican, whereas he, being white, could pull it off. So Ken tucked his blond hair under a woman's stocking and smeared some kind of pancake makeup, mocha coffee goop, on his face and looked like one of the maniacs in a Hollywood version of gooned-out Vietnam G.I.'s.

Another thing that happened is that all the ragging, jazzing, merciless personal insults and wisecracks elicited *new* responses. For example, if someone were to call Ernie Salgado "The Jaw" because of his prominent chin, or say that a night in his hometown—Marfa, Texas—held all the excitement of a bricklaying contest in Poland, he might not laugh anymore. Ditto for Eddie Cervantes when they asked him if he was riding Uncle Ebeneezer's back this Christmas. Tony Puente was getting sick of the gags about seeing his wife out on the street corners handing out Bible tracts to winos. And even someone as good-natured as Renee Camacho with the soprano alien voice didn't find the drag queen jokes so funny anymore. Nor did Joe Castillo laugh very much when they said he was about as smart as a sack of rutabagas. And maybe even smiling Joe Vasquez had heard just about one reference too many to his looking like Charles Laughton hanging from a bell. And for sure Robbie Hurt had had it when he got compared to some jive-ass with diamonds in his teeth.

In fact, when they were donning their bulletproof vests and alien duds, things were getting pretty quiet these days. Even in the little squadroom, which was about the size of a family crypt, there wasn't much horsing around anymore. And when they piled into the four-wheel drive to head for the canyons at dusk, the silence was absolutely spooky. Nobody opened his mouth. A new element had been introduced since they learned unequivocally that even living legends might get *hurt* out there.

On the 5th of April a bandit gang made a very good score in Deadman's Canyon with what had to have been the most unfortunate robbery victims who ever lived to tell their story. Eighteen pollos from El Salvador and Guatemala decided to try their luck in Deadman's Canyon that afternoon. In that the sun was still high over the hills, they probably felt they might be more vulnerable to *la migra* but would surely escape the bandits about whom they'd heard so much. They were wrong.

While the party of eighteen men and women took their first rest under a stunted oak in Deadman's Canyon, they were approached by three young men and a large black dog. One of the young men was carrying a .22-caliber rifle. He had the longest hair most of them had ever seen on a man.

In fact he looked exactly like an Apache from an American movie. His hair was so long it hung all the way down his back to his belt. And he wore a dark-blue bandanna around his forehead just like an Apache or an American hippie. And he wore a brown vest over a white long-sleeve shirt, making him look even more like a movie Indian.

Since he had a big ugly dog and a rifle, they hoped he was just out hunting jackrabbits in the canyons, especially since one of his companions was a boy. But the boy was carrying a big rock. And the third young man was hefting an iron bar.

And perhaps because the eighteen pilgrims didn't look like border Mexicans, or for some other reason, the one with the long hair and the .22-caliber rifle said something very silly. He said, 'We're *judiciales.* Give us your money."

It was almost funny, except that he had a wild and glassy-eyed look and his rifle was clearly not a toy. The long-haired bandit searched one of the pilgrims and found only some Salvadoran money. He crammed the useless stuff in his pocket and the three left in disgust, not even bothering to search the rest. The pilgrims thought they were in luck.

But thirty minutes later, while they crouched waiting for a Border Patrol vehicle in the far distance to clear out, three *more* men approached. These three were older and they said almost the same thing: "We're state police. Give us your money."

It seemed that all the bandits liked to pose as police. But *judiciales* didn't carry clubs and machetes and broken bottles. The nine men and nine women were terrified into giving up their life savings. Three junkie thugs strolled off that afternoon with over 5,000 U.S. dollars.

Then, while the pilgrim party wailed and keened and wept and wondered how they were going to get to Los Angeles or back to El Salvador and Guatemala without one dollar left, yet *another* group of men approached them, twelve men. And *still* the sun had not set in Deadman's

Canyon. The twelve men were crestfallen to learn that the pilgrims had already been robbed. *Twice.* There was nothing left for them but the women.

This was one of the bandit gangs who intimidated through violence. The spokesmen for the Guatemalans saw that it was absolutely hopeless. He perceived savage brains behind black depthless eyes. When he tried to protect the women, the bandits picked up huge rocks. They attacked viciously, driving the wailing male pilgrims back into a ravine, the men begging the bandits to spare the women. Some of the pollos from El Salvador later reported thinking that this could not be real, not *three* bandit attacks.

The bandit gang encircled the weeping women like a mangy dog pack. The women's spoken prayers were met with obscene appraisals by the bandits, who were already arguing about who would get the youngest.

Suddenly a U.S. Border Patrol aircraft swooped over the canyon and banked. One of the male Salvadorans began waving and screaming. *Demanding* to be arrested as an illegal alien.

Within a few minutes a chopper arrived and sent the bandits running back toward Colonia Libertad. The women were saved. The thing they kept repeating over and over as they sat dazed in the Southern substation of the San Diego Police Department was that they had felt so *safe* once they crossed the imaginary line. They had thought that on their trek through Mexico, wherein they had braved danger a hundred times, they might be robbed, but never were. They had thought that the moment they set foot on United States soil, in broad daylight, they were safe at last from bandits. No one believed it when a uniformed cop told them sardonically that there were more robberies in San Diego than in the entire *countries* of El Salvador and Guatemala put together.

Two nights later in Spring Canyon, while the media darlings were re-creating bandit arrests for a television crew, Dick Snider was out and about with his binoculars. He spotted a young man with the longest hair he'd seen in quite a while, something like an Apache with a bandanna headband. He was carrying a .22-caliber rifle. Dick Snider told Manny Lopez, but by the time they could break free from show biz and call it a wrap, the long-haired bandit had vanished.

The next night they arrested two bandits with daggers. There was a fight, and nobody was fooling around, not these days. Ernie Salgado and Joe Vasquez put some lacerations on a bandit's face during the struggle and Ernie thought he'd done a creditable job. He was very surprised when later that night, while having a few for the road at The Anchor Inn, Manny Lopez had a bit too much scotch and said, "Eeeeeeerr-neeeeee, get over here."

Manny would never forget hearing Ernie's wife say that at the party. Then Manny turned a little mean and said, "Gotta run home to mama? Big Marine D.I. How come you're the only one *didn't* shoot the night Joe and Fred got it?"

"Maybe I'm the only one used my head. I didn't shoot the robbers, but I didn't shoot Fred and Joe either."

"Maybe you froze," Manny Lopez said boozily.

"Maybe that's whisky talking," Ernie Salgado said. And he left without finishing the beer.

"You got to have some big *huevos* to look in a gun muzzle," Manny Lopez told the rest. "And you got to have even bigger ones to draw against it and smoke them *down.*"

Perhaps it was best unsaid that network news teams are not interested in ball-clanging mythic heros who go around *arresting* bandits like ordinary cops.

Ernie Salgado said he was indifferent about blowing a hole through the shotgun-wielding kid when he worked SWAT. And about the Viet Cong he had killed face to face during the Tet offensive. But he also thought that unless it was absolutely necessary, he'd like not to kill people. And his feelings for Manny Lopez were turning into something more than resentment. *Much* more.

It was as if someone were playing a record at the wrong rpm. Things were speeding up. It was happening in the canyons faster than they could arrange for the media to cover it. Their luck was limitless, it seemed. For example, the *judiciales* contacted them about that long-haired bandit with the .22 rifle. It seemed that the *judiciales* had him figured to be a dude who had shot and raped a woman in the canyons two years earlier. He had left her for dead and by the time her brother found her and dragged her body back to Mexican soil, she *was* dead. There was no report of the crime on the U.S. side although it was covered in the Tijuana newspapers.

Manny Lopez said, "Okay, we'll see if we can spot this cat and bust him for you."

And since the kid had hair to his ass and a headband like an American "hee-pee," and a .22 rifle, they started calling him "Twenty-two Long."

Just for fun Manny wrote on the chalkboard, TARGET: .22 LONG. And within three days, while they were lollygagging on a hillside in the late afternoon, waiting for sunset and checking out the mobs on the upper soccer field with binoculars, somebody said, "Hey, there's a broad up there squatted down smoking grass."

Then someone else looked through binoculars and said, "Hey, that broad's sure got long hair. She's wearing a blue bandanna around her . . ."

Fifteen minutes later, Tony Puente, Eddie Cervantes, Joe Vasquez and Carlos Chacon were huffing and puffing over Airport Mesa toward Twenty-two Long, who was working on his third joint and was flying higher than any plane leaving the Tijuana airport that day.

It was just that easy. Twenty-two Long turned and saw these panting sweaty pollos standing behind him showing about a hundred teeth under their moustaches, and the pollos said, "*¿Sabes qué? ¿Sabes qué,* asshole?"

And Twenty-two Long was busted. Lifted clear off the ground by his waist-length hair. Hoist with his own petard, as it were. And turned over to the *judiciales.* Of course he confessed, probably after a few bottles of Coke or Bubble-Up or ginger ale. And he led the Mexican authorities to the murder weapon. And because Mexican justice is swift, he was getting ready for prison before Manny Lopez could even figure out how to get the most P.R. mileage out of this one.

Nevertheless, it was impressive. You want a guy on a two-year-old homicide? You got it. Give us about *three* days. What else can we do for international relations?

It was, the Barfers believed, the incredible luck of Manny Lopez. How many times could he be so lucky? Other than breaking a finger or two when punching out bandits, or falling on his face once in a while as they all did, Manny couldn't be hurt, they were convinced. And they could accomplish anything he asked of them. They were feeling elite. Special. They were outside of ordinary police experience. And getting wild.

Joe Vasquez was so outrageous-looking that one day when Big Ugly was uptown he was drawn on by a startled patrolman who thought that some kind of Banana Republic terrorist had gotten into central headquarters.

Meanwhile, old Fred Gil was getting rehabilitated in record time. Perhaps he owed it to his wife, Jan. *Anything* was better than being home with the relentless squabbling. It ended one night with him saying that the only thing she *really* felt bad about was that he didn't get killed.

And her saying, "Well maybe that's right."

And then both regretting it because their little girl was being affected by the bitterness and endless bickering.

They were utterly incompatible, Jan liking to drink and go out raising hell, and Fred wanting peace and quiet. At first he couldn't sit in a chair with that bullet in his hip. When he walked he dragged a leg behind him like Lon Chaney's mummy. But he exercised nearly every waking moment.

He asked to go back to duty and they put him to work filing juvenile reports. He hated it. His lower extremities would go to sleep because of scar tissue touching nerves. After two weeks of this, and evenings fighting with Jan, he faked full recovery and said, "I guess I'm ready to go back in the canyons." There were things worse than getting shot.

Jan Gil was the life of any party, and was only too happy to go one-on-one with Manny Lopez when BARF threw their frequent little bashes. No one else could joust verbally with Manny, but she could, and just as profanely. Jan Gil said she couldn't stand him, and told the other wives he had an ego like Fidel Castro. Manny just figured, what the hell, she was probably in love with him. Of course Fred Gil was mortified, but Jan Gil's balls clanged as loud as Manny's any old day.

And since policemen are about as prone to gossip as soap opera heroines, there were lots of unsubstantiated rumors flying around that Jan Gil was doing more than going out nights with girl friends, and that also mortified him.

The talk of divorce was constant, and then Fred Gil met a woman during the course of his police duty and fell in love, but good. She was utterly different, this one. She didn't drink or smoke and she kept a spotless house for herself. Like Fred she didn't even swear. And Fred Gil, who felt bad about most everything in life, felt very bad about sneaking around. He told Jan that he wasn't so innocent either. That he'd met a woman. And it *really* hit the fan: threats, accusations, usually in front of the children, and finally a scene in the living room of his new lady, with Jan kicking on the door and calling the "other woman" gamy names. So old Fred Gil packed up and left home. For one day.

He moved in with a detective, and Fred, who couldn't bear a dirty house or disorder of any kind, strolled into the detective's bachelor apartment and almost gagged. He practically had to scrape the crud off the refrigerator just to get it opened. Inside was the detective's supply of groceries—one six-pack of Coors. There were dirty clothes on the floor, in the bathtub, in both sinks, in the flower pots. There were roaches riding the backs of other roaches. Fred Gil went home to his wife. Jan talked him into not filing for divorce until they paid off the bills for the rest of the year. He agreed. It made sense. They were pretty broke. Then a week later, when Fred was at the gym doing a few bench presses, he got a phone call.

It was a lawyer who said, "Fred? I can either serve papers on you there or you can come down to my office."

She had filed, and to add insult to injury the lawyer was a friend of *his* family.

And then, Fred Gil recalled in anguish: "I'll never forget it as long as I live! She showed up in divorce court with a Bible! The woman had never been *in* a church! We weren't even married in a goldang church! And she was dressed like Mary goldanged Poppins!"

She got child support. She got the car. And the house. All Fred got was the mo-ped. And a shock when her daughter, really *his* favorite child, took sides with her mother in the divorce. A natural thing of course, but Fred could only think about how it might never be the same with his adopted daughter and it was the bitterest blow of all.

Well, the nights get pretty cold and uncomfortable out there on a mo-ped, so Fred's sister gave him the use of an old beat-up camper about the size of a bathtub. Fred dragged the thing to the police department parking lot and lived there for a month. It was cold in that camper but at least it could accommodate everything he owned. Yet so could a good-sized backpack. Finally Fred Gil got together enough money to rent an apartment. It was a bachelor apartment. There was a bedroom, a kitchen and a bathroom. There were no pictures on the walls. There wasn't even one little scrawny plant. At least he'd had one little scrawny plant in the camper. Fred Gil was by now popping big red tranquilizers which a physician friend gave to him to diminish the anxiety attacks. He'd done a lot of lonely weeping.

Fred Gil took a look around that lowlife little apartment and remembers saying one word: "Dang!"

Then he took out his service revolver. He thought about it so hard that his hands began to tremble. He thought about smoking it. Then he started shaking all over. Fred Gil had to run from that apartment. He had to run for his life.

The other cops got a big kick out of it when poor old Fred Gil was living in the little camper on the police station parking lot. They had a million jokes they'd lay on old Fred, and they never failed to blow their horns or maybe blast a *siren* when he was asleep and all jangled from the big red pills the friendly croaker had given him. The siren would drive him straight up, crashing his skull against the ceiling, which was low as a coffin lid. The other cops would just *scream* when old Fred Gil would come flip-flapping across the station parking lot in his raggedy cotton robe and rubber thongs, heading to the station to take a crap or a shower.

But everyone said that the funniest sight of all was old Fred Gil riding that freaking mo-ped. The other cops had these hot bikes and sports cars they couldn't really afford, and pickups with back tires that could power a jumbo jet, and here was burly old Fred Gil put-putting down the street on his teeny mo-ped. They practically convulsed when one cop yelled an observation that old Fred looked like the simian prodding the pigskin!

Cops just began keeling over—cackling, hooting, snuffling, screaming—because it was true! Poor old Fred Gil looked *just* like an ape fucking a football.

April was a terrific month for scrapbooks. They managed to get fourteen stories written about them in April. The border was written up large in *U.S. News and World Report.*

April was not a terrific month for a Colonia Libertad bandit named Esquivel, who had seen one spaghetti western too many. He had seen the one where Clint Eastwood runs around in a sarape, and when that sarape goes whipping back there's nothing but hot lead and cold bodies flying around for about five movie minutes, all in slow motion. Esquivel didn't have access to a real gun at the moment but he got hold of an air rifle that looked exactly like an M-1 carbine, and best of all, he got himself an ominous black poncho that looked even more sinister than Clint Eastwood's. And he got another bandit pal and they did a little dope and decided to prowl E-2 Canyon and see how much money they could make. Whatever they made, it wasn't *nearly* enough.

The varsity and junior varsity hadn't had time to split up that afternoon before they stumbled upon a whole mob of illegal aliens nesting in the brush of E-2 Canyon about a hundred yards north of the border line. There were Manny Lopez, Eddie Cervantes, and Tony Puente of the varsity. And Ernie Salgado, Carlos Chacon and Renee Camacho of the junior varsity. Only Joe Vasquez wasn't present, since he had to provide cover that night because both Robbie Hurt and Ken Kelly were off duty.

Manny asked the startled covey of aliens what they were waiting for and got the answer when a man stood up far across the canyon and began waving his arms. There was just enough daylight left to see him, and the sixteen aliens jumped to their feet and began hustling down the trails toward the guide who was signaling.

The guide was an enterprising young fellow who was delighted to see that six new pollos had joined his party of sixteen, and he wasted no time wheeling and dealing with the newcomers. He said he was sorry he couldn't get them all the way to Los Angeles, but he could transport them to Main Street in Chula Vista for forty bucks a head.

So Manny Lopez whispered to the other Barfers that they might as well take down this dude for wildcatting. They waited until the aliens started moving off as directed and then they put the badge on him and told him he wasn't going to Chula Vista that night.

So he shrugged, because what the hell, it's no big deal to spend a day or two in a U.S. jail, which was actually about the most comfortable place around. But there was an alien couple sticking to the guy, and Manny Lopez figured now that they knew the Barfers were cops, he'd have to do something with them.

They walked back to Joe Vasquez, who was waiting in the four-wheel-drive Chevy Suburban, mightily bummed because now he had to provide cover and wait in consummate frustration and listen to weird noises and gunshots in the canyons and not know anything. After he took charge of the wildcatting guide, the others walked their alien couple toward the port of entry to turn them over to the Border Patrol.

While the Barfers were trucking along the trails with the couple, Manny Lopez started talking to them. They had left four children behind in central Mexico. The husband had a nice sincere face and he was looking from one cop to the other, trying to figure out this strange business of American cops dressing up like pollos. His wife was a very shy woman who was probably only thinking of the kids left behind and wondering how long it would take to make enough money to return to them with some kind of nest egg.

While they were walking, the man told Manny Lopez that his working day was from sunup to sunset, seven days a week. He was a *campesino* and had the hands to prove it. Then he couldn't contain his curiosity and he said to Manny Lopez: "Please, can you tell me how often does an American policeman buy groceries?"

"My wife does it." Manny shrugged. "She makes the big buy every two weeks when I get paid."

"How much does it cost her to buy food?" the man asked.

Manny shrugged again and said, "I don't know. Maybe two hundred? Maybe a lot more. I don't really know."

"Dollars?" the man gasped. "U.S. dollars?"

"Yeah, dollars," Manny said. "You think I mean pesos?"

Then the alien couple could only walk in silence. It was too much. Policemen getting paid money like that. What a country!

The man said to Manny Lopez: "For working every day as long as there is sunlight I get paid enough money to buy tortillas, beans, sometimes rice, and sometimes a little sugar and a little coffee. I can't buy beef. I try to buy a chicken once a week because the children need meat, but that chicken costs one day's wages so I can't always buy it."

And of course by now all the other Barfers were listening and moaning and groaning, saying, "Let's not turn em over to the Border Patrol. Let em go! Shit!"

"I *got* to turn you over to the Border Patrol," Manny Lopez told the man. "You might tell somebody who we are and it might be a bandit. It's risky."

And all the other Barfers, the least sentimental of whom was about eighty-five times more sentimental than Manny Lopez, were yelling, "Cut em loose! Fuck this! Let em go."

And Manny was saying, "What's the big deal about

spending a day with the Border Patrol? They'll be back here by Tuesday night, goddamnit!"

Everyone was bitching and moaning except the man, who, speaking for himself and his wife, was defending Manny and saying he understood Manny's dilemma perfectly and he shouldn't make exceptions. And all this was interrupted suddenly by two bandits from Colonia Libertad who'd seen one spaghetti western too many.

It was dark now, really dark. As black as Manny's heart, someone mumbled, and Manny said to shut up, fucker. And they were several yards apart on the trail and doing their best to see five feet in front of them when Manny saw two shapes just above the trail in front of him. One of them was wearing a big old black sarape or poncho, just like Clint Eastwood, and he was satisfied when he saw these pollos, especially since one of them was a woman.

When Manny, who was in the lead with the alien couple right behind him, got within a few feet of the silent bandits, the one with the poncho said, "What smuggler do you belong to?"

And Manny made up a name. "We belong to Morro."

The two bandits looked them over, especially the woman hiding behind Manny Lopez, and were more than assured that these couldn't be part of that group of San Diego cops who prowled these canyons screwing up their business. The one with the poncho then did his Clint Eastwood impersonation and swept back the poncho and threw down on Manny Lopez with his M-1 carbine air rifle, and said, "Give us your money!"

And Manny looked around and saw that his Barfers were straggling along far behind and he had to let them catch up, so he said, "Don't hurt us. Don't hurt us."

And he started cowering and whimpering and generally going into character, but of course there was nothing funny about an M-1 carbine which he thought was real. And when the others came stumbling and bumping along and crashing into the ones who'd been stopped by the bandits and saw that goddamn rifle pointed at them, everyone froze waiting for "*¿Sabes qué?*"

The last one up the trail was Tony Puente. And he wasn't wearing his glasses and it was dark and he hadn't heard any conversation as yet except that he knew there was a holdup going on. Tony Puente squinted up ahead and could clearly see a man. And he saw that the man was holding something and he squinted a little more. And it looked to Tony Puente just like a stick in the robber's hands. A skinny old *stick.* And this was pretty funny. On a night when the varsity and junior varsity were teamed up, two bandits jumped them with a skinny little old stick! This was *really* funny. Were those bandits ever going to get their asses kicked.

Then Tony Puente heard one bandit say more forcefully "Give us your money!"

And he was practically giggling when he yelled out from the rear of the queue: "Don't give them shit, the pricks!"

The others couldn't believe it! They were all starting to sweat buckets looking down the barrel of an M-1 carbine and Tony Puente was back there yelling don't give them shit? Calling them pricks?

Manny Lopez said, "Shut up," to Tony Puente, and he started snapping his fingers, hoping that Tony might pick up on it.

Snap, snap, snap, but it was lost on Tony, who couldn't figure out why Manny hadn't said something like "*¿Sabes qué,* motherfucker? I'm gonna stick that stick right up your ass!"

Another problem was that Manny was trying to push the woman down to the ground, because something real bad was going to happen and he wasn't ready to make his move just yet.

And all of a sudden Tony Puente, who was having a hell

of a good time, yelled out, "I'm not giving you anything. In fact, I think you're nothing but *putos.* Hey, thief! Fuck your mother!"

And now *all* the Barfers were groaning and sighing, and fidgeting and wanting to shoot Tony Puente because everyone but he could see that goddamn M-1 carbine pointed down their throats!

And Manny Lopez was saying through clenched teeth: "Shut up, Tony. Shut *up,* Tony."

And everyone except Tony Puente knew that if they lived through this, he sure as hell better start wearing those fucking glasses!

And then Manny managed to get the woman more or less out of the way and he said, "*¿Sabes qué?*"

When he yelled *"Barf!"* there was the most godawful racket heard yet in those canyons, what with the number of Barfers who were together that night. They fired about thirty rounds at the two bandits. They missed one entirely and thought they'd even missed Clint Eastwood, who turned and started flying toward the border with his poncho trailing like a cape.

Eddie Cervantes started after the guy and the firing was still going on and he turned to see Carlos Chacon shooting at the guy and he figured he was going to suffer the same fate as Joe Castillo and Fred Gil, and he started screaming at Carlos and calling him every kind of name when the bandit with the poncho fell flat on his face. Eddie Cervantes was on top of the guy, worrying about the ploy of knives up the sleeves and also worrying that Carlos was going to blow him off the body.

The bandit didn't put up much of a fight. He was shot through the armpit. His companion escaped in the darkness.

The wounded bandit was taken to the hospital, and the homicide detectives once again had to truck on out to the canyons for yet another officer-involved shooting, and stagger around in the coyote crap and mumble about these

Barfers being *way* more trouble than they were worth.

But the alien couple who had almost gotten their heads blown off weren't complaining at all. In fact, the man asked very respectfully if he could inform a superior officer about how kind Manny Lopez and his men had been and how the Barfers had saved them from the bandits.

The night ended as usual with lots of booze being poured to celebrate, except that there were some very bitter comments from Eddie Cervantes to Carlos Chacon about shooting carelessly. Then a few insults started flying back and forth. They were starting to be wary of each other.

Almost every Barfer was having problems at home, what with the riotous drinking going on all night. They got so they'd work like mad trying to get some kind of an arrest in the early part of the evening so they could make it to The Anchor Inn before the bar closed, or if it was too late, get on out to The Wing and unwind a little before going home. It was getting more and more impossible to sleep without a few drinks. And pretty soon on their nights off their wives started to notice that even at home they needed a few.

The heaviest drinker was Robbie Hurt. He'd be eager to stop at a bar even if only one other Barfer was willing. He didn't go alone, because of course that might mean he had a problem. But pretty soon his wife, Yolie, would find him zoned out in front of the television with a drink in his hands.

If Yolie complained, he'd get irritable and say, "I'm only doing what all men do. A few drinks won't hurt me."

He was absolutely wrong. A few drinks one night almost killed him.

As Robbie looked back on those days, he would sigh and say, "Yolie was the epitome of a Mexican wife. She got it from her mother's side. She'd have dinner ready. She was acquiescent. She was agreeable. She'd work ten hours a day at her job and then take care of me. She made it easy to do what I was doing. Too bad she didn't take after her father's side of the family and come on more like a black chick. And kick my ass!"

He was twenty-six years old and it was so incredibly easy. The Barfers would just come banging into a bar after they got off duty and the groupies would fight each other to get at these hardballers.

And they'd lead off the conversation with: "Well, ladies, you'll get to read it in tomorrow's papers, but lemme tell you what we did *tonight*!" It was *too* easy. And though some of them stuck to beer drinking, Robbie was drinking hard liquor.

And after he'd had a few he had an easier time with the wisecracks. He was of course still working the cover team instead of being able to walk with the others, *because* he was black. Therefore, black jokes increased his frustration and he wasn't laughing anymore. And if a macho type like Eddie Cervantes or Joe Castillo would say in front of a groupie: "Whadda *you* know about it, Robbie?" he would be offended and refuse to talk at all. And he'd drink.

They came to call him "Hurt Feelings," and Eddie Cervantes made no attempt to understand, saying, "They never shoulda had anyone but Mexicans on this squad in the first place."

Manny Lopez used to take Robbie aside and stroke him by saying, "Robbie, we *need* you. Don't pay any attention to Eddie. That's the way Mexicans are. They make fun of everybody. We *need* you."

Then, after a time, Manny the manipulator took a new tack. When Robbie would come to him and threaten to quit BARF, Manny would say, "Fuck you, Robbie! Go ahead and quit. This Barf squad's gonna make your career but if you wanna quit, do it." Then he'd yell, "Hey, guys, Robbie just quit again!"

And Robbie Hurt would go off and sulk and think about his police career. He didn't quit, but he *did* drink.

Then he fell madly in love with a lady bartender. It had to be true love, but every time he saw her he had about ten ounces of booze in his belly. She was a white girl, a brunette, a little hefty but nice. She loved music and so did Robbie, so one night he took her to see *The Wiz* when it was appearing on stage in San Diego.

It was the first time he had had a date with another woman since his marriage. He was suffering what the cops called the Secret Service Syndrome. He was looking all around the theater for someone who might know Yolie. He was a wreck and was trying to work out an alibi instead of watching the show, which had cost him plenty. He couldn't very well tell a spy she was his sister, could he? He didn't have his eyes on the stage for three minutes at a time. He decided never to do that again.

Robbie was feeling so guilty that he ran right out and bought two more tickets to *The Wiz.* The seats were even more expensive. He took Yolie, and when they got to the part where Dorothy and her dog go to Emerald City and the Wiz sings his solo, Robbie said, "Wait till you hear *this* part! This guy can really . . ."

And he just hung there in mid-sentence with his mouth agape. And sure enough, Yolie said, "How do *you* know?"

"I been reading about it," Robbie said. "It's in all the papers!"

It was too complicated, so he decided not to continue this. He wasn't cut out for it. He wasn't sure he was in love with the bartender anyway, except he was absolutely sure of it whenever he was with her, because whenever he was with her he'd sit and guzzle a pint or two, and it made his romance glow with a hard gemlike flame, or whatever.

Robbie was driving a 260Z Datsun at that time. It was a hot car, but he wanted a Porsche. The young man had expensive tastes. Once he had to have the car pulled out of the mud near Monument Park when he was there at three o'clock in the morning telling a wide-eyed little lollypop all about Gunslinging in No-Man's-Land. Another night when he was leaving his lady bartender, he was caught on a flooded road after a heavy rain and had to say adieu to the Barf squad for nearly two weeks because he almost took down a telephone pole on San Ysidro Boulevard. He woke up in the hospital, where he spent the next ten days, but after the gash on his head healed up and the eye started working again, he was ready for BARF. And more drinking. He was also trying to be as macho as any Mexican cop.

For the first time his wife started criticizing the boozing. It made him cranky. "*You* won't drink with me," he said. "We get so little time together and you won't even sit and talk and have a taste. You make me go *out* to do it. It's not *my* fault."

And then, if Yolie would go off and cry or something, Robbie would go banging out the door yelling, "Okay, *you* don't wanna have a good time. I'm going to The Anchor Inn!"

And he did the right thing with the insurance money he got from the totaled Datsun. He bought the Porsche 924 he'd always dreamed of. It was *much* faster.

Yolie Hurt decided that it was time to have a life of her own. She liked to dance and he didn't. He liked to drink and she didn't. She worked for a company that manufactured contact lenses, and she made some friends there. She wanted him to meet them. He tried a time or two. He'd sit and listen to them and wonder where they were really coming from, these lizard-shit civilians. And what did *they* know about anything?

Robbie Hurt was not just a member of a minority group. He was a minority within a minority within a minority. An outsider within an elite force within a police force. He started to think he had nothing in common with *any* civilians, Yolie included.

One night he got home at 4:00 A.M. and said he'd worked late. He'd parked his car under the lights in front of The Anchor Inn, unconsciously hoping she'd see it, since they lived nearby. She had. She accused him.

He said, "Well, you caught me. So let's call it a day. I don't want you anymore." Then for good measure, he said what he knew was a bald-faced lie. He said, "Besides, I think *you're* screwing around, you and your girl friends from work. So why shouldn't I?"

She slapped him. He slapped her back, the only time he had ever struck her. She cried for days. He felt like a low-down dog. He had to get out of this before it killed him. He moved out. He moved back. He couldn't understand what was happening inside his head. The move back was half-hearted.

Robbie Hurt was getting macho, very macho. He demanded a swimming pool. She couldn't swim. He *had* to have a swimming pool to be happy. He wanted dogs and got them, a Doberman and a Labrador. It took her two days to clean up after those monsters. She worked ten hours a day at a good job as a lab tech supervisor, but there was never enough money for him. She was losing so much weight she was looking like a half-starved alien. The other wives noticed it at the many Barf parties Robbie threw at their house.

Yolie noted that Manny Lopez had to show who was boss even at the parties. If someone started hitting the bottle, Manny would hit it harder. Once he outdrank everyone and spent the night at Robbie's house on the bathroom floor. Manny Lopez would not let himself be bested by his macho cops, not even at a party.

And Yolie listened to the merciless wisecracks these Barfers directed toward each other. She knew that Robbie was getting more sensitive than he'd ever been about ethnic jokes.

"You can't be on a walking team, Robbie. Who'd rob a spade? It's the other way around."

Or, "Whaddaya call two brothers in a twelve-room house? Burglars!"

But if Robbie was obviously offended by something, the Barfers would just say, "Go pout, Robbie. Christ, you remind me a my wife!"

Yolie recalled those days with Robbie, saying, "I hope I never know anybody as well as I know him. Not as long as I live. It's like having a twin. I knew just how he was going to react to everything."

Of all the Barfers, she liked Big Ugly, Joe Vasquez, the best. She admired the way he was devoted to his wife and lived a quiet life. And since they too were childless, she liked to talk with Joe and his wife, Vilma, about adopting children.

Then Robbie's running got so blatant that it was apparent he *wanted* to get caught. He wouldn't bother to clean the makeup off his clothes.

He'd actually started giving his phone number to Barf groupies, who would call and hang up when Yolie would say, "This is his *wife*. Can I take a message?"

One called back to say how sorry she was, because Robbie had sworn he was single. On weeknights Yolie would always get these calls and hang-ups.

One girl called and said how sorry she was, but Robbie needed lots of sympathy, since he felt bad about being black, and the caller, being white, could help him.

Another said she was a student at San Diego State and knew Robbie was married, but she was desperate to talk to Yolie because Robbie was lying and cheating. Not on Yolie, but on the student.

Yolie Hurt by now was getting as crazy as a Barfer in the canyons. She made a date to meet this distraught student and was surprised to see that she was a pretty black girl. They met in a Cantonese restaurant and Yolie sat through a tearful lunch discussing Robbie. While they were talking, Robbie strolled in the door looking like a bandit about thirty seconds after Manny Lopez says "*¿Sabes qué?*"

There they were: Robbie, his girl friend, and his wife. The girl begged Robbie not to lie and cheat on her anymore. Yolie, for the first time, started getting her head straight.

She simply said, "There's only one thing for us to do. We should make a soap opera out a this."

And that was that. The marriage was, for all intents, finished. They didn't get a lawyer. They did their own divorce. She gave him everything.

"I'd spoiled him all the way," she said. "No sense stopping."

One night Robbie was pacing on a hillside by the Chevy Suburban with Ken Kelly. They both seethed with frustration because they'd heard three gunshots off in Spring Canyon and could not reach the walking teams by radio for nearly thirty minutes, during which time they both had their GI tracts eaten full of holes by stomach acid until they found out the shots were not fired at or by Barfers. On this night Robbie slipped and fell down a hill, spraining his ankle. He wore a temporary cast for a few days, and when he hobbled into a cops' bar on crutches, there happened to be a clutch of groupies drinking with some detectives and patrol cops.

Someone pointed out the arrival of the Gunslingers, one of whom was on crutches, and the next thing Robbie Hurt knew, he was regaling three wide-eyed lollypops with a story as to how he got his "wound."

"It's a jungle out there, ladies!" he found himself saying. "Yes, we had to shoot a few bandits tonight. And I got hurt chasing one who almost escaped back onto Mexican soil."

And so forth. The astonishing thing was that he was starting to believe it. It was amazing what it could do to your head, this job. He tried to stop his own mouth but couldn't. They were gathered around him. They admired him. No, they *worshiped* him.

Ken Kelly said, "It was like having something very special in your back pocket. I could pull it out when I needed it. Robbie Hurt pulled it out *all* the time."

Robbie never stopped calling Yolie for sisterly advice. She was the only person he could talk to, even after the marriage was over. He said that his ex-wife was the finest human being he had ever known in his whole life. He always said he should have cleaned up his act and saved the marriage. He said the loneliness after they parted made him think of suicide. He said he wept out of loneliness.

He said all of this, but there was something he was up against that was so seductive, so irresistible, so overpowering that he couldn't cope. He was up against something that had overwhelmed many a man older and wiser than Robbie Hurt. This something was a *Bitch.* And the sinister Bitch had a name. She was called *Celebrity.*

CHAPTER · 13

LINES AND SHADOWS

THE BARFERS WERE BECOMING CONSUMED BY THE PUBLICity blitz. They were spending their time giving interviews (that is, Manny Lopez was) and speeches (also handled by Manny) and the others were starting to feel like the character actor who never gets the girl. Some of them, Eddie Cervantes especially, were dying to become leading men.

"Hey, I can't help it if they wanted *me* at the Rotary luncheon," Manny Lopez would say defensively. "Listen, fuckers, you're free to make speeches or go on television or hire press agents if you want. Come *with* me next time."

But they never did, except once when Tony Puente tagged along to a Kiwanis speech. He was awed by the way Manny played to the audience. Tony became convinced that Manny could become police chief, or mayor of San Diego, or governor of California, for chrissake. Dick Snider may have dreamed up the idea, but BARF was Manny's baby. He shaped it, he sold it, he represented it, and if it ever died it would be he who killed it.

Eddie and the others might bitch and complain all they

wanted about Manny getting the publicity, but a few of them had to concede that none of them could begin to do what Manny could.

Someone said, "Imagine Joe Castillo or Big Ugly having to address the Rotary Club? Sure. Like pulling teeth. Your own."

Manny had natural gifts. You only had to watch him sometime, up there in his disco suit and gold chains, the witticisms tumbling out of his impish, gap-toothed mouth, his pseudo-Asian eyes darting around the room to lock in on every chick short of menopause, his droopy moustache jumping under that pseudo-Armenian nose, and that eyebrow squiggling and crawling up his forehead into a perfect question mark. As he pointed his finger like a gun and told them how he drew one from the shoulder holster and one from the belt and smoked them down in Deadman's Canyon.

He could make them gasp or make them laugh as he chose. All you could hear was the click of ballpoint pens as local politicians started making notes about getting this little hardball son of a bitch on the campaign committee. There weren't any movie stars in San Diego and only a few big sports stars. And there sure as hell wasn't a genuine mythic hero before this dude came along. Who cared if he was a Republican or a Democrat? This freaking Mexican was the last of the Gunslingers!

In April their activity report showed that Manny was spending his thirtieth birthday re-creating bandit busting in the canyons for various television crews. The Barfers were in fact actors now, in more ways than one. But an actor better by God get in proper character when he's doing real-life bandit busting or somebody might get hurt. It was on their minds, but except for Eddie Cervantes and sometimes Ernie Salgado, they didn't argue very much with Manny Lopez about what made copy and what made sense.

Once they were in character, back to playing the pollo

parts, a smuggler actually told them there was very little bandit activity in the hills these days because of one Sergeant Manny Lopez and his San Diego cops who were scaring the hell out of everybody.

When things got slow out there on warm spring nights, the other Barfers were grateful for the respite. It was on such nights that they liked to lie on a hilltop and listen to the music from the Mexican side, and crack jokes and *try* to get back some of the camaraderie they were losing as they came to fear each other's guns and Manny's restless, driven ways.

They'd talk about bandits shot full of holes who lived. And then: "If I get grazed in the ass I'll probably bleed to death." Or, "Joe Castillo don't gotta worry, long as he gets it in the head." Or, "Manny's okay if it's a heart shot." And so forth.

But if they started griping too much or began to lose interest, Manny could always figure a way to entertain them for a while. For instance, one afternoon while they were loafing there in Deadman's Canyon, feeling bummed and mean, they happened to observe a small party of women passing on the greasy clay trail. It was still daylight and the young women were scared and moving in a hurry. Pretty soon a group of lowlife Colonia Libertad play-smugglers came finger-popping along the trail, signaling for the women. The leader said to the Barfers: "Did you see some little *pollitas* walk this way?"

And Manny, who was bored, said, "Why do you want to know?"

And the guy giggled and said, "They think I'm going to guide them to San Ysidro. But we're taking them down in the canyon."

"For what?" Manny asked, and the guy looked at Manny like he was a festered pimple and said, "To fuck them, stupid."

"Maybe they won't like that," Manny Lopez said ominously.

"They'll *learn* to like it," the guy grinned.

And by now the other Barfers were looking at Manny, and that eyebrow had locked in and the little eye beneath was really looking evil and he walked over real friendly to the would-be rapist and said, "Well, *'mano,* I do happen to know where the girls are. They're hiding right over there."

And all the Barfers got to their feet to follow Manny, who led the would-be rapist along the grease-slick trail to the edge of a gully so that when he fell he might just break his neck, and Manny said something like: "I think now you should grab your balls and cough."

And when the puzzled Mexican asked why, Manny said, "For old times' sake. The next time you feel for those nuts you'll need a catcher's mitt to find them."

And then he didn't bother to say "*¿Sabes qué?*" and the would-be rapist probably felt like his balls were sailing clear to the bullring when Manny kicked them for a field goal and the other Barfers started beating up his rapist pals for good measure and everyone was running in all directions. They eventually walked the limping rapist cradling his wounded glands over to the Mexican *judiciales,* since evil intent in America is not a crime.

The *judicial* in charge didn't like rapists any more than Manny Lopez, so when Manny told him the story he decided the guy needed one more, and POW! He knocked the guy cold, and said, "*That's* for having impure thoughts."

If Manny didn't keep them grimly entertained, they tended to get wilder out there in those lonely hills. Once they decided to build a fire of their own, like the pollos do. They tried setting fire to an old tire, and for a tense thirty minutes the whole goddamned canyon was in danger of going up in a conflagration.

Another time they were listlessly walking along the border fence on the west side of I-5 when some Tijuana kids started throwing rocks at them. They started throwing rocks back and pretty soon there was a first-class rock-throwing melee going on, until some Mexican citizen got sick and tired of rocks banging off his roof and called the Tijuana cops, who showed up and fired a *shot* at them. Which sent them running like hell into the darkness, deciding that they take rock throwing seriously down there and maybe they better quit dicking around so much.

And they weren't the only people getting goofy in those canyons. The U.S. Border Patrol, with one of the most thankless and frustrating jobs of all time, also had its share of head problems. One evening when the Barfers had to arrest a group of pollos who got in the way of a possible bandit ambush, they called the Border Patrol and delivered the pollos to them. One of the aliens happened to be wearing a scruffy old U.S. Army dress jacket complete with insignia, pins and badges. The border patrolman receiving the prisoners went absolutely bonkers. He made the baffled pollo stand at attention in front of the jeep headlights. He pulled each little pin and infantry badge off the jacket and snapped them in half like he was breaking a saber.

"This man never served in our armed forces!" he shrieked. "He has no *right* to wear these!"

The Barfers at first thought it was a gag, and Big Ugly started to do a drum roll on the jeep until the border patrolman showed them eyes ten times more nutty than Ken Kelly's. And they knew this guy was serious.

The pollo never for a minute thought this *migra* wasn't serious, and he started shaking when the border patrolman pulled out a pocket knife and cut off the brass buttons.

As summer approached they were doing well enough—that is, they were arresting a few bandits here and there, nothing worth talking to a Kiwanis luncheon about, but guys with knives and icepicks who only scared the living shit out of them. Guys who smelled like garbage. Nothing worthy of mention on the eleven o'clock news. And one particularly warm evening, Manny decided that they were going to hit those canyons and they were going to walk until they got robbed. He was sick of this peace and quiet. They loaded up, all of them, and were dropped off by Robbie Hurt and Ken Kelly in the vicinity of Airport Mesa. They started walking west toward the sunset. Toward the goddamn ocean! Manny Lopez wouldn't stop.

Old Fred Gil sure enough slipped and fell in a pile of shit. Ditto for Renee Camacho, who that night was wearing high-heeled leather dress shoes such as the aliens wear in their pathetic attempts to get dressed up. His ankles started swelling after the first two miles. He was limping after the third. Manny wouldn't stop. They walked down the gullies, up the escarpments, clear to Interstate 5. They heard rattlers just after dark.

"Look out! A fucking snake!" somebody yelled, and they almost started shooting.

"Don't say 'look out,' goddamnit!" Manny Lopez yelled. "Talk Spanish. Say '*¡Trucha!*' or something."

So somebody yelled, "*¡Trucha!* A fucking snake!"

The mosquitoes were enjoying the balmy early summer evening. They were attacking in swarms and everyone was slapping and yelping. Their hands and faces were swollen before the fourth mile. They were wearing bulletproof vests and lugging all their armament, and Renee Camacho was carrying a shotgun. Manny Lopez wouldn't stop for a drink. He was a man possessed.

At one point he told everyone he wasn't going to put up with any more bitching and moaning. It was eight miles to the ocean from where they started, in the black of night, sometimes not even on trails but on rock-hard clay, through cactus and thorn bushes. Carlos Chacon at a bloated 235 pounds said he was going to die, and just when everyone thought that God had abandoned them, Manny Lopez twisted his ankle and fell flat on his belly in a shallow pool of foul and fetid water.

Manny could yell all he wanted, but it didn't do any good. All the little hardball turds, two of whom literally smelled like turds, were absolutely rolling around the ground. They were snuffling, cackling, squealing, hooting. There was no control whatsoever. The most feeble wino in Tijuana could have strolled through a hole in the fence and disarmed them all. It was another hour until they were wheezing and blowing and panting by the seashore, too exhausted to giggle at the thought of Manny Lopez going down on his pseudo-Armenian nose. They called it The Death March.

At least Manny never lost his sense of humor during the dry spell. The next night, when they were on the west side near Stewart's Barn, a gathering point for aliens, they found fifty people hiding inside waiting for their guides. It was one o'clock in the morning and Manny wouldn't let them knock off early, even though they hadn't seen bandits for days. The aliens inside the barn were mostly sleeping by now and it looked as though their guides weren't going to show up.

The Barfers took a breather and a couple of them snuggled down into their coats, sprawling on the ground and waiting for Manny's inner fire to go out. And while they sat, a guide happened in, stepping over sleeping aliens, looking for the party he was to lead. The guide looked down and saw a pollo glaring up at him. The pollo had a bandanna covering his balding bean which was so insect-bitten it looked a rotten mango. The guide looked curiously at the funny eyebrow on this glaring pollo which was sidewinding up among all the red bumps made by mosquitoes, ravenous sand fleas, and savage red ants.

The guide squatted down and said to the pollo: "Who are you waiting for?"

"Our guide."

"You have to be careful in this barn," the guide said, looking around. "*La migra* makes checks around here and there's a bunch of San Diego cops running around dressed like you."

"Is that a fact?" the pollo said.

"They tried to beat me up one time," the guide said. "But I kicked their asses."

The eyebrow suddenly started getting all spiky and the pollo said, "You did?"

"You should let me lead you," the guide said. "Those bastards are afraid of me. I'm the meanest son of a bitch on either side of the border."

By now all the Barfers were wide awake and listening with some interest. Pretty soon Manny yawned and scratched his balls and sighed and said to the guide: "Tell me, how can you tell they're cops when you see them?"

"Easy," the guide said. "I just pat their pockets for the badge. These pussies got this chickenshit little gold badge and they can't go anywhere without it, the *putos.*"

Manny motioned for Renee to come closer and Manny put an arm conspiratorially around the guide and said, "Well, tell me, does the badge look like this?"

It's doubtful that the guide ever saw the shield in Manny's palm, but if he wanted to see its imprint he'd only have to look in the mirror for the next three days or so. Because Manny, holding him behind the neck with one hand, slammed that badge right into the guy's forehead so hard it sounded like a rifle shot.

The other aliens wondered why their guide went running from the barn like a cat on fire. And the Barfers started to forgive Manny for The Death March. Just when you started to hate the guy, he'd do something good for your morale.

The wounded Barfers, Fred Gil and Joe Castillo, had been back to duty for some time by now. Joe Castillo had had talks with his doctor about more things than the damaged nerves and tendons which refused to give his fingers normal feeling. He talked with the doctor about the canyons and what they were doing out there. The physician, who had served in Vietnam, said, "You might find yourself pulling your gun before you should. You might be too fast now. Or you might be too slow and maybe that's worse. I don't know. This isn't war; it's police work. I don't know what to tell you."

Joe Castillo tried to explain it to the doctor by saying, "I think I'll be okay as soon as I can build my mind back up to a state of *frenzy*. Then I'll be ready to work the canyons."

Police work? Requiring a state of . . . *frenzy*?

Meanwhile, old Fred Gil was having his own little crisis. Ever since he had come back to duty he hadn't been able to relax during the role playing. Whenever potential robbers approached and Fred was squatting down acting subservient, he was ever prepared, with his hand on his gun and the adrenaline practically lifting him to his feet. It was hard to stay down while Manny or someone talked to bandits. It was hard to keep that gun inside his clothing. Fred didn't know it, but almost all the Barfers by this time *also* had their guns half-drawn at the mere approach of a human being in the darkness.

On Fred's first night back from the wounding, Manny took him on a walking tour to where the shooting had occurred. The bloody bandages and gauze wrappings were still on the ground.

Are they testing me? Fred Gil wondered. But he never asked. He covered up the anxiety with a joke. He had always done that in Vietnam. Cover it all with a joke.

His hip didn't always work exactly right, especially when descending steep slopes. Once he had to *roll* painfully down a rock-studded embankment when the others were running from some potential bandits in the hide-and-seek manner of aliens. They would hide but not *too* well. And he didn't like it at all when Manny started breaking them into two-man walking teams instead of three or four, so as to cover more ground when action was scarce. One night when he was walking with Renee Camacho, they encountered what looked like a mass exodus of Tijuana, as far as the eye could see.

What if this tide of aliens thought that he and Renee were bandits and stoned them to death? There must have been hundreds marching, silent as ghosts. They passed in the night on the little trail without a word.

Fred Gil now preferred to work on the east side, because there was less brush and shrubbery, and the better terrain let you see the silhouettes approaching in the darkness. Not like the west side, where they'd come right *at* you from the brush, the only warning being the smell of garbage a split second before you saw them. Specters plummeting. Right *at* you.

One night on the west side, they had to cross through a canyon right next to a sinking sand pit. There was a natural little tunnel in the canyon formed by the brush itself, a tunnel of brush and mesquite. They had to get through by crawling inside that natural tube on their hands and knees. Fred Gil was crawling halfway through before he discovered that now he liked confinement even less than usual. In fact, it was suffocating him.

This was a night when two bandits with big clubs had attacked Renee. After the Barfers arrested them and were trying to get them through that tunnel of brush, they saw *fifteen* silhouettes on top of the gully, and voices began ordering the cops to release their *socio.* The shadows ran alongside the gully as they dragged their screaming prisoners through the blind and black tunnel of brush. They were sweat-drenched, bloody, slippery, beating their prisoners into submission and dragging them, and imagining fifteen specters plummeting. Feeling fifteen machetes and knives hacking through the mesquite, hacking through *them.* Just as it looked as though the shadows were going to swoop, they were gone. They disappeared without a sound.

Fred Gil had never been so aware that he was the *oldest* Barfer. He had never been so aware of impending middle age. He started looking for liver spots.

The Ku Klux Klan created a little media stir for a while by gathering at the border, having decided that some good old vigilantism was needed to stop the flow of illegal aliens into California. The San Diego police chief announced that the Barf squad would be out there to deal with any violence, and the implication was clear that Chief William Kolender, the first Jewish police chief, wasn't fond of the Klan. A Mexican newspaper did a very funny cartoon showing a group of sheet-covered Klansmen who had discovered a spy in their midst. When the headsheet is pulled off the spy by the Grand Dragon, the spy is none other than you-know-who with an evil grin saying, "*¿Sabes qué?*"

Renee Camacho, the boy tenor, heretofore the jolliest, warmest and most sensitive Barfer of them all, began to lose his sense of humor. So did they all. There wasn't so much fun and games at lineup anymore. They'd have a somber little briefing and out they'd go. In the past, Renee used to entertain them with mime and impressions.

One night Renee was slugged by a bandit. He put his gun at the assailant's head and it was all he could do to keep from killing the guy. He'd never felt like this before. He went out with the boys and got good and drunk that night.

Another time when he was taking a bandit into the substation—a robber who had scared the crap out of him—the bandit began calling him obscene names. The robber was handcuffed. Renee leaped on him and got him in a headlock and began hammering his face with a fist, all the time saying, "You think you're bad? You're a *puto*! Here! You rape women? Here! You terrorize children? Here!"

And he was hammering the screaming bandit's face into hamburger when he looked up and saw a uniformed supervisor watching him. The bandit was covered with blood and Renee was absolutely positive that he was going to suffer the fate of Ken Kelly, becoming the *second* San Diego policeman indicted and convicted in a civilian court for criminal assault.

He looked at the supervisor as if to say, "Well, I'm busted." And maybe deep down he was *relieved,* because this proved he wasn't fit to go out there anymore. But the supervisor turned and walked away as though he hadn't seen a thing.

Renee couldn't believe what he had become. It didn't seem possible.

It was happening to all of them. If they encountered potential bandits who, because of the growing Barf reputation, decided after a few probing questions to let them pass, Manny might just say, "*¿Sabes qué?*" And they'd jump on the bandits and beat them up just for drill.

"Teaching the crooks that there was a price to pay for operating in the canyons," Manny called it.

Renee didn't like *any* of it anymore. He went to see his best friend, Herbert Camacho, and told his father that maybe someone should take a look at the Barf squad because maybe they were turning into *weird* guys out there in no-man's-land.

Then they began to run into an old nemesis: El Loco. The bandit in the ski mask was getting on everyone's nerves after six months of eluding them. One dark night the junior varsity encountered him near his favorite hole in the fence by E-2 Canyon. They saw a man dressed in black wearing a ski mask. He faded into the shadows. They saw another man with a rifle. He looked as though he was putting a round in the chamber.

The junior varsity hit the ground behind a mound of earth and a voice called out: "You take care of business on your side and we'll take care of business on our side."

When they hooked up with the varsity later that night, Joe Castillo told Manny Lopez what had happened and Manny was beside himself.

"Listen, fuckers," he said, "why didn't you pop a few caps in their direction to show them we mean business?"

Pop a few caps? Just like that? Well, why not? This wasn't police work anymore and they weren't policemen. They were some kind of untamed bug-eyed little canyon crawlers, and everyone—other cops at the station, their wives at home, their neighbors, *everyone*—was looking at them like they'd just crept out from under a rock, and that's because on any given night, they *had*.

So what the hell, pop a few caps and maybe get in a big shootout with some bandits and maybe wake up the town, allowing the newscasters to say, "Border shooting! Film at eleven!"

Then one night Manny Lopez got to talk to Loco once again. They were walking near E-2 Canyon trying to make contact with the elusive bandit leader when they heard a voice. Manny recognized it as the voice he had heard once before when he passed a cigarette through the fence to the man in the ski mask. A voice, coming from someone who could have seen them only as silhouettes, called out: *"Oye,* Lopez! Is it you?"

And after they hit the deck, Manny yelled back, "Come on over, Loco! Let's talk."

But Loco answered, "No no, Lopez. I like it here in my country. Why don't you stay there and I'll stay here. And why don't you just let me have a little of your territory? I require *very* little and you don't need it!"

But Manny wasn't in the mood to screw around with Loco. He wanted Loco worse than tomorrow's headlines. He went bonkers and yelled, "You motherfucker, I'm gonna get you! You understand, *puto*? You're mine!"

But Loco wanted only to be reasonable and yelled back,

"I got no problem with you, Lopez. I don't want to fuck with you. Leave me alone!"

Then he was gone and Manny was screaming his head off at empty darkness.

The following night Manny was rampaging around the little briefing room with a big cigar in his mouth, scrawling something on the chalkboard in letters two feet high: TARGET: EL LOCO!

Bandits they had captured described El Loco as being about thirty years old, and in fact he was *just* that age, two months older than Manny. They knew Loco to be about 5 feet 9 or 5 feet 10 inches tall and about 170 pounds, making him about Manny's size. It was said that he was bearded but was almost never without his ski mask, and nobody knew exactly why.

Manny Lopez had many regrets about Loco. He regretted the night he'd passed a cigarette to the ski-masked bandit through the chain link border fence when Loco was uneasily trying to figure out if Manny was really a pollo.

"I coulda got him that night," Manny would complain. "At least I coulda grabbed his fucking finger and broke it!"

Manny was obsessed with the bandit, who reportedly controlled half a mile of E-2 Canyon. It made Manny Lopez crazy that some bandit called it *his* turf.

One night Manny came very very close to catching Loco. That was a lucky night for Manny. Three bandits had tried to rob them with knives. A fourth was some distance away and when he came forward to join the robbery in progress, they saw that he wore dark clothing. And a *ski mask.*

It was a night when the other Barfers suddenly found themselves fighting the bandits while Manny was hot after the one in the ski mask, yelling, *"Barf! Barf! Barf! Barf!"* which could be heard clear to Ensenada because Manny Lopez *wanted* this son of a bitch.

It was a dark night and they ran blindly. Loco fell.

Manny yelped with joy. Then Manny tripped and fell so hard that the cylinder of his gun popped open. Manny snapped it shut and resumed running.

"Barf! Barf! Barf!"

The sound of it made Loco run *faster,* driving hard for the fence. Manny got close enough to hear him pant, to *smell* him. Loco smelled like garbage. Manny saw a knife flash in a sliver of moonlight. Manny fell again. Loco hit the hole in the fence and dived through, black and sleek as flowing oil. Loco was in the Republic of Mexico and vanished in the brush.

Manny stood on his side of the international fence and yelled, "I'm gonna *kill* you, fucker! I almost got you! You lucky fucker, I almost *got* you!"

Then Manny happened to look down at his snub-nosed revolver. It felt funny. He opened the cylinder. The bullets had fallen out when he fell. The gun was empty.

"*I'm* the lucky fucker," Manny Lopez said later. "Lucky I didn't catch him."

The last meeting with El Loco took place on the 9th of July and it proved to be the most unbelievable and terrifying moment yet. When it was over some of them weren't sure who or what to fear anymore. It was the night that Manny Lopez vanished.

The weather was clear except for scattered summer clouds that day. The temperature was seventy-five degrees. It was a perfect San Diego day. In E-2 Canyon, approximately one-half mile east of the port of entry, there is, for the benefit of tourists, a chain link fence ten feet high with rolled concertina wire running along the top of it. Of course the fence ends a short distance farther east, and even where it exists it is ridiculously easy to defeat. But never mind, there it is.

There is an unimproved dirt road that runs south of and parallel to the border from east to west, leading directly to the rear of a railroad yard by the international port of entry. The canyon runs north and south and at the bottom is a wash wherein excess water is accommodated by a thirty-six-inch metal culvert, which on the north side is partially obstructed by rocks and boulders and debris of all sorts. This drainage pipe runs under the international boundary to the south where it empties out into a steep wash or gully, which is also boulder-strewn and filled with rocks, old tires, broken glass, beer cans. The international border at this point is, by surveyors' reckoning, five feet south of the southern end of the metal drainage pipe. The hills are steep leading up to the shacks lit by kerosene lamps wherein reside the Tijuana poor who work where they can, as well as the smugglers and addicts and bandits who work in the U.S. canyons.

The importance of the exact location of surveyors' landmarks was that Manny Lopez had strict orders never to venture south of the imaginary line, and always to know exactly where he and his men were. No one wanted to provoke the authorities of a country that owed billions of dollars to United States banks and that now, with the Mexican oil craze in force, might actually be able to *repay* the loans.

The Barfers were on a fishing expedition specifically designed to catch the *big* one. They had received a report of fifteen aliens being robbed by a gang led by a ski-masked bandit who had scrambled through that culvert going south. Of course aliens had been robbed all over E-2 Canyon, but that drainage pipe was smack in the middle of Loco's territory and seemed a likely ambush site for the bandit to repeat. There was absolutely no one, with the exception of Manny Lopez, who liked the idea.

Renee Camacho, who was included with the varsity that evening, *hated* the idea when Manny made the announcement at lineup.

Manny said, "The border marker is actually a few feet south of the south end a that little tunnel. Guess what we're gonna do tonight? We're gonna *sit* in that tunnel!"

The reason Renee Camacho wasn't thrilled was that he detested the very idea of sitting in a tunnel that was thirty-six inches in diameter. He'd detest the idea of sitting in a tunnel that was thirty-six *feet* in diameter. He, like Fred Gil, hated confinement of any kind, but *machismo* forbade overt expressions of something as normal as fear, so he kept his mouth shut and went along.

The plan was that if bandits should approach from the north—that is from the U.S. side—the Barfers sitting in the south end of the pipe would leap out their end and cover their partners through the international fence. And vice versa.

The pipe was twenty feet six inches long. Manny Lopez decided to take his position close to the southern end, closest to Mexican soil. Eddie Cervantes was to sit a few feet north of him. Then Tony Puente. And, thankfully, Renee Camacho got to sit closest to the opening on the north. Still, he would be inside. He would be confined.

Carlos Chacon was brought along as an afterthought and told to position himself in a nest of sagebrush a few yards north of the tube on the U.S. side where he could observe any bandits approaching from that direction.

The Barfers discovered they were in for total misery from the moment they arrived. The drainage pipe was full of garbage, glass, dank urine, human feces. To endure this? And for what? It was a thousand to one they'd catch Loco or anybody else. Manny Lopez was becoming a madman. But Manny Lopez was also the luckiest madman any of them had ever met.

Outside the pipe it was dusk. Dusty light, seldom hard

and clear in those canyons, revealed a coyote, innocent as a house cat, stalking its own shadow among all the shadows in the canyon. Just like them. And silver puddles of light, heavy with póllution particles from the swarming Mexican city, reassured them. Beautiful polluted light, like storm light. And then it was night.

Renee was carrying the shotgun and the Handie-Talkie under his alien jacket. He whispered into the radio every fifteen minutes that all was quiet. He was also being brave by confronting his claustrophobia head-on. He was drenched with sweat and freezing on a warm night. In his words, he was a *wreck.*

There was a moon. It was a fine summer night—a good bandit night, Manny reckoned. He had no doubt whatsoever that Loco would show. If not tonight, *soon.* He'd sit there through the *winter* to get Loco. They were in that foul and dreadful pipe at 7:30 P.M., squeezing into something like fetal position after their legs had gone to sleep and their necks and backs had gone from pain to numbness to pain. They had to keep exercising their fingers to help the circulation. Furry spiders kept creeping around the walls of the pipe, making a man shudder from his tailbone to the top of his head. It was absolutely black within the pipe, and one started to imagine things: a lazy fat tarantula dangling like a hairy-legged corpse from the tunnel roof, suddenly leaping to attack! Spider eyes burning, spider teeth clicking like bandit rocks.

They stared straight ahead as time stopped. It was like looking at the inside of your eyelids in a coffin. Renee kept turning to either end of the pipe for a glimpse, for reassurance that there was another world somewhere. He got it from the shuddering wail of a jackrabbit dying in fear. Then the screech of a hawk triumphant. Then silence.

A lone cricket's chrip sounded like a handcuff's ratchet. Another farther off sounded like the scrape of a footstep. Then the shrill of mosquitoes passing through. Then silence.

It was more than an hour, but seemed like three, when a man was heard approaching the south end of the pipe. Imaginations were overripe: Images of a slavering bandit with black gums and jagged teeth, smelling like garbage. Concealing his *hands.*

It was just a man. A pollo, perhaps. He looked inside and saw Manny. He asked what they were waiting for. Manny said they were waiting for a guide. The man nodded and moved on.

Another hour crept by. Time moved as slowly as the black furry spiders. There were only the sounds of crickets and faint music in the distance and sweat plinking on their shoes. There was more than one Barfer thinking about having a very serious meeting with Manny. There was only so much that one could be expected to give to the police department and the good people of San Diego. Somewhere lately they had gone far past that.

They were thinking thoughts along these lines and thinking how magnificent a cold beer was going to taste and wondering if the smell of urine and human feces would *ever* leave their clothing and their nostrils, when Manny Lopez disappeared. Vanished! Up in smoke. Now you see him, now you don't.

The Barfers who had been in the pipe told the story to detectives and their colleagues later that night.

Eddie Cervantes, who was sitting closest to Manny and who had been looking north for just a second, said, "It was all of a sudden! There was nothing going on! And all of a fucking sudden LOPEZ IS OUT! He's out, man! Out!"

Renee Camacho said, "Do you understand what happened? He was there and then HE WAS GONE!"

Tony Puente said, "Just like that. Manny *vanished*!"

It is clear when you talk to each member of the Barf squad, those who were in the drainage pipe and those who weren't, that this moment marked a turning point in the very ambivalent feelings each member of that experiment had toward his leader, Manny Lopez. Regardless of what they may have felt prior to the moment that Manny vanished, it is clear that the feeling would be either altered or intensified from that moment.

Manny disappeared like smoke because his adversary, who was just Manny's size and age, was a shockingly strong man. Manny Lopez was, like the others, sitting silently and enduring the stench and the misery and the darkness when a shadow appeared in the mouth of the tunnel. Manny hadn't heard a thing. A shadow was just *there.* Then a human head. The human head wore a ski mask. The human head smelled like garbage.

Manny didn't have time to snap his fingers or hiss to Eddie Cervantes. He didn't have time to draw his revolver. He didn't have time fully to comprehend to whom the head belonged when the head whispered: "What's happening?"

Then the head had an arm, and the arm reached inside the pipe and grabbed Manny's arm like a vise, and Manny Lopez was jerked from a sitting position right through the opening of that tube. And he was *gone.*

It took a strong man to do that. Manny found himself flying through the night, crashing down onto glass and boulders and jagged rocks. Tumbling, dragged, crashing down a gully in the grasp of Loco himself. Manny Lopez came to rest in the country of Mexico on a warm and moonlit Mexican night with only scattered clouds overhead.

What Manny saw was this: a bandit standing to his left pointing at his face a rifle which turned out not to be real. A second bandit standing in front pointing a handgun which was apparently very real. A third bandit standing to his right pointing what looked like a handgun which was apparently very real. And there was Loco's hand, *clamped* on to Manny's gun arm like a bear trap, holding a knife in his free hand. Manny Lopez was on his knees surrounded by four bandits looking down at him. All smelling *worse* than garbage.

Renee Camacho, Tony Puente and Eddie Cervantes by now had come alive and realized that Manny Lopez was gone, and Renee heard Manny in his alien voice crying out: "Don't hurt me! Please don't hurt me!"

It is unknown what the four bandits saw or thought during the next ten seconds, when all hell broke loose, but one can imagine there might have been a little curiosity at this bruised and battered little pollo who, cowering in the grasp of El Loco himself, cried out, "Please don't hurt me!" while his right eyebrow squiggled back toward Chula Vista.

The incredible, terrible, *horrifying* fact of the matter, as far as all the other Barfers were concerned, was that with four armed bandits standing over him, Manny Lopez had *them* exactly where he wanted them.

Manny got his hand to his waistband while Loco still held the arm. Then he jerked free and drew, firing from left to right.

Renee Camacho heard BOP BOP BOP BOP BOP! "AAAAYEEEEEEEEEEEE!"

Manny's first shot was at the man with the rifle. The next at the bandit with the pistol. Then one into Loco *point-blank.* Then two more at the fourth man, who was holding an unknown object. Then his five-shot revolver was empty.

Eddie Cervantes was out and shooting and Manny was screaming, *"Barf barf barf barf!"*

Renee Camacho scrambled out the north end of the pipe, firing the shotgun at a running figure, and Carlos Chacon heard KAPLOOM KAPLOOM! and leaped up in time to see a man on the Mexican side scream and tumble down a hill into a gully.

Tony Puente couldn't get out of the goddamn pipe because Renee Camacho was frozen there blocking his exit, still firing the shotgun.

Tony could hear muffled pistol shots and hear Eddie Cervantes screaming, "Get cover! Get cover!"

Then Renee Camacho dropped his shotgun and snapped off five pistol shots: BOP BOP BOP BOP BOP! and someone kept screaming, "AAAAAYYYEEEEEEEEEEEE!"

Two things happened later that night. One, a man staggered into a Tijuana hospital with his legs torn apart by #4 buckshot, which consisted of 27 pellets of .25-caliber shot. He was arrested by *judiciales.* Second, a man shot through the chest joined a party uninvited in a little house near the Mexican border. He dampened the festive spirit by crashing through the patio, his chest covered with blood, scaring the hell out of the partygoers, only to stumble out again, never to be found.

Eddie Cervantes had fired one round and raced after a bandit for half a block into Mexico, firing a last round at the fleeing robber before turning and running like hell back toward the border.

Renee was yelling, "Where's Manny? Where's Manny?" and someone was hollering at him over the radio and Carlos was standing by the fence on the north side screaming, "Where's Lopez?"

Then they heard Manny yell, "I got Loco! Gimme some *help*!" Manny Lopez and El Loco were at the bottom of the gully beating the living shit out of each other.

Then PLOOM PLOOM PLOOM PLOOM!

Four shots were suddenly fired at the Barfers from the darkness, wanging off the border fence and sending them flying in all directions. Loco fought and resisted all the way back down the fence line to the nearest hole, even though badly wounded, even as Manny pistol-whipped him and dragged him through. Loco was feeling the shock of *real* pain by now and was screaming curses.

Tony Puente heard a BOP! and WANG! as another small-caliber slug ricocheted, and overhead the Border Patrol helicopter was roaring in.

Then Carlos Chacon heard four *more* rounds fired in

their direction from the darkness south of the border.

When all the pandemonium had subsided a bit and Loco was safely back on the U.S. side and the cover team and junior varsity were rushing into the canyon, they all gathered around the wounded bandit, who was flat on his back feeling the full impact of Manny's bullet, which had broken his thigh and lodged in his hip. Someone shone a flashlight in Loco's face and Manny jerked off the ski mask for them all to take a look.

He was dirty and bearded and hairy. He cried out in agony every few seconds. And if it had been a western movie, the victorious Gunslinger might at this point have expressed a little compassion for a fallen adversary. But Manny Lopez wasn't much for westerns except maybe *The Searchers,* where John Wayne *scalped* his fallen foe.

Manny Lopez, with all the compassion of a Mafia car-bomber, knelt over the writhing bandit, saying things like: "I hope you die of gangrene. I hope it broke bones. I hope it hurts like cancer."

A few interesting things occurred after they got Loco to the hospital. First, they found out why he always wore a mask. His name was Sanchez and he was a bit shy about being recognized because he was an escapee from the California state prison at Lompoc. He didn't want any trouble with American lawmen looking for fugitives.

While Loco was at the hospital, he made a statement to one of the Barfers which everyone thought was unintentionally hilarious. Loco said, "Just because you got me, don't think it's going to stop. Tell Lopez he can't stop it."

The Barfers got to release quite a bit of stress and tension when they heard about *that* one. It was the funniest thing they'd heard lately.

Someone said, "Did you tell the dumb bastard that Manny Lopez doesn't give a shit if they murder every pollo from here to Yucatan? Did you tell the dumb bastard that

Manny's already on the phone with a press release? Did you tell him Manny *never* wants it to end?"

A thing they discovered then was that they had been mistaken when they thought that bandits smelled like garbage. It became clear in the substation when Manny was pointing at the ulcerous needle marks and pustules on the arms of a bandit junkie brought in by the junior varsity. This bandit was horrible to look at, with a low feral forehead and mucus-clogged cavernous nostrils, with mossy scattered teeth and rotting white gum tissue. He had to cough balls of rusty phlegm every few minutes and they could look at the yellow fingernails and drum-tight jaundiced flesh and imagine fly's eggs. He smelled *deathly.*

Then Manny accidentally poked one of the flaming needle abscesses and the abscess popped and pus shot all over him. The smell of putrefied gas and decay filled the room. *That's* what bandits smelled like. In that so much of the tissue of their bodies was infected and abscessed, they smelled of putrefaction. Flesh dying or dead.

So now there was another little nightmarish notion. As Manny Lopez led them toward the next headline, they could do a little mind fucking with this brand-new idea: Bandits even *smelled* like death. Bandits smelled like *murder.*

And there was something else to contend with, something crazy and confusing that night. Manny Lopez was sitting there chatty and cheerful, getting ready for the reporters. Eddie Cervantes, Tony Puente and Renee Camacho were bumping into things, trying to sort out all *kinds* of emotions, having just shot people and nearly been shot after having witnessed the incredible horrifying moment when Manny vanished. In short, they were responding to enormous stress in a normal fashion. But Manny Lopez looked as though he'd just been to a good football game and his team had kicked a field goal, at the gun.

His response to all of this wasn't human, they said. And worse than that, they were starting to believe that somehow the bastard was invulnerable. They began to get nightmarish ideas that they were all going to be murdered and there he'd be, chatty and cheerful, like he'd got the date with the homecoming queen.

It was pretty hard for some of them to admit it, given the demands of Mexican *machismo,* but despite claims to the contrary it was latent in every utterance concerning Manny Lopez from that night on. They didn't know why for sure, but they came to *fear* him. Not the way they feared murder, but *real* fear nonetheless.

There was yet another mind bender on the night Manny vanished, something to fry your brain over. The way it looked down there in the Mexican gully. Loco and Manny, the two of them. The same height and weight, born just *days* of each other. Separated in life by an imaginary line. Sanchez and Lopez. Under a Mexican sky: thrashing, moaning, cursing each other in the same language. Looking like twins in the darkness, twin silhouettes. Forcing you to think, what if Sanchez had been born north and Lopez south of a shadowy line. Would it *still* have ended like this? Was a choice made somewhere? Or was it all decreed by the Drawer of Imaginary Lines?

CHAPTER · 14

EXORCISM

ANXIETY DREAMS ARE RAMPANT AMONG POLICE OFFICERS. In the dreams the cop is shooting at a gunman who refuses to die or fall or even drop his gun. The cop keeps firing but the bullets have no effect. However, very few cops have the dream come to life.

On the night of Loco's capture, Renee Camacho had fired the shotgun twice at a bandit who was aiming a gun at him. The bandit dropped but got up and pointed it again. Renee fired a third time, and then fired a fourth when the man turned and ran.

It was disturbing, but not as disturbing as what Renee Camacho felt when he heard that the man he shot was alive in a Tijuana hospital. He felt profound *disappointment.* Then fear for himself for feeling such disappointment.

"What's happening to me?" he asked his father, friend and confidant, Herbert Camacho.

"Renee, I know you think it's not right for a policeman to have such feelings," his father said as they shared a beer in his little barbershop at Thirteenth and Market Streets.

"I've never *been* in a situation like this, Dad!" Renee Camacho's tenor voice quivered even as he recounted the moment.

"You're doing a very different kind of police work, *mi hijo,*" the barber told Renee, his only child except for an orphaned nephew the Camachos had raised as their own.

"But I was *sorry* he lived!" Renee said. "Next thing you know, I'll *kill* a bandit who's only reaching to scratch an itch!"

Herbert Camacho, who was perhaps already aware of a cancer which would kill him, said, "If these feelings make you shoot too soon, I'd rather have it that way. I'd rather have you kill someone and be wrong than hesitate and *be* killed."

Distilled to cop language: *Better to be tried by twelve than carried by six.*

Renee had always been a lad quick to smile and be happy, but throughout the many troubled conversations he had with his father, there was seldom mentioned the alternative. The alternative was so simple and so complicated that not a Barfer could manage it.

The alternative was to walk up to Manny Lopez and say, "I quit. I've had enough. I want to go back to uniformed patrol." Period.

It was sacrilege, a breach of the *machismo* code of both cops and Mexicans, and in this way they were very close to being *real* Mexicans.

But there was someone who might have been thinking of it before any of them, that is, thinking of a way to deal with it before it happened. Manny Lopez began badmouthing the young cop who had left the squad after the ninety-day moratorium, which now seemed a generation ago. He said that cop was a quitter. He told them that anyone who quit BARF would quit anything, any challenge for the rest of his life. He told them how they'd hate themselves and never be worth a damn if they quit.

There was not as yet much talk among themselves about fear. Only about those fears that it was possible to discuss, those that didn't violate the code. For instance, Eddie Cervantes often talked about the rampant disease among bandits: hepatitis, venereal disease, tuberculosis, the overwhelming smell of decaying flesh and what it implied.

"I'm scared," he would say. But then would quickly add: "I mean, I'm scared to go home and kiss my kids."

Other little things were happening. When they'd go to the range to practice with the shotgun, Barfers who had previously been good shots began to experience difficulties with accuracy and loading. They would line up in a semicircle and fire on multiple targets with shotguns and revolvers, and the lead shavings would jump from the cylinders right into the next shooter's face and the gunpowder would surge into the nostrils as Manny Lopez yelled target numbers to shoot.

Robbie Hurt, who was right-handed, had a dominant left eye and they belatedly discovered that he could hardly shoot a shotgun at all, which wasn't comforting. Ernie Salgado, who could, kept screwing up, and Manny Lopez started yelling at him. Renee Camacho by this time could hardly move, he had so many bullets stashed all over his goddamn body. He was nearly as much of a walking armory as Joe Castillo. And Joe had a dark secret he was not sharing with any human being. It was the same secret that Renee Camacho and Ernie Salgado and Eddie Cervantes and Fred Gil were also keeping to themselves. The secret was that they couldn't shake a feeling of doom. Each one had it and thought he was the only one who did.

They needed a murder hospice: *We're here to prepare you for a man who will appear in the darkness like a ghost. He will smell like death. . . .*

Renee Camacho by now was always looking at his wife's pregnant stomach and wondering what their child would look like. He'd break into a sweat when a hot shiver swept over him. Then things started to happen: the sky *did* look bluer. Grass *did* look greener!

Joe Castillo kept having a similar feeling. I want to enjoy life. I want to be *alive.* And because he wanted it so badly, he began drinking and carousing all the more and treating himself more shabbily. "I walked around not giving a *shit,*" is how he put it.

They all started to have that feeling. I don't give a damn. Who cares? What's any of it worth? They *all* began feeling like a minority within a minority within a minority.

They didn't want any part of ordinary police chores. When they were assigned to a policing detail for a Mexican holiday, they resented it. "Why us? Why do *we* have to do it?"

Manny Lopez said, "Because you're Mexicans, you dumb fuckers!"

They felt so isolated, so elite *(We who are about to die . . .)* that they isolated themselves and *acted* elite. Whether or not the patrol cops resented the way they looked, dressed, behaved, their *perception* was that they were objects of resentment and jealousy. The homicide detectives clearly resented them, since homicide detectives quite understandably didn't care to spend their nights in those hills because these vigilantes were shooting the canyons to pieces. Almost a law unto themselves, they remained the darlings and pets of the media and politicians—The Last of The Gunslingers.

Once Fred Gil tried to make a stab at the old hardball, merciless kind of ribbing they used to do when BARF was new, when they were *young,* about a century ago. He found a pair of glasses and plastic teeth left over from a Halloween costume and he made himself up like Charlie Chan but, according to Manny Lopez, looked more like a Filipino bookmaker, so Manny gave a yell to Carlos Chacon, who was married to a Filipino girl.

Manny said, "Hey, Carlos, your brother-in-law's here!"

And sure enough Carlos bought it, and came down the hall wondering what the hell his brother-in-law was . . .

Then Carlos was looking at old Fred Gil in buckteeth and glasses with his eyes pulled back with Scotch tape, and Carlos bared his wolfish incisors, and his Rasputin eyes popped and he screamed, "FUCK YOU, GIL!"

And poor old Fred Gil and all the others began to figure out that they didn't even know themselves anymore, and much of the fun and fellowship was gone forever.

They started to come to work looking like something that fell off a boxcar, or was pushed off by a railroad bull. They'd work in their yards or wash their cars or haul fertilizer or whatever, and they'd come to work. Rank. Unshaven. Eddie Cervantes, the gung-ho Marine reservist, let his hair grow way past the Halls of Montezuma and even stopped going to reserve meetings.

They'd tell their wives and friends, and fellow cops who worked patrol and detectives, that they *had* to dress and look and smell like that. That out in the canyons they had to *be* aliens. That their performances might make the difference in whether they lived or died. Then they'd look at some ex-partner who had to wear a police uniform every day and follow rules of conduct suitable to the department and the city and the state and the U.S.A., and they'd say, "Aw, fuck it! How would *you* know?" The implication being that some cop brother who didn't work BARF was, in the final analysis, the same as a lizard-shit civilian.

All of their paranoia, a hundred times more potent than ordinary police paranoia, was realized when Joe Vasquez went uptown to central headquarters on some errand for Manny Lopez, and was challenged by a startled uniformed cop who took one look at the scruffy, rank, raggedy-ass canyon crawler with a bulge under his shirt and drew down on him, making Big Ugly grab some air and yell, "Hold it hold it hold it! I'm a *cop,* goddamnit!"

Did it prove to them that Big Ugly and the rest of them

had terrific wardrobes? Alas, it only convinced them they had *nothing* in common with their former peer group, and the steel ratchets tightened around this beleaguered little group and they turned inward.

And then in would come Manny Lopez, fresh from a little speech to some students at San Diego State, and his thinning hair would be blow-dried and styled and he'd be still all excited, with his gold religious medal gleaming and his pinky ring sparkling and his disco duds immaculate. And he'd smell of Jade East or Brut or something, and start telling them about this little twenty-three-year-old gerbil that kept *throwing* her goddamn phone number at him, asking him if Gunslingers wear bikini briefs, because she was doing this survey.

And Manny, with a Santa Fe Corona Grande stuffed in his teeth, would be giving them his impish grin, and then someone, usually Eddie Cervantes, would say, "How ya gonna walk tonight?"

And Manny would say, "Whaddaya mean?"

And Eddie Cervantes would look at Manny with those sad, down-turned eyes and say, "Well, we *might* get a few bandits to hit on us. But not unless you put on a wig."

"A wig? Whaddaya *talking* about?"

"Well, you ain't gonna pass for an alien smelling like an uptown whore, but maybe with a wig they might try to *rape* you."

And then Ernie Salgado, who by now also despised Manny Lopez, might say, "Hey, Manny, when do *we* get to go to a luncheon?"

Manny found himself more and more on the defensive, so he'd say, "I told you a million times, come with me *anytime*! Remind me when ya wanna go. Remind me next time, fuckers!"

Manny Lopez was nobody's fool. He was aware of the growing envy and resentment of him from the outside *and* within his own squad. He discussed it with superiors like

Dick Snider, who by now was under strict orders to remain an ordinary uniformed watch commander and leave this BARF business to Manny.

Manny Lopez had lots of opinions about Mexican-American cops, and when he expressed them, it was like one of his briefings. He pointed his finger like a gun: "There are minority groups and there are minority groups," Manny Lopez reasoned. "The black cops speak as one. They intimidate. Not the Mexicans. We're like fucking Arabs, always squabbling among ourselves. Mexicans're aggressive policemen, very eager to please the whites, but Mexicans aren't raised to cherish academic things, so they don't tend to do well on written civil service exams. And since they're not good communicators, they don't do well on oral exams either. They become frustrated. They can accept a white guy making sergeant, or even a black guy. Just being a cop is stressful enough, but being a Mexican cop with all these problems? And if a Mexican cop like me just happens to be a good public speaker? They'll *never* forgive you! And here I was the head a the whole goddamn police association! Mexicans're the most jealous motherfuckers alive and *that's* what I had to contend with in my own squad. I got so I hated to come to work, not because a bandits, but because of all the nasty looks and bitching about my publicity. I *tried* to give them credit. I didn't *write* the fucking stories!"

One day Manny Lopez, while off duty, happened upon a traffic accident and pulled a woman from a flaming car. He ended up in the newspapers once again. He came to work like Roberto Duran to a prizefight. He roared in and threw the newspaper on the table, saying, "Okay, fuckers, who wants to be first to start bitching about me stealing the glory WHEN I'M ALONE IN MY OWN GODDAMN NEIGHBORHOOD IN MY OWN GODDAMN CAR ON MY OWN GODDAMN TIME?"

It all started reminding people of the movie *The Treasure of the Sierra Madre,* where the gold prospectors start out as bosom buddies but pretty soon they're watching each other like rattlesnakes. And it even got to that.

Carlos Chacon took to walking *behind* Joe Castillo, always keeping someone between them when they were out in the canyons at night. Joe had made *too* many comments about Carlos having shot him, and about how Carlos should be shot so *he* might learn what it feels like. And after he had a few drinks he'd say it *to* Carlos, and he wasn't joking.

It had finally come down to the last reel of *The Treasure of the Sierra Madre.* They were starting to fear each other more than the bandits.

There wasn't a wife who didn't want her husband to quit. There wasn't a marriage not suffering under the strain of it. But most of the Barfers were responding true to the code of *machismo;* they were toughing it out with the help of the greatest ally a macho young cop ever had, *booze.* Occasionally one of them would fall in love for a few weeks, or so they were convinced during this loony period of their lives.

And some of the camp followers who came looking for The Last of The Gunslingers were gems. There was one they called The Snake who was a reject groupie from another police department. She came to San Diego looking for greener pastures and a new bunch of cops. She was about thirty years old and wore cat's-eye glasses twenty years after everyone but the actors on *Saturday Night Live.* The glasses kept sliding off her nose so she was always looking at you over the top of them, but she had a great body. She lurked in those bars that cashed payroll checks for cops. When she first started dating San Diego policemen, she had only two tattoos: one was a bunch of roses on her ass and the other was her kid's name on her belly. Then she fell for a motor cop and had a San Diego Police Department badge tattooed on the tender flesh of her upper thigh.

The first Barfer to go home with The Snake was dubbed The Reptile Curator by the others. He found the motor cop's uniforms hanging in her bedroom and it made him nervous. The motor cop was a supervisor. The motor cop wore *very* big uniforms *(We who are about to die . . .).*

Just when the Barfers started to think that The Snake had no redeeming qualities, they learned of some charitable work she did. It seemed that she worked in a county home for the elderly, and she would let the codgers "touch" her, because it made them feel younger, she said. In fact, she was discovered jerking off the old coots, but nobody complained. It beat the hell out of Geritol any day.

There were also Barf groupies from solid professional backgrounds. There were nurses who worked at free clinics near the border: white, middle-class, educated. The Barfers made themselves especially larger than life with the nurses. And there were schoolteachers, also white and middle-class, just out of graduate school and looking like commencement night at Brigham Young. All clean-cut and eager.

"They wanted to teach in the poverty areas," a Barfer said, "so they came to San Ysidro to save the little Mexicans. I never knew there were people that naïve about life." And then he added: "Except *us.*"

Perhaps the strangest of the groupies was a new one introduced to them by Fat Mindy. She'd been out of circulation for a while because she'd fallen in love with a border patrolman. He was in love with her, too. He wanted to leave his wife for her, but it all turned sour. He tried to OD on pills a couple of times which she thought showed he wasn't serious, because if they're serious, cops always shoot themselves, don't they? The Border Patrol finally had to transfer him to El Paso because the guy got really goofy over her.

She fell out of love then and immediately into love with Ken Kelly. She liked macho guys and the King was muscular and chewed cigars a lot. There was always a bit of tobacco leaf clinging to his orange-rind walrus moustache. But it was probably his Jack Nicholson impression that got to her, with him pulling his scraggly blond hair back on the sides of his head and looking all cobra-eyed like the actor, except that Ken's eyes were blue. The new groupie couldn't resist him, and another groupie assured all of them that this girl was an all-time, world-class comer.

She'd come if you touched her with your toe, the fascinated Barfers were told. Or your knee. Or your goddamn elbow!

She looked like those aristocratic girls up in Northern Division, moist lips, moist eyes, orthodontic smiles, bodies pearly or buttercup in the sun. Girls with skis strapped to their BMWs. But she said she liked pot and ludes and uppers and none of the Barfers used anything but booze, so this made them nervous. Nevertheless, the King, who was frustrated by being forever a spear carrier, was ready for some *action.* For the "ultimate experience," as advertised by Fat Mindy.

"Sex, drugs, rock 'n roll!" Ken Kelly screamed, looking all demented. "Bee bob a doo bop, a bam bam boo!"

Ken Kelly got boiled on vodka for courage and showed up at Fat Mindy's apartment as ordered, and sure enough the new girl was waiting for him. Eating a peanut butter sandwich.

She was dressed like a Gainsborough portrait, or maybe Little Bo Peep, and when she said, "Have some peanut butter?" it sounded like the movie he saw on television where Gregory Peck asks Ingrid Bergman if she wants ham or liverwurst and when she answers it sounds like a goddamn symphony. *Liverwurst!* Peanut butter!

And then as he was reclining on the sofa thinking he may have overdone it with the booze, she blindsided him with: "Do you believe in God?"

"Sure," Ken Kelly shrugged. "I'm a Lutheran. Why?"

And suddenly she began to tremble and edge away. She got slanty-eyed and *cold.* She was turning to ice before his eyes. This very same number who could reportedly get off by touching your fucking elbow!

And she said, "I worship the devil."

"I like to raise a little hell myself," Ken Kelly giggled.

"No, I mean it," she informed him, licking her peanut butter with the darting tongue of a *serpent.* "I adore the Prince of Darkness."

Now Ken Kelly had his turn to squirm a bit and he tried to think of something to change the subject, because this kind of woofing wasn't as funny as she probably thought it was. His walrus moustache was twitching like mad and he knew it.

Then she swallowed a capsule, and since drugs could get him fired from the police department, he wasn't thrilled about that either. Then she said, "I belong to this . . . society. We like to fuck."

"Now you're talking!" Ken Kelly cried. "Most a my friends also like . . ."

"On altars. In real churches if possible. Or when necessary we can re-create an altar."

Ken Kelly suddenly started going into his Jack Nicholson impression without even trying, because he also does it when he's *scared.* He started raking his limp blond hair back over the top of his ears, the moustache flapping like crazy.

"Do you do acid?" she asked. "Or maybe peyote?"

"No, I drink beer mostly," Ken Kelly said, and his blue eyes darted toward an ominous closed door. He wondered if there was a guy behind it dressed in an iron bra and leather mask! He was getting very sorry he wasn't wearing a gun.

"You'd have to get used to *some* of it, King," she said. "Especially the killing part."

"The killing part," he said. "*What* killing part?"

"Dogs. We kill dogs and drink their blood while it's hot and fresh. Does this shock you?"

"Oh, *hell* no!" Ken Kelly cried. "This is probably just the tame stuff, right? Shit, I'm not shocked!" And then he started looking up at the ceiling and his blue eyes got so bughouse she said, "What're you looking for?"

And he answered, "Oh, nothing. I'm not looking for anything. JUST A FUCKING LIGHTNING BOLT IS ALL!"

And that was it. He was as flaccid as fetuccini. World-class comer or not, *this* romance was over before it began. The Barfers just couldn't be as devil-may-care as people wanted them to be.

Ken Kelly spent the remainder of the night driving around and thinking about what had become of his young life. Dragged through the courts like a criminal for assaulting a number one prick asshole. Worrying every moment about his mother's terminal cancer. Living with a good woman in a marriage gone sour. He felt lower, meaner, sorrier than alien turds. He probably *deserved* a blood-drinking puppy drowner. And then the frustration every night, sitting in the darkness with Robbie Hurt, both full of fear and tension like the others, but worse than the others, because they didn't *know* what's happening out there, and they didn't get the release by being *part* of it. They never knew anything. And then hearing gunshots in the night and running helter skelter, and no release for the adrenaline rush. *Never.*

"I felt like an unexploded bomb with a jiggly fuse," he said.

He got home at 9:00 A.M. His wife asked one question: "Where've you been?"

"We had a tough night," he said. "I drove to Tecate because I just couldn't come home and sleep. I finally got tired and had to pull over beside the road. I just woke up."

Joyce didn't bother to answer. She kicked him out on the spot, clothes and all. He draped the clothes on the back of his motorcycle. He looked like a ragman on two wheels.

He moved in with another cop who, they said, ran a home for wayward policemen and was always taking in strays. The other cop had been drummed out of the vice squad because they decided he wasn't macho enough to kick ass and take names. In fact, he was so "sensitive" that the rumormongers decided he might be a fruit, but Ken Kelly said he didn't care if the guy had his legs waxed and carried a designer gun. Being a pansy seemed pretty normal, given his experiences these days.

He had been married for ten years. Joyce was a Japanese-American girl he'd known since the seventh grade. He was in love with her and he loved his kids, so what was he doing with people who killed dogs and hated Lutherans? It was the first time Ken Kelly suspected he was losing his mind, and that maybe this Barf job didn't cause it but it certainly wasn't making it any better.

He only went home after Manny Lopez had a telephone conversation with Joyce. Manny Lopez wasn't much of a marriage counselor, but Ken Kelly was afraid of him.

Manny Lopez said, "Listen, fucker, you can screw around all you want, but you gotta go *home*! Understand? Go *home*!"

So Ken Kelly went home. Things didn't get better for a long time. They couldn't, not while he was out there in those canyons at night with at *least* a middleweight head problem.

If any of the Barfers had something hot going, Manny would usually oblige. "You owe me, fucker," he'd say when giving the night off and covering if a wife called. "You owe me!"

They'd leave him a bottle of Chivas Regal or a handful of Santa Fe Corona Grandes by way of thanks.

So they had them: schoolteachers, nurses, waitresses, blood drinkers, gerontological dummy floggers. They had them *all*. And the marriages suffered accordingly. Most of the boys staggered home at dawn, slept all day, got up, failed to shave or shower and went back to the canyons. And the next night the cycle was repeated.

But while a few of the Barfers had to "stretch their

legs," as they called it when they got kicked out of the house by mama, some of the others stuck it out and reaped the whirlwind.

Tony Puente was a sensitive fellow, in tune with other people's feelings but quiet enough to keep his to himself. Because he was the oldest, next to Fred Gil, they sometimes called him Pops and took a few of their problems to him. Nobody took problems to Manny because they figured that in the first place he wasn't interested in personal problems, and in the second place he couldn't care *less*.

Tony Puente had his own big problem over and above all the other ordinary ones, such as feeling anxious about murder. He had the most formidable rival for his wife's devotion that any man ever had—God. She read the Bible no less than two hours a night, and that was in addition to services and meetings, and dispensing religious tracts, and other missionary duties in the neighborhoods of San Diego.

When their arguments would rage, she had an irrefutable position. "Why should *you* complain? All you do is go to work, come home drunk, sleep all day and go to work again."

Joe Castillo said, "She was always real nice to us when we carried Tony home drunk. She fed us baloney and mustard sandwiches. Just like they make at the jail."

That would be all she would ever remember about the BARF experiment, Tony coming home drunk.

Dene Puente had immersed herself in a religion that espoused the suppression of self and worldly acquisitiveness. It made Tony goofy because as a Mexican he'd spent his life trying to better himself and *acquire* all the material things his family needed or wanted. Yet he never thought he should have married another Mexican. It was clear to everyone who knew him that he was utterly in love with the woman he married when she was sixteen.

The BARF job became obsessive, even after the

Puentes started having troubles with an adolescent son. It was easy to make mistakes with the boy when the only reality seemed to be out there in the canyons at night.

And then Tony would come home totally boiled, and stinking of the canyons and aliens and stale booze, his brain still sizzling, overflowing with needs of every kind. And naturally she'd be asleep and he'd start thinking.

He'd lie there and want to shoot them down like bandits in the canyons, her fellow religionists. Next Christmas he was going to buy a tree so big they'd have to bring it in on a sixteen-wheeler. He was going to have a crane set it up in the front yard and he was going to say "There!" to every goddamned deacon or elder or minister or priest or whatever they called them in her church. "THAT'S WHAT I THINK ABOUT A RELIGION THAT DOESN'T LIKE CHRISTMAS TREES!"

But then Tony Puente would have to get himself quieted down because he tended to want to weep in frustration over this. Beneath his quiet ways he was a very emotional man. And what could he offer her for depriving her and his kids of a husband and father while he chased a fascination in the canyons at night?

And it was then that a very subtle and fearful thing started happening inside his own heart. He never admitted it to anyone, especially not his wife, but he was, despite every instinct and wish, starting to, well, *admire* what she was doing. He had lost his own belief in priests and church and there was an emptiness. She seemed fulfilled and he was scared to admit he *envied* that part of it. Faith was what he was lacking at this time of life. Faith in something. She had a ton of it.

But how could he admire what he also despised? And how could he anxiously want to get out in the canyons at night and at the same time hate it? It was too much to figure out. But he was an intelligent fellow, and unconsciously they remained in his head, these questions.

Then one night, with a skinful of hooch, he decided to

have it out once and for all. He was going to meet his rival head-on. They had a terrible row. He fogged his glasses with all the screaming and it ended with her in the living room crying her eyes out.

Tony Puente was going to show her. He was going to show the whole world. He was going to *destroy.* He gathered up every religious tract and book and Bible she owned. He had armfuls of the stuff. If this was devil's work, so be it!

Tony took all the religious literature to the kitchen and turned on every burner on the gas range. Moments like this demanded grand gestures. He threw a few pamphlets on the fire, intending to burn them one piece at a time, defying her wimpy, lizard-shit God to *do* something about it.

And as Tony was staggering around the living room realizing he'd had more booze than he thought, and Dene was crying so hard she could hardly breathe, he happened to turn around. The goddamn kitchen was an inferno!

Only the proximity of the sink saved the house. But after he finished throwing pots of water on the fire, he wasn't through. He grabbed armloads of her clothes. He threw them out the back door. Then he threw *her* out the back door and locked it.

He staggered into the bedroom and fell into bed. When he woke up with a hellacious hangover and a luau in his liver, he figured to find her in bed next to him. He was alone. He went into the living room expecting to find her asleep on the sofa. She wasn't.

He panicked. He had all the morbid fantasies that policemen have when they're worrying about loved ones. He started thinking of her stumbling down the street at night and being picked up by a fiend, and looking like corpses he'd seen. The car! Maybe she was safe in a motel! He ran to the garage and found the car. She was asleep in the back seat.

He was beaten. He spent the next three hours telling her how relieved he was and how sorry he was and what a total son of a bitch he was and all the other things that someone with an overly developed sense of personal responsibility and guilt says at a time like that. He carried all her clothes inside. He wanted to wash them and iron them. He felt like washing and ironing his goddamn tongue.

When he got to the substation that night, this private taciturn fellow *had* to spill his guts. If he didn't tell somebody, he might blow like a land mine. He told *everybody* about it, how he nearly burned the house down.

The other Barfers loved it because it took their minds off their own domestic problems. Ken Kelly said it was fantastic, just like the big scene in *The Exorcist* but in reverse! It made Ken especially glad that he'd boogied on the devil diddler. "It just goes to show," he said, "you can't dick around with God."

For Tony Puente, so consumed by religious turmoil, his *own* as well as his wife's, the canyon walks filled a void. His only reality, he said. Something like a ritual need.

The BARF experiment had shifted into another gear. It was going somewhere and no one knew where and no one could stop it, or so it seemed to the Barfers. Only *ten days* after the capture of Loco, there occurred another incident which involved not just the Barf squad but the highest level of law-enforcement officers on *both* sides of the border.

It would not be fully adjudicated by the civil court of San Diego for years to come. Of all the BARF experiences, this one would be the most controversial and bitter and divisive.

CHAPTER · 15

THE CELLAR

FOR THE LAWMEN SOUTH OF THE IMAGINARY LINE, *LA mordida* was a fact of life. One relied on *mordida* to feed a family, and it was ever thus, since the white men started shaking down the Aztecs like common thugs.

La ley de fuga was also a fact of life south of the imaginary line. If someone were to flee from law officers, regardless of the crime, he ran a very real risk of being shot. Everyone knew the rules of the game which hadn't changed for centuries.

The Barfers got reports in the month of July concerning both facts of life. On one of the reports the Barfers were told by some pollos that they had been picked up by a team of Tijuana policemen who caught them crossing into the U.S. in the vicinity of Colonia Libertad, and that they were given a little tour around Tijuana in a patrol car until the officers made the point that they might be willing to forgo a visit to their *comandante* if the pollos would make it worthwhile.

The pollos coughed up all they had, $40 U.S., and the

policemen drove them back to the international fence and bade them a hearty farewell.

The incident involving *la ley de fuga* affected them directly. It was nearly 11:00 P.M. when the varsity, joined by Joe Castillo, was walking just south of Monument Road. Ernie Salgado, who was providing cover that night, heard a gunshot from the vicinity of the drainage pipe and radioed the walking team to hop on over and check it out.

When Manny and the others arrived, they saw a man holding a group of pollos at gunpoint. The man had a partner and that partner shined a flashlight beam on the approaching Barfers and ordered them to cross into Mexico at once. He also stated loud and clear that he was an immigration officer.

The Barfers did not identify themselves to the Mexican officer. They took cover and pulled their guns and watched. The two men, plainclothes immigration officers, took their catch of fifteen aliens back into Mexico. When the Barfers were leaving the vicinity of the drainage pipe they happened on a man and woman hiding in a nest of mesquite. The couple, after the Barfers identified themselves as San Diego policemen, told them that when they fled from the immigration officers who had just arrested their companions, they were fired on.

Indignation in the BARF report signed by Manny Lopez concerned the fact that the Mexican immigration cops were doing their thing on U.S. soil. The report said:

> It is felt that an extremely dangerous situation was created by the actions of the plainclothes immigration officers in that they entered the U.S. while armed with handguns and indiscriminately fired their weapons. The illegal actions of these Mexican immigration officers must be brought to the attention of their superiors in order to avoid an international confrontation and to prevent the needless

shooting of an unarmed illegal alien in the United States.

If the frontal lobes of the human brain anticipate events, and if in the right hemisphere we find sensitivity and in the left we find critical and analytical processes, Manny Lopez had one task before him if the BARF experiment was going to satisfy his conscious and unconscious needs: he had to purée their frontal lobes and right and left hemispheres into something like Reddi Wip. Manny Lopez had to dive on down to the area of the brain where *aggression* lives, where one finds the impulse to follow leaders blindly. This might be called the cellar of the brain. They were, during these fearsome times, *living* in Manny's cellar.

Forty-year-old Chuey Hernandez was a jolly sort of fellow. His gold incisor gleamed when he smiled, as much a status symbol in Mexico as a dental prosthetic. There wasn't always a lot to smile about in that he had a whole bunch of people to support, one child of his own and seven belonging to his wife from her former marriage, as well as his aging mother.

He had served in the Mexican Army before being accepted by the Tijuana Municipal Police, and most of his adult life had been spent wearing a uniform. He had the equivalent of a grade school education.

About the best thing that had happened to Chuey in a while was that President Lopez Portillo was coming to Tijuana for a visit and there would be a big ceremony at La Playa. Chuey Hernandez played cornet in the police band. He'd been playing the cornet for twenty-five years. He had loved *la banda de guerra,* the drum and bugle corps, all his life.

This was quite an honor for Chuey Hernandez and he

was up for it that afternoon of July 16 when he came on duty. First, he got the old horn shined by a guy with a polishing wheel. Then he started looking at his equipment. The uniform was brand-new, but Chuey Hernandez looked sadly at his hat.

The hat was all beat-up and crushed, like in old Army Air Corps movies. Chuey Hernandez had a talk with another cop who was much slimmer but had the same head size. Pedro Espindola told Chuey Hernandez that he had a brand-new hat at home, and since he wore a helmet on duty, he offered to sell it. A tiny moment in life Pedro Espindola would come to regret as long as he lived.

Pedro Espindola left his patrol car at the police station and they both hopped into Chuey Hernandez' patrol car and headed off to the Espindola home in Zona Norte while Chuey Hernandez worried about his upper lip. He believed that the upper lip of a cornet player will fall asleep without daily practice. He worried that his upper lip might decide to fall asleep when he was playing for the President of Mexico.

Hard wind. Flitting shadow and iron sunlight. Blood-beaked birds of prey were driven down by hard wind. The omnipresent summer smoke at the borderline vanished. The varsity and junior varsity were mingled that evening, broken into two groups operating close enough to be seen by each other even after sunset. Manny Lopez, Tony Puente, Joe Vasquez and Joe Castillo were on one walking team. Ernie Salgado, Renee Camacho and Carlos Chacon were on the other. Manny's team was working by the heaps of rock and bottles and trash and debris where the drainage pipe empties north during the wet season. There was plenty of cover there behind mounds of earth and concrete, where they could watch the second team should some bandits cross from Mexican soil to rob them. The second team, the real decoy in this operation, was hanging around right beside the fence talking to some pollos who were getting ready to cross after dark.

It was a pretty relaxed affair and the pollos were, like most, friendly and generous. They were getting up their courage with some tequila and they offered a drink to the Barfers, who politely declined, conjuring images of Mexican contagion.

The men on the south side of the fence asked the Barfers curiously why they continued waiting even after darkness fell.

"*La migra*'s pretty heavy tonight," Carlos Chacon told them, and a pollo said, "Well, maybe *we* better wait for a while, too."

So they just stood by the cyclone fence and drank tequila and chatted.

At 9:50 P.M. Ernie Salgado saw a car coming down the highway. The car slowed and Ernie began watching it.

It had gotten dark suddenly. Chuey Hernandez saw some men loitering by the border fence. He stopped his patrol car and he and Pedro Espindola decided to have a look.

Chuey Hernandez turned on the red and blue siren lights and stepped out of the car, saying, "What are you doing there? Get over to the patrol car!"

Pollos almost always did what they were told and so did this pair. Chuey Hernandez took their bottle of tequila and broke it on the ground by the roadside.

With the two drinkers in the back seat, Chuey Hernandez was about to turn off the blue and red siren lights and had actually started the car forward when Pedro Espindola said, "Hold it. I see people in the gully."

Chuey Hernandez moved the car forward about twenty-five meters—it would later say in an official report. It was parked almost directly over the big drainage pipe where the cyclone fence is rolled and torn and stretched and rendered useless by the people of the night. The cyclone fence abruptly terminates at a point where tourists won't notice. It is a fence going nowhere.

Young Joe Castillo was crouched beside his mentor and idol, Manny Lopez. They were behind chunks of concrete which had been washed away by winter rains and replaced again and again. It was like a military bunker behind all that. Joe Castillo was whispering to his sergeant while Chuey Hernandez was arresting the drinkers.

Joe Castillo later said, "We saw the Mexican cops shaking these guys down. We figured it for an extortion."

Regardless of whether or not it was an arrest for public drinking or drunkeness, "extortion" was taking place on the south side of the fence, in the Republic of Mexico. And these Mexican cops were possibly the ones reported to be robbing and extorting pollos, sometimes on American soil. And if they weren't, they'd do it if they had the chance because all Mexican cops were crooks. To the last man. Such was the state of mind of the Barfers.

Chuey Hernandez held the flashlight in his left hand, keeping his gun hand free, and walked toward the fence shining his light down into the gully. He remembered seeing an old dead tree uprooted by floods and reaching toward the sky, roots-first, like huge arthritic hands clawing heavenward. Then he saw the figures down behind the uprooted trees and broken concrete. The chunks of concrete were pale as gravestones in the moonlight. Chuey Hernandez drew his revolver and stepped closer to the fence.

He yelled at the two figures. He said, "What are you doing over there? Get back here!"

Manny Lopez yelled back: "Give us a break, chief! We already made it! Leave us alone!"

The die was cast. It was preordained from that moment. Every step in the little border drama was inevitable.

Chuey Hernandez walked right down to the fence and

caught the two figures in his beam. They dodged his light. They ducked down. He would always remember the one wearing a bandanna around his head—a *cholo* bandanna, Chuey Hernandez called it.

Chuey Hernandez had never seen pollos behave like this. They could have easily run away in the darkness, but they didn't. Guides would not hang around the fence like that. In the experience of Chuey Hernandez, the only ones who would hang around the fence were smugglers of aliens, guns, or narcotics. Or perhaps they were alien robbers. Chuey Hernandez advanced toward the fence pointing his gun at the man in the Levi jacket with the *cholo* bandanna around his head.

It was then that Renee Camacho heard Chuey Hernandez yell, "Get back over here, you spiders!"

And then Manny Lopez, wearing a bandanna around his mosquito-bitten skull, stood up, exposing his body, and made a controversial statement. He yelled, "Leave us alone! We don't have any money!"

But Chuey Hernandez had not asked for money. The statement said it all. It revealed exactly what was in the mind of Manny Lopez.

Chuey Hernandez was furious. He began cocking and uncocking his revolver. It was so eerily quiet that they could hear the sound distinctly, the oily metallic click as the hammer fell and was cocked, and fell and was cocked. Chuey Hernandez crouched under the fence and stepped toward the United States of America.

The Barfers began moving from concealment as Chuey Hernandez walked down into the gully, his flashlight illuminating Manny Lopez, who was now standing at a higher elevation, above the head of Chuey Hernandez, looking down on him.

Chuey Hernandez glanced back behind him as Pedro Espindola advanced cautiously toward the fence, a slender, bullet-shaped silhouette in his police helmet.

By now Chuey Hernandez was well aware of other figures in the darkness. He was facing Manny Lopez and Joe Castillo above him. Off behind him and to his right were Renee Camacho, Joe Vasquez, Tony Puente, Carlos Chacon and Ernie Salgado.

Chuey Hernandez was angry and he was *scared.* He said, "Come out of there, you bastards, or I'll *get* you out with a bullet!"

And he pointed the gun up at Manny Lopez, standing on the mound of concrete by the uprooted tree. Manny pushed Joe Castillo's head, whispering, "Stay down! Stay down!"

Chuey Hernandez' bravado was wavering at this point and he turned to Pedro Espindola and said, "They don't want to come!"

His partner said, "Let's *see* if they don't want to come!"

And he began scrambling down into the ravine with Chuey Hernandez, who yelled again: "You son of a bitch! You bastards! Come *out*!"

For the record, Chuey Hernandez was at this point probably standing six feet inside U.S. territory. Pedro Espindola was three feet closer to his homeland. For the record, Chuey Hernandez and Pedro Espindola were both in the state of California, U.S.A., exhibiting a deadly weapon in violation of Section 417 of the California penal code. For the benefit of lawyers, it was later noted that Section 467 of the California penal code was also violated. The Tijuana policemen were in possession of deadly weapons with intent to assault. Perhaps.

A criminal investigator for the district attorney's office of San Diego County would later make a notation in his narrative report. The notation made by the investigator was that at this moment, if Manny Lopez had identified himself as a police officer, the incident under investigation would probably never have occurred. The investigator of course did not understand about myth and legend and folklore.

Joe Castillo and Joe Vasquez separately said later: "When Manny braced the fat cop, it was *just* like *Gunsmoke.*"

And that was probably as well put as could be.

Manny Lopez stood looking down at the Tijuana cops with his badge down beside one leg and his gun down beside the other. The Tijuana cops at this moment could see neither. Then Manny Lopez leaped. It was a six-foot drop to the bottom of the gully. He slid slightly upon impact, staggering two or three steps in the direction of Chuey Hernandez, and they were suddenly at arm's length in the darkness.

A lot of things happened simultaneously, or nearly so. No one will ever know in precisely which order things happened, and really it's not relevant except to lawyers and judges and others who might deny that this was predestined and inevitable from the moment that Manny Lopez challenged the authority and *machismo* of the two Tijuana policemen.

For everyone else, the inevitable fact was this: Manny Lopez leaped from the embankment to the feet of the wary Mexican cops. He brought up two things, one in each hand: a badge and a gun. He yelled, "*¡Policía! ¡Policía!*"

As Pedro Espindola yelled, "He's got a *gun*!"

Chuey Hernandez reacted to the movement by jerking up *his* pistol, striking Manny Lopez in the chest with it.

Manny Lopez raised his left arm in defense and fell to his left.

Simultaneously *all* Barfers were aiming their already drawn guns. Some aimed *two* guns. One Barfer saw a badge in Manny's hand. The others didn't see it. Four saw Chuey Hernandez fire a shot. Three did not see who fired first.

All of this occurred in a fraction of a second.

There were fireballs, and one huge endless explosion in the ears of Chuey Hernandez. He felt no pain whatsoever. He was cranking off rounds at shadows. One second he was firing and the next he felt his feet go right out from under him.

Tony Puente fired two shots at Chuey Hernandez.

Ernie Salgado fired five shots at Pedro Espindola.

Joe Castillo, firing two guns, shot nine rounds at both Pedro Espindola and Chuey Hernandez.

Joe Vasquez fired one shotgun round in the direction of both Tijuana cops, and when the shotgun jammed he got off three revolver shots at Pedro Espindola.

Renee Camacho fired five rounds at both of them.

Carlos Chacon, firing two guns, shot once at Chuey Hernandez and five times at Pedro Espindola.

Manny Lopez, as he was falling to the ground, fired three times at Chuey Hernandez.

Pedro Espindola emptied his gun while scrambling back toward the border. Chuey Hernandez got off five rounds before he had the weightless feeling and left his feet.

Nine officers of two countries fired forty-nine rounds of ammunition at each other in the darkness at close range. And when all was said and done, the two who lived south of the imaginary line hadn't the faintest idea why it had happened. And some of the seven who lived north of the imaginary line, after some painful reflection, were not sure if *they* knew why. They were foredoomed to perform. And they did.

Suddenly, everyone was *screaming.*

"I'M HIT!"

"Barf! Barf! Barf! Barf! Barf!"

"I'M HIT, GODDAMNIT!"

"CEASE FIRE CEASE FIRE."

"I'M HIT, YOU BASTARDS!"

"GET HIM GET GET GET HIM GET HIM!"

Incredibly enough, Pedro Espindola was scrambling toward the pipe, up the embankment!

People were cursing, yelling, screaming, ducking, trying to reload weapons. Pedro Espindola was scrambling as though in a dream. Chuey Hernandez was crawling, clawing at the dirt, trying to take himself *home.* San Diego detectives would find his finger marks in the dust.

Chuey Hernandez would not be playing his cornet for the President of Mexico. Chuey Hernandez, during the screaming and pandemonium immediately following the endless explosion that still echoed in his ears, was following the instincts of all wounded creatures. He was crawling on his belly for home. He crawled exactly six feet. His finger marks were in the soil of his homeland. All but his legs were inside the Republic of Mexico. As he clawed his way home.

Then Chuey Hernandez remembers only a body falling hard on him. Someone placed a shotgun at his head and his gun was snatched away. And someone rolled him over on his back and began slapping him across the face and cursing him.

Manny Lopez put the gun of Chuey Hernandez into his belt and handcuffed his own wrist to the wounded Tijuana policeman.

Manny Lopez kept yelling, "Who's hit? Is anybody hit?"

Carlos Chacon screamed, "I'm hit in an *artery*!"

Manny Lopez began jerking on Chuey Hernandez, jerking him upright, and someone else slapped Chuey Hernandez across the face and Manny Lopez screamed, "You fucking thief!"

And Chuey Hernandez remembers how it *confused* him. Thief? What does he mean? What does he *mean*?

"What's going on?" Chuey Hernandez kept repeating. "What's going on?" He kept staring at his handcuffed wrist, disbelieving.

"Don't play dumb, you asshole!" somebody said, and he was slapped again.

Manny Lopez yelled, "Did I get hit or not? What the fuck?" And he started feeling his own body with the hand that wasn't cuffed to Chuey Hernandez, saying, "Somebody check me! I *know* I got hit!"

Now Chuey Hernandez felt a ferocious ache in his stomach. It was the worst stomachache he ever had and he was being dragged along the ground on that stomach. Then his arm started hurting bad enough to make him cry.

Chuey Hernandez was jerked to his feet and was amazed to see that he could walk. He remembers walking perhaps one hundred meters to some trees. Suddenly he started choking and couldn't breathe and became *more* terrified. Then someone said, "*Pinche* robber! I hope you *die*!"

Of all the things that happened that night, the most perplexing to Chuey Hernandez was that later, when the area was swarming with activity, and a helicopter and an ambulance were there, someone leaned over him as he lay on a gurney ready to be put in an ambulance. He couldn't say whether it was the tall one who accompanied him in the ambulance (meaning Ernie Salgado) or the leader (meaning Manny Lopez) or another one. He has a memory of someone slapping him and calling him a robber.

Robber? It was so strange he wanted to laugh and cry. He was having lucid thoughts and he wanted to talk. He thought *they* were robbers when he went into that gully. No pollo ever behaved like that—ducking in and out of the light beam, not running away, yet not obeying. And now *they* were calling *him* a robber? But why? How could it be? If they were policemen, why hadn't they simply said so the first moment he saw them? To Chuey Hernandez none of it made any sense whatsoever. He hadn't any idea at all what they were talking about.

Then the one who was slapping him said, "If our partner dies, *you're* going to die and rot in hell!"

It was the first time he'd known that one of them had been shot. He had no idea whatever as to the fate of Pedro Espindola or even that he had escaped. He then decided they were all crazy and there was no point trying to talk. It didn't make sense. Or maybe *he* was crazy!

Carlos Chacon had vivid memories of the massive shootout which Ernie Salgado said sounded like a Vietnam firefight. Carlos remembered emptying one gun but did not remember taking out the other one. He could feel the heat from the muzzle flashes and the lead shavings striking him. And smell the burn of gunpowder. He saw Chuey Hernandez a few feet away firing at him. One of the rounds from Carlos Chacon's gun struck Chuey Hernandez in the Sam Browne, ripped through and entered the side of his body and into the stomach, settling by the navel. Another passed through his arm.

After Chuey Hernandez was down, they mostly fired at the skinny cop who was shooting and backing away. Carlos Chacon felt a shock and went down. Then Pedro Espindola was down and Carlos Chacon clearly saw rounds exploding into the body of Pedro Espindola as he was crawling toward the pipe.

Then Carlos Chacon began screaming: *"I'm hit!"*

While they were kneeling over Carlos Chacon, tearing his bulletproof vest away, the Tijuana patrol car started up and drove away!

They had been looking for the skinny cop, expecting to find him lying in wait by the pipe, or dead. Then the car left. Was there a *third* one? The skinny one *must* be hiding in the pipe waiting to ambush them. Did one of the drunks drive the goddamn car away?

They later discovered that Officer Pedro Espindola, suffering four wounds, three in the back and one in the leg, dragged his body through the drainage pipe, up onto the highway, crawled into the patrol car, and escaped.

The Barfers were learning that Mexican cops were as hard to kill as Mexican bandits. There were some very tough people down there.

Carlos Chacon was on the ground screaming, "DON'T MOVE ME!" And Manny Lopez was on his feet trying to quell the pandemonium by yelling orders.

Tony Puente got on the Handie-Talkie and screamed, "Goddamnit! I can't make it work!"

So Manny Lopez took it and turned it on, allowing Tony to start screaming *into* it.

Everything was interrupted just then. They heard several sirens approaching. Then they heard dozens of sirens approaching. From the south! The sky was lit for a mile by red and blue siren lights, and the sound of those Tijuana police sirens scared the living hell out of every man.

Then Manny Lopez yelled, "Let's *go*!"

But there were two wounded men and somebody was trying to get a dressing on the arm of Carlos Chacon, who was yelling about an artery, and Carlos Chacon remembers thinking: If I'm hit in the artery, I'll be dead in three minutes!

And Joe Castillo, who hated Carlos Chacon, wounded or not, remembers thinking: Artery? So what? He's got no blood in his veins, the *pussy*! I got shot by *him* and I wasn't screaming about a goddamn artery. Screaming like a pig!

Then Carlos Chacon yelled, "If I start to go, give me mouth-to-mouth!"

And *somebody*, probably Joe Castillo, yelled back, "Fuck your mouth-to-mouth, you faggot!"

And then everybody—shooters, wounded, jokers, maniacs, all of them—started trying to truck on out, because those blue and white patrol cars, as well as plainclothes cars of the *judiciales*, were all *over* that highway. Suddenly they could see nothing but those pale *guayabera* shirts out there in the darkness. And they heard the sound of thirty men hitting that cyclone fence and they knew that the *judiciales* were coming! And somebody might soon be drinking soda pop through his fucking nose if he even *lived* that long! And then they saw clearly in silhouette that one of the *judiciales* was carrying a Tommy gun!

A Border Patrol helicopter responding to the chaos on the airwaves swooped in, illuminating the whole pack of them huddling there trying to tend to the wounded, and Manny got on the Handie-Talkie and said, "Tell those border patrolmen to turn off the light or I'll shoot the fucking chopper down!"

Except that they weren't going to shoot *anything* down. They had shot their *wad.* Everybody had either used up his ammunition or dropped it in the confusion of reloading.

Three Barfers started yelling simultaneously: "I'M OUT A AMMO!"

The wounded were carried, dragged, pushed, pulled, and—with the head of Chuey Hernandez in the painful headlock of Manny Lopez—everyone started running north toward the sound of an ambulance approaching from the substation. Toward Ken Kelly and Robbie Hurt, who were careening over the dirt road in two vehicles, each having what he was sure was his third or fourth heart attack of the month.

While all of this was going on, Joe Vasquez, who had the shotgun that night and had finally gotten it unjammed, was staying closest to the fence, covering the retreat. He was fascinated watching all those cars screaming up the Mexican highway, sliding and skidding to a stop near the hole in the fence.

Within seconds the first dozen uniformed cops hit that cyclone fence. Then the *judiciales* roared up. Then another patrol car. Then another. Then six patrol cars, traveling two abreast and damn the oncoming traffic! Then half a dozen plainclothes cars containing more *judiciales.* Then Joe Vasquez saw the *judicial* with the Tommy gun and he thought: That's it. Time to go.

He turned around and yelled, "That's it! Time to . . ."

He was talking to himself. They had *gone.* When the chopper was hovering overhead, lighting them like quail, the noise had obscured all the frantic commands. The rest of them, carrying and dragging Carlos Chacon and Chuey Hernandez, had simply *gone.*

Big Ugly was left behind. He was all alone. The *guayabera* shirts were running ahead of the uniformed cops. They were running in his direction with flashlight beams criss-crossing the brush.

There was a surprised border patrolman parked in a jeep on the mesa that night who saw a fierce-looking pollo screaming toward him at a pace that would qualify for the police Olympics.

Joe Vasquez found the Border Patrol on the high point and started waving his badge in the lights, yelling, "Get me out a here!"

The Mexican police began firing, probably at some poor pollos caught in the brush. They were on the radio to the San Diego sheriff's helicopter saying, "Help us. Some bandits shot our men!"

Pedro Espindola never knew until later that Manny and his men were cops. He made it to the hospital still conscious. He survived his four wounds and eventually returned to duty.

Chuey Hernandez suffered two bullet wounds that night. One lodged in the abdominal area; the other passed through his arm. The San Diego crime lab determined that he had been shot by Carlos Chacon. Chuey Hernandez was in the hospital in San Diego for fifteen days. When his wife, Miki, came to see him, she couldn't stop crying. The two of them talked with San Diego police detectives but at first neither could understand why Chuey had been shot. Within a few days she no longer had access to her husband because of rules pertaining to prisoners. She was allowed to visit him during prisoners' visiting hours after he was officially charged with criminal assault. Chuey Hernandez never wanted his mother to know, because she had a serious heart condition. Even though she lived with him, the whole family kept the secret scrupulously. The old woman was told that her son was taken to a San Diego hospital for a hernia operation.

Chuey Hernandez was lucky. His wife was a nurse and

could help him when he was released from the hospital. Of course she had to take a leave from her nursing job to tend to her husband during his recuperation at home. Chuey Hernandez also needed a criminal lawyer to defend him against the charges in San Diego. The lawyer required $1,500 for his services, but Chuey Hernandez earned only about $45 a week. They were able to borrow the money against their house. According to the banker, the house was worth $3,000. The medical bills and lawyer's fees finally proved overwhelming and Chuey Hernandez lost his house and had to live in a rented house from that day on. With the children and his mother.

Miki Hernandez had to nurse her husband for two months during the time that their world was crumbling. She had considerable hatred for the San Diego police after that.

Chuey Hernandez returned to duty with the Tijuana Municipal Police and had lots more to worry about than whether his lip would fall asleep.

"I always admired the policemen of San Diego *so* much," he said. "I always wished I could be one. Of course that was only a dream."

It was touch and go for Manuel Smith, the San Diego police liaison officer to Mexico. Upon being called in to conduct the negotiations between the police departments of San Diego and Tijuana, he was shocked to learn that the wounded Tijuana cop was Chuey Hernandez, whom he had known casually from his many dealings with the Mexican police. And with so many relatives all over the Baja Peninsula he was doubly shocked to discover that Chuey's wife, Miki, was a distant cousin of the Smiths'.

Of course it wouldn't be pleasant for any San Diego cop whose job it was to maintain liaison with the Mexican police. The first thing heard publicly was Manny Lopez being interviewed on television to the effect that the Tijuana cops had tried to rob them. And whether Chuey Hernandez was shot six feet north or six feet south of the imaginary line, or whether he jerked the trigger out of reflex when Manny Lopez brought a gun up in his face, or whether the left side of his brain should have understood the sound *¡Policías!* coming from Manny Lopez' lips, or whether the sound did indeed come from Manny Lopez' lips, would be relevant to men and women who manipulate the most ponderous legal machinery on the face of the earth. But none of it was very relevant to the Mexican police, who, like Chuey Hernandez, simply could not *begin* to fathom any of it.

Despite any personal turmoil within, Manuel Smith had to bite the bullet and back his own police department all the way. And he did. He interviewed Chuey Hernandez in the hospital and elicited a statement from the wounded Mexican cop that he had heard the word *¡Policías!* come from Manny Lopez a fraction of a second before the shooting, but that it didn't make any difference because he would never have believed these were any *kind* of cops.

"Why would I try to shoot seven policemen if I knew they were policemen?" Chuey Hernandez cried out in anguish. "I don't understand!"

And when Manuel Smith attempted to elicit a statement tending to verify the BARF allegation that they were about to be robbed by bandit cops, Chuey Hernandez began to sob.

"No one would have thought they were pollos," he said. "Pollos would run away or obey me. *No* pollo ever acted like these. I thought *they* were robbers!"

Then Manuel Smith went south to try to explain it to the Tijuana police, and *judiciales.* To people who were his friends and who were never less than good to him. He found Deputy Chief Verber of the Tijuana Municipal Police. The man was weeping.

He said to Manuel Smith, "Seven of your men? With bulletproof vests and shotguns? And my two officers in full uniform in a police car? Now they're saying my men were bandits? They're saying we're *all* crooks? I don't understand!"

But from that night on, the only thing that seemed important to the U.S. authorities, at least as far as the Mexicans were concerned, was whether Chuey Hernandez was standing a body length north of an imaginary line or a body length south of it. And which pad of flesh on the index finger of which armed policeman was flattened against a metal rod with or without a willful signal from the left side of the brain. And whether or not the unsolicited line from Manny Lopez —"We don't have any money"—was designed to lure and entice Chuey Hernandez or to verify an evil intent to rob already preexisting in the mind of Chuey Hernandez. Or whether it just insulted the hell out of an already angry cop who was being defied by some baffling behavior.

But if one did not hold a degree in jurisprudence and was not concerned with logistical matters involving imaginary lines, or with neurological signals, or coded laws of entrapment, or cultural considerations of *mordida,* then one might, like Joe Castillo, crystallize it all rather succinctly: "It was *just* like on *Gunsmoke*!"

So there it was. Manny Lopez had braced the *bad* cops. He had by now drawn against guns numerous times, something very few lawmen outside of movies have done even once. Something police training has always warned against. He had been publicly glorified for epitomizing a chunk of American myth that may never have existed outside of celluloid: the hardball gunslinging lawman who, when facing the guns of the wicked, will draw. And the fastest gun is not only right; the fastest gun wins the hearts of the West.

There was no point counting the stories written on this one. The Barfers might as well have *weighed* their press notices. Suffice it to say that the mayor of Tijuana finally had to go public and beg the media of both sides to try to forget the border shooting. But the Barfers wouldn't forget it. They were filled with troubled dreams and mixed emotions. They wondered if someone was going to name an airport for Manny Lopez.

There were a few very unforgettable memories for Ken Kelly that night. First, there was the heart attack he and Robbie Hurt were sure they were experiencing when once again they heard gunfire in the night. This time sounding like *war.* And then to hear the static-broken screaming on the radio, and for a minute or a year not to know what was happening or where, and finally to hurtle toward the echo of explosions. The cover team of Ken Kelly and Robbie Hurt, the outsiders, never, but *never* had experienced the release which action provided for the others.

One thing that Ken Kelly took from that evening was the astonishing moment when he was driving away from the hordes of Mexican police flowing through the fence eager to kill the bandits who shot their men. Manny Lopez and Tony Puente were in his vehicle. Tony Puente was trying to talk, with about as much success as a stroke victim. He was hyperventilating slightly and was trying to calm himself by taking deeper breaths, which was exactly wrong, and then he finally sensed or understood the problem and settled back and stopped sighing, panting, sighing. Ken Kelly thought that Tony might just break down and cry, and why the hell not? He was entitled.

Finally, Tony Puente was able to utter things in monosyllables. He said, "God . . ." and after a pause of five seconds: ". . . damn!"

Tony Puente was reacting and behaving pretty much like all the others. In fact, when they got to the substation, more than one had to go to the bathroom and walked into a closed door without opening it.

But in the car alongside Tony Puente was his leader, Manny Lopez. And Manny was saying, "I guess if all those dudes caught us we'd be righteously dead by now. Only thing bothers me, I was sure I got hit. I must be losing my fucking mind. Oh, well."

Oh, well. Then he stopped talking and asked Ken Kelly what time it was and Ken figured Manny was wondering whether he should maybe handle the first batch of reporters all by himself, and could he get to the saloon before it closed what with all the paperwork and television interviews?

Ken Kelly started getting a headache. Manny Lopez looked only about as annoyed as he got when Ken Kelly ran away from home. Ken was sure that Manny was going to ask if he'd heard the baseball score.

What scared the living crap out of Ken Kelly is that he suddenly got a whole new fix on Manny Lopez: This bastard's *crazy*! This bastard would draw on The Holy Ghost!

Carlos Chacon was not hit in an artery. He was treated for a bullet in the upper arm, and was released from the hospital that night only to get seriously infected and be off duty for three months.

On the night of the international shootout there happened to be a police graduation class throwing a big bash at the pistol range. When the alarm went off, the Southern substation was full of brass from that party. They would come up to each Barfer saying things like, "How ya doing, son?"

There were several interviews given to the press by ranking officers who, the Barfers said, would visit the canyons about as soon as an iguana grew eyebrows. The kind, the street cops say, who make command decisions only if the astrological signs, biorhythmic charts and sunspots are correct. Or when the tea leaves tell them.

Very late that night Manny Lopez finally showed some emotion. He pulled off his jacket, went to a mirror to check himself out and cried happily, "See! I knew I was hit!"

The first round fired by Chuey Hernandez had gone

through the collar of his flak jacket and creased the strap on the way out.

Manny said, "I was starting to think I was nuts!"

Which caused Ken Kelly to look around at the other Barfers staring into space.

The BARF experiment had now resulted in the shooting of six lawmen, three from each side of the imaginary line. And *all* by other lawmen.

CHAPTER · 16

PILATE

IF THERE WAS EVER ANY DOUBT, IT HAD VANISHED AFTER the shooting of the Tijuana policemen. Manny said it: "Dick Snider had the idea, but I formed and directed and *shaped* it. BARF was *my* thing."

And indeed it was. Barfers like Ernie Salgado and Eddie Cervantes, who were by now overtly critical of their leader's celebrity, might not like it, but everyone else knew: Manny Lopez *was* the Barf squad.

He was adored by the media. As far as other cops were concerned, some felt like asking for his autograph and some felt he should work for another city, say Havana, Cuba. There were lots of opinions about Manny Lopez but one thing was certain: Chief of Police William Kolender supported the BARF leader. Very much, in fact.

On the night of the big shootout, the little Southern substation was awash with all kinds of people: department brass, detectives, officials of the Mexican police. And more reporters than San Diego had seen since Patricia Hearst was confined in the Metropolitan Correctional Center.

It was tough enough under ordinary circumstances for detectives to separate witnesses and participants in police shootings, let alone under these conditions. During the course of the evening when the Barfers were sitting in a squadroom, ordered by homicide detectives not to talk to one another about the case, a couple of them held a short conversation in Spanish.

The homicide detectives got very mad. The Barfers claimed they were only asking each other who was going to buy the beer and where they were going to drink it. The homicide detectives said that was bullshit. After they'd been ordered not to communicate, it was funny that a little small talk about beer had to be done in Spanish.

The Barfers said they *liked* to talk Spanish. The detectives said it was an awfully long conversation just to say who was going to get the beer. The Barfers said that it takes longer to say things in Spanish than it does in English.

And so forth. As if Barfers and homicide detectives weren't getting on one another's nerves enough these days, there had to arise a squabble about this. No one seemed to have considered that such problems might never arise if it were not that in a police department with fifteen detectives working Homicide, there was only *one* Mexican-American. The San Diego Police Department just didn't seem to know where it *lived.*

In any case, language conflicts or not, the Barfers were beginning to feel the noose tightening ever more snugly. They became convinced that homicide detectives were natural enemies of their mission.

Homicide detectives began to ask openly: What *is* the mission? If it's to create heroes, well, these heroes could be a real pain in the ass. Homicide was openly critical of the shootout, and especially of Manny Lopez.

Two of the homicide detectives had opinions about the entire affair.

"I don't think San Diego policemen have any business

out there in the first place," was how one of them said it.

His partner put it this way: "I don't think what they're doing out there *is* police work. And I think Manny Lopez *insulted* those two cops into coming across."

Manny Lopez was waiting to see what was going to happen to Chuey Hernandez. He told his men that the D.A. had *better* file charges on the Tijuana cop. On Monday after the big weekend, Chief William Kolender scheduled a press conference regarding the shooting of the Tijuana policemen.

Former chiefs were law and order types who, if they were ever asked to speak at a service club luncheon, would quote from the evangelists or J. Edgar Hoover. William Kolender was something different for a career lawman. Large, imposing, young for a chief, he had a good image with the media, the politicians, the public *and* the cops. It takes a juggler.

In truth, he had made positive changes for the beleaguered minority cops in a city that was one-fifth black and brown. But the choice jobs remained top-heavy with whites, so he knew how far to go. He pushed, but not *too* hard.

It was quite a sight when Chief Kolender, dressed like General Motors, stood side by side with his boss Gunslinger, dressed like Saturday night in a singles bar, representing, as it were, the divergence in a police department heading in new directions. Manny Lopez was in a way a tribute to the innovation of the fledgling chief. Everyone knew that there would never have been a Barf squad under previous administrations. For sure, after the first controversial shooting it would have been disbanded. So on the one hand Chief Kolender was considered freethinking for recognizing the need to protect illegal aliens within the city of San Diego, and on the other hand, was hard-nosed enough to back his men when the international confrontations started.

But juggling is never easy business, and any chief of police whose job is subject to political appointment has to take advantage of positive press while the taking is good. BARF was bringing positive press and good public relations to the department the likes of which the television show *Dragnet* had brought to the L.A.P.D. decades earlier.

Chief Kolender genuinely admired Manny Lopez. He often said, "I've never *seen* such gutsy work. Would *you* go out there and do what BARF does? *I* wouldn't."

So despite what homicide detectives thought and said privately, the shooting of the Mexican policemen was publicly and privately defended by the chief. On the Monday following the international shootout, during the chief's press conference, the Barfers were asked by the press relations officer to wait outside central headquarters so as not to steal the limelight from Chief Kolender, who after all was not one of the Gunslingers, and couldn't compete.

The Barfers waited at a local cop bar called Bernie's. Within minutes Manny Lopez received a call at the bar. Deputy Chief Robert Burgreen was on the phone to tell him that the press was on the way. The Barfers were red-hot copy.

Manny Lopez turned to his men and yelled, "Everybody *out a* here! Go to Anthony's Harborside and run up a tab. On *me*!"

Manny Lopez then hustled over to central headquarters, slipped in the side door and went to the office of Deputy Chief Burgreen, who said, "Chief Kolender is *not* going to recommend that charges be filed on Hernandez."

And Manny Lopez said, "That's *it.* I quit."

"Don't you want to think about this?" the deputy chief asked.

"They didn't file on the immigration officer when he almost shot me! Now they're not gonna file on this cop who shot one a my men? I ain't got more than a hundred I.Q. if I take this shit again."

Thirty minutes later the deputy chief led Manny Lopez into the office of the chief of police, saying, "Manny's upset."

The chief of police was writing on a legal pad. Without looking up, he said, "Oh? And what's he upset about?"

Manny Lopez tried to remind himself that this was the superchief himself. He said, "I'll tell you what I'm upset about, Chief. They're not filing charges on Hernandez!"

"I know," the chief answered. "Homicide says it's a very weak case."

Then Manny Lopez surprised both his superiors and himself by pounding on the desk, saying, "Fuck Homicide! Fuck this shit! You didn't ask *my* side of it. I quit! I quit!"

And the chief said, "Do you mean the *department*?"

That stopped him, because he sure as hell didn't mean the police department, only the Barf squad. So he added, "Well, I hadn't thought about *that.*"

Suddenly he started seeing his whole career slipping away and this was the scariest thing that had happened to him lately. He needed time to think, because the chief was calling his bluff.

Something else occurred to him. "Those fuckers're running a tab on me!" Manny cried. "I gotta go see my guys. They're at Anthony's."

And Deputy Chief Burgreen said, "Do you mind if we come with you? I'll pick up the tab."

"No, *I'll* pick it up," the chief of police said.

By the time they arrived at Anthony's Harborside that afternoon, the San Diego press relations representative had already informed the other Barfers that charges were not going to be filed on Chuey Hernandez. And since Manny Lopez was never a piker, especially when someone else was picking up the tab, he grabbed a waitress and said, "Four bottles a good wine for my guys."

The chief of police surprised them all by saying to the Barfers: "I believe in you people. I've just talked to Manny and I'm going to ask the D.A. to *issue* charges on the Mexican officer."

Manny Lopez figured he had won a major victory. He got good and drunk that night. Only one thing spoiled the evening for Manny. It was when Deputy Chief Burgreen said aloud, "The thing that worries me about this is the danger. I'm afraid Manny's going to get killed out there."

Instantly, Eddie Cervantes' down-turned eyes started throbbing and bulging, and he cried, "Manny's gonna get killed! Why only *Manny*?"

"Of course I'm equally concerned with all of you," the deputy chief added. "I only meant that Manny is . . . he's always out in front. That's what I meant."

Later, Manny Lopez tried to placate a scowling Eddie Cervantes by saying, "Listen, fucker, things come out that way. I *always* tell the reporters that Cervantes did this or Salgado did that. I don't write the stories, fucker. I don't *write* em!"

The next morning Manny was shaving, with a monstrous hangover, when his ten-year-old son came in and said, "What'd you do wrong, Dad? On television they just said they dropped charges on the guy you shot."

"THEY DID WHAT?" Manny Lopez screamed, almost cutting his own throat.

As he was pulling on a jacket, ready to go out the door with his head feeling all mushy and inflamed, he said to his wife: "I'm gonna get fired today. Good-bye."

When the BARF sergeant got to the chief's office, it was the first and only time he ever saw William Kolender uneasy.

"Chief, you promised you were gonna see that they issued charges!" Manny Lopez said.

"The case isn't strong," Chief Kolender said. And then he stood up, came around his desk and put his arm on the shoulder of the shorter man. He said, "Manny, I don't know *what* I'm going to be able to do."

"Fuck it, Chief, I quit!" Manny Lopez said.

And then Chief Kolender, who was no slouch at handling legendary Gunslingers as well as ordinary macho cops, said, "Manny if *you* quit, *I'll* get fired."

It was worthy of Manny Lopez himself, this piece of work: If *you* quit, *I'll* get fired. The implication being that Manny Lopez was such a fabled and mythic and legendary celebrity that he could displace the chief of police. And by implication, maybe the mayor. And shit, Governor Jerry Brown wasn't even safe!

It was like a diva refusing to sing until the impresario takes her in his arms and says, "But, Divinity, *I'll* be finished if you don't sing!"

Deep down she *knows* it's bullshit, but it sounds so glorious she goes out there and gets so many curtain calls the stagehands get hernias.

Then the chief added, "What if we issue assault charges and bind him over for trial at a preliminary hearing? Will *that* be enough for you?"

And Manny Lopez, now a king breaker as well as everything else, said, "Sure. I don't care if he never goes to trial. At least bind him over and that shows we didn't fuck up. Okay! And, Chief, how about coming down to the station some night and telling my guys how much you think a them? It might be *nice.*"

There *was* a person connected to the Barf squad by umbilical cord whom the chief did not particularly appreciate, nor did Deputy Chief Burgreen. Nor did lots of other ranking brass who felt that BARF was the tail wagging the dog. That was the man who had created it, Lieutenant Dick Snider.

Dick Snider at this point was like poor old Victor Frankenstein: nobody remembered his *intent.* And Dick Snider, as was his way, remained totally loyal to his mutant creation. He accepted the official interpretation—that is, the Manny Lopez interpretation of the international shootout—without much soul searching. Though he had long since been officially relieved of duty as the BARF officer-in-charge, unofficially, as a Southern Division watch commander, he was still the Barfers' uncle. Manny almost always showed him the courtesy of keeping him informed. Dick Snider repaid the courtesy with total allegiance to BARF, alienating the department brass in the process.

Of course the alienation of the department brass had probably begun many months earlier when Dick Snider, through his one-man canyon crawling and publicity campaign, got the experiment going in the first place. When a deputy chief or inspector would suggest something like keeping the Barfers farther than fifty yards from the international border, Dick Snider would reply, "We already have one invisible line to work with. Don't give us another. Either let us work or disband us."

Deputy Chief Burgreen, whom the troops refer to as Bobby, and who looked like a blow-dried middle-aged cherub, spoke for the administration when he said, "Lieutenant Snider was *not* interested in evaluations, route slips, councilmanic reports. He was vocal, a street cop, not an administrator, but his rank demanded an administrator. He might be a good guy and he might even be a good street cop. But he was *not* a good lieutenant."

The department's position on the BARF creator was dramatized during a meeting of the big chief and several of his immediate subordinates during the difficult weeks following the international shootout. There was some serious talk about disbanding BARF.

Manny Lopez, Dick Snider and the captain of Southern Division were there to opt for continuing the experiment. There were ideas being tossed around as to the feasibility of uniformed cops patrolling the canyons. There were suggestions of begging for federal troops to be stationed in the hills. There were suggestions that the city should somehow cede the land to the federal government and let Uncle Sam worry about all of it. Finally, there was a growing consensus that the BARF experiment was just too dangerous.

Manny Lopez was showing his reptilian sidewinding eyebrow and pointing his finger like a gun and talking triple time in his disingenuous style that charmed the chief of police, and he said, "We're *safer* than the guys on the street! They're not ready for it when some dude smokes them down while they're writing a traffic ticket! But my guys're *always* ready!"

Dick Snider then removed his dangling cigarette and in his country drawl tried to add his thoughts. "Chief, I think what Manny is trying to say is . . ."

"Lieutenant, we *know* your position," a deputy chief interrupted icily. "I was talking to Manny."

And that was it. Manny Lopez returned to the Barfers and told them sadly that Burl the Pearl was no longer as big as John Wayne. He'd just been sawed off at the knees.

Manny said, "Snider's sweet-guy personality . . . his . . . *niceness*—it's a detriment to me now."

Manny added something else when he'd had a Chivas or two that evening after work: "I got a relationship with the politicians. I got a relationship with the chief. I'm *surrounded* by news media. I love Dick Snider, but he can't help BARF anymore."

Manny Lopez genuinely admired Dick Snider for qualities he did not himself possess. Manny privately said, "I had this interview with a young reporter and I told him that me and my guys have a Don Quixote syndrome. And sure enough he does this flowery piece about us fighting windmills. Well, maybe part of it was true, at least so far as Dick Snider's concerned. Saving people would be *his* motive. But the fact is, BARF was giving me this tremendous feeling! That I could do *anything* out there in those canyons! *That* was my motive."

Dick Snider, as correctly pointed out by Manny Lopez, did not have the temperament or the glibness to slug it out with the brass. Debate was an *outlet* for Manny Lopez. He was very good at it. Dick Snider had no outlet. And now Dick Snider knew for sure that they didn't need him. And didn't *want* him.

As for Manny, the meeting ended when the chief of police stopped all argument by saying, "I don't think you gentlemen understand. Manny's saying that if it's not his way he's not leading the squad anymore."

The experiment was permitted to continue. And Chief Kolender tacitly approved whacking Dick Snider off at the knees that afternoon.

One day when the city council of San Diego drew up a resolution to honor the Barfers with a piece of parchment full of fancy "whereofs," the chief of police was supposed to make a speech on behalf of his men. Except that Manny Lopez was suddenly asked to say a few words. Manny wisely stood up and thanked all the politicians present *and* the chief of police for giving his men the chance to do what they did. He got a standing ovation from all.

When the chief did make speeches about the border crime problem he said it should be made a federal responsibility and he spoke like a Republican about the lack of direction in the Jimmy Carter administration. When Manny gave speeches it was about facing bandits in the night and drawing against the drop. It was easy to guess whom people wanted to hear, Republicans and Democrats alike.

Dick Snider was never heard to verbalize a whit of resentment about being effectively banished from any further decisions regarding his brainchild. BARF belonged exclusively to Manny Lopez. Even when his career was, in the words of Deputy Chief Burgreen, "on the slide," Dick Snider was uncomplaining.

Just so long as they kept it going, just so long as Manny and his men were arresting bandits and protecting the aliens of the canyons, in *his* city, in *his* country.

As Manny put it: "Dick Snider's motives were *pure* till

the end. He was the only one of us whose motives were always pure. And the brass not only couldn't forgive him for it, they couldn't even *believe* it."

As to the danger to the Barfers themselves, Dick Snider would only say, "If there was a threat of robbery and rape and murder to the millionaires of La Jolla, we'd all be asked to *give* our lives if necessary. Without question."

During the weeks to come, during a media barrage on both sides of the border about the international shootout, Chief of Police Kolender, true to his word, did come to Southern Division to reassure Manny's men of what a hell of a bunch of gutsy hardballers they really were, and what a job they were doing out there, and that he was behind them all the way.

The chief addressed the Barfers on their own turf just before they went out canyon crawling. After the pep talk he said, "The charges against the Tijuana policeman may be dismissed after the preliminary hearing. You should be aware of that."

And suddenly up popped Ken Kelly, who, feeling especially militant and goofy, had the concoction of instant coffee and powdered chocolate smeared all over his face. And he'd wrapped his long blond hair in a bun and covered it all with a stocking cap to be less visible in the hills. He looked like a cocaine-inspired Hollywood version of a loony G.I. in Vietnam, sort of a cross between a punk rocker and a Jivaro headhunter.

Ken Kelly, suffering the results of having been the only San Diego cop ever convicted in court of assaulting a civilian, wiggled his walrus moustache and said, "Chief, how come the Tijuana cop shoots a San Diego cop and walks? And I dust a number one prick asshole with a flashlight and get honked? How come?"

And the chief of police changed the subject by saying, "Who're *you*?" Then he smiled and added, "You are one of the most *ominous* people I've ever seen in my life!"

The Barfers were all tickled by that because Ken Kelly *did* look pretty loony, all right. They were flattered as hell that the chief had stroked them, whether or not charges were dropped on Chuey Hernandez.

The chief ended it by saying of the Tijuana lawman: "He paid some pretty heavy dues, you know."

The one thing that the chief also said during that meeting which filled the Barfers with *all* kinds of conflicting emotions was this: "I have to be honest about something else. It's been a miracle that nobody's been killed yet. I'm awfully worried about you guys. I've had many second thoughts about letting it continue. If someone'd get killed, well, I just don't want to go to police funerals. I'd stop it then."

The Barfers did *lots* of soul-searching over this one. If one of them gets killed, BARF is stopped? Then why not stop it now, because the way it's going it's a sure bet! There seemed to be a bunch of things wrong with the philosophy behind a statement that their job was worth getting shot over, but not *fatally.*

It seemed like a warning. As soon as one of them died, the rest would be getting new jobs. Don't die if you like your job. Die if you *don't* like it! Oh, their brains were parboiled by *this* one. The chief sort of absolved himself, it seemed. He *said* he wanted to stop it. He'd warned them: Don't die or you'll lose your job. Was he saying that he was blameless if one of them got smoked?

Suddenly the chief of police looked exactly like Pontius Pilate in a Hart Schaffner & Marx.

CHAPTER · 17

PHANTOMS

THE BARF SQUAD HAD DONE A NUMBER ON THE BANDITS. They'd really knocked down the alien robberies on the streets of San Ysidro. Street thugs couldn't miss the publicity generated by the Barfers. Even though all of the shootings had taken place in the canyons, there had been some pretty good thumpings administered in San Ysidro, so there were easier ways to make a dishonest buck, the hoodlums decided.

As to the canyons where the real bandits plied their trade, even they were not unaware of the Barfers' celebrity. Not that the bandits were ever going to stop being bandits, but no one wanted to get shot to death by these canyon-crawling San Diego cops who were maniacal enough to burn down Tijuana Municipal Police if they got in the way. At least that was the word filtering back through the alien grapevine.

The real bandits from the south were survivors though. They began to alter their tactics and rob aliens right *at* the line. This was riskier because the *judiciales* didn't like crimes taking place on Mexican soil. Still, the Barf squad was making them do it, at least for now. The robberies began occurring within a few feet of the tumbledown cyclone fence—where the fence even existed. And where it did not exist, which was in most areas patrolled by BARF, the bandits became acutely aware of such things as concrete monuments and other man-made markers which defined an imaginary line.

As dangerous as it was to commit what the *judiciales* considered an enormous crime, namely armed robbery on the soil of Mexico, the bandits had decided that it was safer for now to risk the wrath of the Mexican lawmen than to encounter the Barf squad.

So the Barfers found they were working themselves out of a job. The number of significant bandit arrests after the shooting of the Tijuana policemen plunged. And actually, there were a few Barfers giving silent thanks for this turn of events. But Manny Lopez was going bonkers.

The Loco shootout, followed within days by the international shootout, had been powerful stuff and had produced even more changes in Manny Lopez: "I felt I could do *anything* out there."

There was much *more* driving him than the publicity, which the Barfers believed was his sole motivation. Manny Lopez was starting to feel some seductive and overpowering emotions that many a man before him had felt down through history: Alexander, Bonaparte, Hitler, Dustin Hoffman. Manny Lopez was beginning to feel omnipotent.

Since the mountain wouldn't come to Mahomet, Manny was going *south*. When he made the matter-of-fact announcement in the tiny little Barf squadroom one night in later summer, several Barfers said that it was like the captain of a jumbo jet announcing that the next sound you hear will be the bomb exploding in the cockpit. Or maybe getting a call from Lana Banana saying, "Gee, fellas, I've started getting these little sores and the doctor says I should call every one a my friends and . . ."

It was *that* kind of announcement. People wanted to speak right up, but nobody could even talk at the moment. People wanted to say a whole lot of things to Manny Lopez but everyone was waiting for someone else to begin. There was a certain amount of *machismo* required just to be a cop, of course. And there was about eighty-seven times as much required to be a Barfer nowadays. And even by being of Mexican blood, thereby culturally programmed with enough *machismo* to get yourself in all sorts of trouble all your life, there are certain things you do *not* do. Not for duty, not for glory, not to prove God knows what to God knows whom. And one of the things you don't do is go *south.*

What Manny Lopez was telling them was that since they couldn't catch any bandits on American soil these days, maybe they should, you know, just fudge a little? Just trip on down past that imaginary line or, where that beat-up little old fence is standing, just slip on through one of the holes? And walk on the *south* side. Only a *few* paces, you understand. Therein fooling the shit out of these smartass bandits who were frustrating them with their new tactic. And just think how many good bandit busts they could make before the robbers got the word. A regular blitzkreig! Can you dig it, fuckers?

Manny was showing his impish grin when he said it. His gap-toothed boyish smile was just full of fun and his eyebrow had squiggled and locked into the question mark as he envisioned shocking the crap out of some robbers right down there on the dirt belonging to the Republic of Mexico.

There were so many things wrong with this idea that everyone was dumbstruck. Not the least wrong was that word had already come back from pretty reliable sources that some *judiciales* and Tijuana police wanted *revenge.* There were even rumors that Mexican lawmen had put together a few pesos and promises. That it would be given to anyone who returned a favor. *Bring me the head of Manny Lopez!* And by implication, his men.

There were all sorts of rumors of this kind flying around. And whether or not the rumor of a price on Manny's head was true, just common sense told them that if they were caught by some Tijuana lawmen on the Mexican side after what they'd done to Chuey Hernandez and Pedro Espindola, well . . .

When they left the briefing that night—and everyone looked like a bat had sucked his blood, and not a word was spoken, not a *peep*—Ken Kelly made a remark that absolutely no one found funny. He said maybe they should start carrying cyanide capsules in their teeth.

It was during these weeks of walking south of the imaginary line, more fearful of Tijuana lawmen than they were of bandits who smelled like murder, that they began to talk among themselves, and with wives, and best friends. After being properly lubricated, of course, because hardball macho Gunslingers don't talk about such things while sober. It was about this time that they began talking about *Fear.*

And any discussion of Fear necessarily included a discussion of Manny Lopez. Not as to whether each man feared him; that was *absolutely* against the code of *machismo* to discuss openly, although it is virtually certain that they did, with the possible exception of Big Ugly. The reason being that Joe Vasquez respected and admired and even liked Manny Lopez too much to fear him as the others did.

Big Ugly put it this way: "Maybe we should a got more credit out there, but the thing is I always knew Manny wouldn't make us do nothing he wouldn't do. And I knew that whatever it was, he could probably do it better than any of us. Thing is, Manny was born to lead. I never came to hate him like some a the other guys."

Fred Gil said, "Manny gave you the feeling that you wouldn't want to cross him and *not* have him on your side."

Ernie Salgado said, "I worked for a lot a sergeants and

lieutenants when I was in Nam. I saw them come and go and die. But I never met a leader like him. The nearest thing I can say is I started to feel like I felt toward my D.I. when I was a Marine recruit." And that could be interpreted easily enough.

The outsiders like Robbie Hurt and Ken Kelly, who were not raised under the cultural code of *machismo,* were more direct.

"We were *scared* of him. Period," Robbie Hurt said. "Whatever it was Manny felt, that *he* called fear, it wasn't what I felt, what I called fear."

It no longer did them any good at all to know that Manny Lopez would never ask them to do something he wouldn't do. That was the *trouble.* They *knew* he'd do it, whatever he asked! Manny was a family man with bright handsome children, yet each Barfer came to the inescapable conclusion that Manny Lopez simply did not *know* self-preserving fear. And that knowledge became the most frightening thing of all.

"It's like the way you're scared of psychotics," Ken Kelly said of their fear of Manny. "Unpredictable, dangerous, *lucky* psychotics."

Manny had them always looking over their shoulders: Is he just a spot on the horizon, or is he about to land on my head like a falling safe?

"I knew they were scared a me," Manny Lopez was quoted as saying. "It had to be that way. We weren't doing *regular* police work."

Regular police work? Not even close. When Eddie Cervantes got back from his vacation in Fresno, having heard the news of the international shootout on television, he was surprised to feel no ambivalence about the most publicized shooting yet. He thought he'd be envious not to have been there. He thought he might feel left out when the others talked about it because he had been the most vocal about Manny Lopez hogging the headlines.

Strangely enough, he wasn't jealous at all. He couldn't escape the notion that it was a miracle one of them hadn't died that night. And if he had been there, fifteen pounds bloated from all the drinking he had done as a Barfer, he might have just filled up that one little pocket of empty air which forty-plus police bullets whizzed through harmlessly. He just might have been the one who *died* out there that night.

He had been thinking a lot about little pockets of empty air with bullets whizzing through, and about near misses to a human artery when knives flashed past, and all kinds of other mind-diddling games like that. And every man had to laugh that year when, in the baseball playoffs, an announcer uttered the inevitable cliché: "Baseball is a game of inches." *They* could tell the dumb shit about a game of *inches.*

Eddie Cervantes, with his sad down-turned eyes and Tex-Mex cadence, had enough *machismo* and anger in him to confront Manny Lopez, and he started doing it without letup. About everything. He used the word *okay* excessively, and it would sound like this: "Okay, Manny, you know I ain't afraid to do nothing okay and since I'm the smallest guy everyone out in those hills picks on me okay and I had my share a shit out there okay but there ain't no sense doing stupid things out there okay cause there ain't no sense *dying* for this since nobody appreciates it anyways. Okay?"

And Manny Lopez would say to Eddie Cervantes, "What's the matter? You chickenshit?"

"You think so?" Eddie Cervantes would say, getting madder and madder. "Just because you're a sergeant okay I don't need to take that shit okay. I think you're fucked! Okay?"

"Well, I think you're a pussy if you don't wanna do your job," Manny Lopez would answer.

"Well, you want a piece a my ass, I ain't afraid," Eddie Cervantes would say.

And then everybody would jump in and break it up,

because if someone actually hit Manny, it might be like hitting the Pope or something, and they'd all die on the spot.

Then Manny Lopez would say, "If someone's a pussy or a *puto,* then stay in the station! I'm going out there and kick ass! And Eddie Cervantes, whose balls are big as Carlos Chacon's ass, is gonna be *right* beside me!"

And Eddie Cervantes' sad down-turned eyes would drop a foot lower and he'd say, "We're gonna go out okay and kick ass. Okay."

"You fuckin *Aries.*" Manny Lopez would grin with an arm around the shortest Barfer because Eddie was born on April 4th and Manny Lopez on April 3rd, two years earlier. "I *knew* you wouldn't quit."

And out they'd go for another fun-filled night walking south of the imaginary line. One night when the junior varsity was on just such a fishing expedition they heard an eerie voice from the shacks on a hill in Colonia Libertad. It sounded like La Llorona, the weeping woman from ancient Mexican legend who roams the land at night looking for her children. Or maybe they figured it was Chano B. Gomez, Jr., yelling from the upper soccer field.

It was a spooky voice that froze them in their tracks. Then the eerie moaning stopped. Fear blew and rattled through the canyon like balls of mesquite. They heard only distant voices in the night: men, women, babies, dogs.

Then a voice like a knife in the guts. Every man flinched or crouched. Every man looked for the shadow of death to the south. A voice belonging to whom? A bandit? A *judicial*?

Who *was* it? And how could the owner of the voice have possibly known that the shadows walking south of the line were San Diego policemen? It was impossible!

A voice cried out: "Sergeant Loooooo-pez! Is that you?"

Renee Camacho couldn't escape the feeling of dread. Nothing helped anymore. He spent much more time talking to his father, Herbert Camacho. The barber told his only child all the comforting things, and he told his father how he couldn't rid himself of the urge to shoot approaching bandits *before* they had a chance to pull a weapon.

"I feel like doing it that way and putting on paper what should have happened," Renee confessed. "I'm even getting disappointed in Snider. Maybe he should step in and get the men rotated out a the hills, or maybe someone should monitor our emotional condition. I think some a the guys are getting to be *weird* guys!"

Dick Snider was the kind of white guy Herbert Camacho admired, one who spoke Spanish and knew the culture, an *emotional* man, the barber said. He remembered telling the BARF lieutenant: "You take care a my son. You take *care* a him now!"

But Dick Snider had been pushed further and further out of it, and Renee Camacho told his father it seemed hopeless. He had lots of talks with his father.

Other Barfers were noticing the change in the happy-go-lucky young fellow that Renee had been. He, like many of them, started to seem distant and even unfriendly to other cops at Southern substation. Barfers didn't talk in the locker room. They sometimes didn't seem to hear a greeting. Other cops thought they were wallowing in elitism and publicity. They didn't know the truth.

Barfers started fearing improbable things: that the bandits might lie in wait for them, to rid the canyons of these San Diego cops who had so hurt business. They started in terror every time a jackrabbit rustled the underbrush. A slinking coyote became a man waiting to *murder* them. Shapes of stunted oak flew at them in the shadows. A groaning tree could take the breath out of a man. Their guns were never out of their hands now. Their guns were getting rust-pitted from sweaty palms and aching clenched fingers.

Sometimes they'd hear a few rounds of gunfire just across the border. Once they heard a burst from an *auto-*

matic weapon and Manny wanted to stroll on over and check it out. They were halfway there before every man, talking triple time, persuaded him to STOP!

And tics? There were Barfers developing blinks, stammers, headaches, indigestion, back pain. Ken Kelly said the place was ticking like Switzerland.

The pressure at home was becoming tremendous for almost all of them. "Border shooting. Film at eleven!" It was uttered once too often by television news readers and the girls were all getting a little loony too. Sharlynn Camacho had made Renee promise a hundred times that after the baby was born . . .

He *couldn't* get his mind off that baby. What would it be, a boy or a girl? Would it look Mexican, or white like her? Would it be tall or short? Then of course, would he ever *see* his baby?

And as though he could read minds, Manny Lopez one evening took Renee Camacho aside and said, "Renee, you're one a the guys I *really* depend on. I know *you'd* never let me down."

The talk among themselves was now on one subject: *quitting.* They weren't talking about groupies anymore, or partying after work or scrapbooks or Manny hogging headlines. They were talking about *survival.* And then they started talking about it at lineup, in the presence of their sergeant.

Eddie Cervantes started things out by saying, "I guess you heard, Manny, that I got a chance okay to transfer to the school task force. Okay?"

"Why don't you just say it," Manny Lopez answered, as his eyebrow locked in.

"Huh?"

"School task force, my ass. You're getting scared."

"Scared? Me?"

"Yeah, you."

"I was scared, I'd a quit long ago."

"Ralph Nader oughtta recall your balls! You wanna be a *pussy*? Go ahead, quit!"

"Okay, I'll show you if I'm a pussy!"

"There's only one way to show anybody," Manny Lopez said dryly. "That's to go out there and kick *ass.*"

"Okay, motherfucker," Eddie Cervantes said. "You know what? I ain't quitting okay? I'm staying!"

"I figured it was just your old lady fucking up your head or something," Manny Lopez grinned. "I'm buying the beer tonight!"

And then, four hours later, as he was squatting by some rock pile smelling sweat and fear and rot and human excrement, Eddie Cervantes would think one thought: I'm gonna get killed. Tonight's the night. And all his friends were starting to say he was stupid. That no one *cared* about this border. That he would die for Manny's glory.

Ernie Salgado was also speaking his mind even more directly on the forbidden topic. "You want somebody to say it," the Vietnam vet told Manny one night. "I'm scared. I'm especially scared to be doing crazy things like walking south."

"Sure, and your wife's pregnant," Manny Lopez said disgustedly.

"You know she is," Ernie Salgado said. "And you know she's had miscarriages and . . ."

"Eeeeer-neeeee, get over here!" Manny Lopez mimicked the moment he would never let go, when Susan Salgado called to Ernie at the party.

"The thing I'm saying," Ernie Salgado continued, "is that I'm *not* quitting. But I *am* scared about how we're doing things now."

"Okay, you're scared," Manny Lopez sighed. "I always knew that since you wouldn't shoot that time."

Most were running to fat by now, bloated boozy coils of fat. Several were waking each night at the drinker's hour with night sweats and irregular heartbeats. Some reported nightmares of smothering, then a glaze of fog and mist, then awake.

Once, when they were walking by a sinister wall of brush in Deadman's Canyon, the clack and clatter of wings drew three guns from their holsters. A dove scared the heart right out of three human beings. The dove went flaring off like the spirit of these young men. One admitted that he absolutely believed his heart was in a fatal stall. Flameout at zero feet sea level.

Fred Gil had lately begun asking himself a question for which there seemed to be no simple or even logical answer. It was actually the most complex and difficult and maddening question of his life: Why didn't I become a plumber?

And then one day all the Barfers more or less implied privately that if one of them would walk right in there and hang it up, the rest would follow. Old Fred Gil—with credentials, being one of the wounded, and the oldest—was a logical choice. He walked right in to Manny and said "heck" or "goldang" and did it. He quit and went back to patrol.

But nobody else followed him. Not yet.

"I used to feel real bad after I left," Fred Gil said. "They sort a hung me out to dry. The others didn't quit. Then I used to read about something they'd done and I'd feel real bad that I shoulda been there with them. I got real angry with myself for quitting."

Old Fred Gil—thirty-seven years of age, judo champ, Vietnam vet, Barf survivor with a bullet in his hip—he figured he'd finally proved the man right. He'd proved it to a father who hadn't raised him. He had *quit.* Old Fred Gil wondered if he was a mama's boy after all.

Renee Camacho hadn't gone home that night he shot one of Loco's bandits. He had called Sharlynn and said, "I can't come home just yet."

She said, "Renee, why don't you come home and let's talk about it."

"I just can't," he told her. "I just can't come home."

She said she understood. She told him to come home when he was ready.

"She was a pretty good wife," he said. "A pretty good cop's wife."

Renee Camacho drove to the home of a police friend who lived in El Cajon, but he never found satisfactory answers to all the questions he posed as he and his friend passed the entire night at a kitchen table.

Renee Camacho told his friend: "I really felt like I was gonna get killed. And it scared me and here I shot somebody with the shotgun and I don't know if I killed him and I feel *good* about it. And . . . and that's *not* good! That's the worst thing of all. And after I shot him, he went down and I ran up and I took out my thirty-eight and I wanted to find him and shoot him some more and I just wanted to kill him and now I have anger and awful guilty feelings about it and . . ."

The friend had served as a Green Beret in Vietnam and tried to reassure Renee that his anger and guilt were normal. But the next burst of questions wasn't quite so easy to deal with.

Renee said, "But am I doing the *right* thing? Is this all worthwhile? Is this whole job we're doing the right thing or the wrong thing? Am I on a macho trip or what? Should I just go back to being a regular cop where I'm sure that I'm doing the right thing? Is this worth it? Why am I out there doing these things?"

Renee Camacho longed to feel *pure* remorse, but couldn't. Anger kept getting in the way, and the fantasy of sticking his snub-nosed gun in the face of a man he shot, and firing five rounds.

And then the boy tenor began asking himself the most difficult questions of all: Am I learning things about myself that I never should have learned? Who am I, *really*?

It was on such a day, when all of life was out of sync and he felt like a record playing at the wrong speed, that one of his former friends from patrol passed him at the substation and said, "Nice job on the crook you brought in the other night. Guess he needed a transfusion after you beat the shit out a him. I'd be in the *joint* doing that to an arrestee, but I guess there ain't no rules for the Barf hot dogs, is there?"

Finally, Herbert Camacho looked at his tortured child during one of the trips to the barbershop, and said, "You must only do this job if you believe in it, Renee. You've helped people who were being hurt. But you must *believe* in what you're doing or stop."

Renee Camacho adored this man, who was perhaps already secretly starting to die. Renee said to his wife: "My dad thinks I'm brave. I'm being *brave* for my dad."

He stayed. And then one fine night at summer's end when they were actually on the proper side of the imaginary line, a group of three bandits tried to rob the junior varsity walking team with knives and clubs, and Renee Camacho, after the arrest went down, found himself running across the canyons after one of the robbers. Running hell-bent for the *fence.*

There was no moon. They were both falling. The bandit hit the fence hole but did not flow through as bandits usually did. He snagged his pants on the wire. Renee dived through on top of him. The man was kicking and punching, and clawing and biting like a rabid coyote. The man, of course, smelled like death.

Renee Camacho was yelling, "*Barf barf barf barf,* GODDAMNIT!" and punching at the bandit and missing and getting punched, and he got his gun out and the bandit smacked the gun sending it clattering into the rocks, and now Renee was himself snarling like a coyote and slamming his fists into the face of the smaller man, who was weakening. And suddenly a car pulled up on the dirt road and the men fighting hand-to-hand in the dirt were lit by headlight beams. Renee looked up and saw red and blue lights.

And suddenly he realized where he was: over one hundred feet *south* of the imaginary line. Two car doors slammed and Renee jerked the bandit up and got the man's neck in a choke hold and the robber started wheezing and gasping.

Just as one of two Tijuana policemen said, "Let him *go*!"

"I'm a San Diego police officer!" Renee Camacho yelled. "He just tried to rob me! He's my prisoner!"

The taller of the two said, "Let him *go.* He'll come with us as *our* prisoner. You're on Mexican land."

But Renee began backing slowly toward the fence, dragging his prisoner with him, holding the bandit around the neck.

The Tijuana cops began looking at each other and advancing slowly, and there was no doubt this time on whose soil they stood.

And Renee was using the bandit as a shield and he could only repeat with a mouth as dry as the Tijuana River: "Now, I'm a San Diego policeman! Now, I'm a policeman! You know that. You *know* that!"

Of *course* the Tijuana policemen knew that, and knew that this San Diego policeman had also known Chuey Hernandez and Pedro Espindola were policemen when he helped shoot them full of holes. They knew all of this. And they moved ever closer and looked at each other again.

To Renee they looked like soda pop interludes, or cattle prods in the nuts. They looked like tags on his toe. In Spanish. And Renee kept backing slowly, toward America. Going *home.*

Just then Renee heard the fence rattling and thought he was surrounded. He heard footsteps padding up behind him! But it was Manny Lopez, who yelled, "Go call your supervisors if you have a problem! This man is our prisoner and we're going *back* with him!"

Renee Camacho looked at the waffling cops. And back at Manny. And picked up his gun from the ground. And back to Manny. And at the two cops, who were thinking about it.

And he expected to hear it any second, the most horrifying words in the language of man: "*¿Sabes qué?*"

Manny whispered in English: "If they draw, *ice* them."

The Tijuana cops did not draw. They stood silently by the fence and let the two Barfers drag their prisoner through the hole back to American soil, beating him into submission.

Renee Camacho was soaked from his head to his crotch. They'd won another game. A game of inches. But in this lunatic game, the odds of winning were getting longer and longer and longer. And what if Manny was unconsciously saying the prayer of the compulsive gambler? Dear Lord, please let me . . . *lose.* They'd cash in *with* him!

Manny Lopez told them a story about personal fear. He said that one night, for no apparent reason, after having been out of the field for a number of days, he was walking through the canyon wearing a brand-new bulletproof vest and even more heavily armed than usual, when he saw a large group of aliens rise up as though from the land itself. Manny said that there were fifty or more in the group and that suddenly they were just *there.* A few yards in front of him coming his way.

Manny said that his knees began to tremble. He was wearing two pairs of pants like an alien, and his legs were buckling and shimmying so much he had to look down because he was afraid Tony Puente and Eddie Cervantes might see. He said he thought he was going a little crazy because of those shaking trembling buckling knees. He said that as the aliens trudged silently past, his legs began to steady themselves and he was able to continue. He said he never felt anything that bad again and could not figure out the why of it. He told them the story to illustrate that just because they felt overwhelming fear on a given night, it didn't mean that they would feel it every night.

Ken Kelly said privately that it simply illustrated that Manny Lopez on occasion had a lucid moment. He was, by now, utterly convinced that the Barf sergeant was psychotic. But very soon Manny Lopez was going to be saying the same thing about Ken Kelly and they were going to have Ken's head shrunk to *prove* it.

The upshot of Manny's story was that not a Barfer believed Manny Lopez. To a man they did not believe that their leader ever felt the emotion they knew as an average run-of-the-mill explosion of terror, and horror of being murdered. And this knowledge, more than everything else, instilled more fear. Fear of *him.*

Renee Camacho said, "There was something about the man. He'd make you think, somehow he'll *get* me if I cross him. Maybe not now, maybe later. Somehow. He's an intimidator. Manny the Intimidator. He'd make you look over your shoulder and think: What the hell's this guy *up* to?"

It was simple for Manny to deal with his protégé, Joe Castillo, even after disenchantment with Manny's methods led the young cop to stop wearing gold chains and pinky rings and disco suits. When Joe Castillo once had a few too many in a local saloon and threatened to quit, Manny simply said, "Okay, you got it. I'll have you back in patrol by tomorrow."

It might be music to half a dozen other ears in that bar, but to Joe Castillo it was a shell burst. The young cop said, "Who'd you get to replace me that fast?"

"Don't worry about it," Manny Lopez said. "Lots a guys wanna join BARF."

"But I been with you since the start!" Joe Castillo cried, and then several other boozy voices jumped in and said things like: "Hey, Manny, don't you have *any* loyalty to your men?" And, "You can't dump on Joe like that!" And so forth.

Five minutes later Joe Castillo was vastly relieved that

he was still a Barfer, and Manny had his arms around Joe and Renee, saying "I *love* you guys!"

And Ken Kelly said, "I wonder what kind a background music oughtta be played behind this love story?"

Maybe a suitable musical score could come from *Snow White and the Seven Dwarfs,* as they trooped out to the canyons the next night, wondering if Manny Lopez had diddled their minds once again.

The Barfers were getting just about goofy enough for kidnapping about then, and one afternoon before the sun went down, they did it. They were resting on the hill just over Deadman's Canyon waiting for dark, and except for Manny, they weren't in any hurry for it to come. Just then two urchins came toddling over the rise. One of them was about five years old and the other was maybe a year older. They were accompanied by a muddy, colorless, bag-of-bones little mutt.

The six-year-old was a *huero,* fair-skinned with big gray eyes, and he strode right up to the group of pollos sprawled on the ground and said, "Where are you guys going?"

"Los Angeles," Manny Lopez answered.

"You got a guide?" he asked, and of course all the Barfers were eye-rolling and poking each other and generally suppressing giggles, and Manny said, "No, we don't."

And the kid replied, "We'll take you to San Ysidro."

And now the Barfers were really busting a gut and Manny said, "How much?"

And the little kid said, "A dime!" Which was no doubt the prearranged tariff the little wildcatters had decided upon. And after getting the dime they'd probably turn and run like hell with their mudball pooch back to Colonia Libertad.

So Manny stood up and strolled over and looked down at the barefoot vagabonds with burrs and stickers in their hair, and clothes that might never have been washed, and their little dog that *surely* had never been washed, and Manny reached his hand slowly inside his jacket and got hold of the piece in his shoulder holster, and turned to the Barfers with his eyebrow all squiggled in place, and with a wicked little grin said to them: "*¿Sabes qué?*"

And they simply exploded. Everybody was squealing and snuffling and cackling and howling and the little kids got very pissed off with this weird bunch of pollos laughing at them when they were trying to do serious business, and the oldest one very indignantly said to Manny: "Hey, *cabrón,* see this partner of mine? He's a bad guy. You better give us the dime!"

And Manny said, "Get the fuck out a here!"

So the baby bandits did that. They got the fuck out of there. They retreated about ten paces, which was still within range of their skinny little arms, and they picked up a pile of stones with their grubby little hands, and the next thing the Barfers knew, the baby bandits were throwing stones at them. Point-blank.

And the *next* thing the Barfers knew, the stones were bouncing off them!

And Manny Lopez started screaming, "Hey, you little assholes, this ain't funny no more! Knock it off!"

But the baby bandits just kept it up. Bing! Bing! Bing! Stones came ricocheting off their shoulders and knees. The little bastards were deadly accurate. So Manny went thundering over to the mudball pooch just sitting there wagging his mud-caked tail and taking in all the action, and Manny grabbed the mutt before he could hustle away.

"Knock it off, you fuckers!" Manny screamed. "Or I'll kidnap your dog!"

The little crooks were unstoppable. Manny got his answer: Bing! A stone came sailing through the air and skimmed off Manny's balding bean and he screamed, "That is *it*!"

And while the tiny bandits stood there wailing and crying, Manny Lopez started highballing it back to the cover team with the whining little mud hen in his arms and the Barfers tagging after him.

One of the baby bandits cried, "Give us back our dog, you bastard!" and Manny yelled back, "This'll teach you to rob helpless pollos, you little fuckers!"

They were reduced to dognapping. Eddie Cervantes took the pooch home and called him Migra for the border cops. But happy endings weren't in the cards, it seemed, for any creatures of the canyons, The little dog just couldn't adjust to baths and flea powder and nutritious chow. He moped around and didn't like America much at all. One day he took off. Heading south. Rehabilitation just wasn't as easy as some folks thought.

And once, in Deadman's Canyon a clutch of bandits approached the entire group, varsity and junior varsity alike. They didn't choose the small men of the varsity for some reason. They walked right past Eddie Cervantes and Tony Puente and Manny Lopez and went at the bigger men, Carlos Chacon and Ernie Salgado, and tried them with a knife. The Barfers of course all jumped on the robbers and beat the crap out of them and threw them down and disarmed them and handcuffed them. But suddenly a group of thugs poured out of the shacks on the hillside, heaving rocks down on the Barfers as the bandits screamed, "*¡Socios!* Help!" to their pals.

Then a strange thing happened. Another significant crowd of people came out of their shacks. Not bandits, not addicts, not smugglers. Just people. Just the poor people of Colonia Libertad. And they started yelling at the thugs to stop throwing rocks. In fact they became hostile to the thugs, and the rock throwing stopped.

Then a *very* strange thing happened. The crowd of people, the poor people of the border, began hollering things at the Barfers. They started yelling, "Shoot them! Put them in jail! Drive them away forever! And we *thank* you!"

They knew who the Barfers were, for sure. It was amazing. Then they started putting their hands together. Then they began applauding! There were lots of weird things happening in these canyons but this was one of the weirdest to the beleaguered group of cops. In this strangest of all amphitheaters, with the Barfers and the bandits performing on the floor of Deadman's Canyon and the people of Mexico up on the hillsides, they were *applauded.*

But of course, being a cynic like most cops, Tony Puente had to undercut it by saying, "Maybe that's just a rival bandit family glad we're getting rid a competition."

There were occasions when Barfers saw things that weren't there. One night Ernie Salgado was screaming at everyone to watch out for a fleeing bandit who was hiding in a bush. Everyone surrounded the bush. There was no bandit. It was like Carlos Chacon seeing a gun that wasn't there. You see phantom shapes in the canyons at night. Sometimes if you're not careful you can see a phantom in the daytime.

You might just go to Thirty-one Flavors for a butterscotch sundae and grab a number from the ticket machine because there's a big crowd waiting for ice cream, and maybe you're thinking that it's just two hours from the time you have to report to lineup for this little appointment with some murderers in the canyons. And the kid calling out the number for service is talking to you and you don't notice and he says, "Your *number's* up!"

And you're suddenly panting and sweating ice drops, and the kid's saying something like: "What'll ya have? Hot fudge? Strawberry ice?"

Or how about a double scoop of hot lead? How about icing down your tonsils with some cold steel? The kid behind the counter becomes a leering death's-head bandit. And you can smell the rotting flesh. You leave the store without your butterscotch sundae. *Trembling.*

You start to think you're crazy, but if you try to tell Manny he'll just call you a pussy and say, "What the hell, Jimmy Carter saw a killer rabbit, and he's *only* the fucking President."

On the outskirts of just about any city in America is a place like National City, just a few minutes from uptown San Diego. Nasty City, the residents call it. It's the kind of place that reassures you if you've been getting paranoid about America's impotence. When you begin to think that the Cuban Coast Guard might just decide to capture everything south of Illinois.

National City will take care of that for you if you just walk into any saloon on the boulevard, where you'll notice that people can file steel on their whiskers and that most of them resemble Willie Nelson or Johnny Cash. If you're feeling suicidal, you don't have to do anything terribly stupid like dumping on the U.S. of A. Just try poor-mouthing the San Diego Chicken.

If you watch and listen to the image makers and communicators in the media centers of New York, Washington and Hollywood, you can get a crazy head from an impression of America gone soft. But just travel to the outskirts of the big city and discover that it hasn't all gone the way of mud flaps and running boards.

Ray Wood was a lawyer in National City, a young guy with busted teeth who looked like a beanbag chair and dressed like an all-night poker game at the Elks' Lodge. He looked like the kind of guy who checked the coin chutes of pay phones, and just *automatically* felt under couch cushions.

Ray Wood wasn't one of those uptight lawyers that cops distrust, one of those three-piece suiters forever checking to see if his fly's unzipped. Ray Wood never checked and it was never zipped. He slouched into his office at the end of a tough day in court, and literally hung his coat on the floor.

The office looked like one of those prefab Quonset huts in Tijuana where you can buy Mexican insurance to cover your booze-soaked Ensenada run. There was a sign on the wall saying: BLESS THE IRISH. The cops figured that anyone like this has to be straight, so they trusted him.

There were three people waiting for him one afternoon after Manny Lopez had decreed that the boys go south. It was extremely unusual for any lawyer to be doing this kind of business with healthy young dudes aged twenty-four, twenty-eight and twenty-nine years respectively. They were staring somberly at the lawyer, who could see that this prearranged meeting was going to be about as pleasant as a clap check.

The young men were Joe Castillo, Eddie Cervantes, and the lawyer's childhood pal Renee Camacho. They gravely examined the document the lawyer handed to each of them.

The document began: *I, being of sound mind, a resident of San Diego, California, declare that this is my last will and testament.*

CHAPTER · 18

BARF

DICK SNIDER LURKED ON THE FRINGE. HE WAS STILL A Southern Division watch commander and still the godfather of the Barf squad. Sometimes he'd have a beer with the boys, and after a few, one of them might start hinting that Manny was having them do something that the department might not approve of.

But as Ken Kelly put it: "Lieutenant Snider would tell us that he'd have a talk with Manny. But he didn't really wanna hear bad things about Manny Lopez. He knew that nobody else coulda made BARF what it was, the biggest publicity machine the department ever had and the only protection the aliens had. And maybe Manny was another side a Burl Snider's fantasy life? Maybe Burl Snider was the superego and Manny was the id? Maybe."

Ken Kelly often spoke in psychiatric terms. He probably learned them firsthand. He was soon to have his head shrunk.

"I just never felt much purpose," Ken Kelly would say. "Neither did Robbie Hurt. There we'd be, sitting in the brush for hours, listening to rabbits and coyotes and skunks and rattlers crawling around us. Sometimes having people just appear out a nowhere, scaring the shit out a both of us. And they'd look at us ragpicking bozos and wonder if we were waiting for scorpion stings or what.

"The sound a gunfire used to make us *psycho* because we never *knew* anything till after the fact. When we got scared there was never a payoff. We just felt useless. No wonder poor Robbie became an alcoholic."

And what did Ken Kelly become, living with this frustration of being, and not being, part of the Barf squad? These two young men, one black and one white, who could not be part of it because of their color, were, as he put it, like a double shot of nitroglycerine.

This was just after the San Diego district attorney's investigator had a little conversation with the homicide leader of the *judiciales* in Tijuana. It seems that the *judiciales* were handling their own investigation of the shooting of the Tijuana cops. And the Mexican homicide leader told the district attorney's man that if their findings were such that the Mexican government decided to issue *arrest warrants* for Manny Lopez and his men, well, it would be the *judiciales'* job to serve those warrants.

Of course the Mexican lawman knew that he couldn't just stroll into the San Diego Police Department and throw handcuffs on Manny and the boys, and take them back to Mexico for trial. Yet there were ominous implications in what he said. The *judiciales* were working along the international border now, trying to arrest robbers on their side, the homicide leader said. And they might just run into the Barf squad.

When the district attorney's man asked if *judiciales* would really consider coming across into the canyons to kidnap the Barfers, the homicide leader said they would do what was *required.*

The Barf squad received the information but it changed

nothing. Manny Lopez still had them walking south of the line. So there were cracks made about the *judiciales* hanging Manny by his heels like Mussolini and other such jokes that no one found funny. And there were more Barfers pondering a last will and testament.

"This job just ain't dangerous enough," Ken Kelly said to Manny at lineup. "Why don't we milk rattlesnakes or jerk off tarantulas on our lunch break?"

One night the Barfers were walking in the drainage ditch near Monument Road and Dairy Mart Road, near the place where they had shot down Chuey Hernandez and his partner. The ditch comes across the border and during the rainy season spills runoff into a cow pasture near Stewart's Barn, often used as a resting place for illegal aliens on their nightly crossings.

Ken Kelly and Robbie Hurt were discussing the exact location of the Barfers in the drainage ditch. The others were possibly on the *wrong* side of the line, since the fence was damn close to being the actual boundary. But of course a few feet didn't matter if a squad of *judiciales* prowling the darkness suddenly ambushed them after figuring that real pollos wouldn't be hanging around that fence for so long, a fact that Chuey Hernandez found strange on the night *he* went to investigate.

Just then a U.S. Border Patrol chopper came roaring in out of nowhere and spotted the Barfers hiding in the ditch. The chopper hovered above them and lit them with a spotlight. The pilot started issuing Spanish commands over his loudspeaker. He started ordering this little group of bogus pollos to get their asses back to Mexico.

But Manny Lopez told his men to stay put, and he tried to raise someone on the Handie-Talkie which never worked properly out there beyond the pale. So, much like the Tijuana policemen, the border patrolmen in the helicopter started getting a little testy because this group of pollos there by the fence wouldn't run away and wouldn't obey. They were just staying put, which was very strange.

Meanwhile, Ken Kelly and Robbie Hurt were going bonzo because the Border Patrol helicopter was making such a commotion that cars were starting to stop there on the Mexican highway, and what if one of them was a Tijuana police car?

Ken Kelly and Robbie Hurt were doing their damnedest to get through on their own radios with no success, and finally the Border Patrol pilot had enough of this shit and he started blasting his *siren* and swooping down a little lower.

Ken Kelly was nearly in tears and was screaming all kinds of things that the F.C.C. wouldn't approve of over the radio, but nobody heard him and by now the pilot was getting just about as mad as Chuey Hernandez got the night he was shot down. And he *dived*!

Ken Kelly stopped breathing because he was sure the chopper was going right in on top of the Barfers in a fireball, but this pilot was a hot dog, and *good.* He was also good and *mad.* He stopped his dive a few yards from the ground and blew up a cyclone of sand and brush and flying tarantulas, and the Barfers were all on their bellies protecting their eyes and faces and weapons and balls or whatever, and Ken Kelly started screaming hopelessly, "They're trying to cut our dicks off!"

And just then they saw a car slam to a stop on the highway and Ken Kelly was seeing phantoms and was positive it must be the *judiciales.* With Tommy guns!

Well, even the Barfers weren't yet crazy enough to shoot down a Border Patrol helicopter, and finally the pilot either figured out who these lunatic pollos must be, or he was called out of the area. He took off very suddenly.

Ken Kelly said, "I was absolutely sure that if it had been *judiciales* on the highway our guys woulda been executed on the spot. They woulda just disavowed all knowledge, like they say on *Mission Impossible.*"

When it was over, his troops told Manny that it was time, *definitely* time, to "chase the elusive southern burglar."

There was always a burglary series somewhere, and to justify coming in from the canyons they would write in their daily activity report that they were working on a burglar, which meant they would jump into plainclothers' cars and drive straight to a fast-food joint or, on a night like this, straight to The Anchor Inn for a drink. And nobody was drinking beer this night; they needed tequila shooters.

Renee Camacho was livid and Tony Puente couldn't stop swearing. Manny Lopez, who had gone to the substation, was the object of just about every obscenity ever invented in English or Spanish. They decided that it was time to *do* something.

They figured that the horrible explanation was that Manny was *glad* the chopper came in attracting attention. He wanted *more* Tijuana cops to come on over for another celebrated shootout. It seemed crazy but all of this was crazy.

Ordinarily at the end of their shift, they trooped into the BARF office, where Manny would have a message or two written on the chalkboard about the plan for the next night. So they all came trudging in as usual except that their eyes were all red from tequila shooters and sandblasted from the whirlwind blown up by the helicopter. Tony Puente, as the senior man, had drawn the short straw.

He was a quiet chap, not very outspoken at any time, and of course he was afraid of Manny, as they all were.

When Manny said, "Is there anything else?" preparatory to dismissing his troops, Tony Puente removed his glasses, wiped them nervously, put them back on, sighed once or twice and said, "Yeah, Manny, there is. Close the door."

But Tony Puente just couldn't come out and say all the things they told him to say. Things like: "This shit's getting old!" Or, "We're tired a hanging our asses out for your headlines!" Or, "We've had it!"

It just wasn't Tony's style. He began tentatively and diplomatically. He said, "Manny, this is hard for us. I don't know how to say it but we got thoughts . . ."

"Yeah, so say it," Manny said.

"It's like we got the feeling that we shouldn't be doing certain things cause we're gonna get ambushed. And like tonight, with that chopper . . . we all talked it over and we feel you put us through shit that we didn't need to be put through and . . ."

"Our cover was blown by that chopper!" Eddie Cervantes said.

"There was absolutely no reason to stay there and get lit up for Tijuana cops!" Ernie Salgado said.

"No alien robber in his right mind would come in and work the area after that!" Eddie Cervantes said.

"What were we doing there, trying to bait *more* Tijuana cops?" Ernie Salgado said.

"My wife's pregnant," Renee Camacho said.

"*My* wife's pregnant," Ernie Salgado said.

"I'm not getting killed for this," Eddie Cervantes said. "I wanna see my kids grow up."

Not everyone was attacking. The younger ones—Joe Castillo, Carlos Chacon, Robbie Hurt—were *mumbling.* Big Ugly, Joe Vasquez, wasn't saying anything but even he was bobbing his head in agreement. Manny Lopez could see they were about to pop their chains.

Then they just talked themselves out. Everyone got very quiet and noticed that Manny's eyebrow had crawled to Point Loma. Manny was in his "*¿Sabes qué?*" mode. Everybody's sphincter slammed so tight a sand flea couldn't have crawled in, which had actually happened out there in those vermin-infested canyons.

They were expecting the worst. Would he single people out? What would he *call* them? Kill me in combat but please don't call me a pussy!

But suddenly Manny's eyebrow came floating back down on his head. Then he got this look of melancholy resignation, like a hangman, or a proctologist, or an actor's agent. The kind of look that says, "It's a dirty job but *somebody's* gotta do it."

Manny's mouth kind of turned down under his Zapata moustache and his little Asian-looking eyes got all misty and Manny put his hands in his lap and dropped his little head as though gathering himself. And when he looked up he made a speech about his *sons*! His *dear* sons!

Manny Lopez began it thus: "When I talk of you I call you *mis hijos.* And sometimes I call you guys *mis hijitos.* And that means I'm feeling *extra* caring about you. The things I go through uptown with the chiefs . . . the things I go through for *you,* well, I don't tell you because I don't wanna worry you and . . ." Then he reaches up and goddamnit! It looks like Manny's wiping away a motherfucking *tear*! And he says, "Okay, I hear you, I hear you. I get your drift. I just want you to understand that whatever I've done it's only for you and . . . Okay! I *hear* you. We'll make a few changes, *mis hijitos.*" Then he gives them his impish grin and says "Now! Let's go down to The Anchor Inn because I got a Master Charge that'll pay for all the drinks you fuckers can *hold*!"

There wasn't a dry eye in the house. They were ecstatic. They'd won! Manny Lopez! *What* a guy! They hit The Anchor Inn like a freight train.

Ken Kelly wondered about it. Manny the high-living dude whose credit cards were always pushed to the max? Manny ordered a round. He told them he *loved* every one of them. They got all warm and rosy and started chattering about the groupie schoolteachers. Maybe *they'd* show up tonight. We'll give some apples to the teacher! Bring on the whole freaking school board!

Manny tossed down his Chivas while somebody was telling jokes, and he excused himself with a wink, saying, "I gotta go to a *meeting*."

Everyone started winking back. A meeting. Sure. Hey hey, Manny! A meeting! Sure!

When Manny left, Ken Kelly, who often talked of reincarnation, said, "Last time around, Manny was either Joan of Arc or Heinrich Himmler. Or maybe he was W. C. Fields? He could con Orphan Annie into chain-saw massacre."

Then he called their attention to the fact that maybe they were only about as complex as a game of Bingo. Manny had stiffed them with the bar tab.

"He knows us like ya know your dick!" Ken Kelly cried.

And within a week they were all back to walking south of the invisible line.

Shortly thereafter it broke wide open. Predictably, it was Eddie Cervantes who bit the bullet. They were having their night's briefing as usual. Dick Snider walked into the tiny squadroom as he sometimes did and was leaning against the wall, showing his permanent squint from the dangling cigarette. He looked even taller in the suntan uniform of the San Diego police.

Eddie Cervantes suddenly threw a whole lot of sand into Manny's gargantuan jockstrap. He said to Dick Snider: "Lieutenant, I don't think it's wise for us to be operating south a the line."

And of course Dick Snider's eroded jaw crunched against his Sam Browne and the cigarette was barely attached to his lower lip. Even the squinted eye got bigger than the shield on his chest, and he said, "You're what?"

Eddie Cervantes softened it a bit, since Manny's eyebrow had crawled halfway down his back. Everyone had only one thought at the moment: Manny was looking exactly as he did when he said *¿Sabes qué?*

Eddie Cervantes plunged ahead and told Dick Snider how they'd been strolling "a few feet" south sometimes because all the bandit activity seemed to be at the border line or south. And how they hadn't been able to take down any good crooks lately because of the robbers staying where they belonged, but all in all, wasn't it a little "chancy" to be doing it this way? He didn't even have to say what the chief of police and the deputy chiefs and the inspectors and Amy Carter, or whoever advised Jimmy, would say if they learned that *after* an international shootout with a country that had become an oil producer, a bunch of hardball little turds had rolled on *south* to do their thing.

Dick Snider said, "Manny, I'd like to talk to you after lineup." And he left without comment.

Manny Lopez showed them a Richard Nixon glower for about three seconds or three days, and didn't say a word. Then he took the number two wooden pencil he was gripping and threw it like a knife at the face of Eddie Cervantes, who nearly caught it in one of his sad eyes.

And then there was all the macho posturing, with Manny snarling, "You pussy! You pussy!"

And Ken Kelly trying to patch things up by saying, "You are what you eat!"

And of course all the other Barfers began jumping up and reminding them that this was a police station. Manny Lopez blazed out to talk with Dick Snider.

This made it easier for Eddie Cervantes to leave the squad quietly and accept the new job with the school task force, a day-shift job with weekends off, doing ordinary normal sane police work. Manny in the end tried to be gracious by saying how this was a career opportunity for Eddie and how he was happy for Eddie. But nobody believed him.

First Fred Gil, now Eddie Cervantes. The Barf squad was shrinking. And Dick Snider issued a direct order that they would *not* walk south of the imaginary line.

One evening when the Barfers were out "chasing the elusive southern burglar," after having tossed down more than a few shooters at a saloon, Ken Kelly couldn't get his mind off two things: his impending day in court with a judge who was finally going to sentence him for the criminal assault, and his mother dying. Of course what was happening in the canyons was no doubt mixed up with these other very dark thoughts. He was quietly riding along in an unmarked car with Renee Camacho driving when Ken just cocked his fist and shattered the windshield of the police car.

Renee couldn't believe it! Ken couldn't believe it! The windshield was a spider web of broken glass. Renee had to drive off the road and stop. Unfortunately, Manny was in a plainclothes car following and he screeched in behind them and jumped out yelling, "What the hell happened?"

Renee, who was still shaky, said, "Manny, it's very simple. A brick came flying over the wall and . . ."

"No, that *ain't* what happened!" Manny said, looking at Ken, who was unconsciously doing his Jack Nicholson impression. Manny then said, "Okay, what the hell happened, Ken?"

Ken Kelly wanted to say a lot of things. He wanted to say: Manny, I just went to court on this scum bucket that creamed somebody with a two-by-four just for fun and they dropped the charge. And there's so many mass murderers getting acquitted and paroled that if the Mansons hadn't been dumb enough to kill celebrities, Susan Atkins'd be living in Mission Valley giving Tupperware parties for Charlie. And me, I'm convicted and waiting sentence just for hitting a number one prick asshole with a flashlight and my mother's dying of cancer and my little off-duty business selling emergency equipment blew up in my face and I'm losing my investment and my marriage is about as sound as a Chicago ballot box and I mortgaged my house for the business that blew up in my face so the only thing that ain't happened is I ain't found out my minister's fucking my wife!

That's what he wanted to say. All he *could* say was: "I'm flipping out, Manny. I don't know what's happening except I'm flipping *out*!"

Thirty minutes later, Ken Kelly was sitting in the BARF office with Dick Snider when Manny came in with some papers and shut the door. Manny said, "I'm sure you want a representative of the Police Officers Association here, don't you?"

"What for?" Ken Kelly asked bleakly.

"This is a predisciplinary interview," Manny said.

"Well then, I guess I could call my lawyer," Ken Kelly said to Dick Snider. "But I don't wanna have a lawyer except that the city's making me crazy because they're mad about having to pay that maggot mouth I hit with the flashlight a lot a bucks because his eye doesn't work too good anymore. All because I hit this bag a pus with a little four-cell flashlight? What was it, a magnum flashlight? With hollow-point batteries? Lieutenant, my lawyer says I oughtta go to a hypnotist to see if I was cognizant of what I did or was it unconsciousness of fact? Or did it result from a perceived threat based on my experience as a police officer? But trouble is I got too many skeletons in my closet to have a hypnotist fucking with my *mind*! I don't know *what* to do! Ya understand? Ya understand what I'm saying?"

Dick Snider just smoked and nodded at Ken Kelly from time to time and finally he put his big leathery hand on the young cop's shoulder and said, "Son, I think you have a real *problem*. I think you need psychiatric help."

Ken Kelly looked up painfully at Dick Snider, the man he hoped he'd get as a father next time if reincarnation is what it's cracked up to be.

And Mr. Sensitivity, Manny Lopez, shook his head sadly and clucked, "Yep, King, you're a fucking nut case. Wacko. A banana is what you are. We gotta get you a fucking lobotomy or something."

Dick Snider ordered Ken Kelly to take a week's vacation and not to report for duty unless he had a note from a psychiatrist attesting to his mental health.

Ken Kelly was sore about the forced vacation, but during that week he was glad Dick Snider had ordered it. He completed his psychiatric work-up and came back to the Southern substation full of enthusiasm. He met with Manny Lopez and said, "This was a *righteous* shrink! He was one that did a work-up on Patty Hearst! That's heavy duty! He canceled his appointments for the whole day and part a the next day just for me! I spilled my guts, Manny. I told him about the first time I pounded my pud and which hand I used. I told him I stole pears when I was four years old. I told him the first time I got a hard-on seeing bare tits. And at the end I say, 'Tell me, Doc, am I a banana or not? Do I need a lobotomy or what?' And he says, 'On the contrary, I wish the San Diego Police Department had *more* officers like you!' Manny! I ain't a nut case!"

Ken Kelly had a letter from the head doctor to prove he wasn't a nut case or a banana after all. Ken Kelly couldn't have been happier when he walked into the office of Captain Joslin, the commander of the substation. Until the captain said, "I've got bad news for you, Kelly. The inspector said you're a liability. I've got to take you off your present job."

Ken Kelly was devastated. It took every ounce of self-control to hold together. He said, "Captain, please don't send me out a the division at least. Put me on a patrol unit, as close to the border as possible. So I can help them sometimes."

"You got it," the captain nodded.

Later, Ken Kelly said, "I've heard that every sane person contemplates suicide sometime. Well, I made up for all the insane people who never did. I never thought a smoking it—that'd be too dirty, too many reports for other cops. But a traffic accident? A little bit of overtime for some traffic cop and that's all? No detectives, no lab man, no insurance man saying they can't pay off on suicides? A cop bites it on-duty in a car? Happens all the time."

Ken Kelly had these thoughts when, on his first night back to patrol, he was screaming down I-5 at one hundred miles per hour. Thinking how *easy* it would be. Then he got *real* scared. He called in sick. He didn't come to work for a few days.

"I was unbelievably bitchy. Then I was a zombie," he said. "My old lady was closer than ever to dumping me. My world was *over.*"

He never knew why, but BARF was the only thing he wanted in life. Was it the carousing? The camaraderie? Was it a perverse thrill of screaming *Barf!* in the night? Was it the threat? *Was* he a banana?

He'd tried to go to Nam dozens of times when he was in the Air Force, but could never leave the Mojave Desert, not in three years. BARF was something he thought would be significant, a new kind of police work. Even though he was the wrong color, he went out and *got* it on his own. And now he'd lost it.

When he returned from his "sick" days off, he was called into the captain's office. Captain Joslin looked at the dejected young cop and said, "Do you want back in BARF *that* badly?"

Ken Kelly couldn't even speak. He could only nod and hold his breath.

The captain said, "Okay, I talked the inspector into it. You're going back."

He was in a daze when he walked into the miserable little squadroom after a week's absence. Renee Camacho and Joe Vasquez hugged him and kissed him on the cheek Mexican-style and said they were going to party for a week.

Ken Kelly started blubbering and had to wipe his eyes on his sleeve. He said to Dick Snider: "Lieutenant, I hope that if I get reincarnated as a foxy chick I can give the captain a blowjob for this!"

Dick Snider told him he didn't think that would be necessary. A simple *thank you* was enough.

They had been at it nearly a year. Summer started to end more abruptly than usual, with rain. And there were very few bandits. Manny took them on a mini-Death March, and his daily activity report estimated that they covered ten miles and had seen only fifteen illegal aliens all night. But they did see a fire. Stewart's Barn was ablaze and was destroyed. There would be no more aliens hiding there after they'd crossed. It seemed like an omen of change. Something familiar was gone. The rumor began instantly that a border patrolman had torched it.

On October 5th, the log of Manny Lopez read: "It was very quiet due to the rain. We contacted two subjects who stated that they had been robbed on the Mexican side just prior to entering the U.S. We are getting more and more reports of robberies just south of the fence."

And then Manny Lopez added a sardonic closing line: "I wonder why the bandits won't come across?"

Late one night right by the fence, right near Interstate 5, so close to the U.S. Customs House that you could hit a government employee with a rock, Manny Lopez put Renee Camacho on the fence as a decoy. It was well lit there. Renee had come to hate light. Light was jeopardy. Light was danger. He wanted to be in the dark at all times.

"Talk to guys," Manny told him. "Tell them you got money."

Renee stood there alone. Manny and the others were thirty yards away in the darkness. Two men approached the fence from the south. One of them was wearing a T-shirt on this warm night. He was about thirty years old. He was incredibly filthy and had a homemade tattoo on his forearm. He had curled puffy lips and swollen white gums. He said to Renee: "The patrol's coming. Come back over the fence."

"No, I'm waiting for my guide," Renee answered in his lilting pollo singsong. "I'm waiting for my guide."

"The patrol's *coming*!" the man repeated, and he turned to his partner who had approached from the darkness. His partner was an ugly man with hair like a Zulu and heavy lips. His smell was overpowering. It made Renee dizzy. He had jaundiced eyes, pupils bright as sapphire in the yellow whites.

He said, "Come back. We're trying to help you."

"No, I have to stay here," Renee told them in his alien voice.

"Bastard, I said come *back*!" the Zulu said, and Renee felt his hot breath. He smelled like *murder*. Like the slavering maniacs of the nightmares.

"If you don't come, I'm coming over there and dragging you back," the man said with that corpse-death-murder breath. His leer was saw-toothed, as hideous as a moray eel.

Renee Camacho was squatted down. Renee Camacho wanted to stand up shooting. He wanted to shoot the son of a bitch to death. He wanted to blast the eel head before it murdered him. There was a nice big hole in the fence, a hole leading to Mexico and murder.

The bandits whispered to each other. The bandits took a good look at Renee and at the darkness and they walked away into the night. When Manny came running up, Renee's legs were still weak.

"What'd they say?" Manny asked.

"They wanted me to go over there. So they could rob me."

"Well, you shoulda done it!" Manny said.

Renee turned and looked his sergeant in the eye and said, "I'm not going across that line, Manny."

Manny looked back at him. He and Renee had known each other since they were players on the same high school football team. Renee and Manny went back a long way.

Manny said nothing and they went on to other business that night. It was the last night Renee would ever be faced with a bandit smelling like murder. He knew that the next bandit who even approached him with a stick in his hand would *die.* Therefore he knew that he *had* to quit.

Renee was dry-mouthed that night when he managed to corner Manny at the substation. He was of course expecting the kind of lambasting that Eddie Cervantes got. He was expecting lots of yelling. All of it: Chickenshit! Gutless! Pussy!

He was almost as tense as he'd been out by the fence with the eel-faced bandit. He asked Manny to come into the office and Renee closed the door.

Renee was very solemn. "Manny, I've done more than a year," he began. "And I have this . . . *commitment* to my wife. I . . . promised her I'd quit after the baby was born and . . . you know what, Manny? Well . . . I guess I'm just burned out, is all."

Then, after the most pregnant pause Renee could ever remember, Manny said, "I've seen it in your eyes for a while now. I understand, Renee. I understand."

And that was all. Renee couldn't believe it. No pussy? No chickenshit? No gutless? No *puto*? Just: "I understand." Manny was amazing.

At last the turning earth promised light. And release from the shadows. But when Renee got back to uniform duty it was very hard for him to watch the Barfers getting ready to go out in the canyons. They were friendly of course, and Joe Castillo came to him and said, "You did the right thing, Renee. It's not worth it. You did the right thing."

They were friendly, and yet he too was an outsider now. The third to go.

One afternoon when the Barfers reported to work, they found that an anonymous writer had scrawled another acronym on their chalkboard. It seemed an eternity ago that the lieutenant had written B.A.R.F. for Border Alien Robbery Force.

This time it was different. And in their present state, it was the truest, most meaningful and profound acronym any of them had ever seen. When they went out to the canyons that night, the sorrowful truth of it was clanging in their heads like a gong. The acronym once again spelled BARF. But the words were different:

Beaners
Are
Really
Fucked

CHAPTER · 19

LAST HURRAH

NEWSPAPER ARTICLES IN SEPTEMBER MADE THE DRAMATIC announcement: SAN DIEGO POLICE MAY GO HOLLYWOOD!

It had to happen. Hollywood hit the border. The Barf squad was courted by a motion picture company. Manny Lopez was of course going bonkers and so were they all. The wives were *more* excited. Everybody started casting the picture. And even Barfers knew that as far as Hollywood was concerned there was no such thing as a Mexican actor, so it was De Niro and Pacino. And Burt Reynolds might be able to play a Mexican. But how about a blond? Goddamn! If you lace his granola with angel dust to make him look like a lunatic, guess who could play King Kelly? Only Robert Fucking Redford!

They wondered if Coppola would direct? And how about music?

When Hollywood showed up, the Barfers were ready to "do" lunch. Ray Wood, the National City lawyer and writer of death documents, was to "take a meeting" with people whose Third World gardeners dressed better than he did.

Ray Wood got his suit pressed that week and tried to wear matching socks and shaved the lint balls off his shirt collar with a razor. Ray Wood had to do a deal!

The Barfers gave Hollywood an "option." The Barfers fell in love with the Hollywood folks and took them home and threw a big party with all the beer and tequila you could drink and the wives made snacks and sandwiches and everybody was just dying because maybe Warren Beatty or somebody *could* pass as a Mexican. This was some kind of a week.

There were a bunch of jokes flying around to the effect that the producers should get the bald guy to play Manny, just like in that *other* Manny Lopez story. The "bald guy" was Sean Connery. The other Manny Lopez story was *The Man Who Would Be King.*

The Hollywood contingent was warm and congenial and the Barfers couldn't believe that bigshots like this could be such regular guys, and the Barfers were trying to impress them with all kinds of macho charades, because what the hell, they wanted to do a movie about hardball Gunslingers didn't they? And being the amateur drinkers they really were, the Barfers proved it with a contest involving tequila shooters. They did the whole business: tequila, lime sucking, licking the salt off the wrist, all of it. The Hollywood producers went along like troopers and had a few, but didn't try to match the boys shot for shot. And the Barfers got blotto and fell in love with everything about these movie guys, and wallowed in some of the most glorious word pictures ever painted which took on the hue of tequila gold.

The Barfers learned about motion picture "points" and got dizzy trying to figure out how much their points would be worth if the picture grossed, say, 30 million!

Some of the Barfers ran out and bought swimming pools. And for referring a fellow Barfer to the swimming pool builder, each of them got a hundred-dollar discount.

They did all this after receiving $250 each for their option.

The Barfers, like most cops, were cynical in the ways of street people, and doubtful as to the innate goodness of mankind, but they hadn't any idea about Hollywood and were unaware that in Hollywood there were people who looked about as macho as Mr. Rogers or John Dean and yet were more ruthless than Loco on his meanest day.

The producers went back to Hollywood and Truth, which was: Whoever made money on a movie about a bunch of beaners? There's only one goddamn role for a white man for chrissake! Two if you count the big Okie lieutenant. What the fuck were you *smoking* when you got this dumb idea?

The Barfers never saw the Hollywood producers again. They had to go to the police credit union to borrow enough to pay for the swimming pools. All that background music in their heads just faded away.

October went bust. There wasn't much doing in the canyons and the brass uptown kept pulling them out to work a burglary or robbery series in various parts of San Diego.

November was cold at night but a bit more active in the canyons. They arrested a group of bandits in Washerwoman Flats who had shot at a fleeing alien and beaten another half to death. There were the usual minor injuries: sprains, cactus infections, lacerations. Carlos Chacon got beaned by a rock thrower and had to spend a night in the hospital for observation. The closest they got to some nurturing publicity was when they did a Gunslingers versus Bandits re-creation for public television.

As their second Christmas approached, the Barf squad finally got one replacement: a veteran cop named Gil Padillo. Small, salty, he was an aggressive type whose thrusting head, they claimed, entered a room five minutes before his body. He despised Manny Lopez at once, but never got the chance to fear him because time was running out on the BARF experiment.

It did seem sometimes that the Barfers attracted trouble wherever they went. On the 9th of December they were assigned uptown to help with the armed robberies that take place every Christmas season. And on that particular day there was a pair of very busy robbers at work in the San Diego area.

At two-thirty in the afternoon in National City, two young black men wearing pearl earrings committed an armed robbery, firing one shot from a .357 magnum and escaping in a white Chevrolet pickup truck.

An hour later they pulled a robbery at the FedCo store in San Diego near Fifty-fourth Street and Euclid.

At seven o'clock that evening they did it again at the College Grove shopping center, and fired at one of the robbery victims as they fled.

A few minutes later they appeared at the Big Bear Market on Federal and snatched a woman's purse, punching her around for good measure. They popped a round at a potential hero who came to the rescue. They had missed all their victims with the powerful handgun, but it wasn't because they weren't trying.

A few minutes after their last robbery of the evening, they were spotted by two San Diego reserve cops driving south on Forty-seventh Street. The reserves followed them without broadcasting that fact and without using emergency lights and siren. It was probable that they were a bit shy or uncertain, as reserve cops are wont to be, but while caravanning down toward Market Street they passed a patrol car containing a pair of regular officers who weren't shy, as well as a "cool" car containing Barfers Carlos Chacon and his partner Joe Vasquez.

The pickup truck made a sudden U-turn over Highway 805 and reversed its direction, and a full-scale lights and siren pursuit was commenced through holiday traffic on uptown streets. While the pursuit was heading east on G Street, the first patrol unit was shot at twice by the robbers. When they got to the U-junction with Boylston Street, two more shots whanged off the asphalt with some mighty big muzzle blasts lighting up the night.

One patrol cop returned fire twice from his pursuit car and then a couple of police units tried paralleling the pickup truck on the next street. After a lot of squealing and careening, the robbers were tooling on down Boylston right toward Carlos Chacon and Joe Vasquez, who were out of their car and waiting.

As the robbers whizzed past Carlos Chacon, he fired five shotgun rounds and Big Ugly fired six revolver rounds, blowing that pickup truck all over the street. The robbers had enough, right then and there, and coasted to a stop peacefully.

Carlos Chacon—with those incredibly expressive eyes which could show hostility, joy, rage, fear, during a conversation on the relative merits of shave lotion—was by far the Barf squad's most prolific Gunslinger. He had nearly outslung Manny Lopez.

Carlos had lived a violent childhood, first with a man who beat his mother and beat him. He had shot his best friend to death in a moment of carelessness. He had shot two of his fellow Barfers in a moment of canyon combat. He had shot Chuey Hernandez. When Carlos carried the shotgun out in the canyons and was ready to use it, they would all hit the deck.

"I was worried that I was crazy and dangerous," Ken Kelly said. "Carlos thought he was sane and in control and he was a *hundred* times more dangerous."

Whether or not Carlos Chacon was "dangerous," one thing was for sure: this very young Gunslinger did not shrink from violence. And he wasn't through shooting.

The squad was running out of gas in more ways than one. Manny Lopez was getting administrative chores and was sometimes staying in the station all night or having to run uptown for some meeting or other. He was still kept busy with speeches and interviews, but not nearly as many as before.

Despite vows to put down his wife's fellow religionists, Tony Puente did not make good his vow to buy a Christmas tree so big they'd have to bring it on a crane. In fact, the tree was *smaller* than any tree he'd ever gotten before. And this year when he decorated the house he didn't try to prove anything. The decorations were sparse. And he even started asking her *questions* about her religion. He was getting tired.

The night of January 25th promised to be chilly and damp. Walking with Manny that night were Tony Puente, Joe Castillo, Carlos Chacon and Joe Vasquez. Robbie Hurt was with Ernie Salgado on the cover team. The new Barfer, Gil Padillo, had the night off, as did Ken Kelly.

Ken Kelly and Joe Vasquez, the Barfer Ken liked best, were about the only ones left with enough energy to entertain the squad. Big Ugly liked to get dressed in a medical smock, so Ken dubbed him Doctor Violence. They'd do make-believe examinations of drunks brought into the substation.

Joe Vasquez, holding a little knee-banger mallet, would say in a Viennese accent: "I'm giving zis man a free psychiatric checkup."

And Ken Kelly would invariably reply, "That's awfully *white* of you, Doctor."

And Joe Vasquez and the other Mexican cops would say, "Hey, watch it, watch it!" to Ken Kelly.

But all the laughs were forced. There weren't even many smiles left in them anymore.

That night they were dragging themselves wearily toward the border after having done a whole lot of walking. Actually, they were tired all the time, it seemed. Some were secretly trying to line up transfers to new jobs, and even Manny Lopez was getting sick of what he perceived to be the lack of appreciation of everyone around him. His Barfers nowadays were bitching and complaining about everything. He was starting to dread what he used to love most, the news stories about the squad, because if only his name was mentioned the snide remarks would start.

The new Barfer was good at snide remarks, and it seemed that every week or so some brass hat uptown would make Manny defend their existence, with the inevitable admonition that if someone got killed, BARF was all over.

So even Manny was getting tired as he led them up a hill that night looking for an early moon and seeing very few aliens and wishing they had gloves because their hands were already getting cold.

All the boozing was catching up with them too. Robbie Hurt was the worst, but several of the others were bloaty and swollen like bullfrogs. In addition to their ordinary fear of being murdered, they had that kind of paranoia peculiar to excessive drinkers. There were demons riding each back, clawing at their throats, breathing hot in their ears. Whispering fearfully. It was like a bellyful of cold earth.

So they were weary and feeling old, these young men. Dick Snider said they were aging before his eyes and he worried what his experiment had wrought.

There had been reports of a gang of bandits in that canyon who'd been walking up to parties of aliens and stabbing the nearest pollo without warning, just to get the attention of the survivors. This was on the mind of Manny Lopez as they climbed, and for a flash he thought he saw human silhouettes on the skyline. Then the shapes were gone, but not the thought of stabbing bandits. Suddenly dark shadows loomed above them. Then the shadows plummeted.

The other Barfers were traversing the canyon's edge. They saw the shadows bearing down quickly at a forty-five-degree angle. Manny started snapping his fingers like an alien guide, but it wasn't necessary. All of them were watching the shaggy specters take shape and the Barfers began to fan out in a line five abreast. These shapes were approaching too forcefully, with too much purpose.

Manny was first, then Tony Puente, carrying the alien tote bag containing flares, radio and first aid kit. Then Joe Vasquez. Then Joe Castillo with his malfunctioning hand, standing next to Carlos Chacon, the man who had shot that hand and was hated for it. Whenever Carlos was next to Joe Castillo in a potential confrontation like this, he had two things on his mind: the bandits, and whether Joe was crazy enough to make good the threats of revenge he made when drunk.

Every man there knew this was a robbery for sure. Each was snapping finger signals back to the next man. They didn't squat pollo-style when the three shapes got close. The shapes belonged to three young men in their twenties, three heroin addicts as it turned out. Three bandits.

The three bandits didn't skirt around them as pollos would do. They didn't send one man up to talk politely as pollos would do. The three walked right up and blocked their way and one said, "Where are you going?"

"That way." Manny Lopez pointed.

Tony Puente pretended he was out of breath from the climb, and he was, but not as much as he pretended. Tony began sucking at the air and wiping his brow and he put down his tote bag as though to rest. So as to have his hands free when Manny said *¿Sabes qué?*

Another of the bandits said, "*La migra* is over there. You better not go that way. You better rest here."

And Manny Lopez started going into his pollo routine and said, "Oooooooh? *¿La migra?* Thank you."

Tony Puente started squinting at one bandit, then the second, then the third. He was not wearing his glasses. They were all on a path over the canyon. If a man would move a few steps in the darkness you could just about lose him, and everyone's head was jerking this way and that, and people were starting to perspire, and then an extraordinary thing happened. The first time it had ever happened out there in the night.

"*¿Sabes qué?*"

What the hell? We're not ready! They haven't threatened to rob us! They haven't asked for money! They haven't shown *weapons*!

Tony Puente looked down the line. Who said that? We're not ready, goddamnit!

Joe Vasquez *saw* who said it. The remarkable thing is that while looking right at the bandit who said it, Big Ugly, the most malleable and obedient Barfer, more than any of them a product of training, actually *got* ready when the bandit inadvertently gave the code words.

Manny Lopez thought: Hey, asshole! That's *my* line!

The bandit repeated it. "*¿Sabes qué?*" You know what? Then he told them what. He laid the old, *we're plainclothes cops* story on them which they'd heard a dozen times out there.

"We're *judiciales,*" the bandit said. "And we're going to need a little of your money before we can let you go on."

Tony Puente decided to move a few steps to get between the nearest bandit and the border.

The bandit perhaps didn't like him moving, because it happened. Very very fast. The bandit lunged for Tony Puente. He grabbed Tony, and Tony grabbed him. Then everyone made his move.

Joe Vasquez had been told earlier that if he ever had to drop someone quick without the bandit's motor reflexes coming into play, he had to take off the back of the head.

Joe Vasquez in that microsecond saw something that Tony Puente, being partially night-blind, did *not* see. And Big Ugly jumped on the back of the bandit who had grabbed Tony Puente. In this bizarre nightmare instant the young men embraced in a three-way bear hug there over the chasm. They did an eerie little bear-hug dance, in the moonlight, on the edge of the precipice.

And there was screaming: *"Barf barf barf barf!"*

And there was the sound of hissing leather as guns were whipping out.

PLOOM! BOP BOP BOP BOP!

Joe Vasquez broke the bear hug long enough to place his two-inch .38 up against the back of the skull of the bandit and . . .

It was unquestionably the loudest explosion Tony Puente had ever heard. Louder than all forty-nine rounds fired the night of the international shootout. Louder than any shotgun round in all these months he had walked these canyons.

The round was fired in his face. His eyes were burned by the muzzle flash and stung by lead shavings. He was blinded. He was *shocked.*

At the same second, or a second later, Manny Lopez was screaming something and seeing a bandit lunging at him with a knife as Manny fired.

The bandit was spun around and started running. Then Manny shot at him one more time. And the man ran. Manny began chasing him.

Then PLOOM! Carlos Chacon fired the shotgun point-blank into the chest of the third bandit. But the man simply turned nonchalantly and walked away. And this was like the recurring nightmare of policemen. They don't go down! You can't make these bastards go down! You shoot them and they either run away or they just turn nonchalantly as if to say, "Is that the *best* you can do?" And they stroll off along the edge of Deadman's Canyon.

Manny Lopez had emptied his five-shot revolver and he was chasing his man over the canyon screaming, "You fucker! Stop or I'll *kill* you!" But he couldn't kill anybody. His gun was empty. They ran, and ran some more. Then the bandit ran out of gas and slowed nearly to a walk and Manny staggered up and booted him in the stomach and the bandit went down at last. Then Manny booted him twice more in the stomach and *Manny* went down. They lay side by side gazing at the stars, the bandit moaning in exhaustion and pain and Manny gasping for breath, thinking dizzily that he had to cut down on the booze. And then the bandit started to get up. Manny Lopez slugged him with a hand he'd broken twice. And the bandit groaned and lay back down. Then the bandit started holding his elbow and screaming. One of the shots had hit him after all and the pain had belatedly struck. A Barfer ran up with handcuffs, since Manny didn't have any.

Carlos Chacon went for a walk toward his strolling bandit, who looked as though he might take a little nap. The bandit lay right down there in the dirt and put his face down sideways with his hands underneath him.

Carlos Chacon's Rasputin eyes were even more so then, and he was sweating buckets because he had shot the guy point-blank and missed. The bandit was just lying there playing possum, with his hands underneath him. No doubt holding a weapon.

Carlos was creeping up in the moonlight screaming, "MOVE AND I'M GONNA KILL YOU, YOU BASTARD! MOVE! GO AHEAD!"

Carlos would creep a few steps closer and say, "TAKE THOSE HANDS OUT FROM UNDER THERE, YOU SON OF A BITCH! YOU HEAR ME?"

And still nothing. So Carlos got a step closer and said, "ALL RIGHT, I'M GONNA KILL YOU, GODDAMNIT!"

Carlos was standing over him. And *still* the guy wouldn't move. So Carlos squatted down ever so slowly and pulled one hand out and knelt on it. The guy didn't respond.

So Carlos very slowly rolled him over, and as Dick Snider later put it: "There was a hole in his chest you could throw a cat through."

Carlos hadn't missed. But he learned that, unlike everything he'd been told, people don't always get blown to the ground when you shoot them with a shotgun at point-blank range. Sometimes they just turn nonchalantly and take a little stroll for themselves.

Carlos did his Bram Stoker number, leering at the dead man and poking his eye which was half open. Carlos ripped open the ragged bloody shirt and saw the ragged bloody holes oozing.

Carlos Chacon said, "I remember how I felt. *Good.* I felt good. I really *enjoyed* killing that guy. I wanted to do it some more!"

Just then Manny Lopez came running up, and seeing his youngest cop all bent over the body of a dead bandit, thinking Carlos was going into some kind of remorseful shock, Manny started screaming in Carlos Chacon's ear: "FUCK HIM! HE'S AN ANIMAL! HE DESERVED IT!"

And Carlos, who wasn't feeling the least bit of fear now that danger had passed, got scared shitless as Manny Lopez screamed in his face: "FUCK HIM! HE'S DEAD! GOOD FOR THE COCKSUCKER!"

Carlos was baffled for an instant. He thought Manny was mad at him, and he was confused and frightened. Then he figured it out and said, "Manny! I don't need reassurance! I *loved* it!"

During the moment or so in which all this took place, the greatest shock of all was experienced by Tony Puente. After having been in the three-way bear hug—the death hug, three panting silent young men in a death-dance polka —one of the embracers suddenly let go and the world's most gigantic explosion went off in the face of Tony Puente, and his polka partner dropped his head on Tony's shoulder like a sophomore at a prom, and his brain fluid started gumming up and welling down his neck and Tony was still embracing him, dancing, and saying, "Oh no oh no oh no!"

Tony Puente laid his dancing partner on the ground and saw it *all* leaking then, behind the ear: fluid, blood, brain matter itself, and Tony started yelling at Joe Vasquez: "JOE, YOU FUCKED UP! YOU KILLED THE GUY! HE WASN'T HURTING ME, JOE!"

But Big Ugly was already hauling ass after Manny and *his* bandit, so he didn't hear Tony's yelling.

When Joe Vasquez came running back he said, "Are you okay, Tony?"

"Why did you *shoot* him?" Tony cried.

Big Ugly said, "Tony! He was trying to stab you!"

"I didn't see any knife," Tony said.

Joe Vasquez pointed down under the body of the bandit, who was moaning and gagging. And there it was. A long blade with the handle wrapped in tape. A stabbing knife.

The Border Patrol came flying in with a helicopter after the calls went out. They landed thirty feet from the crime scene and blew *everything* into Deadman's Canyon, and Manny Lopez said, "Aw fuck it!" and they started dragging the two living bandits out.

Ken Kelly was enjoying his night off by trying to get things back together with his wife. In fact they were on the floor watching television and making love when he heard something that the wives had heard for fifteen months now. "Border shooting! Film at eleven!"

That was the end of the lovemaking. Especially when the announcer added, "At least *one* dead!" He didn't say *who.*

Ken Kelly sped down I-5, crying. He lived twelve minutes from the station. He made it in five. He found Carlos Chacon at the station looking like a homerun hitter doing a high five. He decided that Carlos was more psycho than

Manny Lopez. He saw Joe Vasquez looking like *trouble.* Manny Lopez asked Ken to go to the hospital and report back on the head-shot bandit.

Ken Kelly had to force his way into the intensive care unit after a lot of arguing. He was there for four hours. He had never actually seen anyone die before. After a time he and a starched nurse of the old school were left alone with the patient.

Ken Kelly became interested in all of it. The bandit had a wrapping around his entire head. Only his face showed. He was a good looking guy about Ken's age. His arms were covered with tattoos and heroin tracks. Both this bandit and the other even had *neck* tracks. But he was powerful looking. Ken stared and thought, I wouldn't want to fight him.

The bandit was breathing and moaning from time to time. He was hooked to a machine that gave digital readouts: blood pressure, pulse, respiration. The nurse was sucking brain matter out of his throat because he was leaking.

It was interesting to watch the pulse and blood pressure and respiration building. The patient's system was taking over and fighting to live.

"His blood pressure's super," Ken observed. But his pulse was 180 and climbing. Then Ken said, "Isn't there something we can *do* for him?" Ken Kelly was pulling for the bandit.

The patient was wearing a cross and it got to Ken, who was Lutheran enough not to like women who worshipped devils. He was mightily disturbed by this young man's dying.

The nurse said, "Don't get upset just because a doctor's not here. He's had irrevocable brain damage. The only use he has to the world now is that he's got a good heart and lungs. If we had permission we'd take his organs. He's young and strong."

And Ken got mad and sad at the same time, and thought: The stupid bastard. Barf hadn't even planned to go out that night which is why Ken had the night off. The stupid bad-luck bastard.

And then Ken thought: He's got a good heart and lungs. It's the nicest thing anybody can think of to say about this dying young guy.

In the next hour his blood pressure, pulse and respiration started to drop. Then it jumped a little and then it dropped. Then up a notch and down a few more. His vital signs were way down and then his pulse got down to forty-six. Ken Kelly would never forget the number. Because then the little humming noise started.

The nurse looked at her watch and said, "Well, I don't have to suction him out anymore."

Ken was left all alone with the bandit and he thought: This is amazing! This is an amazing fucking thing! This guy's really dead!

And Ken simply couldn't help himself and he was afraid someone would see him and think he was some kind of pussy or wimp or something but he couldn't help himself. He put his hand on the bandaged head and whispered, "God bless you."

Ken Kelly telephoned the Southern substation and reported the bandit's death to Ernie Salgado. Then he asked to speak to Joe Vasquez.

When Big Ugly got on the phone Ken said, "Joe, I wanted you to know that the guy just died. I was here with him the whole time and I just wanted you to know."

Ken heard a strange voice that was nothing like his friend, smiling uncomplaining Joe Vasquez, who rarely went out partying with the guys, and called his wife his best friend, and talked about adopting a baby because they couldn't seem to have any.

The voice Ken heard, which was Joe but *wasn't* Joe, said, "I don't give a shit! Fuck him!"

"Well," Ken Kelly said, "I just wanted you to know I blessed him for you. I just wanted you to know."

But Joe Vasquez didn't reply. And he never talked about it to Ken Kelly or any of the other Barfers.

Big Ugly always talked in a sincere, halting fashion. He smiled easily and genuinely. When he finally talked about that night he said, "It's a weird thing. People more or less congratulate you cause you killed somebody. Ernie was on the phone and he came in and shook my hand and said, 'Congratulations. You got your first one.'"

"Thanks," Joe Vasquez said to Ernie. But then he thought: This isn't a good thing. He didn't like the feeling.

Joe Vasquez had to deal with questions. People would say, "What was the guy like you killed?"

And Joe Vasquez would say, "I don't know. I don't remember. I don't even know his name. He was just some Mexican. Just some hype. I don't care to know his name."

Joe Vasquez, the most stoic and private of any of them, spoke about it briefly to his wife and once to his parents. Everyone told him that he'd saved Tony Puente's life and he decided that further comment was pointless.

Joe Vasquez would only say, "I had to deal with it for quite a while. Like, for a long time I was saying things like: 'Yeah, I shot the guy and the guy died.' Like, he *died* of his injuries. He *died.* I never could say I *killed* him. That I *killed* the guy. It took me a while to say I killed the guy."

Before that night, Joe Vasquez had been experiencing a burgeoning kind of excitement out in the canyons. It had grown to an unbearable intensity. And then it literally all blew up in his face.

"I guess that was my last hurrah," Joe Vasquez said. And some things were never the same for him after that.

Joe Vasquez usually talked in drug terms, a "quarter" being .25 gram of heroin, worth $25. The final thing he would say on the subject was: "They robbed us to get drugs. The one that lived told that to the detectives. I used to think that if I'da known that this guy needed a fix that bad I'da went and scored a quarter for him, you know, rather than take his life. I felt that strong about it for a long time. It's something that's gonna, you know, *be* there the rest a my life."

About the bandit Carlos Chacon killed, Joe Vasquez said, "Carlos is weird. He's a weird person. He gets excited about weird things."

Carlos Chacon said he wanted the nine .32-caliber shotgun pellets they dug out of his bandit's chest. For a necklace. Carlos was joking, *maybe.* But he *did* order autopsy shots of the dead bandits from the coroner. Some Barfer scrapbooks contained more memorabilia than others.

The next day they all went out to the canyon with homicide detectives to reenact the shooting and they found something startling. The chopper had blown everything that attested to the shooting right off into Deadman's Canyon, and yet, in the exact spot that Carlos Chacon and Joe Vasquez had killed the bandits, the people of Colonia Libertad had placed markers. There on the ground were two crosses formed by rocks. The people of Mexico believed in marking the fall of a sparrow and other creatures of the canyon.

CHAPTER · 20

DARK CROSSING

SO FINALLY THE BARF SQUAD HAD MANAGED TO KILL A couple of people. It had been getting eerie what with all the people being shot down out there and nobody dying. It had been too much like the policeman's recurring nightmare of the killer who won't die no matter how many times you shoot him. Now that two bandits had died there was a secret wave of relief sweeping over some of them who hadn't forgotten that the chief of police had said that if someone died out there he would discontinue the experiment.

In their heart of hearts some of them were praying that the chief would let the death of two bandits satisfy the requirement and stop this Thing before it killed them all.

In fact, he did. And the next couple of months were like being reborn. Of course there were adjustments to make for people who hadn't done ordinary sane normal police work for so long. Manny Lopez warned the brass that they couldn't expect his people not to overreact now that they were to return to regular duty.

This was now the time of Confession. And there is no one in the world, not anyone in history, not Saint Augustine, not Paul after being coldcocked by a bandit, or whoever it was, on the road to Damascus, nobody in the Vatican itself, who has *ever* had the need to confess like your average faith-shaken, stress-ridden American cop. They are the all-time world champ Confessors. Once you get them going they can't *stop* confessing. They'll start spilling and singing ten times louder and longer than the most eager confessor at a *judiciales* soda pop interrogation.

Everyone who has been a police department's Internal Affairs headhunter, or a district attorney's hatchet man, or part of one of the million or so "crime commissions" which purportedly uncover malfeasance, marvels at the confessor mentality of police officers. It's part of their makeup and it's what makes them such terrific victims, especially since they're usually too macho even to *know* they're victims. That's why the early conversation at police reunions and retirement parties usually entails discovering how many of the old classmates have seen whatever it is they see deep in the darkness of their own gun muzzles just before they smoke it.

In any case, the Barfers started confessing. There were Barf wives weeping all over town as the boys told them about the waitresses and the nurses and the schoolteachers and all the goddamn blood drinkers and geriatric titillaters, all those who ran amok amongst them, obsessed with the myths and legends of America. And how they didn't want to be the last of the Gunslingers anymore and just wanted to settle down to being ordinary sane normal cops and husbands and fathers. *Mea culpa, mea culpa.*

So there was weeping and confessing and forgiving, and some of the more unstable Barfers were trying to pull themselves together and there were lots of promises about how things would be different and how they were going to cut out the booze and how they would never look at another woman as long as they lived. *Mea maxima culpa.*

And then, right around April Fool's Day 1978, the Barf wives read some very ominous headlines in the San Diego newspapers. Such as: BORDER BANDIT ACTIVITY ON THE RISE.

On April 5th a boy pollo was summarily shot to death by a bandit gang operating on the west side.

By the 12th of April the Gunslingers were right back in the hills slinging like *crazy.*

By 7:40 P.M. that night, the Barfers had already been confronted by three knife-wielding bandits who, just before Manny could say "*¿Sabes qué?*" were scared off by a Border Parol helicopter which came swooping in and screwing up the Barfers' timing.

Manny Lopez chased one toward the border fence and fired a round at the crook as soon as he was nearly close enough to get stabbed. The shot missed but the terrified bandit hit the deck and knocked himself out anyway.

And before the department brass even had time to reassess the wisdom of reactivating this dangerous experiment, in fact on the very *next* night, there was another shootout. With a deadlier gang. And this time Manny Lopez had an epiphany. It was such an awesome moment in the life of the thirty-one-year-old Barf sergeant that some people claimed it actually drove him sane.

The murder that had occurred on April 5th was in the canyon two miles west of the port of entry. The entire Barf squad went out there now, with the cover team of Robbie Hurt and Ken Kelly parking some distance away from the walking teams. As it turned out, too far away.

The early evening was a drag. Robbie and Ken talked about the probationary sentence and fine the court had given Ken for hitting the citizen with a flashlight, which sent Ken back to the credit union for another loan to keep from wearing stripes. Then they bitched about Ernie Salgado being on the radio this night because he yelled. And they especially hated it when Carlos Chacon was the radio man, because his excitement level made communication almost impossible.

Ken Kelly explained: "When they're upset it's like trying to convince your wife that lipstick stains are all part a the job. You just *can't*, especially when you have so many priors. It's no good saying, 'Unless you got pictures, it wasn't me!' "

In short, you couldn't calm them down when they were on the air during hot times.

Manny and his other six Barfers decided to sit alongside a path one hundred feet north of the international border, a path beaten rock-hard by the feet of the alien armies of the night. The path was a wide one that tunneled through thick brush on both sides and ran north toward prosperity. At about ten minutes past ten, with no stars and very little moonlight, the Barfers heard cries of terror and the sound of running and every man was up and had guns drawn and was fanning out as two silhouettes came toward them.

The Barfers leaped out and grabbed the runners, who thought they were dead and were uttering cries for mercy and begging for their lives and were uncomprehending until they were made to understand that these were San Diego policemen. Then they started pointing behind them in terror.

These two aliens had been ambushed by three bandits wearing ski masks. One had a gun, another a knife, and the third, *¿quien sabe?* The two aliens tried escaping back to Mexico but were cut off by the pursuing bandits and had to veer off in the darkness and run north, right into the Barf squad.

The Barfers heard the part about the ski masks and gun and got very tense because they figured they had their gang of murderers, and just then they heard some more running footsteps and there wasn't even time to set up a proper ambush because here they came! Right out of the darkness!

The newest and smallest Barfer, Gil Padillo, had the shotgun. Manny Lopez heard a metallic click and yelled, "They got a gun!"

When the first two masked bandits charged nearly on

top of them, Gil Padillo let go with a shotgun blast. Carlos Chacon fired. Joe Castillo fired two guns. The first bandit stopped and screamed and started shooting back.

There was *another* point-blank gunfight in absolute darkness. The muzzle flashes lit up tall silhouettes and ski masks.

In addition to driving Manny Lopez sane, this shootout drove Ken Kelly and Robbie Hurt crazy. For these outsiders, fate had saved the worst for last. The cover team was waiting a couple of miles west of a riding stable. There is an escarpment which rises about five hundred feet to a mesa. The border fence south tumbles into nearly impassable terrain, at least for a vehicle, and then there is Smuggler's Gulch, five hundred yards across and three hundred feet deep.

When Ken and Robbie heard the gunfire it sounded distant, like someone breaking concrete with a hammer. They leaped into their vehicles and drove straight through the brush, straight up the escarpment. They skidded and slid and just about lost two police vehicles and stopped.

Ernie Salgado came on the tactical channel, broken by static, screaming, "WE NEED YOU! WE NEED YOU!"

And thus began the moment they'd avoided till the very end. Both outsiders went utterly bughouse. Ken had fifteen parachute flares, extra ammunition, a shotgun, first aid kit, bulletproof vests and radio. Robbie had nearly as much equipment. The grade was perhaps forty-five degrees, through nearly impenetrable brush after a rainy season.

All the outsiders could hear was *"Barf barf barf!"* being screamed in the distance and the BOP! of gunfire and each other's moans and panting and breathing which very quickly sounded phlegmy. Neither of the young men had ever worked *this* hard in his entire life. Within three minutes each was beyond pain and sweat-drenched and Ernie Salgado's voice kept screaming over the radio.

Just as they started seeing hallucinatory bandits and

rattlesnakes, Ernie's voice broke in again, screaming, ". . . helicopter!" And that was all they got.

Ken dropped his bag and shotgun and radio and started losing ammo and Robbie also started dropping things as they hacked through the brush with arms and legs and shotguns. And while Ernie screamed unintelligibly on the goddamn Handie-Talkie, Robbie went into a death rattle and started croaking things to Ken with his last gasp. "This . . . is . . . your . . . god . . . damn . . . FAULT!"

Ken knew he meant that it was Ken's idea to park where they did. But Ken croaked back, "Aw, go . . . fu . . . fu . . . fu . . ."

It was no use. His breathing sounded like a rasp on hardwood. He couldn't even gurgle an obscenity, and they both saved their last bit of energy to hack through another tunnel of brush.

The Barfers didn't know if the bandits were hit. After the tall bandits fired back, they vanished. And Barfers were reloading and running and screaming and ducking and doing the usual things and the two aliens were down on their knees praying for the chance to get *out* of this freaking country and back to Mexico alive. Suddenly two helicopters, Border Patrol and sheriff's department, came roaring in, having heard most of the transmission of Ernie Salgado.

When Ken and Robbie get to the top and collapse, they go into the giddy state wherein they start jabbering nonsense like: "Who's gonna buy the beer tonight if we live?" And, "Nice night to go crazy!" Things like that.

Then Tony Puente comes on the radio to say that no Barfers are hit but three bandits are hiding somewhere in five acres of brush, and the bandits have at least one handgun.

Suddenly Ken spots the red and blue lights of the Tijuana police gum-balling down the highway, having also picked up the broadcast. And he starts popping off parachute flares. Only he's so exhausted and suffering something like hyperthymia that he's damn near shooting down the two helicopters with the flares and he can't stop and the goddamn sky over the U.S. *and* Mexico is totally alight!

Robbie sees Ken looking up with a little demented smile, and it's clear that Ken's bewitched by the soaring popping floating flares. And then the sheriff's helicopter comes *attacking* through the flare pattern, and the chopper's blades are blowing the shit out of the cover team and all their equipment. Ken is so crazy by now, and so is Robbie, that they'd like to pop one right *at* the freaking helicopter bubble and Ken thinks of how the Italian-made helicopter sounds just *like* a dago machine as it hovers overtop with the whining thumping blades sounding like: GUINEA GUINEA, WOP WOP WOP!

Ken Kelly starts jabbering that he'll never eat lasagna again—*Guinea Guinea, WOP WOP WOP!*—but the pilot just waves fraternally and blows the shit out of *everything.* And now with scorpions and tarantulas and flying skunks soaring through this hurricane, Ken and Robbie are falling off the mesa and picture themselves tumbling into a rattlesnake convention just as they hear PLOOM!

A bandit made a break for the international fence and someone cranked one off. At least they all *thought* it was a bandit but they never knew because he made it into Mexico. And though they could see Tijuana police gathering over there, they never saw the man again.

Ken Kelly spent an hour on the mesa popping off flares, and the search continued until the choppers were running out of fuel and there were Tijuana cops everywhere. And San Diego cops everywhere. And news media from both sides everywhere. And they figured Chano B. Gomez, Jr., was probably over there selling tamales to the mobs watching this nutty carnival.

Ken Kelly had indeed lost the gear bag with guns and

ammo in it and Manny Lopez would soon be chewing him a new one because expensive police equipment is a lot more important than inexpensive bandits, and *everyone* would have to look for the goddamn gear bag and Ken figured he might as well shoot himself but he couldn't because he'd lost the frigging *gun*!

During the search Manny Lopez found a red ski mask and a knife with an eight-inch blade, and finally the Border Patrol chopper lit up a patch of brush and reported a man hiding there. Manny and Joe Vasquez pounced on a tall guy, who put up a hell of a fight before they thumped him into submission. They found a poncho lying nearby and with it a black leather holster, but that was all.

When the bandit search was discontinued that night, Ken Kelly reported that several reporters down on Monument Road were really pissed off at them because they hadn't killed somebody, or if they had, they let the goddamn body get away.

Ken Kelly asked, "Why do people wanna play with your dick when you shoot somebody?"

Two shootings in two nights was a bit much even for the ambivalent brass of the San Diego Police Department. This experiment was finally and forever deemed too dangerous, and within a few days BARF ceased to exist.

And so said the San Diego newspapers, making it a sad day for the media, for mythmakers, and for lovers of latter-day Gunslingers.

One wonders what might have happened to the Barf leader had the experiment been allowed to continue. Manny Lopez had experienced something exceedingly strange out there, something that troubled him and gave him pause and made him lie awake thinking about where this experiment had taken *him*.

He had pursued the fleeing bandit immediately after the gunfire. Even the new Barfer—who despised Manny

Lopez and hadn't been with them on all those occasions when Manny's conduct had made the others scared of him —had to say, "You don't *do* that. *Nobody* does what he did."

Manny was hot on the tail of a gun-toting bandit. A bandit who could have stopped at any second in the darkness and shot his pursuer to death at point-blank range. Yet Manny *continued* running all alone through the night toward the sound of fleeing footsteps. And the threat was *very* real, because the next day during a thorough search with detectives, they found a .22 automatic and empty cartridge cases.

While Manny was running that night he had this epiphany, the first and last he ever had. Manny Lopez thought: I am *invincible.* And the wonder of it enveloped him like an impenetrable shield. And he thought: This is my purpose. The why had become clear to the young sergeant. His reason for being was revealed.

Manny ran faster and faster. A few more steps and he'd fly! But that was nothing. Danger was nothing. Women, power, glory—nothing. Before him was something *infinitely* more thrilling. An idea. Manny ran toward it as others have, saints and madmen. It lay before him like a line of shadow. Only a step or two and he would cross. The idea was this: I am not mortal.

But he would never make that dark crossing. He stopped. So suddenly he nearly hurtled on his face. He twisted his head about like a scorpion in a jar. Looking, listening—for what? He didn't care about the bandit now. He saw nothing. He heard nothing but his own desperate breathing and hammering heart, and he thought: This is wrong. I'm thinking wrong things. Wrong!

Manny Lopez, the man they were all convinced had never known fear, began to feel something *like* fear. Of *himself.* He kept thinking about it through the evening and all night and the next day: I am invincible. I am not mortal. It was all wrong!

Manny had always said that if he ever quit the Barf squad it would only be because he was sick of defending his policies to the brass or to his own men, sick of sniping and jealousy. Though he was devoted to his family, he would never have quit for them. And never for personal safety. But Manny Lopez for the first time wondered if something wrong had happened in his own head.

Ken Kelly had always said, "Of *course* we were afraid of him. We're all afraid of psychotics, aren't we? We're terrified of unpredictable *lucky* psychotics."

Dick Snider had always claimed, "There was nobody who was crazy enough to do it except Manny Lopez."

The very last night in the canyons was by far the most terrifying of all. Everyone was secretly certain he would be murdered on the very last night. Still they walked the canyons, sweating it out to the end. Absolutely nothing happened. It was the quietest night of the year.

Manny Lopez had often said he *never* wanted it to stop. That in the BARF experiment he had found out who he *was*. But now things had changed.

Perhaps the experiment was ended not a moment too soon. Even *worse* things may have happened to all of them if they'd tried to continue the crazy experiment under a leader who perhaps had been driven sane.

CHAPTER · 21

BASTARD CHILDREN

THE CHIEF OF POLICE TRIED TO REWARD THE BARFERS BY creating a plainclothes gang detail for them. There were a number of adjustments to make as the months passed, while they were doing ordinary sane normal police work. A great deal of dissatisfaction began to set in. Several of them seemed to fall prey to various kinds of disappointment and depression based on they knew not what.

They felt betrayed in a sense. They had been part of a grand experiment. A bunch of minority cops were going to show the white majority what they could do. But people were criticizing in hindsight many things they had done. Until *they* became uncertain of what they had done. There was talk that relations between the police on both sides of the border could never be repaired.

When BARF was discontinued, U.S. government spokesmen said that there was going to be a beefed-up presence of federal officers on the border. The beefed-up presence never materialized. When the experiment had begun, they were sure that the department would be so proud of them that minority cops would finally be numbered proportionately among the investigative squads of the department, but there was still only token representation.

Even the good intentions of the police chief in creating the gang detail seemed a further segregation of the Barfers instead of integration into choice jobs, as they'd dreamed.

More than one said, "We felt like bastard children."

And some of the friends who had started out together would never be friends again. And that troubled them and seemed to fill them with a deeper kind of disappointment.

Finally, Barfers started drifting away, away from the police department itself. Joe Castillo took his wounded fluttering fingers to the San Diego Marshal's Office. He left the police department for a job wherein he served subpoenas and guarded courtrooms and admitted he was *bored,* and could talk only about the good old days when he was a Gunslinger.

One day BARF attorney Ray Wood, on his way to court, was startled to see a citizen being jammed up and choked out by a marshal in a courtroom corridor. The marshal was Joe Castillo. Some Barf habits died hard, it seemed. And as more time passed, Joe Castillo quit the marshal's office and joined the sheriff's department. But still there was this restlessness. In 1983 he left his wife and filed for divorce.

Renee Camacho lived through his worst time. He watched his father die from a colon cancer that went right to the bone. The boy tenor was devastated. Very few young men were so close to a father, and Renee found that he didn't care about anything, least of all the work he was doing in the Child Abuse Unit, dealing with people who beat and burned and tortured and sodomized their children.

This only child of Herbert Camacho was unable to deal with any of it anymore. He came to work and put his case load away and went through the motions. Finally he left police work entirely and moved to Los Angeles, taking a job in a photo-developing store.

About the BARF experiment, Renee said, "I was confused about all of it from the day the chief said he wanted to stop us because somebody was gonna get killed. I thought of *course* somebody's gonna get killed. And if this job isn't worth that, we shouldn't be *doing* it. From that moment on none of it made sense and I guess my heart was gone out of it."

In 1983, Renee Camacho, having gone through something very much like a youthful version of mid-life crisis, moved back to his world in San Diego and tried to return to the police department. It was noted that he had not been diligent in his last days as a cop. During the time that his father was dying. Police administrators are also products of a profession that sees not only the worst of people, but ordinary people at their worst. And anyway, bureaucrats have never been known for sentimentality. Renee was considered unfit for rehiring. He was accepted by the sheriff's department.

When asked what he got from the BARF experiment, he could only say, "Well, I got a chance to make my dad proud of me. I was brave. For my dad."

After killing the bandit, Big Ugly discovered that he wanted a child more than ever. Joe Vasquez and his wife, Vilma, adopted a baby, a white baby. And then, as so often happens, soon had a baby of their own, a Mexican baby. Big Ugly got himself two beautiful children.

Tony Puente found it more and more difficult to fight with his wife over her religion as each Christmas came and went. He also discovered that, despite himself, he came to buy smaller and smaller Christmas trees each year. Finally, instead of its being so big he needed to truck it in, the Christmas tree was so tiny and scraggly he could practically carry it in his back pocket.

He hoped he wouldn't one day find himself disseminating religious tracts on a street corner, but he was clearly admiring of the faith his wife had. He *hoped* he would never become one of them.

Ernie Salgado and Eddie Cervantes still had difficulty concealing very strong negative feelings about the BARF sergeant. They remembered his humiliating insults as though it were only yesterday.

Old Fred Gil, after all the hard luck, after nearly being killed by a body bag, with a bullet still in his hip, after spending a lifetime trying to prove to an absent father that he wasn't a mama's boy, found a compatible mate and a new life.

His second wife, Judith, had a good job as an office manager, was a slim, attractive blonde, didn't smoke and seldom took a drink and, like Fred, might never say anything worse than "goldang." He did ordinary sane normal police work, and in their spare time they raised show-quality Maltese dogs and entered them in competition. Old Fred Gil finally got a break.

As to the experiment he could say only: "Maybe the answer was in Washington and Mexico City? I don't know. I just don't think ten guys out there was ever an answer."

Of all the Barfers, there was one who stated immediately and unequivocally that he would gladly return to the canyons and do it again. Carlos Chacon felt that they had better jobs with the police department than they would have had without BARF, and he was right. Carlos said that they all "prospered" as a result of the experiment, and he was perhaps not so right. He still had eyes which could show joy, grief, anger, *fear* in ordinary conversation. Carlos Chacon still had violent dreams.

The only other who said that he would return to the canyons was the boss Gunslinger himself, Manny Lopez. A funny thing happened to Manny when he went back to ordinary duty. First, he was named a police officer of the year by *Parade* magazine and the International Association of Chiefs of Police. He was flown to New York for the award and rode in the airplane with his chief, William Kolender.

Americans are fickle about their myths and legends, and pretty soon, when there were no more stories about fabled Gunslingers, people started forgetting all about Manny's exploits. Other cops said Manny doesn't want much from life, only a ticker-tape parade every Friday.

Jimmy Carter went out; Ronald Reagan came in. Mexico went *down.* People could hardly remember the *name* of The Last of The Gunslingers, and even his former Barfers started to doubt that Manny would ever become mayor or police chief. In fact, given all the enemies Manny Lopez had made among the brass when this sergeant had so much power, no one was surprised when he didn't place very high on the promotion list.

Manny found his life becoming empty. He felt as disoriented as a scorpion in a jar. He thought that maybe money was the answer. Manny Lopez became the third to quit the police department. He became an entrepreneur. He started buying and selling grease.

Manny started a little business collecting cooking grease from local restaurants, grease which was then refined and mixed with cattle feed. All those animal fats mixed with molasses and stirred in with feed was supposed to fatten up even the scrawny cows of Mexico. But it turned out that there were too many *other* grease hustlers lurking around McDonald's and Jack-in-the-Box, so Manny had the idea of processing the stuff south of the border in Tecate.

But there aren't any Kentucky Fried and Burger Kings down there and Manny couldn't find his grease. In fact, what excess grease they have in Mexico they recycle until there's nothing left. Or they sell it to the people. Manny was at it for two years. Manny was a failed grease hustler.

Manny Lopez discovered that his talent lay in law enforcement, but he couldn't go back. There was his pride and ego. So he opened a private investigation agency and figured to make a financial killing, what with being a fabled Gunslinger. He was shocked to discover how quickly people could forget myths and legends.

Finally, Manny Lopez secretly contacted his old friend and mentor, Chief of Police William Kolender. The chief truly liked and admired Manny but the civil service rules prohibited his return as a sergeant. He would have to come back as a patrolman. And that, of course, was unthinkable for a man who had been a legend.

Chief Kolender said of the BARF experiment: "It ruined Manny's career."

And that was that. The chief was a very smart fellow who understood, even if Manny didn't, that life is no picnic for Gunslingers Emeritus, and that Manny could never start again at the bottom.

Perhaps Manny was just a young fellow with lots of brains and style and courage who found himself thrust into an extraordinary moment in time—confronted with the potent force of the bitch Celebrity, and the power of myth, and with it the seductive ideas of destiny and invincibility. And then that incredible moment when mortality was falling away into canyon darkness like shredded alien rags, a moment he feared but never wanted to end.

In his home there is a wall *covered* with pictures and scrolls and plaques and medals. And up there somewhere is the knowledge that it will never be again.

Manny's old enemies—and he made a bunch on both sides of the border—no doubt had a chuckle at the thought of him hustling grease. Say it ain't so, Manny! The Last of The Gunslingers? A failed grease peddler? Manny's coming in for a landing. A crash landing.

But Manny Lopez wasn't through being Manny Lopez.

Five years after the experiment ended, one of his former Barfers, perhaps trying to prove he wasn't so young and impressionable anymore, happened to have a few drinks with his old boss, and decided after too many tequila shooters to put the failed grease peddler in his place.

This ex-Barfer's wife, like many of the wives, used to be just as much afraid of Manny as was her husband. Well, nobody was afraid of a failed grease hustler, and his former subordinate felt like lording it a bit.

He said, "By the way, something I always wanted to find out. My wife told me that at one a the Barf parties you made a serious move on her. She never told me for a long time. Now I wanna *know,* Manny!"

And what could a failed grease peddler say to that? No, it's a lie! Or: I'm shocked! Or: let's let bygones be bygones?

Manny Lopez, who had so many times thrown punches and fired shots when he was literally falling to earth, just looked at his ex-subordinate with a tinge of melancholy and said, "I never wanted you to know this. Your wife told one a the girls that she wanted me more than the rings on her fingers. I wouldn't even *talk* to her after I heard, and I guess she couldn't deal with my rejection. I never wanted you to know this, *mi hijo.*"

And with that, Manny sadly put his hand on the young man's shoulder and patted him consolingly, and left quietly.

"I shoulda blew you away in those canyons when I had the chance!" the cop yelled, after he'd recovered.

But Manny was gone. Stiffing him with the bar tab. And Manny's former subordinate learned that a scorpion in a jar is still a scorpion.

If one possessed any charity at all it was best to remember Manny Lopez as he was when they were forcing him into that moment in time and trying to create a legend. When he was sitting in the blackness of a tube, in the blackness of the night, and suddenly *vanished.* When he was jerked from the pipe by a powerful masked bandit and tumbled down into the land of Mexico and was surrounded by El Loco and three armed cutthroats—literally enveloped by murder. And then for his eyebrow to do its reptilian sidewinding crawl into that perfect question mark because, *¿Sabes qué?* Manny Lopez had *them* right where he wanted them.

CHAPTER · 22

DÉJÀ VU

THE FATE OF THE OUTSIDERS WAS PERHAPS THE MOST DISquieting. As time passed, certain traits, responses, emotions they acquired during the BARF experiment seemed to keep coming up. In 1982 three officers had to undergo psychological counseling in an effort to assess certain traits which might cause either embarrassment to the police department or mortal danger to the officers themselves.

Robbie Hurt had managed to crack up another car, his beloved Porsche, in the parking lot of his local saloon. He and his wife, Yolie, were long divorced, but the thing was he never really left her alone. They lived apart yet he kept calling, and sometimes the three of them—Robbie, Yolie and Robbie's lady friend—would go to dinner or to a movie. And if they were out dancing after dinner he could still display something like jealousy if Yolie was dancing with someone else. Robbie wasn't sure of very much in his personal life, not since the old days when he was seduced by the Bitch, more so than any other Barfer except Manny Lopez.

Robbie entered a program of psychological counseling,

primarily to deal with premature cynicism and his drinking problem, before it could claim his life in another car crackup. He talked to his shrink about BARF and his "problem" and how it had never abated and how it seemed all mixed up with feelings from those days when he was out in the darkness listening and never knowing. And feeling this unbelievable frustration which had to be worse than the present danger the others were experiencing. And how at the end of the shift he just had to drink hard stuff because of this frustration, especially when some of the others would let him know he was an outsider. He didn't talk much though about the thing that was infinitely more destructive than frustration: the Bitch, and how he was seduced. He vowed to cut down on the drinking and believed he would as soon as he found Real Happiness in his forthcoming second marriage.

Ken Kelly was yet *another* Barfer who quit the San Diego Police Department.

Ken Kelly said, "I was angry when BARF ended. Real angry and I stayed angry. What was the point of it? Why did we do it? I felt betrayed."

The National City Police Department is said by San Diego cops to be a hard-nosed police department, a rednecked police department. It's still in the Truman administration, they say. Policemen carry Colt .45's in National City. Or .357 magnums. *Big* guns. The crime rate is the highest in the county. Ken Kelly joined the National City Police Department, where he quickly made sergeant.

In 1982, Ken Kelly underwent something so extraordinary that he wasn't ready to believe it for a while and was ordered *again* to have his head shrunk until he believed it

Sergeant Ken Kelly was on duty the night of January 23, 1982, in an unmarked police car. That car was later named

The Gunship because of Ken Kelly. There was a theft of beer from a 7-Eleven Store. Not a robbery, just a theft of some beer. Three guys in a sports car merely ripped off some suds and boogied. The store manager called the cops, who spotted the car and the car took off and the chase was on. Eventually three patrol units were in the chase, as well as Ken Kelly in The Gunship. The shoplifters looked as though they were going to give it up finally. But on a street where they were pretty well blocked off by police cars, the guy behind the wheel changed his mind after slowing down. He decided to go for it and rammed a police car. Then he backed up and Ken Kelly thought he'd run over a cop because he heard a loud thump.

It turned out to be a cop bumping into his own car, but Ken pulled out his .357 magnum and cranked one off. And fortunately for him as well as for the petty thieves, he missed. He would later get a one-day suspension for firing that shot, but after what was to happen the *next* night, he would be sent to a head doctor.

On the night of January 24th, the very next night, at a time when Ken Kelly didn't even have all his paperwork completed from the shooting the night before, he was back in the field, having just gotten a fight settled, when he heard one of his men in pursuit yet again. Two security cops from "Death Valley Hospital"—so called because the cops say more people die of violence there than are born—happened to be in a market when a bunch of kids came in, snatched some beer and took off in a Dodge van. The security cops decided to play like real cops and started chasing the kids, and some real cops eventually joined in. *Another* batch of suds stealers, and that was all.

At the time of the chase the city cops didn't know for sure *why* the kids had begun running in the first place or who they were. The pursuit rambled all through National City and into San Diego. A National City cop took over as lead chase unit out on Highway 805. Ken Kelly paralleled the chase and found himself in his old stomping grounds of San Diego, blowing by at a hundred miles per hour.

This was just like the night before. This was eerie. This was *déjà vu.* This was *impossible.*

On Market Street, Ken Kelly jumped on the brakes and slammed to a near stop, cranking hard to the left. The chase was southbound on Forty-first Street. Ken Kelly parked the car diagonally, using it as a barricade, and ran around in the headlights and here it came! Just like the night before. Or *was* it the night before? Or was it a *dream*?

The van was loaded with kids. The van swerved from side to side. Ken Kelly took out the .357 magnum. Like a *dream.* They were so close he saw the little numbers on the headlights. He fired once before he knew he'd done it. The van passed him. He fired twice more and knew he'd fired, but didn't feel the big gun kick, not a bit.

The first shot hit the E in DODGE and took it out. The second was to the left and lower. The third shot entered the side of the van just as it flew past.

The van ran out of gas finally. One of the kids inside the van was a sixteen-year-old boy who had been crouched between the seats. The .357 slug crashed through his jaw, through his hand, and smashed into his femur. The boy was the cousin of a police sergeant. His hand was crippled and his face was disfigured.

Ken Kelly spent all of 1982 on an emotional roller coaster. There was strenuous debate as to whether he should be charged with a felony. The district attorney finally decided not to charge him.

He spent time with a psychiatrist by order of his police department and he told the psychiatrist all about the dreamlike events of January 24th which, following the events of January 23rd, couldn't possibly have happened, but did. He talked about his days on the Barf squad and what it meant and didn't mean and it was all very confusing.

"We'd rather be tried by twelve than carried by six!"

Ken Kelly said. "That's what we *always* said working Barf. We took them down hard: fists, saps, gun butts, whatever it took. Until such time as the guy was dead or pretended he was dead or flat-ass surrendered unconditionally. They *wanted* us to shoot people. *Everybody* did. Maybe they didn't say it but we came to know it."

Somehow Ken Kelly got through the year. He worried that his head wasn't quite right, but gradually began feeling better. Then on a spring day in 1983 he started feeling very bad. At first he thought it was the flu. Then he felt worse. He went to a doctor and discovered that his blood pressure read like a major league batting average. Ken got *scared.* A cardiologist examined him and found that physically he was in good shape. The cardiologist advised Ken to see a psychiatrist. It was suggested that he might not be fit for police work anymore.

One night Ken Kelly was driving home in his car. He turned on the radio and a song was playing. The song was "Hit Me With Your Best Shot." He thought it was very ironic. He listened to it on I-5 southbound. He listened to it all the way into Chula Vista. In Chula Vista he suddenly started crying. He couldn't stop crying. He got home and he was still crying.

His older sister and his wife, Joyce, tried to stop him from crying but they couldn't. Pretty soon all three were crying. It went on until he was too exhausted to cry anymore.

The Barfers had been given a lot of awards at the conclusion of the experiment. Not just local stuff. Not just Manny's award in New York. The Attorney General of the United States presented them with an award for their work, even as the United States government chose to ignore the rape-robber-murder situation in the canyons. Perhaps it was the last chance to get some P.R. mileage out of the experiment.

At all of these award ceremonies and banquets and parties there was one person conspicuously absent: the BARF creator, Lieutenant Burl Richard Snider. In fact, he was never even *mentioned* by the speechmakers.

All of the Barfers still loved Dick Snider, and they decided to pitch in for a plaque. They wanted to present it to him at the big bash for the attorney general's award. A deputy chief wouldn't permit it. Though the deputy chief had never set foot in the canyons and had been seen around Southern substation about as often as Halley's comet, he was the one introduced as the man in charge of the BARF experiment. The deputy chief stood up and took a bow and people applauded wildly.

Dick Snider—for all the fuss he made in getting the experiment started, and for all his talk about helping aliens—was never looked upon with fondness by the administration. It held no brief for a lieutenant who refused to be a lieutenant and chose to crawl around the hills with lizards and rattlesnakes. And yet the administration was right. He never stepped into middle management and acted like a lieutenant. He didn't learn to compromise, and couch his terms tactfully, and use discretion.

He had initiated the publicity blitz that brought political notice, which brought the Barf squad into existence. And of course when BARF was hot, nobody could touch it. BARF had a life of its own. And these inspectors and deputy chiefs remembered all this. And how even after a direct order to muzzle himself, Dick Snider refused to understand the political expediencies. He only understood putting crooks in jail. For sure, the Dick Sniders of this world are a pain in the ass to administrators and bureaucrats.

The betrayal he felt was more acute than that of the others. After all, they were out in those miserable canyons for a myriad of reasons: to prove something to absent fathers or dead fathers or fathers soon to die. To prove themselves worthy of white respect. For career advancement. Finally, for love of the Bitch, and appointments with Destiny. And sometimes, only incidentally, to relieve some suffering of innocents.

As Manny himself admitted, "Only Dick Snider had *pure* motives and he kept them till the end."

Dick Snider believed all along that if the people of La Jolla were worth risking lives for, so were the aliens in the canyons. He was the one to decide what the bottom line was: we should only do it and continue it if it's worth dying for.

For him it was. Within one month after BARF was ended, a terrifying thing happened. He had just come back into the Southern substation after a five-hour search for some crooks in San Ysidro. He went into the office to put away his gear and was getting ready to go home when he felt like somebody smacked his chest with a sledgehammer and left the iron inside. He got dizzy. He felt a buzzing in his head. A ferocious pain down the side of his neck. His heart began pounding irregularly. He got up and started walking from his office to the captain's office. He sat down.

The captain's secretary looked at him and said, "Are you okay?"

He was not okay. He didn't remember much else except an ambulance ride with Renee Camacho. He couldn't breathe. He was in the hospital for three days. He thought it was a massive heart attack. It wasn't even a minor one. The doctor talked to him about hyperventilation. The doctor talked about stress. The doctor asked the big cop whether he had experienced any unusual frustrations, disappointments, fears in recent months. It was almost too funny to answer.

Dick Snider went back to duty. The city of San Diego said that the attack could not possibly be job-related. Dick

Snider was taken out of Southern substation and ended up in communications, which was under the street, below a fire station.

Dick Snider was far from the canyons and his cops and the border and all the things that obsessed him for so many years. This unofficial "mayor of San Ysidro" and his grand experiment were no more. And for the aliens, nothing had changed.

Dick Snider's career was in the basement. In fact, a couple of levels lower than a basement. He looked at his new surroundings down there below the street and said, "Good. I thought they might as well bury me. And they have."

As President Ronald Reagan was completing his first year in office and it was apparent that this administration was no more concerned with his obsession than the last one, Dick Snider had another of those moments. It happened at home at ten o'clock in the morning. He thought it was the Big One for sure. It was worse than the last one. He became paralyzed. He could hardly talk by the time he got to the hospital. They had to explain to him what hyperventilation really was, and how sometimes the best thing that can happen is that you pass out, allowing the oxygen and nitrogen to right themselves.

And Dick Snider squinted through his own cigarette smoke and felt that his heart was about as sound as a peso and said in his country drawl: "Believe me, pardner, I'm *trying* to believe it. But I kinda hate to keep passing out just to get myself *right*!"

They decided to send him to a psychiatrist, making him the third member of the experiment to have his head shrunk in 1982. Dick Snider talked all about the BARF experiment. The examining physician was of the opinion that Lieutenant Burl Richard Snider suffered from "psychophysiological cardiovascular reaction and labile hypertension" and should not be continued as a police officer. And that this condition was definitely job-related. In other words, Dick Snider got a stress pension. And yet *another* was gone from police service.

Dick Snider was by now aware of mistakes, and felt guilt about not recognizing certain symptoms in his young men and felt sad about the bitterness some felt toward each other. Dick Snider was not a complicated or sophisticated man. He had the history of western America in his face. He was a son of the Great Depression, a believer in law, and his country, and fairness.

It had been a long time since a young border patrolman got an idea by looking out the window of the bridal suite of the hotel in San Ysidro, watching San Diego cops chasing aliens. The idea being: there is not a significant line between two countries. It's between two *economies.*

The border patrolman had thought about the aliens a whole lot in order not to think of a young son dying—*I couldn't save him!*—and he had this idea that if a human being set foot across that imaginary line, that imaginary *economic* line, the person was entitled to be *saved.*

He had spent half a lifetime on the border and he knew the language and ways of the people, and admired them. They were not unlike himself in most ways. So perhaps it was natural that an uncomplicated man who believed so implicitly in the American way should try to do it American style. That is, if political hot air blows nothing but dust devils, send in a *cleansing* wind.

What did they accomplish finally? He couldn't say for sure. "We probably saved a few lives," he said. "Of course we also took a few." Then he added: "Well, there was that miracle. . . ."

And it was true enough. There is a Mexican woman named Rosa Lugo who saw her little girl in the nightmare of gang rape being saved by a host of wild angels. Try telling *her* it wasn't a Christmas miracle. There was that. Things like that.

But it had finally resulted in so much blood and bitterness and discontent, and ruined careers and sense of betrayal. So much psychic violence, which twice struck him down like a hammer and filled his family with dread.

At a time when Ronald Reagan was announcing economic recovery, and Miguel de la Madrid was clutching the sleeve of a teetering nation, and people were looking toward dangerous foreign enemies and crying quite correctly: "If Mexico goes, look out, America!" At this time in history, Dick Snider preferred not to think of his life on the border. He'd much rather sit at the organ in his little living room and play to relax, and to steady his heartbeat. He couldn't read music but he could play some songs by the numbers. His favorite went:

Sunny, yesterday my life was filled with rain.
Sunny, you smiled at me and really eased the pain.

Now the dark days are gone and the
bright days are here . . .

He was fifty-two years old, his face a web of lines, and as he played, his slate-colored eyes squinted through the smoke of the dangling cigarette, and his big leathery farmer's hands were spread out over the organ keys. He looked up at a plaque on the wall.

It was a modest plaque, not presented at any formal ceremony and certainly not by the police department officially. It was given to him by a group of young men, some of whom were born about the same time as a child he had lost so long ago.

"It's the *only* one," he said in the ubiquitous drawl of country America. "There's only *one* a these."

The plaque read:

To Lt. Snider
The person responsible for
the formation and existence
of the
Border Crime Task Force.

Thanks always,
B.A.R.F.

It was the one thing of sure and certain value his experiment had left him.

CHANO B. GOMEZ, JR.

DESPITE THE OVERALL SENSE OF BETRAYAL THAT MOST OF them reported, which stayed with them over the years, not a one of them could, with certainty, name their betrayer.

One ex-Barfer, given the advantage of time's passing, looked back and tried to fathom the nature of the experiment. He said he could not justify some of the things done during those forays into the canyons. Since Mexico had fallen on such hard times, the aliens were coming as never before. During one month in 1983, nearly fifty thousand were *caught* there in the Chula Vista sector. And with robbery, rape and murder proliferating like the cholla cactus in that rainy winter, he particularly felt the futility of it all.

The question was, what did they get out of it? What thing of value? The ex-Barfer pondered that and tried to be cynical but his face had too much disappointment in it. What did they get out of it? The answer was uttered like a question. With the saddest of smiles, he said, "A couple blowjobs?"

It may be that the only one who totally understood the amorphous experiment in the canyons was the man who could see much of it from his vantage point on the upper soccer field, old Chano B. Gomez, Jr., himself. It might take a tamale vendor to figure it all out finally, about good intentions, and myth and legend, and the good and bad that goes into myth and legend.

As to the Barfers, these children of the working class had been honest and brave and loyal to their mission as they were given to understand it. Perhaps in his own way every man came to know unconsciously what that incredible mission finally was, though they didn't know who commissioned it, or if anyone did. It was to dramatize a dilemma of migration and exploitation so enormous that two governments, two *economies,* had despaired of solving it.

It would be ironic if the little tamale vendor with his goat whiskers and his maracas hissing like rattlesnakes wasn't really shaking those maracas at pollos after all. The final irony would be if those hissing maracas—*Cha cha, cha cha cha!*—were meant to warn not pollos but *them,* the Barfers.

Maybe it would take a foreigner like Chano B. Gomez, Jr., to know how typically American it was to thrust ten young men into a monstrous international dilemma with an implied mission to dramatize it. It made for many a good show down there in the natural amphitheater of Deadman's Canyon, if you were perched on a rock at the top.

They gave their nightly performances and almost everyone applauded. They did it the only way they knew—not ingeniously, merely instinctively—by trying to resurrect in the late twentieth century a mythic hero who never was, not even in the nineteenth century. A myth nevertheless cherished by Americans beyond the memory of philosophers, statesmen, artists and scientists who really lived: the quintessentially American myth and legend of the Gunslinger, who with only a six-shooter and star dares venture beyond the badlands. Beyond all charts. Even to the phantom line between substance and shadow. To draw against the drop.